Charles Bray

A Manual of Anthropology

Charles Bray

A Manual of Anthropology

Reprint of the original, first published in 1871.

1st Edition 2022 | ISBN: 978-3-36812-437-3

Verlag (Publisher): Outlook Verlag GmbH, Zeilweg 44, 60439 Frankfurt, Deutschland
Vertretungsberechtigt (Authorized to represent): E. Roepke, Zeilweg 44, 60439 Frankfurt, Deutschland
Druck (Print): Books on Demand GmbH, In de Tarpen 42, 22848 Norderstedt, Deutschland

THE LIFE

OF

NATHANAEL GREENE,

MAJOR-GENERAL IN THE ARMY OF THE REVOLUTION.

BY

GEORGE WASHINGTON GREENE,

AUTHOR OF " HISTORICAL VIEW OF THE AMERICAN REVOLUTION," " HISTORICAL
STUDIES," etc.

Ὡς φάσαν, οἳ μιν ἴδοντο πονεύμενον · οὐ γὰρ ἔγωγε
Ἤντησ᾽ οὐδὲ ἴδον · περὶ δ᾽ ἄλλων φασὶ γενέσθαι.
ILIAD, IV. 374.

" After this manner said they, who had seen him toiling; but I ne'er
Met him myself, nor saw him : men say he was greater than others."

IN THREE VOLUMES.

VOL. II.

NEW YORK

PUBLISHED BY HURD AND HOUGHTON.

Cambridge: Riverside Press.

1878.

RIVERSIDE, CAMBRIDGE:

STEREOTYPED AND PRINTED BY

H O. HOUGHTON AND COMPANY.

PREFATORY NOTE.

—◆—

The ninth volume of Mr. Bancroft's "History of the United States" contains grave aspersions upon the characters and conduct of many of the leading men of the War of Independence. These aspersions were promptly met by descendants and representatives of those eminent men ; and the admirable pamphlets of Mr. T. C. Amory, Mr. G. L. Schuyler, and Mr. W. B. Reed, leave no doubt as to the claims of Sullivan, Schuyler, and Reed upon the gratitude of the American people and the place to which they are entitled in American History. My own part of this controversy I have republished in full in the Appendix of this volume, in order to give it a more permanent character than it would have as a pamphlet. That the reader might have the means of forming an independent judgment upon Mr. Bancroft's method of treating historical evidence, I reprint his letter to the Editors of the "North American Review," which is virtually an attempt to answer my pamphlet.

G. W. G.

East Greenwich, R. I., *February 9*, 1871.

CONTENTS.

BOOK SECOND.

(*Continued.*)

CHAPTER XXVI.

CHAPTER XXVII.

BOOK THIRD.

FROM HIS APPOINTMENT AS QUARTERMASTER-GENERAL TO HIS APPOINTMENT TO THE COMMAND OF THE SOUTHERN ARMY.

1778-1780.

CHAPTER I.

CHAPTER II.

CHAPTER III.

CHAPTER IV.

CHAPTER V.

CHAPTER VI.

CHAPTER VII.

CHAPTER VIII.

CHAPTER IX.

CHAPTER X.

CHAPTER XI.

CHAPTER XII.

CHAPTER XIII.

APPENDIX.

BOOK SECOND. — (*Continued.*)

CHAPTER XXVI.

THERE was one subject which came oftener, perhaps, than all others, to the minds and tongues and pens, both of officers and of privates, during the leisure hours of this bitter winter; a subject which had first been whispered about as early as October, and was not entirely dismissed from men's minds till the active movements of the new campaign began. I have already alluded to it as the Conway Cabal.

We have seen that the campaign of '77 had drawn down severe censures upon the Commander-in-Chief. Greene, indeed, had written in January: —

"Had our force been equal to General Howe's, or at least as much superior as the northern army was to Burgoyne, he must have shared the same fate. But, alas, we have fought with vastly superior numbers, and although twice defeated have kept the field! History affords but few examples of the kind. The people may think there has not been enough done, but our utmost endeavors have not been wanting; our army with inferior numbers, badly found, badly clothed, worse fed, and newly levied, must have required superior generalship to triumph over superior numbers, well found, well clothed, and veteran soldiers. We cannot conquer the British force at once, but they cannot conquer us at all. The limits of the British government in America is their out-sentinels."

But there were critics, both lay and professional, who saw these things in a different light.

"Why," said they, "was the enemy allowed to leave their shipping and enter Philadelphia without being attacked and harassed on their march? Why was their left wing left unwatched at the battle of Chad's Ford? These are very discouraging things, and ought to be rigorously inquired into. The proper method of attacking, beating, and conquering the enemy, has never yet been adopted by the Commander-in-chief. The many fruitless and unaccountable marches have a great tendency to fill the hospitals with sick, and more men will die this winter than it would have cost lives to conquer the enemy last summer and fall. Raiment, contrary to the good old maxim, has been regarded more than life, and the baggage many times sent away to the great hurt of the army. There was something very mysterious in the sending of generals from head-quarters to order the erasure and evacuation of Red Bank; if they were only fit to judge they ought to have been sent six weeks earlier, and if the forts were not sufficient, to have given orders and directions to have them made so; for if the forts had been properly supplied, the shipping could not have come up, and without a free passage for their shipping, the enemy could not have held the city. Then these generals who were sent merely to judge could not have known that Greene was advancing to support the forts; and when members of the same body act, not in conjunction but in opposition to each other, it argues great weakness in the head. If the enemy come out to forage, as they necessarily must, they ought to be attacked at all events, and if there is no general fit and willing to lead them on, the supreme power, the Congress, that is, ought to send one. It is a very great reproach to America to say there is only one general in it; the great success to the northward was owing to a change of commanders; and the southern army would have been alike successful if a similar change had taken place. The people of America have been guilty of idolatry by making a man their God, and the God of Heaven and earth will convince them by woful experience, that he is only a man; for no good can be expected from the standing army until Baal and his worshippers are banished from camp."

The army, too, was an object of suspicion.

" The general contempt shown to the militia by the standing army is a dangerous omen; in every victory as yet obtained by the Americans, the militia have had the principal share; the liberties of America can only be safe in the hands of the militia; the honorable Congress, in many cases, have been too much led by military men; such precedents may, in time, become dangerous; the increasing of the standing army is not right unless better methods are adopted for supplying the same; no action has yet been lost for want of men able, willing, and fit to fight; the

present army with the militia are sufficient to conquer the
present force of the enemy, at least, they were not long
ago, and finally, if the army is not better managed, numbers will avail nothing." [1]

While these insidious censures were carrying
their poison into private circles, and making their
way through secret channels to Congress, members
of Congress also were fanning the flame of discontent, and preparing the minds of their correspond-
ents for a public expression of hostility to the Commander-in-chief. As early as the 2d of September,
John Adams wrote : —

" Washington has a great body of militia assembled and
assembling, in addition to a grand continental army.
Whether he will strike or not, I can't say. He is very
prudent, you know, and will not unnecessarily hazard his
army. By my own inward feelings I judge I should put
more to risk if I were in his shoes, but perhaps he is right.
Gansevoort has proved that it is possible to hold a post.
Herkimer has shown that it is possible to fight Indians ;
and Stark has proved that it is possible even to attack
lines and posts with militia. I wish the Continental
army would prove that anything can be done. But this
is sedition at least. I am weary, however, I own, with so
much insipidity." [2]

And in October, when the news of the successful defense of Red Bank came, he wrote : —

" Congress will appoint a Thanksgiving ; and one cause
of it ought to be, that the glory of turning the tide of arms
is not immediately due to the Commander-in-chief nor to
southern troops. If it had been, idolatry and adulation

[1] " Thoughts of a Freeman," an
anonymous paper, first published by
Mr. Sparks, *Writings of Washington,*
vol. v. p. 497.

[2] *Letters of John Adams to his Wife,*
vol. i. p. 264.

would have been unbounded : so excessive as to endanger
our liberties, for what I know.   Now we can allow a certain citizen to be wise, virtuous, and good, without thinking
him a deity, or a savior." [1]

How far, under ordinary circumstances, these
complaints might have extended, it is impossible
to say.   But while they were still furtively circulating within their narrow bounds, the brilliant
achievements of the northern army came to give
them an element of strength, without which the
greatest discontents soon cease to alarm.   Within
a few hours of the news of Howe's arrival at the
Head of Elk, came the tidings of the victory of
Bennington.   The first battle of Stillwater was
fought only eight days after the battle of the
Brandywine.   While Washington's weary soldiers
were marching and countermarching in the neighborhood of the Schuylkill, the northern army was
holding Burgoyne at bay near the head-waters of
the Hudson.   But seven days passed between the
decisive second battle of Stillwater and the second
indecisive battle of the " grand army," the battle
of Germantown.   Here then was a successful general to set up against an unsuccessful general : a
Gates who had compelled a well-appointed army
to lay down their arms, to a Washington whose
greatest triumph had been a successful retreat.
Americans can conquer, then.   Militiamen will
fight.   Whose fault must it be when they fail ?

Thus reasoned the malcontents, and Gates was
not the man to detect the fallacy of such reason-

1 *Idem*. vol. ii. p. 14.

ing, or call in question his own qualifications for
the first place. Of moderate talents, with little
force of character, easily accessible to flattery,
easily led and misled by those whom he fancied
his friends, vain, jealous, ambitious and headstrong,
his experience in the English army, in which he
had risen by favor to the rank of major, had
given him a position in the American army, to
which he could never have attained by merit. A
friend of Washington at the breaking out of the
war, he gradually became alienated from him as its
progress opened prospects of personal distinction
which had lain far beyond the bounds of his original aspirations. In his first appointment to the
command of the northern army he had superseded
Sullivan, a better officer than himself, though a
less fortunate one. In his second, he came in time
to reap the fruits of the judicious measures and
skillful operations of Schuyler. He was indebted
to Stark for the victory of Bennington; to Arnold
and Morgan for the victories of Stillwater; in
neither of which did he issue an order on the field
or come under fire.[1] In the intoxication of un-
earned success he had quarreled with Arnold and
put slights upon Morgan. And now when his partisans in the army and in Congress began, in their
letters, to draw unfavorable comparisons between
him and Washington, he complacently accepted
the parallel, and readily imagined himself at the
head of a powerful organization. "The scenes of ·
your play," writes an anonymous correspondent

---

[1] Sparks, *Life of Benedict Arnold*, p. 119.

on the 17th of November, anonymous to us, though known probably to him, " have been changed so expeditiously and with such great management that I am fairly lost in my endeavors to trace my hero through the many great parts of his character. You have saved our northern hemisphere, and in spite of our consummate and repeated blundering, you have changed the constitution of the northern campaign on the part of the enemy from offensive to defensive." [1]

" We want you in different places," wrote James Lovell from Congress on the 27th of November, " but most of all in a third which you are not called to balance about. We want you most near Germantown. Good God! what a situation are we in! how different from what might have been justly expected! You will be astonished when you come to know accurately what numbers have at one time and another been collected near Philadelphia to wear out stockings, shoes, and breeches. Depend upon it for every ten soldiers placed under the command of our Fabius, five recruits will be wanted annually during the war. The brave fellows at Fort Mifflin and Red Bank have despaired of succor and been obliged to quit. The naval department has fallen into circumstances of seeming disgrace. Come to the Board of War if only for a short season. . . . . . Upon a motion made some time ago, General Schuyler is *permitted* to tarry and look after his private affairs, and St. Clair is *permitted* to do the same upon *seeing his name* in a council of war at what is generally by the inconsiderate, called the *grand army.* Since our resolve was forwarded, I see Kalb, Knox, and St. Clair, are a council reporting for the evacuation of Red Bank as incapable of bearing a siege.

[1] Sparks, *Writings of Washington*, vol. v. p. 484.

" Such kind of counsel seems to be the relish of this quarter.

" I expect you will judge me to be in a very sour humor. I am so. For if it was not for the defeat of Burgoyne, and the strong appearances of an European war, our affairs are Fabiused into a very disagreeable posture. Poor McDougal lays at the point of death. Conway has resigned, and many spirited officers are discouraged by an overbalance of languid counsellors. There has indeed appeared a little stroke of discipline in the dismission of Stephens and a number of inferior culprits from the service of the States. I wish this may have a suitable effect upon cowards, thieves, and drunkards, for such are the crimes which have caused the dismissions above mentioned." [1]

The same express, or one that immediately preceded or immediately followed it, brought a letter in the same strain from Conway. "Heaven," he wrote, " has been determined to save your country, or a weak General and bad counsellors would have ruined it."

Gates smiled complacently as he drank in the grateful adulation, and repaying the flatterer in kind, wrote to Conway : —

" Your excellent letter has given me pain ; for at the same time that I am indebted to you for a just idea of the cause of our misfortunes, your judicious observations make me sensible of the difficulty there is in remedying the evils which retard our success. The perfect establishment of military discipline, consistent with the honor and principles which ought to be cherished amongst a free people, is not only the work of genius but time. But, dear General,

---

[1] Gates Papers, in the library of the New York Hist. Soc.

you have sent your resignation, and I assure you I fondly hope it will not be accepted ; it ought not." [1]

But unfortunately for Gates he could not conceal the feelings which these flatteries awakened, and in the dizziness of his exultation, he showed Conway's letter to Wilkinson, the aid whom he had chosen to carry to Congress official information of the surrender of Burgoyne. How much farther the confidence went, and how far Wilkinson entered into the views of his patron and chief, it is impossible to say. His first letter from York is couched in terms of personal devotion, and speaks of the chagrin of Gates' enemies in language which almost implies the consciousness of designs which would not bear open expression.[2] But whatever Wilkinson's wishes may have been, he was unable to control his impulses under the influence of the wine-cup, and in the freedom " of a convivial hour" he repeated to McWilliams, an aid of Lord Stirling, the passage from Conway's letter which I have given above. McWilliams promptly communicated it to Stirling, and Stirling, an upright and honorable man, if not a great one, wrote immediately to Washington : —

" The inclosed was communicated by Colonel Wilkinson to Major McWilliams : such wicked duplicity I shall always consider it my duty to detect." [3]

Washington, when this letter came, was in his camp at Whitemarsh, anxiously watching the op-

[1] Sparks, *Writings of Washington,* vol. v. p. 485.

[2] Gates Papers.

[3] Duer's *Life of Lord Stirling,* p. 182.

erations on the Delaware, and hoping still to pro-
tract the campaign until the ice should come and
help him close the river to the English. He had
already begun to look upon Conway with distrust,
and was not in the least disposed to conceal his
opinion of him. Still he let a night pass before he
acted, and then wrote to him with stern and chill-
ing concision: —

"Sɪʀ, — A letter which I received last night contained
the following paragraph. —

" 'In a letter from General Conway to General Gates he
says — " *Heaven has been determined to save your country,
or a weak General and bad counsellors would have ruined
it.*' "

"I am Sir, your humble servant.

"GEORGE WASHINGTON." [1]

That Gates had long been estranged from him
he already knew ; but so far was he from suspecting him of a base intrigue, that he looked upon
Wilkinson's communication as a kind office of his
former friend to put him upon his guard against
" a secret enemy, or in other words, a dangerous
incendiary." [2]

Conway was not equal to the part which he had
undertaken. Nature had made him an intriguer,
but had denied him the caution and self-control of
a successful conspirator. Plausible, insinuating,
with the military bearing which long service
gives, and somewhat of that ingratiating air and
tone which men acquire by constantly looking to
favor for promotion, he easily made in his first ad-

---

[1] Sparks, *Writings of Washington*, vol. v. p. 139.

[2] Washington to Gates, Sparks, *Writings of Washington*, vol.v. p. 493.

vances the impression of a courteous gentleman and open-hearted soldier. But vain, jealous, and censorious, he could not long conceal the inherent defects of his character. The envy which disturbed his repose clouded his judgment. To his jaundiced eye the present condition of affairs seemed to indicate an early change in the highest departments of the army. The army was dissatisfied with Congress. Congress was suspicious and neglectful of the army. The people clamored for victories which the Commander-in-chief could not give them. What was to prevent a dexterous man from rising through these conflicting passions to rank and fortune?

A wise man would have seen that under them all was a deep-rooted faith in Washington, and a sleepless jealousy of foreign influence. De Kalb's calm eye saw this at a glance; and although he had come to the United States with the terms upon which his patron, De Broglie, was to be put in the place both of Washington and the Congress, in his portfolio, he wrote candidly to the aspiring duke that there was no chance of America's accepting that dictatorship which, at a distance, had seemed so practicable.[1] But Conway was not a wise man, and attaching himself for the moment to Gates and the faction which supported Gates, made no secret either in his letters or in his conversation, of his low opinion of the American General. "No man," he was often heard to say, "was more a gentleman than General Washington, or

[1] For this curious chapter of secret history, I refer the reader to Kapp's admirable life of De Kalb, ch. v.

appeared to more advantage at his table, or in the usual intercourse of life; but as to his talents for the command of an army," and here he would enforce his opinion by an expressive shrug, " they were miserable indeed." [1]

Washington's letter came upon him by surprise; but confiding in the strength of his faction, he resolved to hold his ground, and treat it as an " odious and tyrannical inquisition into the secrets of private correspondence." [2] He even went so far as to present himself twice at head-quarters, and greatly irritated, though not disheartened by the reception that he met with, gave vent to his anger in an impertinent letter. [3]

A thing like this could not long be kept secret. Mifflin, third and ablest in this unworthy triumvirate, soon received the tidings in his retirement at Reading, where he was living, " a chief out of war, complaining though not ill, considerably malcontent, and apparently not in high favor at headquarters." [4] What Conway had failed to see, he saw at once, and wrote to Gates, November, 28 : —

" An extract from General Conway's letter to you has been procured and sent to head-quarters. The extract was a collection of just sentiments, yet such as should not have been entrusted to any of your family. General Washington enclosed it to General Conway without remarks. It was supported, and the freedom of the sentiment was not apologized for ; on the contrary, although some reflec-

1 Graydon, p. 300.

2 Sparks, *Writings of Washington*, vol. v. p. 494. John Laurens, in a letter of January 3d, 1778, says that in his first letter, Conway denied the charge, and tried to explain away the word "weakness."

3 Sparks, *ut. sup.*

4 Graydon, p. 293.

tions were made on some people, yet the practice was pleaded boldly, and no satisfaction given. My dear General: take care of your sincerity and frank disposition: they cannot injure yourself, but may injure some of your best friends." [1]

Gates was alarmed. His answer to Conway's letter, filled with flatteries as gross as Conway's own, was on his table, already "sealed up to be sent," when Mifflin's letter came, and in the first impulse of his fear he wrote in postscript : —

" This moment I received a letter from our worthy friend General Mifflin, who informs me that extracts from your letters to me had been conveyed to General Washington, and that it occasioned an *éclaircissement* in which you acted with all the dignity of a virtuous soldier. I entreat you, dear General, to let me know which of the letters was copied off. It is of the greatest importance that I should detect the person who has been guilty of that act of infidelity. I cannot trace him out unless I have your assistance." [2]

A night's reflection increased instead of calming his agitation.

" Yesterday," he wrote to Mifflin on the 4th of December, " yours of the 28th of November reached my hands.

[1] Sparks, *Writings of Washington*, vol. v. p. 485. The original is among the Gates papers. It is evident from this letter that Conway and Mifflin were in direct communication, for it was only from Conway that the account of the "bold pleading" and "no satisfaction given" could have come.

[2] Gates to Conway, postscript. Albany, 3 Dec. 1777. Sparks, *Writings of Washington*, vol. v. p. 486. It is evident from the expression,

"which of the letters," that more than one letter had passed between Gates and Conway, although Gates does not hesitate to write to Washington, " I never wrote to him in my life but to satisfy his doubts concerning the exposure of his private letter ; nor had any sort of intimacy, nor hardly the smallest acquaintance with him, before our meeting in this town." Sparks, *Writings of Washington*, vol. v. p. 502.

Its contents have inexpressibly distressed me ; for though to this moment I have been ruminating who could be the villain, that has played me this treacherous trick, yet I can find no clue to a discovery. There is scarcely a man living who takes greater care of his papers than I do. I never fail to lock them up and keep the key in my pocket. I assure you, my dear General, I am as cautious to whom I show a private letter as any of my most sensible and scrupulous friends. Yesterday the original of the enclosed to General Conway was sealed up to be sent when I received yours which caused the postscript to be added to it. This untoward affair makes me the more unhappy as a very valuable and polite officer was thrown into a situation which must increase his disgust.

"No punishment is too severe for the wretch who betrayed me, and I doubt not your friendship for me as well as your zeal for our safety will bring the name of the miscreant to public light. To enable you to act with all possible propriety, I enclose copies of my letters to the General and to the President of Congress, on the same subject. Believe that in any matter which shall affect your peace of mind, you will find in me that warmth which your known sincerity convinces me that I shall experience from you." [1]

There is anger enough in this, and a great deal of fear; fear as if Washington's stern eye were upon him; but no remorse, no regret even, at the remembrance of the place he had once held in the confidence of the man whom he was betraying. And yet, but a short time before, he had been shown what a slippery path he had entered upon; for speaking confidentially to Morgan about the discontent of the main army, and the resolution which several of the best officers in it had come

[1] Gates to Mifflin, December 4, 1777. Sparks, *Writings of Washington*, vol. v. p. 486, and Gates Papers.

to of resigning unless there was a change in the
command, the blunt wagoner had answered, "I
have one favor to ask of you, sir, which is never
to mention that detestable subject to me again;
for under no other man than Washington as Commander-in-chief would I ever serve." [1]

Four days pass. His anxiety has slightly subsided. The thought of denying his intimacy with
Conway, or the existence of the offensive passage,
had not yet occurred to him, although he will attempt both by and by. But now he deems it still
possible to give a construction to the letter which
may leave him uncompromised. It is not a question between him and Washington, much less between Washington and Conway; but a dangerous
plot to come at the secrets of the American leaders.
If he can only alarm "the patriotism of the delegates," and divert attention from the subject of
the letter to the manner of obtaining possession
of it, suspicion will pass away from him, and the
responsibility of encouraging treachery be thrown
upon the Commander-in-chief. Therefore on the
8th he writes to him, ... "I conjure your
Excellency to give me all the assistance you can
in tracing out the author of the infidelity which
put extracts from General Conway's letters to
me into your hands. Those letters have been
stealingly copied. . . . . It is, I believe, in
your Excellency's power to do me and the United
States a very important service by detecting a
wretch who may betray me, and capitally injure

[1] Graham's *Life of Morgan*, p. 173.

the very operations under your immediate directions;" and forgetting the five inactive days which he had already let slip by him, he adds, that as "the least loss of time may be attended with the worst consequences" he sends a copy of this letter to the President of Congress, "that the Congress may, in concert with your Excellency, obtain as soon as possible a discovery, which so deeply affects the safety of the States."[1]

But no sooner are these words written than new hesitations arise, and as he had already announced to Mifflin his intended letter to Washington four days before he wrote it, so he now waits three other days before he writes the letter to the President of Congress which he hints at, without distinctly announcing it, in his letter to Washington. Thus in spite of "the danger of the least loss of time" in tracking this treason to its source, it is not till the 11th that he puts the finishing touch to his work of constructive accusation.[2]

But profound as the artifice may have seemed to the author of it, it was not of a kind to ensnare so straightforward a man as Washington. "Your letter of the 8th ultimo," he writes to Gates on the 4th of January, "came to my hands a few days ago, and to my great surprise informed me that a copy of it had been sent to Congress, for what reason I find myself unable to account; but as some end doubtless was intended to be answered by it, I am laid under the disagreeable necessity

1 Gates to Washington. Sparks, cember 11, 1777. Sparks, *Writings Writings of Washington*, vol.v. p. 487. of Washington*, vol. v. p. 487, and
2 Gates to Pres. of Congress, De-   Gates Papers.

of returning my answer through the same channel, lest any member of that honorable body should harbor an unfavorable suspicion of my having practiced some indirect means to come at the contents of the confidential letter between you and General Conway."

This was an ominous beginning. A clear and concise narrative followed; and then a few sentences of mingled indignation and contempt.

" Thus, Sir," he continued, and every sentence has its sting, " Thus, Sir, with an openness and candor which I hope will ever mark my conduct, have I complied with your request. The only concern I feel upon the occasion, finding how matters stand, is that in doing this, I have been obliged to name a gentleman, who, I am persuaded, although I never exchanged a word with him upon the subject, thought he was rather doing an act of justice than committing an act of infidelity; and sure I am that till Lord Stirling's letter came to my hands, I never knew that General Conway, whom I viewed in the light of a stranger to you, was a correspondent of yours; much less did I suspect that I was the subject of your confidential letters. Pardon me, then, for adding, that, so far from conceiving that the safety of the States can be affected or in the smallest degree injured, by a discovery of this kind, or that I should be called upon in such solemn tones to point out the author, I considered the information as coming from yourself and given with a friendly view to forewarn, and consequently, to forearm me against a secret enemy, or in other words a dangerous incendiary; in which character sooner or later this country will know General Conway. But in this, as in other matters of late, I have found myself mistaken." [1]

[1] Washington to Gates, January 4, 1778. Sparks, *Writings of Washington*, vol. v. p. 492.

Two days after these lines were written, further tidings of the existence of a conspiracy reached Washington from another source. Dr. James Craik had been Washington's companion in the old French War, and his intimate friend ever since. No man held a higher place in his esteem, and no man loved and reverenced him more sincerely. Craik's connection with the medical department of the army brought him into contact with all classes of men, and his well-known attachment to the Commander-in-chief brought him into intimate relations with the friends of that great man. While the letters which I have quoted from above were passing between Washington and Gates, Craik was preparing for a visit to Maryland; and just as he was upon the point of leaving camp he was told "that a strong faction was forming against Washington in the new Board of War and in the Congress." His first impulse was to go directly to head-quarters with the intelligence; but remembering that this was a subject more easily talked about out of camp than in it, he checked the impulse and began his journey. "On my arrival at Bethlehem," he wrote to Washington on the 6th of January, "I was told of it there, and was told that I should hear more of it on my way down. I did so, for at Lancaster I was still assured of it. All the way down I heard of it, and I believe it is pretty general over the country. No one would pretend to affix it on particulars, yet all seemed to believe it."

In Congress, the story ran, "some Eastern and some Southern members were at the bottom of it," and among them Richard Henry Lee, who had already been suspected of hostility to Washington. "In the new Board of War, Mifflin was a very active person." "He is plausible, sensible, popular, and ambitious," writes Craik, "and takes great pains to draw over every officer he meets with to his own way of thinking, and is very engaging." By "holding General Gates up to the people and making them believe" that with three times the force of the enemy Washington had done nothing but sacrifice Philadelphia, and neglect favorable occasions of attack, they hoped to shake the confidence of the country in him and prepare the way for a change. "Had I not been assured of these things from such authority that I cannot doubt them," writes the faithful friend, "I should not have troubled you with this." [1]

Still further confirmation came in the course of January and February from Henry Laurens, President of Congress, Patrick Henry, Governor of Virginia, and Joseph Jones, a Virginia delegate. Laurens sent to Washington the anonymous "Thoughts of a Freeman," parts of which I have already quoted. Henry sent him an anonymous letter in a hand-writing which Washington immediately recognized as that of Dr. Rush. And Jones wrote him, "whatever may be the design of these men, and however artfully conducted, I have no doubt but in the end it will redound to

[1] James Craik to George Washington, January 6, 1778. Sparks, *Writings of Washington*, vol. v. p. 493.

their own disgrace."[1] Washington was on his
guard. His friends were rallying round him.

Gates's friends too, had not been idle. To support Conway and Mifflin was to support Gates, and
therefore, when on the 15th of November, Conway
sent in his resignation accompanied by a "long,
complaining, boastful, and somewhat impudent
letter,"[2] addressed to Charles Carrol, though intended for Congress, instead of resenting the insult and accepting his resignation, Congress held it
in abeyance till the 13th of December, and then
" *Resolved*, That two inspectors general be now
appointed," and " proceeding to the election and
the ballots being taken, Brigadier T. Conway
was elected." Nor did they stop here, but resolving " That another major-general be appointed in
the army of the United States," the ballots " were
again taken and Brigadier T. Conway was elected."
The choice of the other inspector was " postponed
to Monday," and when Monday came, suffered to
lie over, not to be revived again till May, when
the cabal having failed, Conway was dropped and
Steuben appointed to that important office.[3]

On the 17th of October a new Board of War had
been formed, and on the 7th of November, Mifflin
was chosen a member of it.[4] As his dislike of
Washington was already known, and his failure in
the Quartermaster's Department was notorious, it
was impossible for Washington's friends to look
upon this appointment in any other light than as

---

[1] Sparks, *ut infra.*

[2] I borrow the words of Mr. Sparks.

[3] *Journals of Congress.*

[4] *Journals of Congress* ad diem.

an open avowal of hostility. But that the friends
of the Commander-in-chief had still a voice in
Congress was shown by the appointment of Harrison, his military secretary and friend. To those
who did not know the man, the choice of Pickering may have seemed equivocal, for he was believed to entertain an unfavorable opinion of
Washington's military talents. Those who knew
him, knew that he was too upright and too high-
minded to be the voluntary accomplice of an intrigue, and too independent and clear-sighted to
become its unconscious instrument. Harrison declined. But on the 27th of November, Gates,
Trumbull, and Peters were chosen to complete the
Board; and two seats having been secured for the
enemies of the Commander-in-chief, the hostile organization was completed by making Gates President. "Resolved," say the journals of that day,
"That Major-general Gates be appointed President
of the Board of War; that Mr. President inform
Major-general Gates of his being appointed President of the new Board of War, expressing the high
sense Congress entertain of the General's abilities
and peculiar fitness to discharge the duties of that
important office, upon the right execution of which
the success of the American cause does eminently
depend; that he inform General Gates that it is
the intention of Congress to continue his rank as
major-general in the army and that he officiate at
the board or in the field, as occasion may require;
that the General be requested to repair to Con-

gress with all convenient despatch to enter on the duties of his new appointment." [1]

The way was now open; and a broad and easy way as it might seem. With Gates at the head of the Board of War, with Mifflin a member of it, and Conway for Inspector-general, might not Washington be disgusted into resignation? In order to make this sure, and prepare the public mind for the change, reports were industriously spread that he had already expressed his intention of resigning. But to these he put an immediate stop, by authorizing the historian Gordon, who had written to inquire of him about them, to say, "that no person had ever heard him drop an expression that had a tendency to resignation. . . . . To report a design of this kind," he continued, " is among the arts which those who are endeavoring to effect a change, are practicing to bring it to pass. . . . . While the public are satisfied with my endeavors I mean not to shrink from the cause. But the moment her voice, not that of faction, calls upon me to resign, I shall do it with as much pleasure as ever the wearied traveller retired to rest." [2]

[1] *Journals of Congress*, November 27, 1777.
Washington to Wm. Gordon, February 15, 1778. Sparks, *Writings of Washington*, vol. v. p. 510. Compare also Craik's letter, *sup.*

CHAPTER XXVII.

THE cabal was again thwarted. It was evident that their webs had been too finely spun. Whatever the strength of Washington's passions might be as a man, they had no control over him as a public man. He was neither to be deceived nor irritated into an incautious step. No way was left to his enemies but the very doubtful way of open assault, and tradition says they did not hesitate to enter upon it. I say tradition, for there is no higher authority for the story. and yet that tradition should have found such a story to preserve, is of itself a proof of the impression which the general fact had made upon the public mind. Tradition says, then, that the cabal numbered their strength in Congress, and found themselves stronger by one vote than their opponents. They resolved upon immediate action. The day was fixed. The parts were assigned. A motion was

to be made for the appointment of a committee to
proceed to head-quarters and arrest the Commander-in-chief. No delay was to be allowed, but
the motion pushed straight on to a vote. We seem
to be dealing with infatuations. But infatuation
is the vital element of conspiracy, and Congress,
we must remember, often consisted of only eighteen members, seldom of more than twenty-two.
Absolute secrecy, however, was impossible, and
Washington's friends were on the alert. A single
vote might turn the scale. Unfortunately, only
two of the New York delegation were present,
Francis Lewis, and William Duer; and Duer being
dangerously ill, Lewis alone was unable to give
force to the representation of the State in such an
emergency. An express was sent to recall Gouverneur Morris from camp whither he had gone as
a member of the committee on the army. The decisive morning came, but Morris had not arrived.
Duer summoned his physician, Dr. John Jones.
" Can I be carried to Congress ? "

" Yes; but at the risk of your life."

" Do you mean that I should expire before reaching the place ? "

" No ; but I would not answer for your leaving
it alive."

" Very well, sir. You have done your duty, and
I will do mine. Prepare a litter for me ; if you
will not, somebody else will, but I prefer your aid."

The litter was prepared, and the sick man put
into it, but before he had fairly started on his
holy errand, Morris arrived, and taking his place

in Congress fresh from camp, and with a thorough knowledge of the temper of the army, the conspirators saw that the occasion had failed them, and desisted.[1]

Desisted, I say, from their open, but not from their covert attacks. There was one man in the army whom it was a special object to detach from Washington, and win over to the faction at all hazards. From his first entrance into the American army, the Marquis de Lafayette had attached himself with a son's affection to the Commander-in-chief, who had met the devotion of the ardent young Frenchman with the warmth of a father. Rich, enterprising, enthusiastic, and ambitious of honorable renown, his accession to the cabal would have been a severe wound to Washington's feelings, and a proportionate triumph for Gates. No efforts, therefore, were spared to entice him. "I am your soldier," said Conway, "prepared to go wherever you bid me," and, courtier by instinct, he plied the young nobleman with flattery and professions of devotion. But if Conway had the instincts of a courtier, Lafayette had the instincts of an honorable man, and although never a quick judge of character, was always a sure judge of principle. The moment that Conway betrayed his hostility to Washington, Lafayette closed his door to him.[2]

---

[1] This singular story is told by William Dunlap in his *History of New York*, vol. ii. p. 133, apparently upon the authority of Morgan Lewis.

[2] Lafayette to Washington, December 30, 1777. Sparks, *Writings of Washington*, vol. v. p. 488.

Congress came to the aid of the intriguer. Ambition was appealed to. A winter campaign against Canada was planned, and Lafayette, under the pretext that, as a Frenchman, he would easily win favor with the French Canadians, was appointed to the command of it, with Conway for his lieutenant. Once separated from Washington, and brought under the daily influence of the veteran plotter, the inexperienced young general, they thought, would find it hard to hold true to his allegiance.

But here again they had overshot their mark. In planning the expedition they had not even consulted Washington. Lafayette was instantly on his guard, and making Washington's approbation the condition of his acceptance, insisted upon De Kalb instead of Conway for his second in command.[1] "I would rather it should be you than another,"[2] said Washington, in reply to Lafayette's appeal for his decision; and comforted by this assurance, the young general repaired to York to receive his instructions. Gates was already there, surrounded by his friends of the hour, and when Lafayette arrived, in the full enjoyment of the pleasures of the table. Eager were the welcomings of the new comer, and profuse the expressions of joy. "The expedition," he was told, "was a glorious one: Canada would be so swiftly overrun,

---

[1] Lafayette to President of Congress, January 31, 1778. State Department, Washington MSS., vol. clvi. pp. 5-7.

[2] Lafayette, *Mémoires*, vol i. p 78, Fragment C.

that if the General-in-chief did not hasten, his sub-
ordinates would outstrip him in the race." Meanwhile, no allusions were made to Washington, nor
to the camp at Valley Forge, where Washington
and his generals were eating a very different
kind of dinners from those which heaped the
abundant table of the lucky hero of Saratoga. Lafayette observed, and listened, and kept his own
counsel. At last the moment came. The festivi-
ties were near their end. " I have a toast to propose," he said, and instantly all eyes were turned
upon him, and every glass was filled to the brim.
" There is one health, gentlemen, which we have
not yet drunk. I have the honor to propose it to
you : The Commander-in-chief of the armies of
the United States."

A thunderbolt could not have startled them
more. None indeed dared to refuse the toast
openly; but some merely raised their glasses to
their lips, while others cautiously put them down
untasted. Silence and constraint suddenly took
the place of boisterous hilarity, and Lafayette, rising and bowing his good-by with a placid smile,
left the disconcerted agitators to their wine and
their meditations.

The expedition failed, and in such a way as
clearly to show that it was less an expedition
against Canada, than an expedition against the
Commander-in-chief. " A Don Quixote expedition
to the northward," Greene calls it in a letter to
William Greene ; and writing about it to Knox, he
says, " I look upon the whole plan to be a crea-

ture of faction lick't into a publick form to increase
the difficulties of the General." [1]

But who were these discontented Congressmen,
and what pent-up grudges could civilians cherish
against a man with whom they had never been
brought into offensive collision? They had even,
in moments of extreme peril, entrusted him with
supreme power, and by many of their recent votes
had expressed their confidence in his character
and talents. It is evident that a part of their
body was still sound. It is equally evident that
a part of them were not; but who or how many,
it is impossible to say. Sectional jealousies would
seem to have had a small part, if any, in these intrigues; [2] for the same common report which
classed Samuel Adams among the intriguers,
pointed also to Richard Henry Lee. The letters
of James Lovell to Gates leave no doubt as to his
sentiments, and of former members Washington

[1] Francis Dana, a member of the
committee sent to camp to consult
with Washington, shows the absurdity of the expedition by a single
sentence — " Good God," he writes
to Gerry on the 16th of February,
"how absurd to attempt an expedition into Canada when you cannot
feed this reduced army."

[2] Such was the opinion of Mr.
Sparks, who has done more than any
other writer to elucidate this obscure
subject, and his opinion is always to
be received with great respect. I do
not, however, find Austin's defense
of the eastern members so conclusive
as he does. Mr. Welles seems to me
to meet the question more fully in

his *Life of Samuel Adams*, ch. 46.
Adams in May writes to Mr. Warren — " Was he, (Hancock) here, he
might, if he pleased, vindicate me
against a report which has given occasion to my friends to rally me, that
I have been called to account and
seriously reprehended at a Boston
town meeting for being in a conspiracy against a very great man."
Adams seems to have been annoyed by the report and felt that it
was unjust. Letters of S. Adams to
President Warren, in the collection
of Winslow Warren, Esq., of Boston.
Sparks, *Writings of Washington*, vol.
v. Appendix vi.

suspected Rush. Conway expressly classes Richard Henry Lee among his friends; but it is to Lee that Washington writes in friendly trust his strongest protest against Conway's promotion.[1] That Conway had warm friends both "within and without doors," and that by some of these friends he was asserted to be the favorite of the army, Lee tells Washington in his answer, but is far from counting himself among them. I hardly know whether to rejoice or to be sorry that the votes by which Gates and Mifflin were placed on the Board of War, and Conway promoted in spite of Washington's opposition, have not been recorded. When Charles Thompson burnt his private letters and memorandums, the details of these humiliating scenes were probably snatched from the grasp of history forever.

Nor with the exception of Gates, Mifflin, and Conway, can we bring home the charge to any leading men in the army. If they had partisans, and some they must have had, they were too insignificant to attract attention. Their names, even, have not been preserved. At Reading, Mifflin and Conway might sneer openly at Washington's generalship, but they would scarcely have dared to whisper their hatred within the lines of Valley Forge.[2] Even among the foreign officers,

[1] Washington to R. H. Lee, October 17, 1777. Passages from Lovell's letters have been given above. The originals are among the Gates Papers in the Library of the N. Y. H. S. Conway's mention of Lee occurs in a letter to Gates, dated Yorktown, June 7. Sparks, *Writings of Washington*, vol. v. p. 373.

[2] "It may be said that the popularity of the Commander-in-chief was a good deal impaired at Reading." Graydon, p. 300.

Conway, with all his intrigues, had failed to win accomplices. "I must render to General Duportail and some other French officers, who have spoken to me," writes Lafayette to Washington on the 30th of December, " the justice to say, that I found them as I could wish upon this occasion, although it has made a great noise amongst many in the army."[1]　The army was true.

And soon, also, it was seen that the country was true. Wherever the slander penetrated, it called forth indignant exclamations. Greene had written to his brother Jacob, on the 7th of February : —

" A horrid faction has been forming to ruin his Excellency and others. Ambition how boundless! Ingratitude how prevalent! But the factions are universally condemned. General Mifflin is said to be at the head of it. And it is strongly suspected that General Gates favors it. Mifflin has quarreled with the General because he would not draw the force off to the southward last summer, and leave the New England States to themselves before the enemy's object was ascertained. It was uncertain whether he intended to go up the North River, to Newport, or to the southward. The General thought it his duty to take a position to give the earliest support to either. Mifflin thought Philadelphia was exposed by it, and went there and raised a prodigious clamor against the measure, and against me for advising it. But the General, like the common father of all, steadily pursued the great Continental interest without regard to partial objects and the discontents of individuals. This faction has been the offspring of that measure. See upon what a monstrous principle the General is persecuted."

And to Knox : —

1 Sparks, *Writings of Washington*, vol. v. p. 488.

" The faction is in great discredit and prodigiously frightened; several very humiliating letters have been wrote to the General, disavowing the contents of a letter wrote to General Gates, and another actually appears in a different style ; but the artifice is too barefaced to deceive anybody. General Gates has censured General Wilkinson for betraying family secrets, and has refused to admit him as Secretary to the Board of War, where the Congress wanted to place him to get him out of the way of the colonels — but more of this hereafter."

Unfortunately for us this hereafter never came; for Knox returned to camp, where the rest of the story was told him by word of mouth.

But returning to the subject in March, Greene writes to his kinsman, William Greene : —

There is another great evil which I very much dread, that is, factions and parties among ourselves. Ambition, that seven-headed monster, begins to mingle its poison in our politics, to spread detraction through the country, to lessen the confidence of the people in the Commander-in-chief, and hurt the reputation of his subordinate officers. . . . . But I am happy to find at this time but little to fear from this evil; all those dissatisfied spirits are sinking in their consequence, and the Congress begins to find their credulity and confidence have been greatly abused. . . . General Conway has been a great incendiary in our army. He is a man of great ambition and little talents; he is a man of intrigue and without principle ; he wishes to be thought a hero, but wants the enterprise.[1] He had the most consummate impudence to publish General Washington deficient in every point of generalship. He was lately made a major-general, which he obtained by the most dirty artifice."

[1] John Laurens calls in question his personal courage. Vide *Correspondence of John Laurens,* p. 192.

While Greene was writing these lines in camp,
his right-minded kinsman had already written to
him from the old homestead in Warwick : —

"It gave me much pain to hear that there was an unreasonable party forming against General Washington ; I
say unreasonable, as I imagine it was carried on without
the least foundation, and for any man or set of men to undertake a matter of so dangerous a consequence (they)
must have lost sight of our grand cause. But I was much
pleased to hear by your letter to your brother Jacob, that
the affair had vanished, for I sincerely believe there is no
greater earthly instrument that promises greater probability of success at the head of our grand cause than General Washington."

I have already hinted that one of the chief
grounds of accusation against Washington was an
attachment to unworthy favorites. "If you had
remained with the army," wrote Gates's anonymous friend in November, "we might have opposed, but could not have counteracted, the deep
rooted system of favoritism which began to shoot
forth at New York, and which now has arrived at
its full growth and maturity."[1] "According to
him" (Mifflin), says Graydon, "the ear of the
Commander-in-chief was exclusively possessed by
Greene, who was represented to be, neither the
most wise, most brave, nor most patriotic of counsellors."[2] "Various reports," wrote Major John
Clarke to Greene on the 10th of January from
York, "have been circulated through the country
to prejudice the people against his Excellency and

[1] Vide *sup.* Sparks, *Writings of*   [2] Graydon, p. 299.
Washington, vol. v. p. 484.

you, and you are said to lead him in every measure, and that he wrote, if he fell, to have you appointed to the command of the army." " General Knox," he adds in a postscript, " equally shares the censure of individuals for having the ear of the General." [1]

Invention too, was busy in forging tales and scenes to suit the calumny. A specimen of them, apparently in the handwriting of James Lovell, has been preserved among the papers of General Gates : —

" Dr. Craik, the Clitus of this army, spoke very freely to a great man on the subject of favoritism and impenetrable reserve, and gave a free opinion on the probable consequences. It was taken kindly, and given out that a change would happen in conduct. The two privy counsellors absented themselves three or four days from table. Reed and Cadwallader were caressed, and appeared as substitutes. But the great man's feelings were too much hurt by the apparent banishment of his dear dear. They were restored, and wonderful to tell he has now two sets of favorites, friends, the one ostensible only, to blind the army, and the other real and at the bottom of every movement. Again, Reed and Cadwallader, though good men, have no commissions in the army, yet their advice is taken on all occasions, and good authority says they sit in all councils of war. Do you recollect a similar adventure ? "

In all of these reports the most prominent name is that of General Mifflin. He even went so far as to say, that Greene, who succeeded him in the Quartermaster's Department, had taken the office in order to be " out of the way of bullets."

[1] Greene MSS.

"Now, I do not think," wrote George Lux to
Greene, from Baltimore, in May, "it would be
amiss for you to take an opportunity of telling
him in a public company, that *it has been reported,
but that you cannot recollect any author*, that he has said
so and so, and ask him if it is true ; if he acknowledges it you will be saved the trouble of producing any author; and if he denies it, it will be
stamping the character of a liar effectually upon
him, for the whole army know he said so." [1]

Greene took a still more decisive course, and
wrote to Mifflin, who denied the charge. "I observe the letters that have passed between you
and Mifflin," wrote Lux, in June, ... "I
would have you, however (if you have any acquaintances at Reading and Carlisle), to communicate contents of their *letters in a letter addressed to
me*, as Mifflin in all those places has used them" —
that is, the expressions mentioned in Lux's letter
of May.

But in this as in all cabals, the danger ceased
with the discovery of the intention. No sooner
was it known that certain officers and a part of
Congress were hostile to Washington, than people
began to ask themselves what these men had done
to prove their superior devotion to their country ?
Washington, it was true, had been compelled to
retreat, but whose fault was it that he had not

1 Of George Lux, Graydon tells
us (pp 328, 329), "Mr. Lux was
the greatest reader, in a certain line,
I have ever known. His historical
knowledge was accurate to minute-
ness." It was probably this quality
that drew Greene towards him. His
letters, of which there are several
among Greene's papers, are filled
with gossip, and fully justify Graydon's estimate of him.

been properly furnished with the means of defense? His judgment had sometimes been at fault; how had these men established the correctness of their own? He had placed in some of his officers a confidence which he withheld from others; were not these chosen counsellors of his respected and honored in an equal degree by all the best officers in the army? Even some of Gates's friends were convinced that Mifflin had failed in his duty as Quartermaster-general.[1] Even some who believed both in Gates and Mifflin must have been annoyed and vexed by the querulous impudence of Conway. It was soon evident that the attempt to displace Washington had failed. "I am happy to inform you," Greene wrote to his brother Jacob on the 17th of March, "that the faction raised against General Washington has sunk into contempt; the party charged denies they had any intention of the kind; but the symptoms have been too visible to doubt the truth. Ambition is a dangerous evil in a free state when it happens to rage in an unprincipled bosom; but we must expect such little ebullitions of discontent and partial views to mingle in our national politics."[2]

Each plotter now began, as men always do when detected, to cast about him for his own safety. Gates, who had opened his correspondence in a lofty and confident tone, gradually fell back upon

[1] "Thoughts of a Freeman." Sparks, *Writings of Washington,* vol. v. p. 498.

[2] Vide also Hamilton to Schuyler and Fitzgerald to Washington, in Sparks, *Writings of Washington,* vol. v. Appendix. Gerry would seem to have doubted the existence of the cabal (Gerry to Knox, Feb. 7, 1778), but his defense of Congress is feeble and unsatisfactory. Vide Austin's *Gerry,* p. 241.

prevarications and contradictory denials. It would
have been easy to put an end to the discussion
concerning Conway's letter by producing the original; but instead of doing this Gates confined himself to the assertion that the obnoxious paragraph
was "in words as well as in substance a wicked
forgery." "It is my wish," answered Washington,
"to give implicit credit to the assurances of every
gentleman; but in the subject of our present
correspondence, I am sorry to confess, there happen
to be some unlucky circumstances, which involun-
tarily compel me to consider the discovery you
mention, not so satisfactory and conclusive, as you
seem to think it. I am so unhappy as to find no
small difficulty in reconciling the spirit and import
of your different letters and sometimes of the
different parts of the same letter with each other."
Then entering into a careful examination of the
subject he convicts Gates of insincerity, and closes
with a frank and pointed expression of his opinion
of Conway.

Driven to the wall by the stern reasoning of the
Commander-in-chief, Gates denied "all personal
connection with Conway," asserted that he was
"of no faction and disliked controversy," and hoped
that Washington would not "spend another
moment upon the subject." "I am as averse to
controversy as any man," wrote Washington in
reply, "and had I not been forced into it, you
never would have had occasion to impute to
me even the shadow of a disposition towards it.
Your repeatedly and solemnly disclaiming any of-

fensive views, in those matters which have been
the subject of our past correspondence, makes me
willing to close with the desire you express, of
burying them hereafter in silence, and as far as
future events will permit, oblivion. My temper
leads me to peace and harmony with all men ; and
it is peculiarly my wish to avoid any personal
'feuds or dissensions with those who are embarked in
the same great national interest with myself, as
every difference of this kind must in its consequences be very injurious." It was evident that
Washington's confidence in Gates had not been restored ; but their correspondence upon the subject
ceased here, and their subsequent correspondence
upon other subjects never resumed its original
cordiality. Gates was conscious that he had not
told the truth, and felt that Washington knew it.[1]

"I learn," George Lux wrote to Greene in
April, " that General Mifflin has publicly declared
that he looked upon his Excellency as the best
friend he ever had in his life, so that is a plain
sign that the Junto has given up all ideas of sup-
planting our excellent General from a confidence
of the impracticability of such an attempt." And
in May : "I am glad that the factious and designing Junto who would sacrifice everything to their
insatiable ambition, are alarmed at their unpopu-
larity on account of their malevolent machinations,
and *now deny* all their practices. It shows they
will be cautious hereafter. I have heard it re-

---

[1] All of these letters are found in Sparks, *Writings of Washington*, vol. v.
Appendix.

ported that General Mifflin has wrote to his Excellency declaring he esteems him above all men, both as an officer and as a gentleman, and his particular friend, and wondered how so many reports injurious to him could have been propagated: now I myself heard him condemn him for his partiality to you and General Knox."[1]

"The scheme," Washington wrote to Landon Carter, on the 30th of May, "originated . . . . with three men who wanted to aggrandize themselves. Finding no support, but on the contrary that their conduct and views, when seen into, were likely to undergo severe reprehension, they shrunk back, disavowed the measure, and professed themselves my warmest admirers."[2]

In the autumn, when Mifflin came forward again in Pennsylvania politics, "he found," writes Joseph Reed to Greene, in November, 1778, "his enmity to the General was a fatal objection; he has, therefore, been obliged to recur to his old ground, that he did not oppose the Commander-in-chief but his favorites (yourself and Knox) who had undue influence over him; this is the language he is obliged to talk or he would have been utterly rejected."[3]

Conway's fall was still more precipitate. In a moment of spite he wrote another of his rude letters to Congress, with a threat of resignation, which sounded so much like an actual one that Congress, under the guidance of Gouverneur Morris, accepted it. Then came explanations and

[1] Greene MSS.
[2] Sparks, *Writings of Washington*, vol. v. p. 390.
[3] Joseph Reed to Greene, November 5, 1778.   Greene MSS.

assurances that he had been misunderstood. "The
gentleman, however," wrote Morris to Washington,
" had been so unlucky as to use the most pointed
terms, and therefore, his aid, from whom the information came, was told that the observations he
made came too late. I am persuaded that he will
attempt to get reinstated, if the least probability
of success appears, but I am equally persuaded
that his attempts will fail.[1]" He did attempt it, as
Morris had foreseen; and from York, whither he
had repaired to urge his suit, he wrote to Gates
on the 7th of June: —

"I never had a sufficient idea of cabals until I reached
this place. My reception, you may imagine, was not a
warm one. I must except Mr. Samuel Adams, Colonel
Richard Henry Lee, and a few others who are attached to
you, but who cannot oppose the torrent. Before my arrival, General Mifflin had joined General Washington's
army, where he commands a division. One Mr. Carroll,
from Maryland, upon whose friendship I depended, is one
of the hottest of the cabal. He told me a few days ago
almost literally that anybody who displeased or did not
admire the Commander-in-chief, ought not to be kept in
the army. Mr. Carroll may be a good papist, but I am
sure the sentiments he expresses are neither Roman nor
Catholic. I expect to depart from this court in a very few
days. If there is any attempt from the enemy upon your
post, I will ask your leave to serve in the quality of a volunteer."[2]

But he had not yet reached the end of his
punishment. Factious and censorious to the last,
and still walking in crooked ways, he was led into

[1] Sparks, *Life of Gouverneur Mor-*   [1] Sparks's *Morris*, vol. i. p. 169.
ris, vol. i. p. 167.

a duel with Cadwallader, and wounded dangerously in the mouth and neck. Then at last, repentance came, and one redeeming act with it; for recalling to mind all that he had done to injure the great man who, at his coming, had received him with kindness, he wrote from what he and all around him believed to be his death-bed : —

" I find myself just able to hold the pen during a few minutes, and take this opportunity of expressing my sincere grief for having done, written, or said anything disagreeable to your Excellency. My career will soon be over; therefore justice and truth prompt me to declare my last sentiments. You are in my eyes the great and good man. May you long enjoy the love, veneration, and esteem of these States whose liberties you have asserted by your virtues." [1]

But the wound was not mortal. He recovered, lived for a few months as Lee lived soon after, deserted and despised by all, and returning to France towards the end of the year, appears no more in history.

And thus ended the Conway Cabal; leaving, as such intrigues always do, the object of its hostility stronger than ever; for from that time, men openly avowing what they had hitherto unconsciously believed, placed their hopes of success, not in the wisdom of Congress, but in the virtues of Washington.

[1] Sparks, *Writings of Washington*, vol. v. p. 517.

BOOK THIRD.

CHAPTER I.

Important Change in Greene's position. — Letter to his Brother
Jacob. — Original Condition of Quartermaster-general's Depart-
ment. — Committee to President of Congress. — Greene to Knox.
— Urged to become Quartermaster-general. — Reluctantly ac-
cepts. — Resolves of Congress — Greene to Washington. — John
Cox, Charles Pettit, and Jeremiah Wadsworth. — Greene enters on
the Duties of his Office. — Letter to Colonel Biddle. — Greene to
President of Congress. — Greene to Washington. — Magazines. —
Dilatory Congress. — Greene to President. — Transportation. —
Goes to Lancaster. — Roads. — Conference with the Legislature. —
Slowness of Congress and Treasury Board. — Question of Appoint-
ments. — Letter to President of Congress.

WE have reached an important period of
Greene's public life, and a change in his position which, while it brought his administrative
powers into fuller play, drew him away, in a measure, from those more brilliant duties of the line
wherein it had become his ambition to excel. He
had been three years in constant service, had
studied his new profession in camp, in the field,
and in the best text-books of the day; had become
known to the country as the general in whom

Washington most confided, and to the army as a counsellor deliberate in inquiry, and prompt in decision.   As yet, however, no opportunity had been afforded him of displaying the fertility of his resources or the force of his will, and much less, that comprehensive grasp of mind which enabled him to master with ease the most complex details of a subject, and reduce them to their appropriate heads. The time for this was now come, and come, too, just as he was suppressing a longing for the tranquillity of private life.   "It is very true, what Cousin Griffin told you," he writes to his brother Jacob on the 17th of March, "that I wanted to retire to private life again, provided it was consistent with the public good; but I never will forsake the cause of my country to indulge in domestic pleasures.   Nevertheless it would be agreeable to retire if no injury was to follow to the public, for the splendor of the camp is but a poor compensation for the sacrifices made to enjoy it."

In the original formation of the department of Quartermaster-general, the appointment of that officer had been left to Washington,[1] who had appointed Thomas Mifflin, a member of his own military family.[2] During the first year Mifflin fulfilled the duties of his office with efficiency and zeal, and resigning of his own accord, Stephen Moylan, another of Washington's aids, was appointed in his stead.[3] He too soon resigned, and

[1] Journals of Congress, July 19, 1775

[2] Sparks, Writings of Washington, vol. iii p 68.

[3] Journals of Congress, June 5, 1776.

Mifflin, by a special resolution of Congress, which had now taken the matter into its own hands, was " authorized and requested to resume " the office; " his rank and pay as Brigadier-general " being continued to him.[1] But Mifflin did not bring back his original zeal; and in the following year, entering, as we have already seen, into a cabal against the Commander-in-chief, withdrew from the army under the pretext of ill-health, and without resigning, virtually abandoned his office. Among the subjects which pressed most upon the attention of the committee of Congress for the reorganization of the army, was the systematic organization of this department, and the choice of a competent officer to put at its head.

" We had flattered ourselves," they write to the President of Congress on the 12th of February, " that before this time the pleasure of Congress would be made known to us respecting the Quartermaster's Department. We fear our letter upon this subject has miscarried, or the consideration of it yielded to other business. You will therefore pardon us, when we again solicit your attention to it as an object of the last importance; on which not only the future success of your arms, but the present existence of your army immediately depends. The influence of this office is so diffusive through every part of your military system, that neither the wisdom of arrangement, the spirit of enterprise, or favorable opportunity will be of any avail, if this great wheel in the machine stops or moves heavily. We find ourselves embarrassed in entering on this subject, lest a bare recital of facts should carry an imputation (which we do not intend) on those gentlemen who have lately conducted it. We are

[1] *Journals of Congress*, Oct. 1, 1776.

sensible great and just allowances are to be made for the
peculiarity of their situation, and we are perhaps not fully
acquainted with their difficulties.   It is our duty to inform
you it is not our intention to censure ; and be assured
nothing but a sense of the obligation we are under to postpone all other considerations to the public safety, would
induce us to perform the unpleasing task.   We find the
property of the Continent dispersed over the whole country ; not an encampment, route of the army, or considerable road but abounds with wagons, left to the mercy of
the weather, and the will of the inhabitants ; large quantities of intrenching tools have in like manner been left in
various hands, under no other security, that we can learn,
than the honesty of those who have them in possession.
Not less than three thousand spades and shovels, and a like
number of tomahawks, have been lately discovered and
collected in the vicinity of the camp by an order from one
of the general officers.   In the same way a quantity of
tents and tent-cloth, after having laid a whole summer in
a farmer's barn, and unknown to the officer of the department, was lately discovered and brought to camp by a
special order from the General.   From these instances, we
presume there may be many other stores yet unknown
and uncollected, which require immediate care and attention.

" When in compliance with the expectations of Congress and the wishes of the country, the army was thrown
into huts, instead of retiring to distant and more convenient quarters, the troops justly expected every comfort
the surrounding country could afford.   Among these, a
providential care in the article of straw would probably
have saved the lives of many of your brave soldiers, who
have now paid the great debt of nature.   Unprovided
with this, or materials to raise them from the cold and wet
earth, sickness and mortality have spread through their
quarters in an astonishing degree.   Notwithstand'ng the

diligence of the physicians and surgeons, of whom we hear no complaint, the sick and dead list has increased one third in the last week's return, which was one third greater than the week preceding; and from the present inclement weather, will probably increase in a much greater proportion. Nothing can equal their sufferings, except the patience and fortitude with which the faithful part of the army endure them. Those of a different character desert in considerable numbers.

"We must also observe that a number of the troops have now for some time been prepared for inoculation; but the operation must be delayed for want of this (straw) and other necessaries within the providence of this department. We need not point out the fatal consequences of this delay, in forming a new army, or the preservation of this. Almost every day furnishes instances of the small-pox in the natural way. Hitherto such vigilance and care have been used, that the contagion has not spread; but surely it is highly incumbent on us, if possible, to annihilate the danger.

"We need not point out the effects this circumstance will have on the new draughted troops, if not carefully guarded; they are too obvious to need enumeration. In conference with the forage-master on this subject (which though in appearance trivial, is really important), he acquainted us that though out of his line, he would have procured it if wagons could have been furnished him for that purpose.

"The want of horses and wagons for the ordinary, as well as extraordinary occasions of the army, presses upon us, if possible with equal force; almost every species of camp transportation is now performed by men, who without a murmur, patiently yoke themselves to carriages of their own making, or load their wood and provisions on their backs. Should the enemy, encouraged by the growing weakness of your troops, be led to make a successful

impression upon your camp, your artillery would now undoubtedly fall into their hands, for want of horses to remove it. But these are smaller and tolerable evils, when
compared with the imminent danger of your troops per-
ishing with famine, or dispersing in search of food. The
commissaries in addition to their supplies of live cattle,
which are precarious, have found a quantity of pork in
New Jersey, of which, by the failure of wagons, not one
barrel has reached the camp.

" The orders were given for that purpose as early as
the 4th of January. In yesterday's conference with the
General, he informed us that some brigades had been four
days without meat, and that even the common soldiers had
been at his quarters to make known their wants. At present
there is not one gentlemen of any rank in this department,
though the duties of the office require a constant and un-
remitting attention. In whatever view, therefore, the object presents itself, we trust you will discern that the most
essential interests are connected with it. The season of
preparation for next campaign is passing swiftly away.
Be assured that its operation will be ineffectual, either for
offense or protection, if an arrangement is not immediately made, and the most vigorous exertions used to procure the necessary supplies. Permit us to say that a
moment's time should not be lost in placing a man of the
most approved abilities and extensive capacity at the head
of the department, who will restore it to some degree of
regularity and order ; whose provident care will immediately relieve the present wants of the army, and extend
itself to those which must be satisfied before we can expect vigor, enterprise, or success. When your committee
reflect upon the increased difficulties of procuring wagons,
horses, tents, and the numerous train of articles dependent
on this office, without which your army cannot even move,
they feel the greatest anxiety lest the utmost skill, diligence, and address will prove ineffectual to satisfy the

growing demand.   All other considerations vanish before this object ; and we most earnestly wish Congress may be impressed, in a proper degree, with its necessity and importance. . . . .   We find, in the course of the campaign, necessary tools and stores have often been wanting, important and seasonable movements of the army delayed, in some instances wholly frustrated, and favorable opportunities lost, through the deficiencies of this department.   The rapid marches of our army, and unforeseen disasters which have attended it during the summer season, partly claim some allowance ; but that disorder and confusion prevail through the department, which require some able hand to reform and reduce it, is a certain and melancholy truth. . . . .   A character has presented itself, which, in a great degree meets our approbation, judgment, and wishes.   We have opened the subject to him and it is now under his consideration.   When we are at liberty we shall introduce him to your notice ; but delicacy forbids our doing it until he has made up his mind on the subject, and given his consent to the nomination." [1]

The character thus spoken of was Greene.   How he felt about exchanging the line for the staff, he tells Knox : —

" The committee of Congress have been urging me for several days to accept of the Quartermaster-general's appointment.   His Excellency, also, presses it upon me exceedingly.   I hate the place, but hardly know what to do ; the General is afraid that the department will be so ill-managed unless some of his friends undertakes it that the operations of the next campaign will in a great measure be frustrated.   The committee urge the same reasons and add that ruin awaits us unless the quartermaster's and

[1] Congress Committee to President of Congress, from Valley Forge, Feb. 12, 1778.   This able letter is in the handwriting of Joseph Reed, and has with great propriety been inserted in his *Life and Correspondence,* vol. i. p. 360.

commissary-general's departments are more economically
managed for the future than they have been for some time
past.   I wish for your advice in the affair, but am obliged
to determine immediately."

Such a pressure, Washington, whom he revered,
appealing to him in the name of personal friendship and love of country ; Reed and Morris, whom
he loved and trusted, urging him in the name
of public and private duty, he could not resist.
" Your task," he said to Washington, " is too great,
to be Commander-in-chief and Quartermaster at
the same time."   " I will serve a year," he said
to the committee, " unconnected with the accounts, without any additional pay to that I have
as major-general."   " But this proposition was rejected as inadmissible ; and on the 25th of February, the committee wrote to the President of Congress that Greene had consented to serve.   They
communicated, at the same time, a new plan for
the organization of the department.   On Monday,
March 2d, Congress, " taking into consideration the
arrangement proposed by the committee, —

" *Resolved*, That the same be adopted instead of that
agreed to on the 5th day of February, and that there be
one quartermaster-general, and two assistant quartermasters-general :

" That these three be allowed, for their trouble and expense, one per cent. upon the moneys issued in the department, to be divided as they shall agree, and including an addition to the pay of wagonmaster-general and his deputy :

" That Major-general Green be appointed Quartermaster-general :

" That John Cox and Charles Pettit, Esq. be appointed
Assistant Quartermasters-general :

" That the forage-masters, wagon-masters, and other officers in the department, be in the appointment of the quartermaster-general, who is to be responsible for their conduct:

" *Resolved*, That Major-general Green retain his rank of major-general in the army.

"*Resolved*, That Major-general Mifflin, late Quartermaster-general, be directed to make out immediately and transmit to Congress and to Major-general Green, Quartermaster-general, a state of the preparations for the next campaign in the Quartermaster-general's department, specifying what articles are in readiness, where deposited, where engaged, and in what quantities; and that he deliver or cause the same to be delivered to Major-general Green, Quartermaster-general, or his order." [1]

A year later, Greene, in a letter to Washington, returns to the circumstances of his acceptance: —

" There is a great difference between being raised to an office and descending to one, which is my case. There is also a great difference between serving where you have a fair prospect of honor and laurels, and where you have no prospect of either, let you discharge your duty ever so well. . . I engaged in this business as well out of compassion to your Excellency as from a regard to the public.

Before I came into the department your Excellency was obliged often to stand Quartermaster. However capable the principal was of doing his duty, he was hardly ever with you. The line and the staff were at war with each other. The country had been plundered in a way that would now breed a kind of civil war between the staff and the inhabitants. The manner of my engaging in

[1] *Journals of Congress*, March 2, 1778. The plan of the 5th of February, alluded to in these resolves, was a suggestion of Mifflin's, and is worth careful consideration as illustrating the crude ideas which prevailed both in the Congress and the Board of War upon this important subject. Vide *Journals* ad ·liem.

eration was of great service to Greene in many trying emergencies.

Greene as Quartermaster-general was to " perform the military duty of the department, attend to all the issues, and direct the purchases." Colonel Cox was to " make all purchases, examine all stores and the like," and Mr. Pettit was to " attend to the keeping of accounts and of cash." . . . .
" Forage-masters, wagon-masters, etc., must of necessity be in the appointment of the quartermaster-general, who is, or ought at least to be responsible for their conduct, as forming a part of the general system."

" We have had great difficulty," writes the committee, " in prevailing upon these gentlemen to undertake the business. They object the advanced season, the confusion of the department, the depreciation of our money, and exhausted state of our resources, as rendering it almost impracticable to do that essential service which they conceive their duty to require of them. Besides which each has private reasons of his own. General Greene was very unwilling to enter into this large field of business, which though it will not and indeed ought not to exclude him from his rank in the line, will of necessity prevent his doing the active duty of a general officer. Colonel Cox, whose private business is known to be very lucrative, was unwilling to quit it and break off engagements which he hath largely entered into for the manufactory of salt and iron and to accept a compensation much short of it, for doing public business to a much larger amount and with increased labors. Mr. Pettit, now Secretary to the State of New Jersey, an office which will make a genteel as well as permanent provision for his family, cannot be expected to quit it without an adequate compensation. In short

Sir, we are confident that nothing but a thorough convic
tion of the absolute necessity of straining every nerve in
the service could have brought the gentleman into office
upon any terms."

Greene, as we have seen, had offered to perform
the military duty of the office for a year without
any addition to his pay as major-general, but his
family expenses. To this the committee, who were
anxious to put the department upon a permanent
footing, would not consent. An adequate salary
would lead, they feared, to a general demand
for increase of salaries; and "when once the
mode is begun no one can tell where it will end
except in public bankruptcy." There were grave
objections to the payment of a commission on the
expenditures; but there was "no possibility of ob-
viating peculation but by drawing forth men of
property, morals, and character." It was decided,
therefore, that the compensation should be a commission of one per cent. upon the money issued in
the department, to be divided as they (Greene,
Cox, and Pettit) shall agree, and including an
addition to the pay of the wagon-master-general
and his deputy which is absolutely necessary."
" The commission of two and a half per cent. now
paid on forage alone will, we believe, exceed the
allowance of the new establishment." Greene
proposed an equal division of profits." [1]

Having made sure of the acceptance of Colonels
Cox and Pettit, Greene, on the 23d of March, en-

---

[1] Letter from the committee signed by Francis Dana, February 25
1778. MSS. Dep. of State.

tered upon the duties of his office. "We have been looking over your plan for the forage-master-general's department," he writes to Colonel Biddle on the same day. "We wish to have a plan of the relative state the forage-master's department stood in to the quartermaster-general's heretofore. . . . . You will give us an account of your former conditions of serving,— who were paid by the month, who received a commission, what it was, and on what it arose. Give us as full a history of the matter as may be necessary for our full information to compare the two plans."

On the 26th he writes to the President of Congress : —

"I received my appointment as Quartermaster-general through the hands of the committee of Congress here at camp, by whose special solicitations I engaged in the business of the department. I am very sensible of the importance of the trust, and the difficulty of putting the business upon a tolerable footing at this advanced season. My utmost exertions, however, shall not be wanting to answer the expectations of the Congress and to accommodate the army; and I am sensible the gentlemen who are appointed my assistants will give me all the aid in their power. The demands are so extensive, and the resources so few, that the shortness of the time in which we must provide the necessaries for the ensuing campaign will not leave us at liberty to make the most advantageous contracts. This is an inconvenience to which the public must be subject, in consequence of the business of the department being taken up at so late a period, and will necessarily call for a large and immediate supply of cash. Colonel Cox will wait upon Congress in a few days, and give them further information upon this head. I hope by this time they are impressed with proper ideas respecting the situation of the department, and they will know how essential it is to the operations of the ensuing campaign that the most speedy preparations should be made. If I am not properly supported, if I am not aided with all the influence of Congress in the several States, I am fully persuaded our utmost endeavors will fall vastly short of the desired effect; the army will be distressed, the public disappointed, and our reputations ruined. I hope, therefore, as I engaged in the business of the department from necessity and not of choice, and the gentlemen also, that are with me, that every possible encouragement will be given to enable us to answer the demands of the army.

" I have not received any returns from General Mifflin, and therefore only conjecture as to the full extent of our wants. I have seen some returns from Colonel Butler, agent for camp equipage, by which I find a great deficiency in the article of tents; the like deficiencies also appear as to horses, carriages, and other capital articles. We are taking every method in our power to draw in supplies as fast as possible, and shall be obliged to extend our views to the neighboring States, which renders our immediate demand for cash very great.

" I find there are very large demands against the Quartermaster-general's department now outstanding. It will be necessary to appoint commissioners for the settlement of these accounts, or to authorize us as a board for that purpose; but unless we are to be furnished with money fully equal to the former claims and the present demands, I could wish to be unconnected with the business, as it will be attended with the most destructive consequences to cramp the present preparations.

" You cannot be insensible that the present depreciated state of our currency and the extravagant prices things are sold at must greatly increase our demand for money. The public expenditure will always be proportionate to the depreciation of money, for the prices of commodities are regulated entirely by that; and as our contracts must be paid in cash, the public will suffer the whole loss. Those who have one thing to barter for another, suffer no injury from the advance of prices. Nothing can correct this evil but a heavy tax.

"I find wagoners are not to be got under 10 pounds per month. This is a most extravagant demand; but necessity will compel us to comply with it; for that appears to be the current price given for private business. Good wagoners will be a valuable acquisition. Horses are scarce and difficult to be got, and hundreds are lost for want of good conduct in the drivers. The loss of one horse amounts to almost a driver's wages for a whole year; those that have been drawn out of the line have been ignorant of their duty, and besides it gives great discontent to the officers, and keeps up a kind of perpetual warfare between the staff and the line.

"It may not be improper for me to assign to Congress the reason why I did not somewhat sooner take upon me the exercise of the office. It was a preliminary condition of my acceptance that the gentlemen appointed as assistants should accept also; they were at a great distance from hence when the appointment arrived, and it necessarily took up a considerable time for them to receive the notification, and make the necessary preparation for coming to camp, so that they did not arrive till Saturday last, and we entered on business immediately afterwards."

What his relations with Washington were to be appears from a letter to him of the same date with that to the President of Congress: —

"I received your Excellency's letter containing a list of the counties in Virginia where wagons might be got, and the properest persons to employ to make the purchases. We shall send one Mr. Johnston Smith. I shall be much obliged to your Excellency for a letter to the inhabitants of Virginia by Mr. Smith, requesting their aid in forwarding the business of the department.

" I shall also be obliged to your Excellency for letters to those gentlemen you recommend ; I shall give them appointments, which I shall forward by Mr. Smith, and wish them to accept and engage in the business. Mr. Smith will set out this afternoon.

" There is one Captain Overton of the 14th Virginia Regiment, that I wish to send upon this business. Please to signify your pleasure in the matter. The time is so short that I have to put the business of the department in readiness, that I wish to put everything in motion that will expedite the business.

" If your Excellency has any particular orders respecting the business of the department in camp you will please to transmit them by Major Blodget, and excuse me for not waiting upon you, being very busily engaged in the arrangement of matters abroad."

On the next day he sends an express into New England [1] with instructions, orders, and commissions, and among them a contractor's commission for his brother Jacob, who had served with him in the State legislature, and was now living in the house at Coventry as superintendent of the iron works.

By the 30th he had studied the subject of magazines, and prepared himself to decide upon the proper places for them. " I agree with you there is not a moment's time to be lost in fixing upon proper places for magazines," he writes to Colonel Clement Biddle : —

" I have been thinking upon the subject, and am of opin-

[1] Letter to General Varnum, March 27, 1778

ion that the following must be the great outlines of the
chain of magazines; the quantity to be laid in of particular
stores upon the river and at intermediate posts to form a
proper communication, must be regulated by circumstances.
200,000 bushels of grain upon the Delaware, and as much
    hay as can be got.
200,000 bushels of grain upon the Schuylkill, and as much
    hay as can be bought.
200,000 bushels of grain at the Head of Elk and the in-
    termediate posts to camp, and as much hay as can
    be bought within forty miles to camp upon that
    route.
100,000 bushels of grain upon the line of communication
    from the Susquehanna to the Schuylkill, from
    Reading through Lancaster to Wright's Ferry, and
    as much hay as can be got.
100,000 bushels of grain from the Delaware to the North
    River, to be proportioned to the consequence of the
    several posts forming the communication, and a nec-
    essary quantity of hay.
40,000 bushels of grain round about Trenttown, within a
    circle of eight or ten miles, and as much hay as can
    be got.

"As there has been a post kept at Trenton it is more
than probable the forage must be principally drawn from
Burlington or Monmouth. The forage at the North River
must be proportioned to the number of troops to be kept
there. I am ignorant of that at present, but believe it
will amount to five thousand, and as it is on the direct
route of communication from the Eastern States, the quantity must be considerable; the river will enable you to
form that magazine very easy.

"In forming your magazines, give all sorts of grain the
preference to wheat. Oats first, corn next, rye next, and
so on. You must get a number of screws made to screw
all the hay, and employ hands to do it either at the farm·

ers' barns or at the magazines. You cannot set about this too soon; there must be a number of forage carts provided to be employed in no other business.

"I shall call upon you this afternoon, if possible. I find my present situation to be very inconvenient for the Quartermaster-general's department, and purpose to move to More Hall as soon as possible.

" I intend to construct some boats as soon as may be to transport forage and stores up and down the Delaware and Schuylkill."

The same day or the next he submits the plan to Washington for approval.

" I approve the above places for magazines," writes Washington on the 31st, " with this proviso, that the one at Trenton shall not in its full extent be immediately formed, and that the others upon that river shall be tolerably high up for security. The quantity is, I presume, the result of estimation. For obvious reasons I should prefer a number of small magazines to a few large ones, and think if they were to be laid in quarterly, or for a term not exceeding four or six months, it would be advisable and proper, as the theatre of war may change, and taxation must reduce the price of every commodity."

Another great source of anxiety was the selection of deputies and agents.

" Having been lately appointed to the office of Quartermaster-general," he writes to General Heath : " I have sent a considerable order for goods and stores in that way, to be purchased by Mr. Benjamin Andrews, merchant in Boston, since which I have heard his character has been called in question, respecting some dealings with General Burgoyne's officers. I had conceived so good an opinion of him as to think him a suitable person to be employed, but at the same time I would not choose to continue him in the employ if his character is so far injured as to hurt his usefulness, or is even become doubtful. I shall, therefore, be much obliged to you to furnish me with the history of this charge against him, together with your sentiments concerning his fitness to be employed as Deputy Quartermaster-general at Boston. I am told Colonel Chase has been employed in that department. I am not certain that I even know his person, as there are several of the name with whom I am perfectly unacquainted; you will farther oblige me by giving me his character, and your opinion of his fitness for the employment.

" You will perceive, from the nature of this letter, that it is confidential, and you may rely on my care that no ill use shall be made of the information you may give me. My aim is to have the business of the department well executed, and having been so long absent from Boston, it will be impossible for me to form a right judgment of characters at so great a distance, without the aid of this kind of intelligence, which no person is better qualified to give than you. Any farther aid which it may be in your power to give me in the department of Quartermaster-general will be a favor done to the public, and will be thankfully recived."

Now, too, begins the struggle with a dilatory Congress. But if they will delay, Greene is resolved that they shall not have ignorance to plead in their defense : —

" You will have been informed by my letter of the 26th of March," he writes to the President on the 3d of April, " that a large sum of money is absolutely necessary for the Quartermaster's department, to enable us to make due preparation for the ensuing campaign, and I expect before this reaches you, Colonel Cox will have stated that necessity to you in a still more pointed light. Hitherto, however, we have not received a single shilling, though we have

daily demands for large sums not only for expenditure here,
but to be distributed into different parts of the country from
whence we expect to draw supplies; and until these dis-
tributions are made, our utmost efforts will not have the
desired effect. I have, therefore, drawn on the Treasury
Board for fifty thousand pounds in favor of Robert Lettis
Hooper, Jr., Esq., an active and useful deputy quartermaster for the district in the neighborhood of Easton, who,
I expect, will lay it out to good advantage. I therefore
hope the draught will be duly honored. I have directed
it to ' the Honorable, the Board of Treasury of the United
States.' I do not know whether the address is right, and
should be glad to have directions in that respect; but however that may be, I hope Mr. Hooper will not be disappointed in his expectations of receiving the cash, as such a
disappointment would be greatly injurious to the service."

As the army is in Pennsylvania, and much depends upon the temper and action of the State
government, he resolves to go to Lancaster and
meet the legislature face to face; first, however,
taking care to make himself master of such parts
of the local laws as relate to the immediate subject of his demand. " If you have, or can procure
the State law respecting the wagon department,"
he writes to Colonel Biddle, Sunday evening,
"please to send it down to me by the bearer. I
wish to consult fully upon the subject before I
write to the State. The General will write when
he has further information."

He has begun, too, with the knotty subject of
transportation, which had hitherto served as a pretext for the delays and failures of the commis-
sariat : —

"This," he writes to Col. Henry Hollingsworth, on the 7th of April, "will be handed you by Mr. John Hall, who offers himself in the Quartermaster-general's department, and comes warmly recommended. I wish you to employ him under you as an assistant, for I am persuaded there is more business than you can execute yourself.

"The Commissary-general has made a demand upon me for a large number of teams to remove a great quantity of provision from the Head of Elk. I wish you to procure all you possibly can either by hire, purchase, or impressment. If you want any further powers, please to write me by express, and they shall be transmitted you immediately. I must beg your utmost exertions to forward the business. I hope you have received my letter requesting you to purchase a large number of horses, and have taken necessary measures accordingly."

By the 10th he is ready to start for Lancaster.

"I received your note by your boy," he writes to Colonel Biddle that day. "I intended you should have gone to Lancaster with me, as I am almost a stranger to all the assembly. If there is no particular objection, I wish you to go still. I have sent your agreement signed. I note your observation respecting Colonel Hollingsworth. I purpose to set off this afternoon, and wish you to be in readiness to go with me. Mrs. Greene's compliments to Mrs. Biddle."

On his way he takes note of the bad roads, and resolves at once to have them repaired.

"The road from camp to this place is exceeding bad," he writes to Charles Pettit from the "Red Lion" on the 11th, "and as it is the greatest communication between camp and Lancaster, and between camp and Yellow Springs, where our principal hospitals are, it is our interest to set about mending it as soon as possible. Apply to his

Excellency for fifty men to work upon this road, and fifty more upon the Reading road.

"I met and overtook several wagons that were stalled yesterday. The sick that were removing, in distress, and the cattle almost ruined by repeated strains in attempting to get through the most difficult parts of the roads. More attention must be paid to the roads than heretofore to save our cattle and our wagon-hire. We must get some good man to survey the road, and to direct the operations of the fatigue parties.

"We have the misfortune to have a rainy morning, which I am afraid will detain me here to-day, as it is now past twelve o'clock."

How it fared with him at Lancaster, face to face with a legislature not altogether pleased with the conduct of the army, the Pennsylvania records show. He presents himself with hands strengthened by a letter from Washington: —

"I beg leave to introduce Major-general Greene to you, who is lately appointed Quartermaster-general. Upon looking over the late law of the State for regulating the manner of providing wagons for the service, he has found out some parts which he conceives might be amended so as more fully to answer the valuable purposes intended. He will lay the wished amendments before you and the Council for your consideration, and if you think with him, that the service will be benefited by them, I have no doubt but you will recommend them to the Assembly at the opening of the next session.

"There is a grievance complained of by many persons, inhabitants of this State, who attend the army in Continental employ as quartermasters, wagon-masters, teamsters, etc. They are called upon to do duty in the militia, and if they do not appear are fined to the amount of their substitute money. This they conceive to be very hard upon them as they are in the service of the States, and ought to be as much exempted as officers or soldiers.

" General Greene will represent this matter fully to you, and point out an equitable mode of redress. He is interested in the matter, as the persons who complain generally belong to his department." [1]

On the 13th of April Greene appeared before the Council, and on the 15th and 18th, the Council entered upon its records : —

" Major-general Greene having on the 13th instant represented to the Council that there may probably be cases of great and immediate necessity for wagons for the use of the army which cannot be supplied in the mode pointed out by the wagon law, so as to answer such emergency; and he expressing an earnest desire of acting in the discharge of his duty as Quartermaster-general in perfect harmony with this State, and of conforming to the laws of it, proposed that some further authority be given by law to him and his deputies in extra cases. The subject being duly considered, this Council are of opinion, that whenever a sudden and extraordinary emergency shall make the impressing of wagons by a military force absolutely necessary, that necessity must, from the nature of things, justify the impressing by force of arms, but that it would be improper to entrust such powers in the military by law. And Major-general Greene having represented to Council that great difficulties had arisen in the procuring of wagon-masters and teamsters, in consequence of the demands made on them for their services in the militia, or for payment of substitution money in lieu of such service : on consideration, the Council are of opinion that wagon-masters and wagon-drivers actually enlisted in the Continental service for a reasonable time are not liable to serve in the militia during the time of their continuing in such service, nor

[1] *Pennsylvania Archives*, 1777–78, p. 405.

subject to the payment of substitution money ; and that an
enlistment in either of these services for six months or
longer time ought to be considered by the lieutenants and
sub-lieutenants of the respective counties of this State as
a good and sufficient cause to forbear levying the substitution money in such cases." [1]

On Greene's return to camp he followed up vig-
orously his endeavors to give life and system to
his department. One of the evils which called
most loudly for immediate correction was the negligence whereby, for want of a responsible head,
the property of the public had been scattered over
all the roads by which the army had marched.
Greene resolved to trace it out. " Your apology is
sufficient," he writes to Varnum on the 17th of
April. " Please to retain the axes for the use of
your brigade. I am very sorry to be obliged to
call for the axes belonging to the regiments in this
way. I hope the necessity won't remain long."

Congress and the Treasury Board still move
slowly. He is determined to make them feel that
if he is to do his work — and he means to do it —
they must do theirs also.

" Having received information from Joseph Borden,
Esq., the loan officer for the State of New Jersey," he
writes to President Laurens on the 20th of April, " that he
has on hand a considerable sum of money which he wishes
to be called out of his hands, as he thinks his situation at
Bordentown not safe, and as Colonel Cox did not obtain a
sufficient quantity of cash from your treasury to distribute
through all the channels which immediately call for it, and
a large sum is wanted in New Jersey to give vigor to the

---

[1] *Colonial Records of Pennsylvania*, vol. xi. p. 467.

purchasing of horses and other necessary supplies, I shall hope to receive by the return of this express an order on the loan officer of New Jersey for one hundred and fifty-thousand dollars. Near one half of that sum he has on hand; the rest we will draw from him as it comes in, or take in certificates which we can negotiate in the country.

"I hope this business will meet with no delay, as the agent for purchasing in New Jersey will wait the return of this express."

Instead of the $150,000 that he asked for, Congress, on a report of the Treasury Board, voted him $50,000.[1]

Among the many troublesome questions that arise is the question of appointments, and the mixing up of civil and military rank — one of the vices of the former system. "My blacksmith is a captain," writes De Kalb. "The numerous assistant quartermasters are for the most part people without any military education, often the common tradesmen, but collectively colonels. . . . . The army swarms with colonels."[2] Greene was determined to bring the question of his own rights to an immediate decision.

"This will be handed to you," he writes to the President of Congress on the first of May, "by Lieut.-Col. Hay, who acted as deputy quartermaster-general to the Northern army the last year by an appointment from Congress. Upon my offering a new deputation, he informed me that as Congress had been pleased to give him the rank of

---

[1] *Journal*, April 24, 1778.

[2] Kapp's *De Kalb*, p. 132. John Laurens writes to his father: "Rank has likewise been vilified by the indiscriminate distribution of it. Wagon-masters, regimental quartermasters, etc., have had titles which cease to be honorable when possessed by such personages." — *Correspondence of John Laurens*, p 83.

lieutenant-colonel in the army with his former appointment, and he could not, without acknowledging that to be
cancelled, accept of a new one, he could not with propriety
accept it at present; that he was ready, nevertheless, to
act under his old appointment or a new one, provided his
military rank were preserved, but wanted to know the
mind of Congress on these points, previously to his entering on business, and therefore would wait upon you for an
explanation.

"The business of a deputy quartermaster-general is so
distinct from any idea of military rank, that I apprehend
they have no necessary connection nor relation. I believe
Colonel Hay to be a very good and active officer, and I
doubt not that he will bring strong testimonials of his merit
from former services; it may, therefore, be very proper
that his military rank should be continued to him; but
this is a matter that as Quartermaster-general I pretend
not to interfere in. So far, however, as relates to the
Quartermaster's department, I conceive the appointment
of all subordinate officers to be clearly within my province,
as well from the nature of the business, which requires
an orderly and regular subordination throughout the department, as from the resolution of Congress on my appointment in which it is expressly mentioned, and which
makes me responsible for the conduct of my deputies to a
degree that would be incompatible with any other mode
of appointment. I have therefore concluded that it was
undoubtedly the intention of Congress in that resolution that all former appointments were wholly superseded
on the appointment of myself and my assistants, and I rest
assured that Congress will give it no other interpretation to Colonel Hay. Were it necessary, I could mention
many inconveniences that would arise from different modes
of appointment; it would give birth to disputes very injurious to the service, were precedence to be claimed by appointments coming through different channels; and the

respect arising from some degree of dependence, and which is necessary to the preservation of due subordination and discipline, would be totally lost. A person lately applied to me with an old appointment from Congress, as deputy quartermaster-general at Baltimore, which I was obliged to disregard, not only because I considered it to be extinct, but because I had, before I had any knowledge of it, appointed another person whom I esteem more fit for the office, in the same place.

"As other instances of the like kind may arise, I have thought it proper thus to explain my ideas of the powers Congress have been pleased to invest me with, and of the propriety of my appointing of all subordinate officers in the Quartermaster's department. At the same time I shall always be ready to gratify their wishes in favor of any particular person, or on any occasion where it may be in my power consistent with that order which must necessarily be preserved in a business of so much importance, and for the well conducting of which I am in so great a degree responsible."

This letter was received and read on the 5th of May, but it was not until the 29th that Congress acted upon it; the committee to which it had been referred reporting that the "appointment of subordinate officers" had been given to the Quartermaster-general; that "Udney Hay, Esq.," could not claim office under his old appointment; and "that no persons hereafter appointed upon the civil staff of the army, shall hold or be entitled to any rank in the army by virtue of such staff appointment."[1]

[1] *Journals of Congress,* Friday, May 29, 1778.

CHAPTER II.

TIME passed swiftly amid these engrossing cares, and a new campaign was at hand. "There seem to be but three general plans of operation, which may be premeditated for the next campaign," wrote Washington on the 20th of April; "one, the attempting to recover Philadelphia, and destroy the enemy's army there; another, the endeavoring to transfer the war to the northward by an enterprise against New York; and a third, the remaining quiet in a secure fortified camp, disciplining and arranging the army till the enemy begin their operations, and then to govern ourselves accordingly. Which of these three plans shall we adopt?" [1]

Opinions differed widely among the general officers to whom these questions were addressed. Greene was for keeping the main body of the army in their present quarters, under the command of

[1] Sparks, *Writings of Washington*, vol. v. p. 319.

General Lee, while Washington with four thousand regulars and the eastern militia made an attempt upon New York. But tidings were already on their way from France which were to give a new aspect to the campaign.

Meanwhile the pressure of Greene's new duties did not prevent him from taking a lively interest in the progress of discipline which, under the intelligent supervision of Steuben, had already reached a higher point than it had ever reached before; nor did the necessity of sometimes providing for the army by impressment harden him against just reclamations.

"The wife of Mr. Jacob Brick," he wrote to General John Lacy on the 21st, "complains that some of your people have taken from her husband one of their horses which they are in want of to enable them to move up to Reading. I wish you to inquire into the matter, and if there is no capital objection, to order the beast to be delivered to the owner again. The war is a sufficient calamity under every possible restraint; but where people are influenced by avarice and private prejudice, they increase the distresses of the inhabitants beyond conception. These evils can only be restrained by the generals, whose duty it is to protect the distressed inhabitants, as well as govern and regulate the affairs of the army. I hope you will pay particular attention to this affair, as the age and distress of the complainants appear to claim it."

"I received your letter of the 21st instant," General Lacy answered from Camp Crooked Billet, on the 27th, "and have made inquiry concerning the horse you mention, which I find has been taken by a person who calls himself a volunteer, and has made a practice of riding with my parties on the lines. I have sent for him to appear before me to answer for his conduct in acting thus without orders. Every precaution has been taken, and repeated orders given my parties, not to distress the inhabitants unless they be found favoring the enemy. In that case, I think it requisite and justifiable to take what may be of immediate benefit to the army.

"Strolling parties, both inhabitants and soldiers on furlough from the army, have made a practice the greatest part of this winter, of skulking about the enemy's lines, where they have committed the most villainous robberies imaginable, under the character of militia. I have given orders to my parties to apprehend and bring them, under confinement, to my camp. Some of them have been taken, and, for want of sufficient proof, were discharged. One or two soldiers I ordered to be sent to head-quarters."

Early in May the welcome tidings of the French alliance reached camp, diffusing confidence and joy. The bitterness of the struggle, many said, is now over, and our independence sure. However this may be, thought Greene, there will be important changes in the plan of campaign, for which I must prepare at once. The enormous sums he was compelled to call for startled him, and he felt that they would startle the country and Congress still more, though all knew that in the actual state of the currency the nominal sum was a very imperfect representation of the real sum. To prepare himself for the attacks which he foresaw, he wrote to Washington on the 3d of May : —

"From the situation in which I found the Quartermas-ter-general's department on my entering upon the office, which is not unknown to your Excellency, it appeared to be absolutely necessary to make very extensive and speedy preparations for the ensuing campaign, especially in horses, teams, tents, and other articles of high price. In consequence of this apparent necessity, I have given extensive orders, almost without limitation, for the purchase of these articles; apprehending from the prospects at that time, the utmost exertions we could make would not procure more than a sufficiency for the necessary accommodation of the army.

" From the intelligence lately received, the aspect of our affairs is essentially changed; and it may be that in consequence of this change, the plan of military operations may undergo such material alterations as may, in a considerable degree, abate the demand for those expensive preparations which some weeks ago were thought indispensably necessary. And as I would not willingly enhance the expenses of the quartermaster-general's department further than prudence and good economy absolutely require, I take the liberty of addressing your Excellency on the occasion, to request the favor of your advice and direction whether the plan above mentioned for obtaining supplies ought to be retrenched, and in what degree, or in other words, in what degree the plan of preparations ought to be continued, and particularly, as the prospect of the local situation of the army may be greatly altered by these changes, what alterations should be made in the plan, lately approved by your Excellency for establishing magazines of forage in the different parts of the country."

Meanwhile it had been resolved to celebrate the French alliance with imposing solemnity. Steuben's memory and invention were brought into play for the important occasion. On the 5th of May the outlines of the festival were announced in general orders. On Wednesday the 6th, the happiest morning that had ever dawned upon the gloomy valley, the army was early a-foot, happy and hopeful as they had never been before. At nine, the brigades were drawn out, to hear their chaplains read the announcement of the alliance from the postscript to the Pennsylvania Gazette of the 2d. Prayers and a thanksgiving sermon, the American Te Deum, followed at the head of each brigade. Next came Steuben's well-earned hour of triumph, and as the first signal-gun boomed through the valley, the troops, stepping briskly into line, were soon all under arms. The inspection came next, exact, rigid, stern; Steuben himself, with his hair powdered and dressed as he had learnt to wear it in the Prussian army, with the bright star of the order of Fidelity on his breast, and bearing himself like one on whom all eyes were fixed, passed slowly through the ranks, scanning them closely with his experienced scrutiny. Barber, Brooks, Davies, Ternant, and Fleury came close in his footsteps, inspecting, first the dress, arms and accoutrements of each brigade, then forming them into battalions, and when all were arranged, announcing, each to his brigadier, with military precision, that the men were ready for their officers. The brigadiers then assigned to each battalion its commanding officer for the day, and the men, loading their muskets, stood with grounded arms, waiting the second gun. It was now half past eleven, and the sun was looking down upon them from a clear sky, calling out with every motion bright gleams and sudden flashes from the polished steel of musket and sword. The whole valley was alive with gay sights and sounds. The signal gun came, drum and fife and bugle gave a joyful response, and taking up its line of march, the whole army, with Stirling commanding on the right, Lafayette on the left, and De Kalb the second line, advanced in five columns to the appointed position on the heights, where Washington and Greene and other officers not on duty had taken their stand to witness the services. O, for a glance at their happy faces on that happy day!

The review ended, Washington and the general officers repaired to a kind of amphitheatre in the centre of the encampment, and when all were ready, the third signal gun was fired, and instantly cannon after cannon followed, one for each State, thirteen in all, with a sound, that swelling upon the ear in gradual progression, rebounded in full chorus from the semicircle of hills, and swept with its canopy of smoke, far down the still bosom of the Schuylkill. When the cannon ceased, the musketry began a running fire from Woodford's right, straight along the first line. The second takes it up on the left, and on it runs, rattling along to the right again. Silence then for a moment as the smoke floats slowly away, revealing the long flashing line of musketeers, the eager artillery, the exultant group around Washington, the ladies mingled with them, and most exultant of all. Then at a given signal, one loud huzza of "Long live the King of France," bursts from ten thousand voices. Thirteen more cannon, one more running fire from right to left and from left to right, and then a huzza for the "friendly European powers." Can-

non again, musketry again, and a huzza for the
American States.

Meanwhile there was great ado and great running to and fro in the amphitheatre, where tables
were already set out and decked for a sumptuous
repast; on the outer circle those of the officers
under tent-cloth stretched on poles; in the centre
those of the guests and officers of higher rank, with
marquees, to protect them from the sun, but all
forming one vast inclosure.[1]   Here Washington,
with Greene and Lafayette and Stirling, were already in waiting, Lafayette conspicuous by his
white scarf.   Here too the ladies who had shared
the hard winter encampment, were collected.
Mrs. Washington, Mrs. Greene, Lady Stirling and
her daughter Lady Kitty, whom Greene mentions
so pleasantly in letters to his wife.   And towards
this spot the officers now turned their steps,
marching in columns, thirteen abreast, with arms
closely linked, in emblem of the union of the thirteen States.   On none was attention more fixed
than on the foreign officers, who represented the
new ally in the popular mind, and were eagerly
greeted by all as the subjects of America's best
friend.   Never before had men seen Washington's
face so radiant.   Pleasant words passed round; the
wine circled merrily in toasts to the king of France,
and the friendly powers, and the Congress, and the
States; the band playing all the while patriotic

[1] According to De Kalb, fifteen
hundred persons sat together at the
tables, "officers with their wives and
the most distinguished people of the
neighborhood." — Kapp's *De Kalb*,
p. 145.

and martial airs. The doubt and the fear and the great suffering are over now, said one to the other, little dreaming, alas! how much blood was yet to flow, and how many of these exultant hearts would cease to beat before the victory that seemed so sure was fully won. As Washington rose to go, the whole company rose with him, clapping their hands, and tossing up their hats, and huzzaing long and loud. When he had gone near a quarter of a mile on his way homeward, he turned his horse, all his suite turning with him, and sent back a loud huzza in reply. While the festivity was yet at its height, a British spy was detected by the guard and seized.

"What shall we do with him?" asked the officer on duty of the officer of the day.

"Let him go back and tell his employers what he has seen. 'Twill pain them far more than to hear of his detection and death." [1]

On the next day there was a council of war to decide upon a plan of operations adapted to the change in the political situation of the country; Gates and Mifflin sitting again, with unabashed brows, in the presence of the man they had striven to undo.[2] The council decided "to remain on the defensive and wait events, not attempting any offensive operation against the enemy, till circumstances should afford a fairer opportunity of striking a successful blow." [3]

---

[1] Sparks, *Writings of Washington*, vol. v. p. 356. Kapp's *Steuben*, p. 139. *De Kalb*, p. 145. Moore's *Diary of the Revolution*, vol. ii. p. 48 *et seq.*

[2] For Washington's opinion, *Vide* Sparks, *Writings of Washington*, vol. vi. p. 371.

[3] Sparks, *Writings of Washington,* vol. vi. p. 360.

But the wished-for opportunity was still delayed. A change was taking place in the English army also. Wearied with the unsuccessful contest, Sir William Howe was giving place to Sir Henry Clinton, the same Clinton whose timely succor at Bunker hill, tradition says, he had never forgiven. An attempt was making, too, to counteract the French alliance by offering new terms of reconciliation, in the hope of producing a division in the country and strengthening the hands of the Tories.[1]

Before this intention was known, Congress had undertaken to strengthen its position by prescribing a new oath of allegiance. The resolution was passed in February, but it was not till May that it was acted upon, thus gaining additional importance from circumstances unforeseen at the time of its passage. The general officers took their oath together before Washington, the others before some general officer, Greene being one of the busiest in this task also, and his name one of the oftenest found in the records still preserved in the Department of State.

In the midst of these occurrences his duties called him back to the scene of the last year's operations in Jersey and on the Hudson; and on the 15th of May we find him writing from Fishkill to General Gates; " You was polite enough to offer to regulate and settle the quartermaster-

---

[1] This was the occasion of the celebrated commission of this year. Most of the documents relative to it are found in Almon, vol. vi. p. 291 et seq.

[2] Vide *Journals of Congress*, February 3, 1778.

general's department at Albany.   I shall be much
obliged to you for doing of it.   You'll be kind
enough to transmit me your regulations and orders thereon as soon as the business is completed."
If Gates was to be kept in command, Greene was
resolved not to give him any opportunity of making trouble in his department.   This excursion
affords him also an opportunity of rendering a
service to his friend Mr. Lott; and the letter that
records it, though not important in itself, is not
without interest as an illustration of some of the
difficulties men had to contend with in the daily
life of those times : —

"Mr. Lott, a gentleman of this place," he writes to
Colonel Wadsworth from Morristown on the 19th of May,
"purchased a small quantity of rum and salt at Boston,
which he cannot get on, owing to the State laws. I should
be obliged to you to give him such a pass, that his property
may come forward ; he wants the salt for his family use ;
part of his spirits he proposes for sale."

"Mr. Lott's character for generosity and hospitality is
too well known to say anything upon the subject. I am
under particular obligations to him ; and shall esteem myself so to you, if you will be kind enough to enable him to
get forward his property. The propriety and the best
forms you are the best judge of, and I therefore submit
this matter to your opinion and discretion."

By the 25th, Greene is back in camp again,
writing to his kinsman William Greene, who had
just been chosen Governor of Rhode Island : —

"I am happy to hear you are elected Governor of
Rhode Island, and beg leave to congratulate you upon the
occasion. I am told Dr. Bradford took some very disin-

genuous means to supplant you.   The duplicity of his conduct met with a deserved punishment.

" I am persuaded you have taken the reins of government from the best of motives, and that you will discharge your trust with the greatest integrity.   Nevertheless don't flatter yourself that the most upright conduct will secure you from reproach.   The pride and ambition of some, the spite and envy of others, will always find occasion through misrepresentation to wound the reputation for a time.   But truth and virtue will triumph at last.   Therefore don't be surprised at the one, nor despair of the other. You have a very difficult and jealous people to manage. They are feeble in their tempers, variable in their measures.   They are warm in their friendships, but subject to sudden and unaccountable changes.   But to do them justice I don't think there is a more patriotic or spirited people upon the continent.   They feel for the calamities of their neighbors, and like generous spirits, lend them a helping hand.   They have done (this) with more liberality than they have ever received in return.

" Your salary will go but a little way towards the defraying the additional expenses of your office.   Splendor and dignity are essential among a mercantile people.   Pomp and parade goes a great way towards governing them ; for the vulgar are generally apt to admire those things they least understand, and merchants despise what don't consist in part of show.   You must, in order to support your reputation, make a figure equal to the importance of your station. There is such a general intercourse throughout the continent that a person becomes contemptible unless he appears characteristical at home.   Having heard many animadversions upon these matters by travellers, I just take the liberty to give you a hint of what you are to expect.

" I beg leave to congratulate you upon the agreeable news from France.   Our political alliance is most excellent. It is strongly reported Spain has acceded to the treaty also.

I don't doubt all Europe in a few months, not in alliance with Great Britain, will declare us free and independent States.

"The enemy are making the greatest preparations imaginable for the evacuation of Philadelphia. Their further intentions and destination is unknown. We have the best intelligence the whole of the British forces are to rendezvous at New York; but whether they are going to leave the continent or go up the North River, remains yet to be discovered. I must confess many circumstances induce a belief they are going off altogether. How happy will America be, like a man just free from a racking pain.

"A French war is confidently asserted. There has been the hottest press in New York and Philadelphia ever known. The enemy took everybody they could lay their hands on, *Quakers* and all.

"Upon the enemy's evacuating Philadelphia we shall move towards the North River, where General Gates is now commanding.

"Pray, how does General Sullivan agree with you? He is a good officer, but loves flattery. That is his weak side. . . . .

"General Lee has joined this army with his usual train of dogs. I feel a singular happiness at the different situation of the American affairs between the time he left us and the time he joins us again.

"Major Ward left this army some time since to join his regiment in Rhode Island. Mrs. Greene is on her way home. Poor girl! she is constantly separated, either from her husband or children, and sometimes, from both."

The difficulties occasioned by the defective organization of the old department come up in a new form, which threatens collision with the Board of War : —

"Considering the weighty affairs," Greene writes to the

President of the Board, on the 27th of May, " which must constantly claim the attention of the Board of War, it gives me no small concern to find myself in a situation which obliges me to ask their interposition. But as it respects a matter in which the public interest, and harmony necessary to the well conducting the business of our respective departments are in no small degree concerned, I am persuaded the application will be excused.

" It has been my constant aim in the appointments I have made, to engage such men in the different branches of my department as were in every point of view most suitable for the business, giving the preference where I conceived it could be done with propriety to those I found in office. But having not been favored with any return of those formerly employed I may, perhaps, have made some changes which might have been avoided, had I obtained better information. The office of deputy quartermaster-general does not, however, necessarily include that of a purchaser of stores, nor are the abilities for the one always attended with a proper capacity for the other. I have in some instances, therefore, thought it expedient to appoint gentlemen skilled in mercantile business to make purchases, to whom I have not offered a deputation in the quartermaster's line. Among these is Mr. Benjamin Andrews, of Boston, to whom in March last, I sent a large order for the purchasing of stores, particularly duck and other materials for tents and knapsacks. I had heard that Colonel Chase was Deputy Quartermaster-general in Boston; and as I knew of no cause of complaint against him, I did not choose to displace him; but at the same time, being wholly unacquainted with his character and mercantile abilities, I thought it most prudent to send an order of so much importance to a gentleman of whose character and fitness for the business I had a more thorough knowledge. He has accordingly made considerable purchases, and some of the goods are now on the way from Boston hither; but he and

his partner, Mr. Otis, complain that they have been much
obstructed by the interference of Colonel Chase, founded,
as is alleged, on authority derived from the Board of War;
that he claims an authority superior to mine, and deter-
mines to bid as high for purchases as any one ; that a large
quantity of duck, tent cloths, etc., lately arrived at Boston,
which the Navy Board intended to deliver to Messrs. Andrews & Otis as purchasers for the Quartermaster's department, till Colonel Chase demanded sufficient to make 4,000
tents, which he said he had orders from the Board of War
of a later date than my order to Messrs. Otis & Andrews,
to get made up and forward immediately, and threatened
to purchase at any rate if the demand were not satisfied.
On the whole they describe Colonel Chase's conduct in this
business as savoring more of resentment, and setting up
one source of authority in competition with another, than a
prudent regard to the good of the service. They have,
therefore, desisted from purchasing articles of this kind,
till the matter shall be further explained, and consented
that Colonel Chase shall receive the duck from the Navy
Board rather than prejudice the public by a contest. How
far this line of conduct may be warranted by instructions
from the Board of War, is not for me to determine ; but I
must, till I have more full information, suppose there is
some mistake in the matter. For however necessary it
might have been for the Board to execute the office of
quartermaster-general while the place was vacant, I cannot admit the supposition that so respectable a body would
continue the exercise of it after they knew it was filled,
without at least notifying the Quartermaster-general of the
part they had taken, that he might regulate his conduct accordingly. But from whatever motive Colonel Chase may
have been actuated, this kind of competition is surely injurious to the public in a high degree. The business is
not only retarded by it, but must finally be effected at a
greater expense by raising the prices of the commodities

purchased, and thwarting measures taken by either party. I cannot, therefore, doubt but the Board will make due inquiry into the affair and give such directions as will be proper on the occasion."

Trouble came from another quarter also. His agents were negligent in their purchases, and the blame would necessarily fall upon him.

"Your favor of the 29th is before me," he writes to Col. R. L. Hooper, one of his deputies, the 31st of May. "The horses you mention are arrived, but I am sorry to inform you there are a great many of them that is barely fit for service, and make but a very indifferent appearance.

"I must beg you to be very particular in the purchases, and orders given to those that purchase for you, that no more bad horses may be brought to camp. The public will find themselves saddled with a great expense in the purchase of horses, and if there is but little or nothing to show for it they will think themselves greatly injured.

"Forward the valises, portmanteaus, knapsacks, canteens and axe slings as fast as possible.

"The enemy still remain in Philadelphia, although there has been appearances of their designing to evacuate it from day to day, for a week past."

What pressed hardest upon his mind at this moment, and what he thought upon the topics and reports of the day, he tells in a letter of June 1st, to Gouverneur Morris : —

"I received your favor of the 5th of May upon the subject of the Quartermaster's department, and intend to follow your advice in order to my own justification, and to silence the faction. I have represented the substance of what I wrote you (only more fully) in a letter to the General, requesting his advice and direction, which he has given much in the same terms as you did. But I am frightened at the expense. I have drawn on the Treasury already for upwards of four millions of dollars, and it seems to be but a breakfast for the department, and hardly that.[1] The land carriage is so extensive and costly, the wants of the army so numerous, and everything selling at such enormous prices that our disbursements will be very great. I dare say they will far exceed your expectations.

" I have written to Congress for their sense and direction upon several matters respecting the department. I beg you will endeavor to bring the matter to issue as soon as possible, as I am much at a loss to know how to proceed.

" The enemy appear, from every piece of intelligence, to be making all necessary preparation to evacuate Philadelphia. I should be glad of your opinion respecting their future operations. Some of the officers think they are going to the West Indies ; others are of opinion that they are going up the North River. There is one objection to this scheme. There is not a sufficient force to coöperate with Sir Henry from Canada. I should think that if Great Britain meant to be serious in her propositions for a reconciliation with America, her forces would be collected together at some secure place, and there wait to see the issue of the commissioner's negotiations.

" Sir Henry Clinton sent out a letter to his Excellency a few days ago, respecting certain acts of Parliament lately passed in favor of America, as he terms it. This letter, I suppose, has been before Congress before this time.

" General McDougall is not well pleased at the manner of his being superseded in the command on the North River. He thinks the public will form some unfavorable sentiments respecting it. General Gates will not meet with the most cordial reception there. However, he will undoubtedly be treated politely. Governor Clinton showed me several letters respecting the operations of last campaign, which will do him much credit in history.

---

[1] The depreciation during June 1778, was four for one. In December it reached six for one.

" Pray how came General Mifflin to be ordered to join this army? This is a phenomenon in politics. General Conway is at last caught in his own trap, and I am most heartily glad of it. I wish every such intriguing spirit may meet with the like disappointment in his ambitious designs. He is a most worthless officer as ever served in our army.

" I suppose you go on pretty much in the old style, puzzling one another with doubts and difficulties, each striving to display the greatest wisdom and ingenuity. What progress have you made in the establishment of the army? The half-pay you have fixed at seven years. Most of the officers are discontented with it, and I am sorry for it."

Soon after Greene became Quartermaster-general he had changed his quarters from the log hut in which he had passed the winter to the house of a Mr. More, one of the few houses of the neighborhood, and which was known in the army as More Hall. Towards the latter part of May his wife returned to Rhode Island.

" Captain Bowen is just going," he writes to her on the 4th of June, " and I have only time to tell you now that I am here in the usual style; writing, scolding, eating, and drinking. But there is no Mrs. Greene to retire to spend an agreeable hour with.

" Colonel Hay writes me you passed the Fishkill in great haste. I hope you got safe home. I received a letter from Billy; he says the children are well; I wish it may be so. Pray write me a full history of family matters; there is nothing will be so agreeable. Kiss the sweet little children over and over again for their absent papa. You must make yourself as happy as possible; write me if you are in want of anything to render you so.

" Mr. More and the family all inquire after you with

great affection and respect, and, I believe, with a degree of
sincerity. Colonel Cox has wrote a most pompous account
of you to Mrs. Cox, as appears by her answer. She desires him to prepare you to see an old-fashion, plain woman,
marked with age and rusticity among the pines. I believe
there is no necessity, for everybody agrees she is one of
the finest women of the age. Mrs. Washington and the
other ladies of camp are daily asking after you. Colonel
Cox and Mr. Pettit desire their most respectful compliments
to the *intruding fair*. Mrs. Knox is in camp and lives with
the General. She professes great regard for you, and often
inquires how and where you are. You will judge of the
regard from former circumstances; but she really seems
sincere.

"I had a letter from Mr. Lott last night; the family
are well.

"Mr. Lebrune is going to join Count Pulaski's legion;
he is gone to Baltimore. He does want to see Mrs.
Greene very much. He thinks he loves her very well.

"Blodget is still at Yorktown, dunning the Congress
for money. Major Burnet is not yet arrived. I had a
letter from Major Loyd a few days past. He is still paying his court to Miss Tilghman. Poor fellow, he is over
head and ears in love.

"Betty has gone out of our family and is married. I
wish to know if you missed anything from among your
clothes. She has delivered me your knife.

"The enemy remain in much the same situation in
Philadelphia as I wrote you before.

"My kind love to all the family, Cousin Griffin and
Sally, Mother Greene, and all other friends."

CHAPTER III.

AT last the army began to move; the British
were evacuating Philadelphia, and Washington was preparing to harass them in their retreat,
and, if possible, fight them on their march. It
was the first active movement since Greene became Quartermaster-general, and the promptness
with which everything that depended upon his
department was done, demonstrated the possibility of what had hitherto been deemed impossible,
and proved that Washington's confidence had not
been misplaced.[1] On the 17th of June a council
of war was held, and the majority were against attacking the enemy on their passage through the
Jerseys, — a decision strongly supported by Lee,
but not wholly approved either by Washington
or Greene.[2] "The country," said Greene, "must

---

[1] Gordon, vol. iii. p. 133. Greene
to Henry Marchant, July 25, 1778.

[2] Sparks, *Writings of Washington,*
vol. v. p. 410. Marshall, vol. i. p. 249.

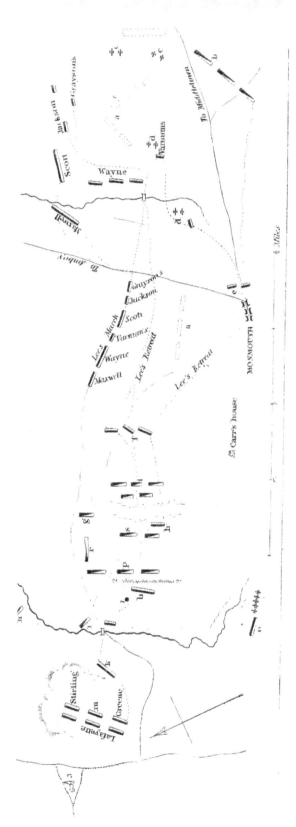

be protected; and if in doing so an engagement should become unavoidable, it would be necessary to fight."[1]

On the next day he wrote to Colonel Pettit: —

"Intelligence has been brought this moment from Philadelphia, that the enemy have evacuated it. Part of our army begins their march towards the Delaware this afternoon, and the whole will be in motion to-morrow morning. Various are the opinions of the general officers respecting the further designs of the enemy. General Lee seems to think they are going towards Maryland. But I am fully of opinion they are going to New York. The balance of evidence at present is much in favor of this conjecture.

"I hope you have brought your business to some issue before this. The sooner you can join us the better. Colonel Cox is going into the city immediately, and I, poor soul, shall be left all alone to do both the field and family duty.

"Stop Colonel Davis from getting any more portmanteaus made, as the officers don't like to pay the cost thereof. I hope you will collect the intention of Congress fully on this point, and the horses and saddles."

Clinton moved slowly, with the intention, as Washington and some of his officers thought, of drawing the Americans "into the lower country, in order, by a rapid movement, to gain their right, and take possession of the strong grounds above them."[2] The Americans moved slowly too, for the weather was oppressive, and the roads heavy with frequent rains and deep sand. On the 21st they crossed the Delaware of happy omen, at Coryell's Ferry, Greene marking out the route and

[1] Marshall, vol. i. p. 249.
[2] Washington to President of Congress. Sparks, *Writings of Washington*, vol. v. p. 423.

order of march and places of encampment; a duty that kept him more than half the time in the saddle. Food it was still difficult to obtain, and, in spite of all his exertions, Wayne's detachment suffered greatly for want of it.[1] At Hopewell, on the 24th, another council was called, and Lee, supported by a majority, still opposed an attack. After a long discussion it was decided "that a detachment of fifteen hundred men be immediately sent to act, as occasion may serve, on the enemy's left flank and rear, in conjunction with the other Continental troops and militia, who are already hanging about them, and that the main body preserve a relative position, so as to be able to act as circumstances may require." [2]

Although Greene signed this resolve as the utmost that could be obtained, yet with Steuben, Duportail, Wayne, Paterson, and Lafayette, he was for raising the number to twenty-five hundred, or at least two thousand ;[3] and still more dissatisfied, the more he reflected upon the subject, he addressed himself to Washington in writing, urging an attack on the enemy's rear by a large detachment, and a general engagement, if the main body could be brought into a favorable position for it.[4] Tradition says that he went still further, and accompanied by Hamilton, repaired to Washington's tent to enforce his views in a personal interview. " I know what you have come for," said Washington, rising

[1] Sparks, *Correspondence of the Revolution*, vol. ii. p. 145.

[2] Sparks, *Writings of Washington,* vol. v. p. 553.

[3] Sparks, *Writings of Washington,* vol. v. p. 553.

[4] Sparks, *ut sup.*

as they approached, " you wish me to fight;" and after a brief discussion, the orders were issued which led to the battle of Monmouth. This and another glimpse through a letter to his wife are all that we see of Greene till we meet him on the battle-field.

" I have not received a single line from you since you left camp, only that by Mr. Lebrune," he writes to her from " Camp Hopewell, near Princeton, New Jersey, June 23, 1778," " I am afraid your letters are stopped and opened by some impudent scoundrel. I have wrote you five or six times. I had the pleasure to hear of you on the road, and that you were well. I hope you got home safe.

" The enemy have evacuated Philadelphia, and are now on their march through the Jerseys; they are at this time about fifteen or twenty miles distant from us at a place called Crossix; we arrived here last night, and shall march for Princeton this afternoon.

" Colonel Cox is at Philadelphia and Mr. Pettit at Congress, and I am left all alone, with business enough for ten men; they both write and desire their compliments to you; they are often paying you the highest compliments; this they do by way of pleasing me, as well as paying a proper tribute to your merit and worth. They profess great friendship for you.

" You cannot conceive how the family at More Hall were distrest at my leaving them; they expected every kind of insult and abuse after I was gone. You are their favorite; they pray for you night and day.

" Mrs. Knox has been in Philadelphia and is now gone to Morristown. She is fatter than ever, which is a great mortification to her. The General is equally fat, and therefore one cannot laugh at the other. They appear to be extravagantly fond of each other; and, I think, are perfectly happy.

" Pray write me the first opportunity of everything and particularly about the children and yourself: my love to all friends."

With the first part of the battle of Monmouth Greene had nothing to do, and hence his name does not appear in Lee's trial. Neither has his own account of it been preserved, and I have nothing to add to what Washington says of him in his report to the President of Congress : —

" General Lee being detached with the advanced corps, the command of the right wing for the occasion was given to General Greene. For the expedition of the march, and to counteract any attempt to turn our right, I had ordered him to file off by the new church, two miles from Englishtown, and fall into the Monmouth road, a small distance in the rear of the Court House, while the rest of the column moved directly on towards the Court House. On intelligence of the retreat, he marched up and took a very advantageous position on the right. The enemy by this time finding themselves warmly opposed in front, made an attempt to turn our left flank ; but they were bravely repulsed and driven back by detached parties of infantry. They also made a movement to our right with as little success, General Greene having advanced a body of troops with artillery to a commanding piece of ground ; which not only disappointed their design of turning our right but severely enfiladed those in front of the left wing." [1]

One of the cannon that did this good work was served by an Irishman, whose wife, Molly, already known throughout the army as having fired the last gun at Fort Clinton, kept him constantly supplied with fresh water from a neighboring spring. At last a shot struck him dead at his post, and no

[1] Sparks, *Writings of Washington*, vol. v. p. 426.

fit person being at hand to take his place, the officer in command ordered the piece to be withdrawn. Molly, seeing her husband fall and hearing the order, dropped her bucket, sprang to the gun, seized the rammer, and vowing vengeance upon the slayer of her husband, kept up a constant fire till the enemy was driven from the field. Whether Greene saw this with his own eyes or not I do not know, but on the next day he presented her to Washington, who gave her a sergeant's commission and had her name put upon the half-pay list.[1]

Greene's labors did not end with the battle; when the fighting was over, the Quartermaster-general's department came back upon him with orders to give and provision to make for the morrow; and it was not till late in the night that he was able to wrap his cloak about him and stretch himself on the ground under the shelter of a tree. We next get a glimpse of him at Brunswick, trying to obtain a new supply of horses to make up for the heavy losses which the army had sustained in the field and on the march, in both of which large numbers had dropped dead from the heat. Then the army marches towards the Hudson, to secure the passes of the Highlands, and the first that we see of Greene is at " Captain Drake's, seven miles from the ferry," writing to Washington on the 16th of July.

" General Varnum is at this place, and has very lately

---

[1] Lossing, *Field Book of the Revolution* vol. ii. p. 155.

[2] Sparks, *Writings of Washington,* vol. v. p. 430.

returned from Rhode Island ; he says that there are fifteen hundred State troops, including the artillery regiments. There is the Continental Battalion, commanded by Colonel Greene, about one hundred and thirty strong. Besides these, 4,500 militia are ordered from Massachusetts, Connecticut, and New Hampshire States, part of which are already arrived, and the others daily coming in. General Varnum thinks there cannot be less than three thousand men already embodied under the command of General Sullivan, that can be depended upon.

" General Varnum thinks that there are not above three thousand of the enemy at Rhode Island and only six frigates.

" I find no place for encamping the troops short of nine miles from the ferry towards Crompond."

Thus the Rhode Island expedition was already taking shape and consistency in Washington's mind, and Greene was, as ever before, deep in his councils.

The next day finds him on the Croton in Westchester, still thinking of Rhode Island, as a letter to his deputy at Providence, Col. Ephraim Bowen, shows, although he dares not yet speak openly.

" Your request by Mr. Martin for cash is gone to the Treasury. I hear this day he has been successful; you may, therefore, expect the money very soon.

" I have written to my brother to furnish you with any articles you may want, that he has purchased, or may purchase for the public use. If you should want you will please to apply accordingly.

" Let us hear the news from your quarter every week, by the post."

On the same day he writes to his wife : —

" I received your agreeable letter of the 8th of this instant, yesterday in the morning.

" I am very sorry to find you are unwell. Why did you ride in the night? What was your hurry? Why do you expose yourself unnecessarily and risk any disagreeable consequences that might follow?

" Sensible of your anxiety, and desirous of giving you the earliest information after the battle of Monmouth, I sent off an express to Fishkill, with a line to Colonel Hay, desiring him to forward your letter by the first opportunity; which I hope you have received long before this.

" You express a strong desire to see the army on the east side of the North River, and urge you have political as well as private reasons for it. Your private reasons I can interpret, but your political ones I cannot divine. You may rest assured that there must be something very uncommon to prevent my coming home; you cannot have a greater desire to see me than I have you and the children. I long to hear the little rogues' prattle. Besides which there are many other matters that I want to settle.

" You write you are politely treated in Boston. I am exceeding happy to hear it. They cannot flatter me more agreeably than by their respect to you. What we love we wish to be regarded, and our partiality leads us to wish that others should feel the same attachment with ourselves, and whenever we find it it produces an agreeable train of sensation.

" You are envious then, I find; why so, Caty? (if) there are others more happy than you, are there not others less so? Look around you, my dear, and see where there are not many whose conditions and prospects are far less eligible than yours. It has ever been my study and ever shall be to render you as happy as possible. But I have been obliged in many instances to sacrifice the present pleasures to our future hopes. This, I am sensible, has done violence to your feelings at the time; but I trust

the motives were so laudable and the consequences will
be so salutary that I shall meet with no difficulty in obtaining your forgiveness hereafter.   At the close of the
war I flatter myself I shall be able to return to your arms
with the same unspotted love and affection as I took the
field.   Surfeited with the pomp and parade of public life
I shall doubly relish domestic pleasures.   To please my
love and educate my children will be a most happy employment; my fortune will be small; but I trust by good
economy we may live respectably."

It is well known, though not generally acknowledged, that Washington had a very quick temper,
and was often led to sudden and violent manifestations of it.   Few of those who lived on an intimate
footing with him were with him long without wit-
nessing, even when they did not draw it upon
themselves, some hasty expression of his irritation; and the more thoughtful of them, adopted for
themselves from the beginning a method of dealing with it suited to their individual character and
position.   " I was always determined," writes
Hamilton to Schuyler, "if there should ever happen a breach between us, never to consent to an
accommodation." [1]   Greene's position was far from
requiring or even justifying so decided a course.
He loved and venerated Washington, looking up
to him as the only man who could guide us safely
through the dangers and perplexities of such a war,
and grateful to him for the fullness with which
he had given him his confidence from the beginning of their intercourse.   When, therefore, Washington gave way to a sudden ebullition of dis-

[1] Hamilton's *Republic of the United States*, vol. ii. p. 174.

content, Greene appealed to him in the language of respectful friendship.

" Your Excellency has made me very unhappy. I can submit very patiently to deserved censure, but it wounds my feelings exceedingly to meet with a rebuke for doing what I conceived to be a proper part of my duty, and in the order of things.

" When I left your Excellency at Haverstraw, you desired me to go forward and reconnoitre the country, and fix upon some proper position to draw the troops together at. I was a stranger to all this part of the country, and could form no judgment of a proper place until I had thoroughly examined the ground.

" Croton River was the only place I could find suitable to the purpose, all circumstances being taken into consideration. I wrote your Excellency what I had done and where I was, that if you had anything in charge I might receive your orders. I wrote you the reasons for my not waiting upon you in person were I had my letters to answer and many matters to regulate in my department, which prevented me from returning. Besides which it was almost half a day's ride, the weather exceeding hot, and myself not a little fatigued. And here I must observe that neither my constitution nor strength is equal to constant exercise.

" I was a stranger to all the lower country. I thought it absolutely necessary for me to come forward. A thorough knowledge of the country is not easily obtained ; such a one, at least, as is necessary to fix upon the most eligible position for forming a camp. The security of the army, the ease and convenience of the troops, as well as to perform the duties of my office with a degree of reputation, all conspired to make me wish to fix upon the proper ground for the purpose. This it was impossible for me to do unless I came on before the troops. And I must confess

I saw no objection, as your Excellency had wrote me nothing to the contrary, and what I wrote naturally led to such a measure.

"I expected you on every hour, and was impatient to get forward that I might be able to give some account of the country when you came up. Before I left Crompond I desired Mr. Pettit to wait upon you at your arrival, and take your orders, and if there was anything special, to forward it by express.

"If I had neglected my duty in pursuit of pleasure, or if I had been wanting in respect to your Excellency, I would have put my hand upon my mouth and been silent upon the occasion; but as I am not conscious of being chargeable with either the one or the other, I cannot help thinking I have been treated with a degree of severity I am in no respect deserving of. And I would just observe here that it is impossible for me to do my duty if I am always at head-quarters. I have ever given my attendance there as much as possible, both from a sense of duty and from inclination; but constant attendance is out of my power, unless I neglect all other matters, the propriety of which and the consequences that will follow, I submit to your Excellency's consideration.

"Your Excellency well knows how I came into this department. It was by your special request, and you must be sensible there is no other man upon earth would have brought me into the business but you. The distress the department was in, the disgrace that must accompany your operations without a change, and the difficulty of engaging a person capable of conducting the business, together with the hopes of meeting your approbation and having your full aid and assistance, reconciled me to the undertaking.

"I flatter myself when your Excellency takes a view of the state things were in when I first engaged, and considers the short time we had to make the preparations for the opening campaign, and reflects with what ease and facility you began your march from Valley Forge and continued it all through the country, notwithstanding we went great part of the way entirely out of the line of preparation, you will do me the justice to say I have not been negligent or inattentive to my duty.

" I have in every respect, since I had my appointment, strove to accommodate the business of the department to the plan of your Excellency's operations. And I can say with great truth that ever since I had the honor to serve under you I have been more attentive to the public interest, and more engaged in the support of your Excellency's character than ever I was to my own ease, interest, or reputation.

" I have never solicited you for a furlough to go home to indulge in pleasure or to improve my interest, which, by the by, I have neglected going on four years. I have never confined myself to my particular line of duty only. Neither have I ever spared myself either by night or day where it has been necessary to promote the public service under your direction. I have never been troublesome to your Excellency to publish anything to my advantage, although I think myself as justly entitled as some others who have been much more fortunate, particularly in the action of the Brandywine.

" I have never suffered my pleasures to interfere with my duty; and I am persuaded I have given too many unequivocal proofs of my attachment to your person and interest to leave a doubt upon your mind to the contrary. I have always given you my opinion with great candor, and executed your orders with equal fidelity. I do not mean to arrogate to myself more merit than I deserve, or wish to exculpate myself from being chargeable with error, and, in some instances, negligence. However I can speak with a becoming pride that I have always endeavored to deserve the public esteem and your Excellency's approbation.

" As I came into the Quartermaster's department with

reluctance, so I shall leave it with pleasure. Your influence brought me in, and the want of your approbation will induce me to go out.

"I am very sensible of many deficiencies, but this is not so justly chargeable to my intentions as to the difficult in circumstances attending the business. It is almost impossible to get good men for conducting all parts of so complex a business. It may, therefore, naturally be expected that many things will wear an unfavorable complexion, but let who will undertake the business, they will find it very difficult, not to say impossible, to regulate it in such a manner as not to leave a door open for censure and furnish a handle of reproach."

Washington's answer has not been preserved, but as the intercourse of the two friends continued upon the same intimate footing as before, it is evident that he acknowledged the force of the appeal.

The French fleet under Count d'Estaing was now on the coast. How can it be employed to the best advantage?

"I would propose writing to the French admiral," writes Greene to Washington, "that there are two objects. One of the two may be improved as a blockade or an investiture, as circumstances and the practicability of entering the harbor of New York should be found.

"The French fleet to take the station at Sandy Hook and block up the harbor. This army to take a position near the White Plains to cut off the land communication, and to all appearances seem to design some serious operations against New York and the troops there.

"General Sullivan to be wrote to desiring to know what force he has that may be confided in in the character of regular troops. What force is from the neighboring States and expected in a few days and what militia can be brought together in eight days' time, and how the magazines are prepared for such a consumption and whether there is boats to make a landing upon Rhode Island ; to learn the strength of the enemy there and the number of their ships and what force.

" In the mean while the admiral to make himself acquainted with the depth of water into New York and the ships and force there.

" On the return of the express from General Sullivan, the admiral to determine, from the inquiry he shall make and the information General Sullivan give, which will be the most eligible object. But if it should be found the fleet can come in the harbor of New York, this army will be ready to coöperate with him as far as the nature of the country and the situation of the enemy will admit.

" The fleet from Sandy Hook can run into Newport in three days' time ; that that station will be favorable for either the one or the other of the measures as should be found hereafter to be the most certain of success.

" I would inform the admiral of the difficulty of approaching New York by land ; of the enemy's strength there : send a verbal account of our own strength and position. I would also send him a copy of the letter to General Sullivan, if it is not thought dangerous, as it is possible it may fall into the enemy's hands."

The channel, as had been feared, was not deep enough for the larger ships of the French squadron, and it was resolved to turn the combined forces of the new allies against Newport.

" You are the most happy man in the world," Greene writes to Sullivan from the White Plains on the 23d of July. " What a child of fortune. The expedition going on against Newport, cannot, I think, fail of success. You are the first General that has ever had an opportunity of coöperat-

ing with the French forces belonging to the United States.
The character of the American soldiers, as well as of their
officers, will be formed from the conduct of the troops and
the success of this expedition. I wish you success with
all my soul, and intend, if possible, to come home to put
things in a proper train in my department, and to take a
command of part of the troops under you. I wish most
ardently to be with you.

"The battle of Monmouth and its consequences I suppose you have heard and seen the particulars of. General
Lee is on trial; the event uncertain as to the determination of the court.

"A certain northern hero gave his Excellency several
broad hints that if he was sent upon the Newport expedition great things would be done. But the General did not
think proper to supersede an officer of distinguished merit
to gratify unjustly a doubtful friend. Had it been necessary my little influence would not have been wanting to
have prevented such a piece of injustice from being done
you.

"The good agreement that has ever subsisted between
us, and the prospect of a noble opportunity of acquiring
reputation, together with the certainty of your doing
justice to every man who distinguishes himself in any
manner whatever, induces me to wish to join you upon this
occasion, not as a northern hero to rob you of your laurels,
but to share them under you.

"I was an adviser of this expedition and therefore am
deeply interested in the event. I wish a little more force
had been sent. The Count d'Estaing will block up the
harbor and you may wait until your plan is ripe for execution. I hope you won't precipitate matters until your
force gets together. Everything depends almost upon the
success of this expedition. Your friends are anxious; your
enemies are watching. *I charge you to be victorious.* The
Marquis de la Fayette is coming to join you. Trust to

your own judgment for forming the plan, as you have everything at stake; and pray give your orders positive for the execution. The late transactions at the battle of Monmouth make me drop these hints. You'll excuse the freedom, I take, and believe me, &c."

It is evident that Greene longs for a part in the expedition which is to free his native State from the presence of a cruel enemy, and afford American soldiers an occasion of proving themselves by the side of the disciplined and tried soldiers of France. It is equally evident that he finds it hard to reconcile himself to the silence in which his services at the Brandywine, Germantown, and Monmouth had been passed over. He had done too much and lived too long in the light of history not to feel that he had earned a place therein; a secondary place indeed as yet, but still one of those pages, the hope of which fills the noblest minds with their highest and purest aspirations.

"There is an expedition going on against Newport," he writes to Major Ephraim Bowen, his deputy at Providence. "The forces that will be collected for this purpose will be considerable. Great exertions, therefore, will be necessary in our department. You must get the most active men to assist you that you possibly can.

"A great number of teams and boats will be wanted upon the occasion. Pray do not let the expedition suffer for want of anything in our line. If tents are likely to be wanted, get all that Mr. Chace, Mr. Andrews, and Mr. Greene have. I think you had better write them to send you all they have on hand.

"I am in hopes to come and assist you myself and join the expedition; but am afraid I cannot obtain the General's assent.

" There is a line of expresses established at the following places, to form an easy communication of intelligence from Providence to this camp. You must fix one at Mr. John Greene's in Coventry, to complete the communication. It must be done immediately."

This Major Bowen was one of the captors of the *Gaspee,* and it was from his lips, in the last days of his protracted and honorable life, that I received the assurance that General Greene, in spite of a current tradition, had no part in that first bold display of colonial daring.

A letter of two days later to Henry Marchant gives us a side light for our picture.

" I am informed the Congress have the appointment of all the agents to be employed for the disposal of British property captured by the French navy. If the information is true, and there is one to be appointed for the State of Rhode Island, I would beg leave to nominate my brother Jacob. You know he has made no small sacrifices and devoted great part of his time to the public service for several years past. If you can procure him this appointment you will lay both him and me under equal obligations. However, you will judge of the justice and propriety of the application and take your measures accordingly.

" The expedition against Newport will be attempted. The French fleet is to block up the harbor, while General Sullivan raises a land force to take off the garrison. I believe and hope I shall have an opportunity to go upon the expedition, first to put the business of my department in a proper trim, and then to join in the execution of the plan.

" I am told you are making great preparations for the reception of the French ambassador. The public audience will be a grand exhibition, the dignity and splendor

will be new in America, and excites a curiosity in me to
see the audience, as I never saw the like.

"I hear General Arnold has rendered himself not a
little unpopular with the officers of the army in Philadelphia, by not giving them an invitation to a ball he gave
the citizens. I am very sorry for this circumstance, as it
will render his situation disagreeable, owing to the clamor
and cabal of those who conceive themselves injured.

"The great exertions that have been in the Quartermaster-general's department contributes greatly to the
success of the army in the operations through New Jersey.
It has been and will be very expensive; but is unavoidable ; and although it is not possible to correct every imposition and stop all abuses in so complex a business, I am
persuaded there has been as much economy as the circumstances of the department and the state of the times
would admit.

"I hope his Excellency will do me the justice to say I
have done my duty. The army must have remained until
this hour at the Valley Forge, had not some person undertaken the business with more spirit and activity than those
formerly in it. However, his Excellency, for fear of being chargeable with partiality, never says anything to the
advantage of his friends. In the action of Brandywine
last campaign, where I think both the public and the General were as much indebted to me for saving the army
from ruin as they have ever been to any one officer in
the course of the war;[1] but I was never mentioned upon
the occasion.

"I marched one brigade of my division, being upon the
left wing, between three and four miles in forty-five minutes. When I came upon the ground I found the whole
of the troops routed and retreating precipitately, and in
the most broken and confused manner. I was ordered

---

[1] This sentence is imperfect, but I
let it stand as I find it. It probably
should read — *This appeared at the
action, &c.*

to cover the retreat, which I effected in such a manner as to save hundreds of our people from falling into the enemy's hands. Almost all of the park of artillery had an opportunity to get off, which must have fallen into their hands; and the left wing, posted at Chad's Ford, got off by the seasonable check I gave the enemy. We were engaged an hour and a quarter, and lost upwards of an hundred men killed and wounded. I maintained the ground until dark, and then drew off the men in good order. We had the whole British force to contend with that had just before routed our whole right wing. This brigade was commanded by General Weedon, and, unfortunately for their own interests, happened to be all Virginians. They being the General's countrymen, and I thought to be one of his favorites, prevented his even mentioning a single circumstance of the affair.

" The battle of Germantown has been as little understood as the other by the public at large, especially the conduct of the left wing of the army. Great pains has been taken to misrepresent the transactions of that day. I trust history will do justice to the reputations of individuals. I have the satisfaction of an approving conscience, and the confirming voice of as able a general as any we have in the service, General McDougall, who knows the report the troops were delayed unnecessarily to be as infamous a falsehood as ever was reported; the troops were carried into action as soon as it was possible, and in good order.

" However, as I said before, I trust history will do justice to those who have made every sacrifice for the public service. It is going on four years since I have spent an hour at home save one that I stopt on my march from Boston to New York. There is no man gone through more fatigue or been more attentive to duty than I have since I belonged to the army. But men and actions have been so miscolored that little benefit is to be expected from a series of good actions. Refined policy is too prevalent for merit to be in much estimation. I expected when we were first formed into an army that we were going upon a truly republican principle, that merit only was the criterion ; but I find a few friends at court is of much greater consequence than all the service a man can perform in the field."

Such were some of the annoyances which were troubling Greene's mind at this moment, and certainly not without reason. Two days later we find him contending with another.

" His Excellency, General Washington," he writes to the President of Congress on the 27th of July, " having been pleased to favor me with a sight of two papers which had been delivered to him by General Gates containing a list of persons employed in the northern department under the direction of the Deputy Quartermaster-general, a copy of which, I am informed, has been transmitted to Congress by General Gates ; the other a resolution of Congress thereon of the 23d of June, which seems to imply a censure on the Quartermaster-general or his deputy in that department, I think it necessary to trouble Congress with the mention of a few facts which, I doubt not, will satisfy them that no part of that censure can justly fall on me.

" In the month of May last, when General Gates was about to take the command on Hudson River, I made a journey to Fishkill in order to examine into and regulate the business of the Quartermaster-general's department. In a conversation with General Gates, he proposed that this business in the northern district should be put under his direction, and offered to take the trouble of making the necessary arrangements, to which I readily consented, and thought myself happy in having committed it to a person I supposed in all respects so well qualified to direct the management of it. On my leaving Fishkill I left a letter for General Gates, informing him what I had done in that district, and referring that of Albany entirely to him, and

I never doubted that if any error or abuses were found, especially in the latter, they would have been immediately corrected, and that I should in due time have been favored with a state of the department. A copy of his letter I shall take the liberty to inclose herewith. Sometime afterwards I was honored with a letter from General Gates which contains all the official information I have been favored with on the subject, a copy of which will also be inclosed. By this letter you will observe there is not the most distant hint of any supernumerary officers being employed, or other abuses or irregularities committed in the Albany district, and I rested satisfied that everything there was properly regulated and going on well. It therefore appeared to me not a little strange that the first intimation I received of an undue number of officers being kept in pay in that quarter, should arise from a resolution of Congress for correcting the abuse, and that, too, founded on a complaint or report transmitted by the very person on whom I relied, at his own request, to remove all causes of complaint. A written statement of facts delivered me by Colonel Lewis, Deputy Quartermaster-general at Albany, of which a copy is inclosed, will make it appear the more extraordinary that such a complaint should be transmitted by General Gates.

" The nature of the business requires that almost every Deputy Quartermaster-general should employ a number of assistants, clerks, and other subordinate officers, and as, from the movements of the army and other circumstances, the business at many posts and districts is fluctuating, and requires, in order to avoid unnecessary expense, that these subordinate officers should have but temporary appointments, I have invariably given in charge to every deputy I have appointed to take especial care to keep no such officer on pay within his district longer than the public service should require it. Colonel Lewis having, as I understood, been appointed immediately by Congress, and being under the eye of the commanding officer of the northern department, I did not think it requisite, especially as I heard no complaints concerning him, and much other business claimed my attention, to send him any particular instructions ; and indeed, as there was but little business expected in his district, and from his character and standing in office, as well as for the reasons before mentioned, I did not consider it at all necessary."

Greene might well feel surprised that the first indication of discontent should come to him in the form of a resolution of Congress : —

" That General Gates be, and he is hereby authorized to dismiss all the supernumerary staff officers in the district under his command. That so much of General Gates' letter of the 17th and the papers inclosed as relates to the supernumerary officers of the staff, be referred to the committee of arrangement ; and that they be directed to report a plan for preventing the extraordinary expense arising from the appointment of such officers." [1]

I would not rashly accuse Gates of malice ; yet when I consider his intimacy with Mifflin, whose hostility to Greene was well known, I find it difficult to repress the suspicion that he was not unwilling to give a false direction to the censures of Congress, and thus prepare the way for a future condemnation of the present Quartermaster-general, and a justification of his predecessor.[2]

[1] *Journal of Congress,* Tuesday, June 23, 1778.

[2] That Gates was capable of doing this is not improbable, if we consider his conduct towards Washington ; *vide* Washington to President of Congress, from Middlebrook, April 14, 1779. Sparks, *Writings of Washington,* vol. vi. p. 214.

CHAPTER IV.

THE letter which we have just read was written on the 27th of July. On the 28th Greene
set out for Rhode Island, a weary three days' ride
over a space which we now cross in six hours. It
is well-nigh three years since we have seen at the
head of his letter, the date that we find there on
the 31st.

"COVENTRY IRON WORKS.

" I arrived at this place last evening about nine o'clock,"
he writes to General Sullivan, " and being a little fatigued,
having rode from camp in three days, I propose to refresh
myself to-day and wait upon you to-morrow, unless there
should be something special that renders my attendance
necessary immediately ; in which case I will set out without
delay. You'll please to inform me by the return of the
express.

" Inclosed is a letter from his Excellency, General

Washington. I have forty ship-carpenters and boat-builders coming on to put things in readiness in the water department for the expedition, and there is a most excellent fellow at the head of them, Major Eyres."

That 31st of July was a happy day at Coventry. What a pleasure, with his strong local attachments, to walk down the green lane once more, and stand upon the bank of the beautiful stream, and hear the familiar sounds of the forge. What a delight to sit again at his own table, under his own roof, with his wife at the head of the board. What a rapture to take his two little ones, the second of whom he had never seen before, in his arms, and " listen to their prattle."

Then friends and neighbors would come in with questions about the army and the officers; Monmouth would be freely discussed; for among those who had left limbs there, was a well-known citizen of East Greenwich, Captain Thomas Arnold, whose wooden leg, the only one in the town, was one of the wonders of my boyhood, when he was still known by the name of Monmouth Tom. Greene's brothers, too, came up from Potowomut! What changes since they last met under that roof! And what a change in him, no longer asking only for means to buy books, and leisure to read them; but with a place in history, and a name known throughout the length and breadth of the land. The bookshelf, too, we may be sure, was not the last place visited, nor was it without a sigh that he turned away from it for the grave duties of the hour.

For after his single day of rest, he went back to

all his cares again. It had been decided that he should have "a command in the troops to be employed in the descent." [1] Lafayette, whose command was divided by this new arrangement, accepted it with a cheerful frankness, which, if other proof were wanting, would of itself prove what high and generous motives he was governed by. "I have received your Excellency's favor by General Greene," he writes to Washington, "and have been much pleased with the arrival of a gentleman who, not only on account of his merit and the justness of his views, but by his knowledge of the country and his popularity in this State, may be very serviceable to the expedition. I willingly part with half my detachment, since you find it for the good of the service, though I had great dependence on them. Anything, my dear General, which you shall order or can wish, will always be infinitely agreeable to me." [2]

On the 2d of August Greene is at East Greenwich, in the old house on the hill, where he had wooed and wedded, with no leisure to think of tender scenes now, but earnestly concerting with Governor William Greene those parts of the expedition which depend upon the civil authority. He is dissatisfied with the act for calling out the militia; and after stating his objections to the Governor by word of mouth, borrows a pen and writes them out for public use.

"Upon inquiry I find there is an order from the council board for drafting one half the whole militia in the State.

[1] Sparks' *Washington*, vol. vi. p. 22.   [2] *Ut sup.* p. 23, note.

I presume the intention of the board was to have one half of all those actually fit for duty drafted, and no others, for the intended expedition. If this was the intention of the board, I am afraid both they and the General will be disappointed in their expectations; there being many drafted that are unfit for duty, and are now getting clearances.

" It will be necessary for the board to issue their orders that one half of the militia fit for actual service be drafted, and none others; or that those that are unfit for duty provide others to serve in their places. If something of this sort don't take place there will be a great diminution of the expected force.

" You will pardon the freedom I take in hinting these matters to your Excellency."

On the 4th, he writes from Providence to Colonel Wadsworth : —

" I am here busy as a bee in a tar-barrel, to speak in a sailor's style. I am happy to inform you that everything in your department seems to equal our wishes; it was the first inquiry I made, and I received the most flattering answers.

" Will you want a quantity of rum? If you should, please to give the price to be delivered at Norfolk. My brothers have some ; any service you can render them consistent with your trust will be duly acknowledged. Please to write me an immediate answer. We intend to give the enemy a cursed flogging. We are almost in readiness."

Thus far, and still for some days longer, everything seemed to promise success. The people were full of confidence ; the hopes even of the timid and cautious were high. " We will show these French soldiers that we can fight as hard as they can," said they whose minds were still filled with old English and colonial prejudices. " We

will show our allies that while we know what they
are doing for us, we are prepared to do our parts
like true men," said they who felt what the French
alliance might be if met and used aright. Greene
established his head-quarters at Tiverton, doing
double duty, Quartermaster-general and commander of a division, at the same time. Almost
every order of the day contains some new charge
for the Quartermaster-general. "The Quartermaster-general is directed to send over all the spare
tents and distribute them among the troops that
are destitute of covering, also all the canteens,"
says an order of August 10th. "The Quartermaster-general to see that the axes and entrench-
ing tools are forwarded immediately after the army
have marched. The Quartermaster-general will
furnish proper tools for the pioneers," say the
orders of the 11th. Then every third day finds
him Major-general for the day.[1] In this increase
of labor he feels the want of another aid; and in
the orders for the 11th, I read, "Major Jacob
Morris is to act as volunteer aid to Major-general
Greene, and to be respected accordingly."

But soon unforeseen difficulties arose. The
French fleet came to off Newport, on the 29th of
July, and began the blockade. But the American
levies were not yet on the ground, and Sullivan was
reluctantly compelled to wait. At last they were
all in, ten thousand men and more, and among the
generals, John Hancock, who as President of Congress had signed both of Greene's commissions.

---

[1] Glover Papers, MSS.

It is agreed that the French and Americans shall advance at the same time, the French landing near Dyer's Island, on the west side, the Americans at Howland's Ferry, on the east side. The British General, divining their intention, withdraws his forces from the strong works he had erected on the north end of the island, and prepares to stand a siege in the lines near Newport. Sullivan, seeing the works empty, throws over on the 9th a strong body to seize them, and crosses with his whole army as speedily as he can, a breach of etiquette which d'Estaing has some difficulty in forgiving, although fully justified by the circumstances. The French troops land on Conanicut. Hemmed in on all sides, General Pigot must surrender.

But while the French fleet are lying at their anchors under the shore of Conanicut and landing their four thousand troops, who were to pass under the command of Lafayette and coöperate with the American army, a British fleet appears off Point Judith, thirty-six sail in all, and thirteen of them ships of the line. D'Estaing hurries his troops on board again, and sails out to meet the enemy, eager for a trial of strength. Could he but have curbed his impatience, and contented himself with defending the mouth of the harbor, his triumph would have been sure.

Then began a struggle for the weather-gage, drawing both fleets far down the coast, till towards the evening of the second day, just as they were upon the point of engaging, a sudden gale arose and scattered them. Lord Howe made for New

York, D'Estaing for Newport, crippled and shattered, both of them, by the violence of the tempest.

Nor did the army escape unharmed, although they had the solid ground under their feet. Their provisions were drenched, their ammunition was wet, their tents were blown down. Some found a sort of shelter under the stone-walls which almost everywhere in Rhode Island take the place of fences. Many could find no shelter. A few are said to have perished from the exposure; "and then" said an eye-witness, "I saw for the first time that men were more hardy than horses,"[1] for a great many horses sank down and died. For two whole days, the 12th and 13th, the storm raged on sea and land. The 14th was passed in efforts to repair the damage it had done, and on the morning of the 15th, the American army moved forward to within two miles of Newport, and began to prepare for regular approaches against the British lines. How Greene's labors were increased by this untoward tempest it is easy to divine.

"I received your two letters by Vester," he writes to his wife on the 16th, from the neat farmhouse on a cross-road between the east and west roads, and about two miles from the lines, where he had taken up his quarters:[2] —

"I am sorry to find you are getting unwell. I am afraid it is the effect of anxiety and fearful apprehension. Re-

---

[1] Cowell's *Spirit of '76 in Rhode Island*, p. 167.
[2] This house is still standing.

member the same good Providence protects all places, and
secures from harm in the most perilous situation. Would
to God it was in my power to give peace to your bosom,
which, I fear, is like the troubled ocean. I feel your distress. My bosom beats with compassion and kind concern
for your welfare, and the more so at this time as your situation is critical.

" I thank you kindly for your concern for my health and
safety ; the former is not very perfect, the latter is in the
book of fate. I wish to live but for your sake and those
little pledges of conjugal affection which Providence has
blessed us with. Those dear little rogues have begun to
command a large share of my affection and attention. O,
that I was at liberty to cultivate their young genius.

" I find it is your intention to return home. I have
sent Vester accordingly with the horse. If you can con-
veniently spare him when you get home I should be glad ;
but don't wish you to send him by any means unless it is
perfectly convenient. I don't wish you to send the grays
by any means, as you will be left without the means of
going abroad upon any occasion whatever.

" Mr. Taylor delivered me your letter. I am too much a
stranger to his history to know how or in what I can serve
him. I could therefore only give a general tender of any
good offices that was in my power to render him at any
time and upon any occasion whatever. I shall be exceedingly glad in an opportunity to oblige him, because it is
your request.

" I received Miss Nancy's pies and puddings, and thank
her kindly. They come very seasonably to our relief, as
we are a little short in our stores, especially of the deli-
cacies of good living.

" Major Franks tells me he has offered his services to
wait upon you home. I would wish you to accept his
kind offer ; he is a very obliging, clever fellow.

" You'll kiss my little son when you get home, and tell

him his papa does love him exceedingly.   Remember me
kindly to all friends at home, and make my best respects
to Mr. Vernon's family.[1]

"The French fleet has not returned.   We are within
two miles of Newport, and are to begin our approaches
to-night."

Every eye was now anxiously turned to the
southern horizon.   What havoc must this tempest
have made at sea which had made so much on
land.   D'Estaing, in departing, had solemnly promised to return ; if alive and free, he would surely
do so ; but who could answer for human life or the
work of human hands in such a war of the elements ?   The ocean lay full in view of both the hostile lines, and Greene could see it from the roof of
his quarters.   From morning till night the watchful
lookout stood with his eyes fixed upon the offing.
The approaches were regularly begun ; cannon and
mortar were busy at their deadly work.   Only let
D'Estaing keep his word, and we will have the
town in forty-eight hours.   At last, on the 19th,
just at night-fall, a sail was seen on the horizon
swiftly holding its way towards the land.   It was
the *Senegal,* a frigate taken from the enemy, bringing a letter from D'Estaing.   Sullivan's heart sank
within him as he read the letter ; for it told that the
fleet had been shattered by the tempest, and must
go into port to refit.   What better port than this,
thought the Americans ; and Greene and Lafayette
were sent to meet the Admiral, and show him how

[1] "There is something exquisitely
touching in the traits of domestic affection which sometimes gleam
through the busy pages of history."—
Milman, *History of Christianity,* **vol.**
iii. p. 124.

completely the enemy were within their power. "If we fail in our negotiation, we shall at least get a good dinner," said Greene, as they stept into the boat. "But he was mistaken," said Lafayette with a smile, when he told me the story years ago at La Grange, "for by the time we got to the *Languedoc*, he was too seasick to think of eating." The *Languedoc* was no longer the proud ship which a few days before had met the fire of the British batteries so gallantly, as with the white lilies at her masthead she sailed boldly into Narraganset bay. Stunted jury-masts held the place of the stately pines that had towered above her deck, as through long years, they had towered amid their brethren of the forest. Her huge hull bore marks of both enemies; for a British seventy-four had attacked her, all crippled as she was by the gale, and poured in a broadside with impunity.

D'Estaing's face was care-worn, though his manner was still cordial and bland. He listened politely to the representation of the American Generals, Greene speaking through Lafayette, for he could not speak French. But the question had already been discussed, and all his officers and "even some American pilots"[1] had declared that his safety depended upon making the best of his way to Boston. This too was the order of the king in case of disaster. In deference to his allies, he called a new council of war; and Greene, as he watched their deliberations, discovered their secret

---

[1] Lafayette to Washington.   Sparks' *Correspondence of the Revolution*, vol ii. p. 184.

motive. D'Estaing was a land officer, and his captains were resolved to prevent him from winning laurels on the sea.[1] The first decision was confirmed, and D'Estaing did not dare to overrule it. Greene, in the hope of strengthening the Admiral's hands, for he would gladly have acceded to Sullivan's request, drew up a protest and presented it.[2]

When the decision was announced to Sullivan, he too drew up a protest, which all signed but Lafayette, who, as he writes to Washington, " had been strangely called there." [3] Laurens was dispatched in a fleet boat to carry it to the Admiral. " It imposes on the commander of the king's squadron," said D'Estaing, "the painful but necessary law of profound silence." [4] Thus there was profound irritation on both sides; old English prejudices starting up from their white ashes; old French prejudices suddenly springing with a rebound from the reaction of enthusiastic sympathy. Sullivan, sometimes ardent too much, said in his orders of the 24th, " He " (the Commander-in-chief) " yet hopes the event will prove America able to procure with her own arms that which her allies refused to assist her in obtaining." Lafayette, deeply wounded, called on him to alter them. " It having been supposed by some persons," say the orders of the 26th, " that by the orders of the 24th inst. the Commander-in-chief

[1] Marshall's *Washington*, vol. i. p. 264.

[2] Sparks' *Correspondence of the Revolution*, vol. ii. p. 168.

[3] *Ut sup.*

[4] Sparks' *Washington*, vol. vi. p. 46.

[5] Glover MSS. Order of the day, August 24.

meant to insinuate that the departure of the French fleet was owing to a fixed determination not to assist in the present enterprise; and as the General could not wish to give the least color to ungenerous and illiberal minds to make such an unfair interpretation, he thinks it necessary to say that as he could not possibly be acquainted with the orders of the French Admiral, he could not determine whether the removal of the fleet was absolutely necessary or not, and therefore did not mean to censure an act which those orders might render absolutely necessary." [1]

Greene had shared fully in Sullivan's hopes, and was as firmly convinced as he that the English General would be unable to sustain the combined attack of the French and American forces. He even went so far as to sign the general protest in the same hope with which he had drawn up his individual protest. But this was as far as he felt authorized to go. "I must add to my letter," writes Lafayette to Washington, "that I have received one from General Greene very different from the expressions I have to complain of. He seems there very sensible of what I feel. I am very happy when placed in a situation to do justice to any one." [2]

How strongly Greene felt, a letter of the 22d to Charles Pettit shows:—

" Your two long letters came to hand last night. I was

---

[1] Glover MSS. General orders for 26th August. This subject has been carefully treated by Mr. Amory in his recent life of Sullivan.

[2] Sparks, *Correspondence of the Revolution*, vol. ii. p. 188.

on board the French fleet.   I have only time to tell you
the devil has got into the fleet; they are about to desert us, and go round to Boston.   The garrison would be
all our own in a few days if the fleet would but only
coöperate with us; but alas they will not.   They have got
a little shattered in the late storm, and are apprehensive
a juncture of Byron's and Howe's fleets may prove their
ruin.   They are, therefore, determined to quit us immediately.   I am afraid our expedition is now at an end.
Like all the former attempts it will terminate with disgrace, because unsuccessful.   Never was I in a more perplexing situation.   To evacuate the Island is death; to
stay may be ruin.   The express is waiting at the door.
I am obliged, therefore, to defer giving you the particulars until a more favorable opportunity, and to renew my
promise of writing you more fully in my next.   My best
respects to General Reed if at camp, and to Colonel Cox
in your next letter."

" What shall we do next " was the difficult question that now presented itself.

" You inform me," writes Greene to Sullivan on the
23d, " that the French fleet have deserted us, and left the
harbor open to receive reinforcements, and that there is
but one of three measures to pursue : to continue the siege
by regular approaches; attempt the garrison by storm;
or effect an immediate retreat, and secure our stores.
You further inform me that the enemy's collective strength
is about 6,000, and that your own force is 8,174 rank and
file, besides a well appointed artillery, and that you expected
a reinforcement in two or three days of 3,000 men.

" In this situation and under these circumstances you
demand my opinion which of the three measures it is your
duty and interest to pursue.

" It will be a folly to continue the siege by regular approaches.   We are so contiguous to New York; and their

strength and security there enable them to detach such a force that upon joining the troops here they would be too formidable for your army. They will be mutinous, difficult to govern, and of little service in our future operations. There are many other reasons that urge a retreat, but these may suffice and would be sufficient in my humble opinion to justify you in effecting one immediately.

"However, as our forces are all collected and in pretty good health, and there will be no additional expense to the public to attempt to possess ourselves of the town by surprise, I shall take the liberty to suggest a plan for your consideration. I am sensible that neither the number nor quality of our troops would justify an attack upon the enemy's lines by open storm; but as many advantages are lost for want of being attempted, it may be well for you to consider how far you can be justified in risking the consequences that may follow the attempt.

"The garrison is said to be 6,000 strong; they are well fortified with lines, redoubts, and abattis; your strength is but little above 8,000. To attack 6,000 regular troops in redoubts, with an expectation of carrying them, would require 15,000 troops of equal or superior quality; you have but about 3,000 regular troops and 5,000 militia. Therefore it is a folly to think of effecting anything by open storm. If anything can be effected it must be by stratagem.

"Upon reconnoitering the works I observe a redoubt round a house at the head of Easton's beach, which commands the pass. If we could possess ourselves of this redoubt we might possibly open a passage within their lines by the way of the beach. I would pick out three hundred men of the best troops in the army, and give the command to a good officer, who should be provided with boats at Satchueset beach, all completely manned with good oarsmen, to land the party some distance south of the redoubt, which they should attempt to possess themselves of by fixed bayonets. I would have a body of troops ready at the entrance of the beach to push over for their support if they should succeed, and the whole army to follow in order and file off to the left and get upon the high grounds back of the town, and there form in good order.

"If the enemy should attack the column as it moved forward there must be detachments to check them and keep them in play while the troops are passing. In order to get a good and sufficient body of troops for the purpose, I would recommend a draft from the militia of all such soldiers as have been in service before, and have them incorporated with the Continental and State troops ; or else to form them into separate corps, and pick a corps of officers to command them from among the militia, State, or Continental troops as it shall be found they can be spared, and as they appear suitable to the command.

"With the rest of the militia I would make sham attacks along their lines from Tamminy hill to our batteries, in order to hold as much of the enemy's force upon the outlines as possible while we get footing within. The militia not to begin their attacks until we give them a signal by a rocket, and the column not to begin to move across the beach until the advance party fire a rocket, which will answer two valuable purposes ; it will serve to direct our own motions, and make the enemy think there are other principal attacks to commence, which will leave them in doubt how to divide their forces.

"The troops posted along in front of the enemy's lines will answer another valuable purpose. It will prevent the enemy from sallying (if we should meet with a repulse) and attempting to cut off our retreat.

"The quartermaster should have as many teams provided, as would take up all our baggage, stores, cannon, and mortars at once — which should move off for the upper end of the Island the moment we begin our motions for the storm. I would recommend the forepart of the night for the attempt as the enemy will be less upon their guard. If we should get footing it will give us time to make the necessary dispositions before they can attack us; and if we meet with a repulse, it will afford us an opportunity to draw off our men with more safety, as our disposition cannot be known in the night.

" If we were not situated as we are I could not recommend this attempt because the chance is not equal; but our particular situation demands every attempt that reason or common sense can justify. I think it, therefore, worthy your attention. I can only assure you, if you should think the measure eligible, I will cheerfully undertake any part of the execution, and will give you every possible aid in my power to render it effectual."

Why this was not attempted we shall see a little further on. Meanwhile let us bring in another side light to help us in our conception of the man.

" Judge Potter," he writes to his wife on the 26th, " is polite enough to call at my quarters and offer his services to bring you a letter. I wrote you this morning by the way of Providence, but for fear that should not come to hand I embrace this opportunity. I am not very well in health. I have been a little troubled with the asthma but have got over it.

" I hope you and the children are well. Patty, you say, is getting on finely. I am sorry you wear such melancholy countenances at Coventry, but it is natural to the family. Jacob is one of Doctor Young's disciples; he is always looking over the black page of human life; never content with fortune's decrees.

" Miss Nancy don't like the note I sent her; she says she won't correspond any more with me. She don't like the insinuation of being an old maid. Poor girl! I am afraid her romantic conceptions of human nature will lead her to pass the flower of life, and then her pride won't permit her to marry. How wretched this state, to be always at war with one's inclinations. I am in hopes to see you in a week or fortnight."

If there is nothing of his disappointment in this letter there is enough of it in the one he writes the next day to General Heath.

"I received your favor of the 18th this evening.

"I have endeavored to keep Colonel Chase fully supplied with cash to satisfy all the demands against the department; but it has not been fully in my power, owing to the difficulty of getting the money from the Treasury. The drafts upon the office are so great that it is almost impossible to answer the demands seasonably.

"The moneys you have advanced to Colonel Chase since my appointment, I presume was to discharge the old arrearages, as I am persuaded his disbursements under me cannot much exceed the sums I have advanced him, and what he writes me he is now in debt.

"I shall transmit Colonel Chase in a few days an order on the loan office in Boston for $150,000, which I hope will be equal to all his wants.

"I thank you for your good wishes for the success of the expedition against Newport, but our hopes are all vanished since the French fleet has left us. The storm has proved a cruel misfortune; it has deprived us of the very foundation of the expedition, which would never have been undertaken but from the assurance of the French fleet and forces coöperating with us. However, the shattered state of the fleet and the Admiral's particular instructions from the court of France obliged him to abandon the enterprise, although he had the fullest evidence of its being crowned with success in a few days.

"Several ships have come into the harbor of Newport yesterday and to-day. A reinforcement is hourly expected.

Our force is melting away very fast. We shall be obliged to depart if there comes in any considerable reinforcements. The enemy are very strongly fortified with redoubts, lines, and abattis. They are almost encircled by water. There is but one narrow side where they can be approached, and that very difficult of access from the make of the ground, and a pond they have formed almost across their front.

" On the back of these are all their fortifications, (so) that it is impossible to storm the garrison, especially as they have more regular troops than we have.

" If we could have got into their rear, which we might have done with the assistance of the shipping, we might have succeeded with great ease. However, Providence has thought proper to order it otherwise ; perhaps for our good, although difficult to conceive of.

" The disappointment is very great and our mortification not less so. To lose such a prize that seemed so much in our power is truly vexatious."

On the next day, the 28th, he repeats the story in a long letter to Washington which may be taken as a narrative of the expedition.

" Your Excellency's favor of the 21st, came to hand the evening of the 25th.

" In my last I communicated to your Excellency the departure of the Count d'Estaing with his fleet, for Boston. This disagreeable event has, as I apprehend, ruined all our operations. It struck such a panic among the militia and volunteers that they began to desert by shoals.   The fleet no sooner set sail than they began to be alarmed for their safety. This misfortune damped the hopes of our army, and gave new spirits to that of the enemy.

" We had a very respectable force as to numbers ; between eight and nine thousand rank and file, upon the ground.   Out of these we attempted to select a particular corps to possess ourselves of the enemy's lines, partly by force, and partly by stratagem ; but we could not make up the necessary number that was thought sufficient to warrant the attempt, which was five thousand, including the Continental and State troops. This body was to consist of men who had been in actual service before, not less than nine months. However, the men were not to be had, and if they could have been found, there was more against it than for it. Colonel Laurens was to have opened the passage by landing within the enemy's lines, and getting possession of a redoubt at the head of Easton's beach. If we had failed in the attempt the whole party must have fallen a sacrifice, for their situation would have been such that there was no possibility of getting off.

"I shall inclose your Excellency a plan of the enemy's works, and of their strength from the best accounts we are able to get. They have never been out of their lines since the siege began till night before last. Colonel Bruce came out with a hundred and fifty men to take off a small picket of ours posted at the neck of Easton's beach. He partly succeeded in the attempt by the carelessness of the old guard. He came over after dark and lay in ambush, (so) that when the new guard went down to take their post the enemy came upon their backs before they discovered them, it being very dark. We lost twenty-four privates and two subalterns. Ten of the picket got off.

"Our strength is now reduced from nine thousand to between four and five thousand. All our heavy cannon on garrison carriages, and heavy superfluous stores of every kind, are removed to the main and to the north end of the Island, where we intend to intrench and to attempt to hold it, and wait the chance of events. General Hancock is gone to Boston to forward the repairs of the fleet, and to prepare the mind of the Count for a speedy return. How far he will succeed I cannot pretend to say. I think it a matter of some doubt yet, whether the enemy will reinforce or take off his garrison. If they expect a superior fleet from Europe they will reinforce ; but if not they will remove the garrison.

" Your Excellency may rest assured that I have done everything in my power to cultivate and promote a good understanding both with the Count and the Marquis, and flatter myself that I am upon very good terms with them both. The Marquis's great thirst for glory and national attachment often run him into errors. However, he did everything to prevail upon the Admiral to coöperate with us that man could do. People censure the Admiral with great freedom, and many are impudent enough to reproach the nation through the Admiral. General Sullivan very imprudently issued something like a censure in general orders. Indeed it was an absolute censure. It opened the mouths of the army in very clamorous strains. The General was obliged to explain it away in a few days. The fermentation seems to be now subsiding and all things appear as if they would go smoothly on. The Marquis is going to Boston also, to hasten the Count's return, and if possible to get the French troops to join the land forces here, which will the more effectually interest the Count in the success of the expedition.

" Five sails of British ships have got into Newport within two days past. We have heard nor seen nothing of the fleet of transports your Excellency mentioned in your letter to General Sullivan of the 23d. If they arrive with a large reinforcement our expedition is at an end, unless it is by the way of blockade, and that will depend upon the French fleet's being superior to that of the British.

" General Sullivan has done everything that could be expected, and could the fleet have coöperated with us as was at first intended, and agreeably to the original plan of the expedition, we must have been successful. I wish it was in my power to confirm General Sullivan's prediction of the 17th, but I cannot flatter myself with such an agreeable issue. I am sensible he is in common very sanguine, but his expectations were not ill founded in the present case. We had every reason to hope for success from our numbers and from the enemy's fears. Indeed, General Pigot was heard to say the garrison must fall unless they were speedily relieved by a British fleet. If we could have made a landing upon the south part of the town two days would have put us in complete possession of it. Nothing was wanting to effect this but the coöperation of the fleet and French forces. The disappointment is vexatious and truly mortifying. The garrison was so important, and the reduction so certain, that I cannot with patience think of the event. The French ship that was missing has got into Boston. The rest of the fleet have not got there yet, or at least we have no accounts of their arrival.

"We are very anxious to learn the condition of Lord Howe's fleet. The French seventy-four that has got into Boston had an engagement with a British sixty-four. The Captain and Lieutenant of the former were both wounded; one lost a leg, the other an arm.

"Our troops are in pretty good health, and well furnished with provisions and everything necessary for carrying on the expedition.

"Our approaches were pushed on with great spirit while we had any hopes of the fleet's coöperating with us, but the people lost all relish for digging after that.

"People are very anxious to hear the issue of General Lee's trial. Various are the conjectures, but everybody agrees he is not acquitted."

And here, for the next three days, his pen was stayed; for the British were reinforced, the Americans retreated, fought a hard battle, won a decisive victory, repelling every attack of their enemy, and effecting a retreat to the main-land without loss of men or baggage.

" For fear you should hear any vulgar reports circulating about the country," writes Greene to his wife from " Camp near Bristol Ferry," August 29, " I have sent George to inform you that we have had a considerable action to-day; we have beat the enemy off the ground where they advanced upon us; the killed and wounded on both sides unknown, but they were considerable for the numbers of troops we had engaged.

" We retreated back here last night, with an intention to hold this part of the Island. The enemy advanced upon us early this morning, and a pretty smart engagement ensued between our light troops and their advance party, and a severe action ensued with nearly the whole right wing. I write upon my horse and have not slept any for two nights, therefore you'll excuse my not writing very legible, as I write upon the field. Colonel Will. Livingston is slightly wounded. My aids all behaved with great gallantry."

Well might he hastily trace these few lines without pausing to dismount; how hastily the half sheet of coarse, dark paper before me bears witness; for every cannon that was fired that day was distinctly heard in Coventry, and the smoke of the battle-field was distinctly seen from the door of his quiet home. A single anecdote of the day has reached me : he had made his quarters in the house of a Quaker named Anthony, and the march of the night had given him a good appetite for his breakfast. He was still at table when the increasing distinctness of the musketry showed that the advance was gradually retreating before the enemy. " The British will have you, General," said the servant woman, alarmed for his safety. " I will have my breakfast first," said he, and tranquilly finished it, as if it were the only thing he had to think of.

On the 31st he resumes his letter to Washington from " Camp Tiverton."

" I wrote the foregoing and intended to have sent it by the express that went off in the morning, but while I was writing I was informed the express was gone ; and the change of situation, and round of events that have since taken place, have prevented my forwarding what I had wrote, as matters seemed to be coming to a crisis.

" On the evening of the 29th the army fell back to the north end of the Island. The next morning the enemy advanced upon us in two columns upon the East and West road. Our light troops, commanded by Colonel Livingston and Colonel Laurens, attacked the heads of the columns about seven o'clock in the morning but were beat back ; they were reinforced with a regiment upon each road. The enemy still proved too strong. General Sullivan formed the army in order of battle, and resolved to wait their approach upon the ground we were encamped on, and sent orders to the light troops to fall back. The enemy came up and formed upon Quaker Hill, a very strong piece of ground within about one mile and a quarter of our line. We were well posted with strong works in our rear, and a strong redoubt in front, partly upon the right of the line.

" In this position a warm cannonade commenced and lasted for several hours, with continual skirmishes in front of both lines. About two o'clock the enemy began to advance in force upon our right, as if they intended to dislodge us from the advanced redoubt. I had the command of the right wing. After advancing four regiments and finding the enemy still gaining ground, I advanced with two more regiments of regular troops, and a brigade of militia, and at the same time General Sullivan ordered

Colonel Livingston with the light troops under his command, to advance. We soon put the enemy to the rout, and I had the pleasure to see them run in worse disorder than they did at the battle of Monmouth. Our troops behaved with great spirit; and the brigade of militia under the command of General Lovell advanced with great resolution and in good order, and stood the fire of the enemy with great firmness. Lieutenant-colonel Livingston, Colonel Jackson, and Colonel Henry B. Livingston did themselves great honor in the transactions of the day, but it's not in my power to do justice to Colonel Laurens, who acted both the general and partisan. His command of regular troops was small, but he did everything possible to be done by their numbers; he had two most excellent officers with him, — Lieutenant-colonel Henry and Major Talbot.

" The enemy fell back to their strong ground, and the day terminated with a cannonade and skirmishes. Both armies continued in their position all day yesterday, cannonading each other every now and then. Last night we effected a very good retreat without the loss of men or stores.

" We have not collected an account of the killed and wounded, but we judge our loss amounts to between two and three hundred, and that of the enemy to much more.

" We are going to be posted all round the shores as guard upon them, and in that state to wait for the return of the fleet, which, by the by, I think will not be in a hurry.

" It is reported that Lord Howe arrived last night with his fleet and the reinforcement mentioned in your Excellency's letter to General Sullivan. If the report is true we got off the Island in very good season.

" The Marquis went to Boston the day before the action and did not return till last night, just as we were leaving the Island. He went to wait upon the Admiral to learn his further intentions, and to get him to return again and complete the expedition if possible.

"I observe your Excellency thinks the enemy design to evacuate New York. If they should, I think they will Newport also; but I am persuaded they will do neither for the present.

" I would write your Excellency a more particular account of the battle and retreat, but I imagine General Sullivan and Colonel Laurens have done it already, and I am myself very much unwell. I have had no sleep for three nights and days, being severely afflicted with the asthma."

For the next few days Greene was stationed on the west shore of Narraganset Bay, with his head-quarters at Coventry, in his own house. But glad as he was to be in it again, he did not return to it with the same elastic tread with which he had left it a short month before. The expedition from which he had expected so much had failed. This in itself was a great disappointment, for, as he tells Reed, he "was dreaming of whole hosts of men and cargoes of generals to grace (their) triumph. But all at once the prospect fled like a shadow." [1] And to add to the mortification of failure public disappointment was venting itself in disingenuous criticisms and unmerited reproaches. Foremost among the discontented were John and Nicholas Brown, two prominent merchants of Providence, whose interests were materially affected by the closing of the bay to their ships. In their opinion the whole expedition had been badly planned and worse executed, and Sullivan had proved himself a bad general. Greene was indignant at these unmerited accusations of a good officer.

[1] Letter to General Reed, October 26, 1778.

"TO JOHN BROWN.[1]

"COVENTRY, *Sept.* 6, 1778.

"SIR, — In all republican governments every person that acts in a public capacity must naturally expect to have observations and strictures made upon his conduct. This is a tax generally laid by all free governments upon their officers, either civil or military, however meritorious. I am not surprised, therefore, to hear the late unsuccessful expedition against Newport fall under some degree of censure; but I must confess I am not a little astonished to hear such a principal character in society as you throw out such illiberal reflections against a gentleman's conduct merely because he took his measures different from your opinion.

"This expedition was planned upon no other consideration than that of the French fleet coöperating with the American troops. The strength of the garrison was considered, and a force ordered to be levied accordingly, that might be sufficient to complete its reduction. In forming the estimate there was the aid of the fleet, and the assistance of 3,500 French forces that were on board the fleet, taken into consideration. The loss of this force with that of the aid of the French fleet was a sufficient reason for abandoning the expedition.

"You say you think the expedition was ill-planned and worse conducted. In the first place, that the forces were drawn together at an improper place. I must beg leave to dissent from you in opinion. Was there any time lost by the Continental troops coming to Providence? There was not; for they all got together some days before the militia. Would it not have been extremely difficult, if not impossible to have brought the forces to have acted in concert with each other, one body at Tivertown and the

---

1 John Brown was a leading merchant of Providence; of whose position and occupations at this period, some interesting particulars are given in the memoirs of Elkanah Watson.

other at Boston Neck; and divided as they were, both parties would have been unequal to the descent. If either party was sufficient of itself, then the other part was superfluous. Besides the objections of a division of forces and the distance apart, there are two other objections against the measure; one is the difficulty of embarking a body of troops from that rugged shore; the delays that storms and high winds might produce. The accidents that might happen in crossing where there is such a large swell agoing; and the languor that a sea-sickness might produce among the men, is one objection; the other is, there were no stores or magazines of any kind at South Kingston to equip and furnish the troops for the attempt; besides which, it was necessary for the General to have all his troops together that he might select out such men and officers as were most suitable for the enterprise. If the troops had been collected at South Kingston, it would have too fully explained our intention, and put the enemy upon their guard; whereas landing upon the north end of the island led the enemy into a belief that we intended to carry the garrison by regular approaches; which would have given us an opportunity of reëmbarking the troops and landing upon the south part of the island, without being mistrusted. This was the plan of attack, and it might have succeeded, had our strength been sufficient, and the disembarkation countenanced by the fleet.

" You cannot suppose that General Sullivan wants spirit or ambition to attempt anything that reason or common sense can justify. It is the business of every general officer that is desirous of distinguishing himself, to count all opportunities to engage with the enemy where the situation and condition of his own forces and that of theirs will admit of it. But the safety of our country is a greater object with every man of principle, than personal glory.

" Before a general officer engages in any hazardous enterprise, he should well consider the consequences of success and failure, whether the circumstances of the community will not render one infinitely more prejudicial than the other can be beneficial. The strength and quality of the troops should be considered that you are about to attack, how they can be approached, and by what means you can secure a retreat. Then you have to take into consideration the number and quality of your own troops, how they are found, what temper they are of, whether they are regular or irregular, and how they are officered. Even the wind and weather are sometimes necessary considerations, and not to be neglected.

"I have heard many people foolish enough to suppose that it was only necessary for a general to lead on his forces to insure success, without regard to the strength or situation of the enemy, or the number or goodness of his own troops. Those that have often been in action can only judge what is to be expected of good, bad, and indifferent troops. Men are often struck with panics, and they are generally subject to that passion in a greater or less degree, according as the force of discipline has formed the mind by habit, to meet danger and death. I dare say many a man has gone from home with a determined resolution to meet the enemy, that has shamefully quitted the field for want of a habitual fortitude. Men often feel courageous at a distance from danger, that faint through fear when they come to be exposed. Pride and sentiment support the officer; habit and enthusiasm the soldier; without these there is no safe reliance upon men.

"I remember you recommended an attempt to effect a landing upon the south part of the island the night we returned from the fleet. But I could not possibly suppose you to be serious, because it was impossible for us to get the boats round seasonably, draw out the men and officers proper for the descent, and effect a landing before day. It was, therefore, impracticable if it had been ever so eligible. But I am far from thinking, under our circumstances, the measure would have been justifiable by reason or common sense in a common view, much less by military maxims. The day after the fleet sailed there was such a great change took place in the two armies, but particularly in ours, whose spirits all sunk upon the departure of the fleet, except the few regular troops (and it had its effect upon them), that nothing could be attempted with the hope of success. The garrison in Newport, that before gave themselves up for lost, now collected new courage, and would have defended themselves with double obstinacy.

"Suppose General Sullivan had attempted a landing, and actually effected it, and the garrison had defeated his troops, what would have been the consequence? The whole would have been made prisoners, and not only the party that landed, but all those that remained in camp, with all our stores of every kind. Was the object important enough for such a risk? Was the chance equal of our succeeding? Every one that will suffer himself to reflect a moment, will readily agree that neither the importance of the object, nor the chance of succeeding, would have warranted the attempt. It must be confessed the loss of such a garrison would have given the British army a deadly wound. But the loss of our army would have put our cause in jeopardy. Remember the effect of the loss of the garrison of Fort Washington. There was men enough there to have defended themselves against all the British army, had they not have been struck with a panic; but being most of them irregular troops, they lost all their confidence when the danger began to grow pressing, and so fell a prey to their own fears.

"But when you take into consideration the little prospect of our effecting a landing where there was batteries almost all round the shores, and where the enemy had cutters to intercept any attempt, and guard-boats to make discoveries, the measure would look more like madness than rational conduct.

" There was another objection to the measure; that was, our force was unequal to the attempt. The party detached to make the landing should have been superior to the whole garrison. The remaining part left in camp to cover the stores, and coöperate occasionally with the detachment after they had effected a landing, should have been equally strong; for both being so circumstanced as to render it necessary to be able independent of each other to resist the whole British garrison, if either had been deficient, it might have proved the ruin of all. If the party that was landed had not been superior to the garrison, they might have been defeated; and not having any ships to cover their retreat, all would have been lost. Or if, during the embarkation the garrison had sallied, the troops left in the camp would have been put to the rout, and nearly the whole have been made prisoners, and all our cannon and stores fallen into their hands.

" These are common and probable events in war, and to be guarded against accordingly. The garrison at Newport was generally thought to be 6,000 strong, including sailors. Our force amounted almost to 9,000; indeed, the field returns made it but 8,174, and the much greater part of these militia; but I would swell it to the utmost extent, and still you see it will fall far short of the necessary number to warrant the measure, even supposing ours to have been all regular troops. Here I cannot help remarking that some people seem desirous of deceiving themselves with regard to our strength. They rather incline to credit the votes of assembly, and the resolves of councils of war with regard to numbers, than returns actually taken upon the grounds. Would not a general officer be a fool to take a measure from numbers voted him for an expedition, without examining them to see how they agreed? Some, I hear, assert that our strength must have been much greater than appears by our returns, from the number of rations that were drawn. I remember

very well last winter at Valley Forge our army drew
32,000 rations, when the most we could muster for duty
was but 7,500; and in all irregular armies, there will be
generally a third more rations drawn than is in a well-
appointed one, to have the same strength upon the
ground. Therefore there can be no safe conclusion drawn
from the circumstance of the rations; their being either
greater or less is no certain evidence of the real strength
of an army.

"I am further informed you think this expedition has
been the worst concerted, and the most disgracefully executed of any one during the war. I must confess I differ widely from you in opinion. I think it prudently concerted, and honorably and faithfully executed. If the
General had attempted to have stormed the lines in common form, he would have met with a disgraceful defeat.
Some people are foolish enough to think that because the
northern army carried Burgoyne's lines, that these might
have been attempted with equal success, not adverting
to the difference of circumstances. These lines were ten
times as strong as those of Burgoyne's; besides which
the enemy came out of their ranks there, and our people
drove them back again, and entered pell-mell with them.
Burgoyne's force was much less than this garrison; his
troops much dispirited; the army that surrounded them
more than as strong again as ours in regular troops.

"Remember the loss of the British army before Ticonderoga last war, in attempting to storm lines inconsiderable
compared with the fortifications at Newport, and defended
with a less number of men in the works than were here.
Recollect the fate of the British army at Bunker's Hill,
attacking slight works defended by new levied troops;
consider the disgrace and defeat that happened to the
Hessians in the attack upon the inconsiderable redoubt
at Red Bank; and then form a judgment what prospect
General Sullivan had of success in making an attack

with an army composed principally of raw militia, upon a garrison as strong as that at Newport, consisting almost wholly of regular troops, and fortified so securely as they were.

" There was but one possible mode of attack by storm, which was proposed to the General; but the men necessary for the attempt could not be found, and consequently the attack could not be made.

" I am told you censure General Sullivan for not bringing on a general action, and urge my opinion as a proof of the propriety. I remember you asked me why there had not been a general action, when you was at the island the evening of the day of the battle. I told you that I had advised to one in the morning; but that I believed the General had taken the more prudent measure. He had fought them by detachment, defeated and disgraced them, without running any great risk.

" Our numbers, at the time we left the enemy's lines, were not much superior to the garrison. We knew they expected a reinforcement hourly. Had any considerable force arrived the night we retreated; landed, and marched out with the old garrison, we should have met with a defeat. The smallness of our numbers, the dispirited state that all troops are in on a retreat, together with the probability of the enemy's having received reinforcement, determined the General not to risk a general action, when he was sure of an advantage in a partial one; and by risking a general one he exposed the whole of the troops to certain ruin. He thought the other measure most advisable; and I think so too, upon cool reflection, although I thought otherwise at the time.

" I have seen as much service almost as any man in the American army, and have been in as many or more actions than any one. I know the character of all our general officers as well as any one; and if I am any judge, the expedition has been prudently and well conducted, and

I am confident there is not a general officer, from the Commander-in-chief to the youngest in the field, that would
have gone greater lengths to have given success to the
expedition than General Sullivan. He is sensible, active,
ambitious, brave, and persevering in his temper; and the
object was sufficiently important to make him despise every
difficulty opposed to his success, as far as he was at liberty
to consult his own reputation; but the public good is of
higher importance than personal glory, and the one is not
to be gratified at the risk and expense of the other.

" I recollect your observation to me on board the fleet, —
that the reputation of the principal officers depended upon
the success of the expedition. I have long since learned
to despise vulgar prejudices, and to regulate my conduct
by maxims more noble than popular sentiment. I have
an honest ambition of meriting the approbation of the public; but I will never go contrary to my judgment, or vio-
late my honor or conscience, for a temporary salute.

" If the Congress, or any particular State, who intrusts
their troops under my command, thinks proper to give orders to run all risks and hazards to carry a point, I would
cheerfully lead on the men; but where it is left discretionary, I must act agreeably to the dictates of my own
judgment.

" People, from consulting their wishes rather than their
reason, and by forming a character of the spirit and firmness of irregular troops, more from general orders sounding their praise, than from any particular knowledge of
their conduct, are led to expect more from such troops
than is in the power of any person to effect with them.

" I would just remark one thing further to you, that
an attack with militia in an open country, where they could
get off upon a defeat, might be very prudent, which would
be very rash and unwarrantable upon an island.

" I have wrote thus much in justification of a person's
character whom I esteem a good officer, and who, I think,

is much more deserving your thanks than reproach, and that of the public also. With regard to myself, it was unnecessary for me to say anything in justification of the measure of calling the troops together at Providence; because I had no voice in it; neither was I opposed to a storm, providing a proper number of men of a suitable quality could be found fit for the attempt. My advice for a general action I think was wrong; and the retreat that followed, everybody must allow, was necessary, and that it was well conducted.

"I have been told that your brother Nicholas let fall some very ungenerous insinuations with regard to me a few days before the action upon the island. These are the rewards and gracious returns I am to expect for years of hard and dangerous service, where every sacrifice of interest, ease, and domestic pleasure has been given up to the service of my country. But I flatter myself I am not dependent upon the State of Rhode Island for either my character or consequence in life. However, I cannot help feeling mortified that those that have been at home, making their fortune, and living in the lap of luxury, and enjoying all the pleasures of domestic life, should be the first to sport with the feelings of officers who have stood as a barrier between them and ruin.

"I am, sir, your most
"Obedient and very humble servant,
"N. GREENE."

The day after this letter was written, brought tidings which made the failure seem even more serious an evil than it had seemed in the beginning.

"By a letter this moment received from Major Courtland," — Greene writes to Sullivan on the 7th of September, — "I find I am not to expect the pleasure of your company to dine with us to-day. Should be glad to know when you can make it convenient.

" Am sorry to hear of the destruction of Bedford. General Clinton deserves to be immortalized for this memorable action. It is highly worthy so great a commander. He has forgot how he run the other day in the Jerseys at the head of all his troops. If he wanted to fight, he had then an opportunity. But there is something so low, dirty, and unworthy in this action, that I am surprised he would be concerned in it; and more especially as he reprobated General Vaughn's conduct up the North River last fall for a similar conduct.[1] I am clear it is the intention of Clinton, if possible, to burn Providence, and he is making these manœuvres at New London and Bedford to divide and draw off our force.

" Tyler's brigade is gone, and I suppose more force will be demanded at the eastward.

" In attempting to cover too much we shall expose everything; some principal objects should be attended to, and the others must take their chance.

" Warwick is now left open. Will you have part of the troops at Pawtuxet ordered there or not? I wish to know your mind upon this matter.

" Should be glad to know the particulars of Bedford affair, and any other intelligence that may come to hand.

" The artillery is wanted at Greenwich; please to order it forward, for fear Mr. Clinton should try his success this way."

Had there been nothing now but his military duties to occupy Greene's attention, he might have given himself up for a few days to the society of his friends, or found a little time for the examination of his private affairs. But there was no pause in the demands of the Quartermaster's department; and toward the middle of September

---

[1] For a concise account of the ourning of Bedford, or Dartmouth, as it was often called, vide Gordon. vol. iii. p. 169.

he mounted his horse again and rode once more over the well-known road to Boston. On the 16th he writes to Washington: —

" BOSTON, September 16, 1778.

" SIR, — The growing extravagance of the people, and the increasing demands for the article of forage in this quarter, has become a very alarming affair. Hay is from sixty to eighty dollars per ton, and upon the rise ; corn is ten dollars a bushel, and oats four, and everything else that will answer for forage in that proportion. Carting is 9s. per mile by the ton, and people much dissatisfied with the price. I have represented to the States of Rhode Island and Connecticut the absolute necessity of legislative interposition to settle the prices of things upon some reasonable footing, of all such articles and services as are necessary for the use of the public in my department. I am going to do the same to the Council of this State. What effect it will have I cannot say ; but if there is not something done to check the extravagance of the people, there are no funds in the universe that will equal the expense.

" The late affray that happened in this place between the people of the town and those of the fleet has been found to originate from a parcel of soldiers belonging to the convention troops, and a party of British sailors which were engaged on board a privateer. The secret enemies of our cause, and the British officers in the neighborhood of this place, are endeavoring to sow the seeds of discord as much as possible between the inhabitants of the place and the French belonging to the fleet. The French officers are well satisfied this is the state of the case, and it fills them with double resentment against the British. The Admiral and all the French officers are now upon an exceedingly good footing with the gentlemen of the town. General Hancock takes unwearied pains to promote a good understanding with the French officers.   His house is full from morning till night.

"I had a letter from the Marquis day before yesterday; he writes me he is endeavoring to represent everything in the most favorable colors to the Court of France, in order to wipe away the prejudices that the letters of some of the more indiscreet may make upon the Court.   All the French officers are extravagantly fond of your Excellency, but the Admiral more so than any of the rest.   They all speak of you with the highest reverence and respect.

"General Hancock made the Admiral a present of your picture.   He was going to receive it on board the fleet by firing a royal salute, but General Hancock thought it might furnish a handle for some of the speculative politicians to remark the danger of characters becoming too important.   He therefore dissuaded the Admiral from carrying the matter into execution.

"I find by your Excellency's letter to General Sullivan that you expect the enemy are going to evacuate New York; and that it's probable they are coming eastward.   I can hardly think they mean to make an attempt upon Boston, notwithstanding the object is important, and unless they attack Boston, there is no other object worthy their attention in New England.

"I am rather inclined to think they mean to leave the United States altogether.   What they hold here now, they hold at a great risk and expense.   But I suppose if they actually intend to quit the continent, they will endeavor to mislead our attention and that of our allies until they can get clear of the coast.   The Admiral is fortifying for the security of his fleet, but I am told his batteries are all open in the rear, which will be but a poor security against a land force.   General Heath thinks there ought to be some Continental troops sent here; but the Council won't turn out the militia, they are so confident the enemy are not coming here.

"If your Excellency thinks the enemy really design an

attack upon Boston, it may not be amiss for you to write your opinion to the council board, for I suspect they think the General here has taken the alarm without sufficient reasons.

" The fortifications round this place are very incomplete, and little or nothing doing upon them.

" I have given General Heath my opinion what posts to take possession of if the enemy should attempt the place before the Continental army gets up.

" From four to five thousand troops have arrived at Halifax; their collective strength will make a formidable army. I wish to know your Excellency's pleasure about my returning to camp. I expect Mrs. Greene will be put to bed every day; she is very desirous of my stay until that event; and as she has set her heart so much upon it, I could wish to gratify her, for fear of some disagreeable consequences, as women sometimes under such circumstances receive great injury by being disappointed.

" General Sullivan granted me leave to come here upon the business of my department. I expect to return in a few days.

" Major Gibbs is with me, and is going to Portsmouth.

" This is the third letter I have wrote since I had a line from your Excellency. Should be glad to hear from you when at leisure.

" I am your Excellency's
" Obedient servant,

" *August* 22.   " N. GREENE."

And again on the 19th : —

" BOSTON, *September* 19, 1778.

"SIR, — Your Excellency's letter of the 15th came to hand last night. I have waited upon General Heath, and have got the state of the clothing department. Mr. Fletcher has forwarded for Springfield from this place between 10 and 12,000 blankets, 7,669 pair of shoes, 8,000 suits of uniforms, and 2,000 shirts. He is forwarding from Portsmouth about 15,000 pair of hose and 10,000 suits of uniform. Messrs. Otis & Andrews have 5,000 suits of uniform in the hands of the tailors. They think they will be complete in a month at the furthest. General Heath has ordered all the cloths out of town, except about ten or twelve days' work for the tailors, which may delay the business some.

"I shall send a man from hence to Springfield, to see whether the clothing forwarded from this place has arrived all safe there ; and if not, to take the necessary steps to get it forward.

"All the clothing that has been sent on for some months past has gone under the care of proper conductors ; but I have now desired General Heath to add a small guard to each brigade of teams. The clothing shall be forwarded as fast as it is possible to get teams ; but there being no powers given the Quartermaster to impress, and the demand for private commerce, renders it difficult to procure a full supply. Merchants are giving 12s. a mile per ton for transportation.

"It is reported here that General Gates has advanced as far as Danbury on his way for this place. General Heath is greatly alarmed at it. He thinks it will be a most degrading circumstance to him, as he has had the command here, to be superseded at the approach of the enemy. Your Excellency's coming would give him pleasure, but anybody else will hurt him exceedingly. I hear General Sullivan declares, by all that is sacred, that he never will submit to an order of General Gates's. I think General Sullivan is wrong ; but I wish he may not be sent, if there is any possibility of avoiding it without involving your Excellency in any new difficulties with General Gates. It is my opinion that none of the Major-generals that took commissions after General Gates's appointment can with any propriety dispute his rank, unless they made that reserve condition at the time of accepting their commissions.

" Was not General Gates, by resolve of Congress, stationed at the post of the North River for the security of the Highlands; and will there not be a propriety in his remaining there, provided the grand army comes to the eastward?

" I thought it my duty to mention these matters with regard to General Heath and Sullivan, that your Excellency might be seasonably advertised.

" In my last I wrote your Excellency that the affray that has happened in this town between the French and the inhabitants, had not made any bad impressions upon the minds of the former; but I am afraid, from several little incidents, the French officers are not altogether satisfied.

" However, they mix with the inhabitants very freely, all except the Count, who remains on board the fleet the much greater part of the time.

" The great and General Court of this State are now sitting here. They have ordered in 3,000 militia to guard Boston, until the Continental army can come to its relief, should the enemy think proper to make a descent here. However, I cannot persuade myself they are coming this way. I think their destination must be to the West Indies. There is a report in town by some of the late arrivals, that a Spanish fleet, with a considerable land force, has arrived in the West Indies. If that should prove true, it may serve as a clue to explain the enemy's movements by.

" I am with the greatest regard,

" Your Excellency's most obedient humble servant,

" NATH. GREENE.

" His Excellency General WASHINGTON."

But the duties of his department were not the only duties that called Greene to Boston. The French fleet was still there, as his letters tell us; and there were still some heart-burnings between

D'Estaing and Sullivan, which it was necessary to assuage. Greene had won the Admiral's confidence. Sullivan's he had always possessed; and thus, when the correspondence between the two seemed to be rapidly verging towards bitterness, he naturally came in as a friendly counsellor to both. How fully D'Estaing appreciated his good offices, will be seen by the following letter : [1] —

"BOSTON ROAD, *October* 1, 1778.

" SIR, — The letter which your Excellency did me the honor of writing to me when you were leaving Boston, was of a nature to console me for the little irregularities which you perceived in General Sullivan's letter, which I took the liberty of communicating to you upon receiving it. It is from you and what you are, that it is doubtless suitable and flattering to judge of the respectable and amiable qualities of the American general officers whom I have not the honor of knowing by correspondence or personally ; it is with cordial warmth that I render homage to truth in assuring you that on every occasion I have had reason to admire their zeal and talents, and to feel personal satisfaction for their behavior with regard to me ; and to add to the motives of duty those of inclination and attachment which I shall always profess to have for them. I shall be enchanted if the assurance and the homage of these sentiments appear to you of any value. With respect to the conduct, more or less moderate, that General Sullivan seems to have adopted in his literary commerce with me, as a zeal and devotion for the common cause, which I glory in, had engaged me to style him my General, he avails himself of the privileges which this title gives, beginning as you saw in his letter, by scolding me unjustly, and finishing by telling me in confidence that he has rivals whom he supposes his enemies. This mix-

---

[1] Written in French, with a translation on a separate sheet.

ture of chagrin and confidence being confined personally
to me, did not offend me.   There is another more important article, and which I am not at liberty to pass in
silence.   I mean the obstinacy which General Sullivan
exhibits in national imputations ; and the abuse of his place
in filling incessantly the public papers which are under
his direction with things which might at length create ill
blood between the individuals of two nations who are
and ought to be united.   It is wounding their interests in
a capital manner to dare by indiscretion or passion to
foment what ought to be extinguished if it exists.   I have
been obliged lately to entreat General Sullivan to reflect
on this subject.   In doing it I observed all the deference
that was due to him ; but my quality as a public person
and that of his well wisher, equally imposed this law on me.

" I hope that your Excellency and your respectable
colleagues will not disapprove my conduct.   To merit
that it should please them will ever be one of my desires,
as well as to prove to you particularly all the consideration which I have for you and them, and the respect with
which I have the honor of being,

" Sir, Your Excellency's
" Most humble and most obedient servant."

On his return to Rhode Island, Greene found the
legislature in session at East Greenwich.   A natural
feeling carried him to this scene of his first public
labors, and on entering the hall he was invited to
a seat upon the floor.   Among the business papers
to be read were letters of Sullivan to the Governor,
written in the first moments of his dissatisfaction
with the French Admiral, and containing strong
expressions of his irritated feelings.   Greene instantly suspected their nature.   " Do not let these
letters be read aloud," said he in a whisper to the

Speaker ; and the whisper passing round the house, the order of the day was called, and a serious danger averted ; for the house was crowded, and such accusations, publicly read, could hardly have failed to have spread over the country, gathering strength as they passed from mouth to mouth, and reviving at a critical moment old and dangerous prejudices.[1]

His thoughts now turn again towards camp. He calls upon his deputy for "the returns."

"For I am exceedingly in want of them to know the general state of the department.

"Mr. Pettit writes me he is in want of a few hundred tents and a number of marquees. Can they be spared from this quarter?

"I shall want a good wagon, well geared, to carry on to camp four or five hundred boxes. Please to get one in readiness." [2]

And still all the while little jostlings occur in the department which he is called upon to regulate.

"Colonel Bowen informs me," he writes to Sullivan from Coventry on the 5th of October, "there is some difficulty respecting the staff officers belonging to the quartermaster's department drawing clothing out of the public stores. All those who do business at the stated prices are, I conceive, as justly entitled to draw as the other officers ; it being impossible for them to support themselves without this privilege. Such of the staff as have been appointed in the grand army, have always had free access to the store with other officers of the line.

---

[1] *Vide* Marshall, vol. i. p. 266.— Johnson, vol. i. p. 116, transfers this incident to Philadelphia, forgetting that Sullivan's conduct was approved by Congress in September, and that Greene did not go to Philadelphia until the following January, when the Rhode Island expedition had ceased to occupy the attention of that body.

[2] Letter to Colonel E. Bowen, Sept. 29, 1778.

" Colonel Bowen desired me to write to you upon the subject, that he might receive your instructions upon this head.

" Mr. Dexter Brown is the subject of this particular application. He is a wagonmaster-general in this department, and refuses to serve unless he can be allowed this privilege. He is said to be a good officer, and the Colonel thinks it will be an injury to the public service to lose him."

On the same day he writes to Washington :—

" COVENTRY, RHODE ISLAND, *October* 5, 1778.

" SIR, — Your Excellency's favor of the 22d of September and the 1st of October, came to hand last evening.

" I am exceedingly sorry for Colonel Baylor's misfortune. The surprise is the worst part of the affair, and no man will more sensibly feel upon the occasion than the Colonel, should he recover.

" Colonel Butler's and Major Lee's surprise made upon the Chasseurs was a complete one. These two events serve to show how much in war depends upon attempts.

" I fancy the enemy are foraging for the use of the garrison at New York, and will withdraw themselves as soon as they have completed their work. Their future operations are merely conjectural. However, as France is not prepared to carry on any offensive operations in the West Indies against any considerable force, a part of the British army will be detached there, to secure the Island against any little attempts. The remainder will continue at New York and Newport, in order to keep us in awe, and to make some further trial to negotiate a peace not only with us, but through us with France.

" The depreciation of our money is an alarming circumstance, and the remedy difficult to be found. Nothing but taxation and a high interest can work an effectual change. Legislative interposition may produce some temporary advantages, but not a radical cure for the evil.

"I shall set out for camp to-morrow, or next day at furthest; the state of the clothing business I shall give your Excellency particular information about at my arrival in camp; but I believe every necessary measure is taken to get it forward, so far as it depends upon my department.

"I was told yesterday that General Sullivan had wrote to your Excellency to have me stationed here this winter. However agreeable it is to be near my family and among my friends, I cannot wish it to take place, as it would be very unfriendly to the business of my department.

"I wrote yesterday to General Sullivan for leave to join the grand army, and expect his answer to-day.

"I have the honor to be,

"With the greatest respect and regard,

"Your Excellency's most obedient humble servant,

"NATH. GREENE."

These were his last public letters from Coventry; and then the light of history faded from the house, and the roar of the forge by day, and the murmurings of the beautiful stream by night, were the only sounds that were heard in the pleasant valley.

And now those sounds also have passed away. The old house still stands on the green hill-side, and still from its door-way and windows you may look out on a wide reach of wooded landscape; but the forge is gone, the little village of the laborers is gone, the foundations of a railroad have encroached upon the bed of the Pawtuxet, and even tradition itself has transmitted to the new generation but faint and imperfect recollections of these early efforts of the productive genius of Rhode Island; a genius which, directed to other branches, has made the smallest, one of the richest and most flourishing States of the Union.[1]

[1] Among the authorities for this chapter are the letters of John Laurens to his father in the *Correspondence of John Laurens*: in which, however, I cannot but think that he has not done justice to Lafayette.

CHAPTER V.

THE active movements of the campaign were now over, yet much doubt was still felt concerning the designs of the enemy. Greene, as we have already seen, believed that their operations would be directed against the West Indies. "A large part of the enemy at New York have embarked," he writes to General Varnum from the "camp at Fredericksburg," on the 24th of October. "Their destination is unknown. Many conjecture they are bound to Boston. I am rather of an opinion they are going to the West Indies. Another embarkation is said to be getting in readiness. Most people are of opinion there will be a total evacuation; but I am not of the number. I think they will leave a garrison, if it is but a small one."

Rhode Island, however, he believed would soon be set free.

"We have been hourly expecting the arrival of the accounts of the evacuation of Newport," he writes to his kinsman William Greene, now Governor of the State.[1] " I was glad to see your proclamation forbidding all kinds of plundering. This line of conduct will do the State great credit. If delinquents are to be punished, let it be by one course of law. It is dangerous to let loose the rabble upon people by way of punishment. Nothing tends more to unhinge government or destroy the morals of society. Such as have behaved unfriendly, bring them to a legal trial. But if I was to advise in this business, I would recommend great moderation. Let none fall a sacrifice but such as may be dangerous hereafter, or are necessary to deter others from a similar conduct. Passion and resentment mix so freely in our politics in a state of civil war that we often listen to the voice of resentment instead of reason, justice, and moderation. Proscription and confiscation are rather to be considered as misfortunes than benefits to government, although we may seem to gain by the measure. Industry and harmony should be the great objects of legislation. These produce plenty, and diffuse general happiness in society. I know your moderation and humanity, and therefore speak the more freely to you on this subject. When passion, rage, and public animosity have subsided, the events of these days will be viewed through a very different medium to what they are at this hour. The name of him who has wantonly sported with human creatures will be held up to after ages with horror and detestation. Those who are at the head of government generally stand responsible for all transactions during their administration. The love and friendship I feel for you, and the desire I have that your administration should be glorious to yourself and honorable to the name, makes me drop these hints."

But while military questions still received a share of his attention, and were still frequently discussed in his letters, the chief of his time

[1] West Point, October 27, 1778.

was necessarily devoted to the absorbing duties of his department. How absorbing and at the same time how perplexing those duties were, may best be seen by his letters. No department was so much exposed to malignant criticism, for no department came into such direct relations with the public purse and private interest.

"I thank you kindly," he writes to Henry Marchant from the camp at Fredericksburg, October 15, 1778, " for your friendly hints upon the state of the Quartermaster's department. I am sensible of the difficulty of conducting such an extensive business without leaving some cause for complaints. But I cannot help thinking the agents employed are nearly in the same predicament that Lord Chesterfield says ministers of state are. They are not so good as they should be, and by no means as bad as they are thought to be. A charge against a quartermaster-general is most like the cry of a mad dog in England. Every one joins in the cry and lends their assistance to pelt him to death. I foresee the amazing expenditure in our department will give rise to many suspicions; and I make no doubt there will be some impositions and many neglects; but the great evil does not originate either in the want of honesty or economy in the management of the business, but in the depreciation of the money and the growing extravagance of the people. I have taken all the pains in my power to fix upon the most deserving charac-ters as agents to act under me, and always gave the most positive instructions to retrench every unnecessary ex-pense.

"It was with great reluctance that I engaged in this business. The committee of Congress and the Commander-in-chief urged it upon me contrary to my wishes. They painted the distress of the army and the ruin that must follow unless that I engaged in the business, as there was

no other to be found who could remove the prejudices of
the army and supply its wants. Before I would undertake
it, both the committee and the General promised to give
me all the aid and assistance in their power.

" How far the business has been conducted to the public
satisfaction I cannot pretend to say ; but I am persuaded
the successes of the campaign are owing to the extraordinary exertions made in this department to accelerate the
motions of the army.[1]

" I readily agree with you that so far as the commission
allowed for doing the public business increases the expense,
so far it is injurious (to) its interest; but I cannot suppose
that I have given an appointment to one person who would
wish to increase the public charge for the sake of enlarging
his commission. However, I may be deceived. I wish it
was possible for the public to get their business done without a commission ; but I am persuaded it is not. Be that as
it may, the evil, if it is one, did not originate with me. The
commission given to most of the deputies in the western
States under the former Quartermaster-general was much
higher than is now given. The Board of War gave larger
commissions for such persons as they employed in the department before I came in than I would give to the same
persons afterwards. I have got people upon the best terms
I could, and I hope there is few if any but what are men
of principle, honor, and honesty. To the eastward I am
confident there is no abuse of the public trust worthy
notice. You may depend upon my keeping a watchful eye
over all the branches of the department, and no impositions
shall pass unnoticed. But as I am at so great a distance
from many parts of the business, abuses may prevail for
some time, unless my friends will be kind enough to give
me seasonable information."

To form a correct estimate of the personal sac-

---

[1] For Washington's opinion, vide Sparks, *Writings of Washington*, vol.
vii. p. 153.

rifice that Greene made in accepting the office of quartermaster-general, we must remember that he was ambitious of a place in history, and " who," he writes to Washington some time after, " ever read of a quartermaster in history as such, or in relating any brilliant exploit?" " You mistake me," he writes in this same letter to Marchant, " if you think I meant to complain of Congress or my friends in it, for not taking more particular notice of me. I freely confess I have ever had an honest ambition of meriting my country's approbation; but I flatter myself I have not been more solicitous to obtain it than studious of deserving it. However, people are very apt to be partial to themselves; but I have sometimes thought my services have deserved more honorable notice than they have met with, not from Congress, but the army."

It is very evident that Greene was not free from the " last infirmity of noble minds."

Another and not the least of his difficulties arose from the frequent doubts and disputes produced by the want of a clear and definite statement of the powers and duties of his department. How far he was responsible for this state of things, he tells us in a letter of the 25th of March, 1779, to the President of Congress:—

" It has been almost impossible to obtain returns from the different branches of the Quartermaster's department for want of the necessary forms to direct the business. This I am endeavoring to complete, and flatter myself the agents in future will be able to make regular returns once a month.

" It was so late in the season last year before I entered upon the business of the Quartermaster's department, and finding it naked, distressed, and in a state of confusion; the wants of the army numerous and pressing; the business multiform and complex; myself and the two gentlemen, my assistants, in a great degree strangers to the economy of it; that I have never had either leisure or opportunity to digest it into such form and order as I could wish, and as I conceive necessary for the just information of Congress, and for my own convenience, ease, and security."

We see but little of the individual amid these engrossing cares. Yet we know that amid them all the domestic affections still held their place, awaking constant longings for his own fireside, and the faces and conversation of friends. Family tradition says that he still found or made time for reading, never going to his pillow until he had composed his mind by a few pages of some favorite author, Horace the oftenest of all. But as winter drew near, he began to look forward to its comparative quiet with an anticipation of enjoyment which he had scarcely dared to indulge before.

" The eastern jaunt," he writes to his wife from camp on the 13th of November, " I am afraid will prove very unfriendly to my wishes, as I am all impatient to see you. Never did I experience more anxious moments. Colonel Cox and Mr. Pettit are gone to Philadelphia. They both desire their most respectful compliments, and insist upon the pleasure of seeing you at Trenton this winter. You know how polite and clever these gentlemen are, and they affirm they are the worst part of the family. What a happy set. Great deductions are to be made from people's professions in polite life; but I verily believe these gentlemen have a great respect and regard for you. The Colonel says Mrs. Cox is very desirous of being of your acquaintance.

"I dined yesterday with his Excellency, who inquired very particularly after you, and renewed his charge to have you at camp very soon. Your last letter contained expressions of doubts and fears about the matter. To be candid with you I don't believe half a kingdom would hire you to stay away; but at the same time, I as candidly confess, I most earnestly wish it, as it will greatly contribute to my happiness to have you with me. However, this pleasure I would willingly forego rather than expose you too much in coming to camp. Should you think upon the whole of setting forward, come on by the way of King's Ferry; that will be the safest and best route. In the Clove there have been several robberies committed lately by *Tories and other villains.* Apply to General Putnam, who will command at King's Ferry, for a small escort of light-horse, who will guard you on to Paramus or Pompton. I have spoke to him upon the subject. Bring Washington with you if the weather is not too cold.

"I have many matters to write you, but my time is so taken up upon matters of business that I can hardly spare a moment to write a friend."

His winter-quarters were once more in the Jerseys, at Middlebrook, with the division of the army which Washington kept near his own person; the rest being distributed in different cantonments for greater convenience of supplies.

Another village of log huts sprang up in the woods, but better built and more commodious than the huts of Valley Forge. Practice had made both officers and men skillful in hutting, and trees were always at hand to supply the best of material in the most convenient form. More than one naked hill-side still bears witness to the local traditions of those winters.

Greene's quarters were at Pluckemin, in a house not far, I believe, from Washington's, though I have not been able to ascertain exactly where it stood. "The American troops are again in huts," Washington writes to Lafayette on the 8th of March, 1779, but in a more agreeable and fertile country than they were in last winter at Valley Forge, and they are better clad and more healthy than they have ever been since the formation of the army."[1]

Part of the new clothing came from France; but that Greene had a large share in bringing about this amelioration his letters abundantly show. Nor was the encampment without its pleasant scenes and appropriate amusements. Mrs. Washington was again at head-quarters, presiding with quiet dignity at her husband's table. Mrs. Greene and Mrs. Knox, Lady Stirling and Lady Kitty, whose name we meet so often in the social records of these days, were within calling distances of each other. Morristown was near, and the Lotts came often to take part in the social gatherings.

"We had a little dance at my quarters a few evenings past," Greene writes to Colonel Wadsworth on the 19th of March. "His Excellency and Mrs. Greene danced upwards of three hours

[1] Sparks, *Writings of Washington*, vol. vi. p. 192. *Vide* also Moore's *Diary of the Revolution*, vol. ii. p. 153.

without once sitting down. Upon the whole we had a pretty little frisk. . . . Miss Cornelia Lott and Miss Betsy Livingston are with Mrs. Greene. This moment they have sent for me to drink tea. I must go."

In February the anniversary of the French alliance was celebrated, as the alliance itself had been celebrated at Valley Forge the year before. But this time instead of the review there was an artillery salute, and in addition to the dinner, fireworks and a ball, Washington joining heartily, as he always seems to have done, in the dance. "There could not have been less than sixty ladies," wrote a correspondent of the "Philadelphia Packet," who was present.[1]

I have grouped together these interludes of hard work and deep anxiety; now I must go back to December, when we find Washington writing from Philadelphia : —

"I have seen nothing since I came here on the 22d instant, to change my opinion of men or measures; but abundant reason to be convinced that our affairs are in a more distressed, ruinous, and deplorable condition than they have been since the commencement of the war. . . . . . If I were to be called upon to draw a picture of the times and of men, from what I have seen, heard, and in part know, I should in one word say that idleness, dissipation, and extravagance seem to have laid fast hold of most of them; that speculation, peculation, and an insatiable thirst for riches seem to have got the better of every other consideration, and almost of every order of men ; that party disputes and personal quarrels are the great business of the

[1] Moore's *Diary of the Revolution*, vol. ii. p. 134.

day; whilst the momentous concerns of an empire, a great
and accumulating debt, ruined finances, depreciated money,
and want of credit, which in its consequences is the want
of everything, are but secondary considerations, and postponed from day to day, from week to week, as if our affairs
wore the most promising aspect.   After drawing this
picture, which from my soul I believe to be a true one, I
need not repeat to you that I am alarmed and wish to see
my countrymen roused.   I have no resentments, neither do
I mean to point at any particular characters.   This I can
declare upon my honor; for I have every attention paid to
me by Congress that I can possibly expect, and I have
reason to think that I stand well in their estimation.   But
in the present situation of things I cannot help asking,
where are Mason, Wythe, Jefferson, Nicholas, Pendleton,
Nelson, and another I could name?"   (B. Harrison, to
whom he was writing.)   "And why, if you are sufficiently
impressed with your danger, do you not, as New York has
done in the case of Mr. Jay, send an extra member or two,
for at least a certain limited time, till the great business
of the nation is put upon a more respectable and happy
establishment?   Our money is now sinking fifty per cent.
a day in this city; and I shall not be surprised if in the
course of a few months a total stop is put to the currency
of it;[1] and yet an assembly, a concert, a dinner or supper
that will cost three or four hundred pounds, will not only

---

[1] The rate of depreciation during
1779, as ascertained by Pelatiah
Webster from the merchant's books,
was —

1779. January, 7, 8, 9.
"   February, 10.
"   March, 10, 11.
"   April, 12 1-2, 14, 16, 22.
"   May, 22, 24.
"   June, 22, 20, 18.
"   July, 18, 19, 20.
"   August, 20.
"   September, 20, 28.

1779. October, 30.
"   November, 32, 45
"   December, 45, 38.

A short History of Paper Money
and Banking in the United States, by
William M. Gouge.

It is greatly to be regretted that
the data are wanting for tracing the
connection between these fluctuations in the currency and the commercial, agricultural, and manufac-
turing interest of the country.

take men off from acting in this business, but even from
thinking of it, while a great part of the officers of our
army, from absolute necessity are quitting the service, and
the more virtuous few rather than do this are sinking by
sure degrees into beggary and want.

"I again repeat to you that this is not an exaggerated
account. That it is an alarming one I do not deny; and
I confess to you that I feel more real distress on account
of the present appearances of things than I have done at
any one time since the commencement of the dispute.
But it is time to bid you adieu. Providence has heretofore taken us up when all other means and hope seemed to
be departing from us."[1]

Early in January, Greene joined the Commander-in-chief in Philadelphia. Of the manner
in which his time was passed there some idea may
be formed from the following paragraph with
which he begins a letter to Washington : —

"The little leisure I have don't afford me a
sufficient opportunity to go largely into the subject your Excellency requested my opinion upon.
I have been obliged to write for two nights past
until after one o'clock in the morning, and am
now writing before sunrise." Then, after a lucid
exposition of his views upon the subject, — the
plan of campaign for the new year, — he adds :
"I am obliged to wait upon the Treasury Board
this morning, which prevents my adding anything
further for the present. But I shall see your
Excellency by and by, and will converse further
upon the subject."

The object of Washington's visit to Philadelphia

[1] Washington to Benjamin Harrison. Sparks, *Writings of Washington,*
vol. vi. p. 150.

was not merely to discuss with Congress the plan of campaign, but to come to an understanding with them upon numerous questions of organization. Not the least among these was the question of half-pay, in which he had to support the cause of the army against men like Samuel Adams and Henry Laurens. It was natural that he should wish to have Greene with him; for upon all these subjects their opinions were in harmony, and each drew strength and aid from the other. Each too was followed by the details of his office. Greene writes to Col. Biddle, on the 20th of January: —

"DEAR SIR, — I am favored with yours of the 9th, 11th, and 14th of this instant. The great scarcity of the article of forage produces too general a cry to leave the least doubt of the reality of the thing. I am happy to hear from camp, that the distress among the cattle grows less and less. Major Forsyth and Mr. Thomson writes me that almost all the public teams are gone, and the country teams comes in in greater plenty than was expected. There has been large sums of money gone eastward both for you and us. I hope nearly equal to the demands. A great sum will be sent to Major Furman in a few days.

"I am sorry to hear the repeated complaints against Col. Bostwyck. I think you had better give Col. Hay orders to provide forage for himself, if Mr. Bostwyck don't supply the post. Let him open a forage account for the purpose. I find the Governor and Council will do nothing more than recommend or enforce the old law; although this is far short of our wishes, yet it is much better to have them with us than against us. I wish most heartily the forage and commissary line could unite their force and measures for getting the wheat manufactured; but I am afraid it is not to be done. The shorts would be a great relief to us.

"I have directed Col. Pettit to keep you in money at all events to pay for forage that is impressed agreeable to law.

"You inquire what you shall give your assistants in the forage department. Don't the resolution of Congress state their pay? I don't know what to say to the expenses. What do you suppose to be absolutely necessary for the purpose of subsistence?

"I shall procure an order from head-quarters for the division of Col. Sheldon's regiment. I agree with Mr. Hubbard they can be subsisted much easier and cheaper in a divided state than together.

"The Governor and Council of this State complain that the State is overborne with cavalry and wagon horses. I have got an order for Pulaski's legion to go down into Kent and Sussex in the Delaware State. I don't think it advisable to order in horses out of Salem County, neither can Maj. Lee's corps be removed. There is nobody willing to receive the horses, and everybody desirous of getting rid of them.

"I drank tea with your good lady and sisters this evening. The spirit of dueling, intrigue, and cabal goes on here as much as ever."

And again on the 22d : —

"The express that brings this will also bring you a sum of money for the use of the army at camp. I believe I have taken such measures for supplying the eastward States that there will be no cause of complaint. Before the arrival of Coocke's express, Mr. Pettit had sent him 33,000 dollars. Mr. Furman can have a full supply by applying. I am doing everything to get things along; but the wheels goes heavily, especially in the forage line. I am in hopes to get away soon ; if not, I am sure the

Quartermaster-general will be broke. We spend money here not by hundreds but by thousands of pounds.

" Colonel Wadsworth is fretting his soul out."

The following letters to Colonel Bowen show how carefully Greene was watching over the public property, what pains he was taking at this very time to secure regular returns from the officers of his department, and how constantly he kept its wants in view. They are but two examples from many.

PHILADELPHIA, *January* 26, 1779.

" SIR, — Major Burnet acknowledged the receipt of your accounts a few days past.

" I am much in want of the returns at your post, of stores of all kinds for the Quartermaster's department, and the cattle and carriages that are public property. I also want from the army under General Sullivan's command, returns of all stores belonging to the Quartermaster's line. You will also give me a return of the men employed for different purposes in the department. I expected these returns with your accounts ; but they did not come to hand.

" If Mr. Jacob Greene should have occasion to draw on you for cash to enable him to complete some orders sent him lately, you will please to furnish him. I shall send him a supply of cash soon, when he can repay your office.

" Make the brigade quartermasters and others who have charge of public property, make you weekly returns, and transmit them to me monthly.

" My best respects to Mrs. .Greene and Mrs. Olney."

PHILADELPHIA, *January* 27, 1779.

" DEAR SIR, — I wrote you the 5th of this instant, to charter, in the State of Rhode Island, and in and about Bedford, in the State of Massachusetts, vessels enough to import 1,000 casks of rice from South Carolina. I wrote to Mr. Benjamin Andrews to charter a sufficient number to import 4,000, in the State of Massachusetts Bay; his unfortunate death I am afraid will disconcert the business.

"I hope you have not failed to complete what was requested of you. It is an object of the highest importance to the interest and welfare of the United States. Pray don't neglect the affair. If you should be able to do more than is requested, please to let Mr. Otis, partner to Mr. Andrews, know it; and if he should decline the business, let Messrs. Miller & Tracy be acquainted with it, as they are requested to take the business up.

"The express is just going, and I have not time to take a copy or correct what I have wrote.

     "I am, sir,
       "Your humble servant,
         "NATHANAEL GREENE, Q. M. G."

Early in February he was in camp again, bringing back with him impressions very like those which we find in Washington's letters of the same period.

"The local policy of all the States," he writes to Varnum on the 9th, "is directly opposed to the great national plan; and if they continue to persevere in it, God knows what the consequences will be. There is a terrible falling off in public virtue since the commencement of the present contest. The loss of morals and the want of public spirit leaves us almost like a rope of sand. However, I believe the State of Rhode Island acts upon as generous principles, and ever has done, as any one State in the Union.

"Luxury and dissipation are very prevalent. These are the common offspring of sudden riches. When I was in Boston last summer, I thought luxury very predominant there; but they were no more to compare with those now prevailing in Philadelphia, than an infant babe to a full grown man. I dined at one table where there were an hundred and sixty dishes; and at several others not far behind.[1] The growing avarice and a declining currency are poor materials to build an independence upon."

One thing, however, comforted him.

"I believe the Congress have it in contemplation to make some further provision for the army; but whether it is in their power is a matter of doubt. I cannot agree with you that the army is despised. It is far from being the case in Philadelphia. The officers were never more respected."

Seventeen hundred and seventy-nine was neither an active nor a hopeful year. It was not till the end of the preceding December that Congress, yielding to the urgent representations of Washington, could bring itself to renounce the absurd plan of an expedition against Canada. The new year found them listless in everything but personal schemes and party dissensions. Personally Washington was treated with confidence and respect. Personally Greene was received with consideration and listened to with attention. But neither Washington nor Greene could overcome the inherent sluggishness of a legislative body called upon to perform the functions of an executive body. Members would still consume time in debate when they should have thought only of action; and still, after the experience of four years of war, repeat the errors and illusions

[1] "It is no less a fact that in every town on the continent luxury flourishes as it would amongst a people who had conquered the world, and were about to pay for their victories by their decline." — *Correspondence of John Laurens*, April 11, 1778.

of the first year. Recruits who, when the war began, might easily have been secured for the whole duration of it, without any expense beyond their food, clothing, and pay, could hardly be obtained now at any price. Drafts took the place of voluntary enlistments, but no State dared to make drafts for the war, or even for three years; so that nine or twelve months were the average term of service for drafted men, and eighteen the utmost limit. Indeed, very few were willing to engage for the war on any terms. To procure recruits Congress offered a bounty of $200. To fill up their quotas the State governments outbid the Congress. Thus every year the army had to be created anew; most of the officers, it is true, remaining, but the men going off as their terms of service expired. Steuben's discipline, indeed, was not thrown away, for it became a part of the general military education of the country; but his labors were to be renewed with each new campaign.

Yet even with all these elements of delay, a tolerable preparation might have been made, and the rudiments of discipline imparted to the new recruits before they were called to the field, if they had been engaged in season. But Congress would never do its own share of the work at the right time, and hence Washington's could never be done in the right way. Untaught by the past, Congress, this year also, manifested the same unwillingness to act which had already produced so much mischief through all the preceding years.

It was not till the 23d of January that they gave
Washington authority to reopen the enlistment
rolls.   It was not till the 9th of March that they
called upon the States for their quotas.   And thus
upon the verge of the campaign, instead of an
army to discipline, there was still an army to
raise.

But this year a new delusion came to add its
baneful influence to the evil influences already so
busily at work.   Now that France is with us, and
Spain so soon to be, it will be impossible for England
to continue the war at such a distance from home.
Her forces, therefore, will speedily be withdrawn,
and the battle-field be transferred from the continent to the islands and the ocean.   Thus
reasoned many Congressmen, not a few out of
Congress, and some in the army.   Neither Washington nor Greene shared this delusion.

The enemy had their delusion too, and suffered
themselves to be led by it to a vain prolongation
of the war, a wanton waste of treasure, and a
wicked waste of life.   The French coöperation,
they reasoned, has signally failed, leaving nothing
but heart-burnings and dissensions behind.   Americans will see now how unable their allies are to
protect them.   The old hatred of France, so
deeply rooted in the Anglo-Saxon heart, will re-
vive.   They will gladly accept the terms which
they so rashly rejected in their hour of ill-
founded hope; and returning to their allegiance,
unite with us in chastising the common enemy of
our peace and prosperity.   To hasten the happy

moment, the English leaders resolved to complete
the conquest of the South, and confine their
operations in the northern and middle States to
such measures as would most effectually keep
alive a constant feeling of insecurity all along the
seaboard.   And thus while the colonies would be
made to feel the powerlessness of France to protect them, France also would be made to feel
that she had nothing to hope from the colonies.
This was the object of Matthews' descent on
Virginia in May, and Tryon's expedition against
Connecticut in July; in both of which towns were
burnt, shipping and stores destroyed, and lives
taken; vain and wanton outrages; for while they
carried desolation to happy firesides, they still
more surely awakened the thirst of vengeance in
the hearts of the sufferers.   It was a poor way of
winning subjects back to King George.

Meanwhile the Americans held the line of the
Hudson, keeping strong positions on both banks,
and with part of their forces within striking distance of the enemy.   Washington had from the
beginning decided to stand on the defensive, and
make up by position for the want of numbers.
But he dealt in July a sharp, quick blow at
Stony Point, which Wayne carried by the bayonet, and another in August upon the hostile
Indians, whom Sullivan defeated and drove back
from the borders.   Henry Lee's brilliant surprise
of Paulus Hook, Clark's daring march against St.
Vincent, and Van Schaick's bold attack of the
Onondagas, were all equally successful.   If the

main army made no great marches and fought no great battles, Washington accomplished none the less the object of his campaign. In September he sums up its results in a letter to Lafayette. " The operations of the enemy this campaign have been confined to the establishment of works of defense, taking a post at King's Ferry, and burning the defenseless towns of New Haven, Fairfield, and Norwalk, on the Sound, within reach of their shipping, where little else was or could be opposed to them than the cries of distressed women and helpless children; but these were offered in vain. Since these notable exploits, they have never stepped out of their works or beyond their lines. How a conduct of this kind is to effect the conquest of America, the wisdom of a North, a Germain, or a Sandwich best can decide. It is too deep and refined for the comprehension of common understandings and the general run of politics." [1] In the South, where the enemy continued to win new ground and strengthen that which they had already won, things wore a different aspect. By the beginning of December the army was once more in winter quarters.

[1] Sparks, *Writings of Washington*, vol. vi. p. 367.

CHAPTER VI.

Quartermaster-general's Department. — The Currency. — Congressional Delays. — Errors and their Consequences. — British Gold and Continental Bills and Certificates. — Privateering. — Trammels on Industry. — Depreciation. — Its Consequences. — State Laws.

INACTIVE and uneventful as this year seems in the general narrative, it was for Greene a year of much hard, annoying, and thankless labor. The Quartermaster's department, bringing him into relations more or less intimate with all classes of men, and always in connection with those questions of personal interest which call out man's worst qualities, was a source of constant disquietude. In spite of all his precautions, some of his agents were untrustworthy, and the blame fell upon him. Some were imprudent, and the people's jealousy is as often excited by imprudence as by guilt. Purchases and contracts were made with scrupulous care ; but the supplies did not always correspond to the samples, nor the delivery to the promise. With money of fixed and recognized value, purchases might have been made to advantage, and transportation obtained at reasonable rates. But such money was not to be had. Of the money that Greene had to buy with, Washington wrote in November, " But I am under no apprehension of a capital injury from any other source than the depreciation of our Continental money. This indeed is truly alarming, and of so serious a nature that every other effort is vain unless something can be done to restore its credit." [1]   Yet while even of this depreciated money it was impossible to obtain a supply adequate to the demands of the department, the people, judging by the name and not by the value, and forgetting that forty-five dollars in paper would not buy what could easily be had for one in silver, accused the Quartermaster and his agents of profuse and wanton expenditure.

But the greatest obstacle to the successful conduct of the department was in the delays and hesitations of Congress. At a time and under circumstances which called for the utmost promptness of decision in order to make promptness of action possible, day after day and week after week were wasted in profitless discussion. Washington's letters as well as Greene's are filled with the evidence of this fundamental error of Congressional policy.

Heavy drafts had been made upon the natural resources of the country, and the faith of the people put to a severe trial. Foresight, rarest and most essential of the elements of statesmanship, had been grievously wanting from the beginning of the contest. It had seemed a noble sacrifice to break off intercourse with the mother country and renounce the luxuries of English manufactures. But this voluntary self-denial of

---

[1] Sparks, *Writings of Washington*, vol. vi. p. 394.

the war of resolutions, brought with it the in-
voluntary self-denials of the war of the sword.
A few years of extensive and general importation
would have secured supplies enough to have carried us well armed and well clad through the first
half of the contest. We have seen what straits
the army of 1775 was reduced to for powder. We
have seen Knox toiling in the middle of December to bring the cannon of Ticonderoga to the
lines before Boston. We have seen with what
exultation the capture of a few transports laden
with military stores was hailed by the army and
country.

As the war continued, occasional supplies came
from France, and each new arrival was greeted
with a joy which bears painful witness to the
necessities it relieved. Yet industry, skill, and
material were not wanting. There was iron, there
were manufactories of arms and powder. The
hand-loom was still the chief instrument in the
manufactory of cloths, and in American houses as
in English homes, the hand-loom and spinning-
wheel were familiar objects. The ground gave its
returns abundantly; all the grain needful for
daily food, and the grasses required for the nour-
ishment of animals. Steam was not yet known
as a motive power, but hundreds of wheels, re-
volving by the impulse of wind or water, prepared meal and flour in sufficiency for all the demands of life. A few years of thoughtful preparation would have spared long years of privation
and suffering.

But even after this first great error had been committed, the remedy was still within our reach. It is not difficult to supply a regular army, for in the consumption of their food, as in the employment of their time, they are governed by fixed laws. But volunteers and militia reject these laws, and before they can be brought under them, consume the resources of a whole campaign. And thus this second great mistake, the neglect to secure from the beginning an army for the war, served to increase each campaign the consumption of food and clothing, arms and ammunition.[1]

Nor was this the only evil. The frequent calls upon the militia took the husbandman from his field when his labor was most needed. The ground that had just been prepared for the seed, the grain that had begun to grow, the harvest that was white for the reaper, were all subject to the chances of a sudden alarm. "Why," the farmer soon began to say, "plant more than I need for my own table?" And sowing a single field, where he had been used to sow six, he forgot that the failure of this field would bring starvation to his own door.[2]

There was another evil chance, too, which in some parts of the country told constantly against us. Wherever the army went, heavy calls were made for forage and food. In most cases, also, where one army went another army followed,

[1] Among many others that might be cited is a letter of Greene to Gouverneur Morris, Sept. 14, 1780. — Greene MSS.

[2] Ramsay, vol. ii. p. 187. Reed to Washington. — *Correspondence of the Revolution*, vol. iii. p. 18, and Reed's *Reed*, vol. ii. p. 224.

each trampling down fields and consuming grain and forage, and leaving fatal marks of its passage. The Americans undertook to pay, but had nothing but Continental bills and loan certificates to pay with. When the English paid, they paid in gold, and wherever they staid long, their gold worked like poison. The English market in New York was well supplied when the American army in the Jerseys was starving.[1]

The relief which commerce might have afforded was, like the farmer's harvest, subject to the chances of war. The chief trade was with the West Indies, but that, as well as the trade with Europe, was attended with constant danger from privateers on the high seas, and cruisers, stimulated by the thirst of gain, on the coast. In both our wars with England, a very important part was played by our privateers. In the first war, the regular navy was too small to afford any adequate protection either to commerce on the high seas or in the seaboard towns. But the daring privateer brought supplies which regular trade was unable to obtain, and inflicted blows upon British navigation which the regular navy was unable to strike. The progress of civilization which is gradually preparing the way for correct views concerning war itself, by the diffusion of sounder views concerning many of its instru-

---

[1] Ramsay, *ut sup.* Washington calls it " that injurious and abominable traffic which is carried on with the city of New York." Sparks, *Writings of Washington*, vol. vi. p. 453. And for one of the forms of injury done by the army, *vide* Greene's orders of the day for September 21, 1780. Whiting's *Revolutionary Orders*, p. 107.

ments and accessories, has made privateering
the subject of international stipulations which degrade it almost to the level of piracy. Men are
already ashamed to trace the fortune of their families to the successful plundering of an enemy's
commerce by letters of marque, as they will some
day be ashamed to trace it to successful plundering by a regular navy. But it would be both
unphilosophical and wicked to judge the belief
of our fathers by the higher standard which their
progress has enabled us to make. Civilized warfare — how strangely the two words already begin to look in their unnatural conjunction — has
been stripped of many of the horrors of the warfare of the darker ages of modern Europe, as
well as of the still greater horrors of the brightest ages of ancient Europe. Each generation has
contributed something to the change, but none,
and least of all our own, enough to justify it in
condemning in the individual what belongs to his
times.

But the good done by successful privateers
during the War of Independence was not an un-
mixed good. If they brought needed wares to our
market, they took much needed men from our
armies. It was a frequent complaint, fully confirmed by the facts, that the sudden fortunes acquired by privateersmen were a serious obstacle
in filling up the rolls of the army. "Why should
not I think of my fortune as well as my neighbor who rides in his coach while I am compelled
to work with my hands," was the natural reason-

ing of men who saw themselves outstripped in the race of life ; and like all pursuits into which the element of chance enters in undue proportions, privateering corrupted the moral sense of the community, and seriously interfered with that systematic industry which is the only true source of national prosperity.

While the productive industry of the country and the industry of exchange were thus trammelled by the presence of an hostile army and the demands of a protecting army, the chief instrument of commercial exchange was exposed to constant danger from the fluctuations of public credit. The war itself was from the beginning a war of faith. Men believed that they were right, and cheerfully staked their lives and fortunes upon this belief. Congress, their agent and representative, had pledged its faith for twenty millions of dollars before the Declaration of Independence had been signed. Part of the people accepted the responsibility, and not only stood by the Congress, but gave their goods and their labor for Continental bills. But the country was not united in its resistance to England. It was as much a point of honor with the Tories to refuse the Continental money as it was with the Whigs to accept it.

As the war continued, doubts arose in the minds of the best of Whigs. Depreciation began when the first nine millions had been put into circulation, slight indeed at first, and almost imperceptible, but soon fatally apparent. It was one and one quarter in January, 1777. It had reached four for one in December. Through 1778 it ranged from four to five and six, finally settling into six for November and December. But in the January following it sank to nine, and in December was at forty-five. It was not till the depreciation had become apparent to all that recourse was had to taxes, loans having already been tried and found insufficient. But the whole amount received from taxes up to September, 1779, was but little over three millions,[1] and already the tax was felt to be a grievous burden. Each State, too, had its debts and its daily struggles with them.

Meanwhile prices everywhere kept pace with the depreciation of the currency and goods rose in the market as money fell, till it took four hundred dollars to buy a hat, and sixteen hundred to buy a suit of clothes.[2] Conventions met and discussed the propriety of fixing a scale of prices. The trial was made, and failed miserably; the natural laws of commerce compelling obedience in spite of the unnatural restraint laid upon them. Congress made laws, but had no power to enforce them. States made laws for the protection of their own citizens, without regard to the necessities of the army, thoughtlessly setting up individual interest in opposition to the general interest, and exposing the military service to dangerous collision with the civil service. The service of

[1] *Journals of Congress*, iii. 352.

[2] Letter from a member of Congress, cited in Wells' *Life of Samuel Adams*, vol. iii. p. 51.

the Quartermaster's department often demanded labor and materials when there was no money to pay them with. State laws required that payment should be made before the service was rendered. More than once it was found impossible to feed the cattle and horses attached to the army, and essential for the transportation of its baggage and stores, without invoking the aid of military law. It was chiefly upon the Quartermaster's department that the burden of thankless labor and unfounded suspicion fell. " We have a thankless task," Greene wrote in June, " with difficulties and prejudices innumerable to contend with." And as month after month passed away, and the difficulties increased, he ceased to hope for relief from the action of Congress. " Congress, I am told," he writes in February 1780, " have appointed another committee on finance. But in all matters of this sort the members themselves have such scattered and heterogeneous ideas that none of them can form a tolerable judgment beforehand what will be the result of any motion or measure set on foot. . . . When necessity presses so hard that something or other must be done, they will then and not before, take some course by way of temporary expedient, trusting, as usual, to accident for the rest." [1]

[1] For a more extended view of the finances I would refer to my _Histor-_ _ical View of the American Revolution_, Lect. V.

CHAPTER VII.

ANOTHER dreary winter began; the severest
and coldest of all the eight winters of the
war. For the old men of my boyhood it was the
standard of extreme cold, and when the wind was
keenest and the snow deepest, they could find no
stronger language to describe them in than to say
that they brought back to their memories the
fearful winter of 1780. On the 3d of January
there was a great snow-storm, which rent the can-
vas walls of tents and marquees like twigs, and
buried men and officers under them like sheep.
" My comrades and myself," says Thacher, " were
roused from sleep by the calls of some officers
for assistance; their marquee had been blown
down, and they were almost smothered in the
storm before they could reach our marquee, only
a few yards." [1] . . . No man could endure

[1] Thacher's *Military Journal*, p.
181. It might have comforted the

American officers somewhat, if they
had known that the same wind was

the violence of the storm many minutes without danger of his life.[1]   When it ceased, it left all the roads blocked up and the fields covered. "We ride over the fences," writes Greene. But for a timely supply of straw, men and officers would have frozen to death; but by spreading their blankets on the straw, kindling large fires at their feet, and piling all the clothes they could collect over them, they succeeded in preserving warmth enough for life ; comfort was beyond their reach. The poor soldiers with their single blanket, scanty clothing, and often naked feet, fared harder still.[2]

Famine, too, stared them in the face. Snow, four, six, and one account says twelve [3] feet deep, covered the ground all around them, and cut them off from their supplies.

"The army is upon the point of disbanding for want of provisions," writes Greene to Colonel Hathaway, at Morristown, " the poor soldiers having been several days without, and there not being more than a sufficiency to serve more than one regiment in this magazine. Provision is scarce at best, but the late terrible storm and the depth of the snow and the drifts in the road, prevents the little stock coming forward which is in readiness at the distant magazines. This is, therefore, to request you to call upon the militia officers and people of your battalion to turn out their teams and break the roads between this and Hackettstown, there being a small quantity of provision there that cannot come on until this is done. The roads must be kept

blowing down some of the enemy's tents that very night. *Vide* Matthews' *Narrative* in *Historical Magazine*, vol. i. p. 103.

[1] Thacher's *Military Journal*, p. 180.

[2] Thacher, *ut sup.*

[3] Kapp's *DeKalb*, p. 169.

open by the inhabitants, or the army cannot be subsisted; and unless good people immediately lend their assistance to forward supplies, the army must disband. The dreadful consequences of such an event I will not torture your feelings with a description of; but remember the surrounding inhabitants will experience the first melancholy effects of such a raging evil. We would give you assistance was it in our power, but the army is stripped as naked of teams as possible, to lessen the consumption of forage, which has reduced us to such shifts as render us unable, with the teams we have, to do the duty we are daily called upon for in camp. You will call to your aid the overseers of highways and every other order of men who can give despatch and success to the business.

"Give no copy of this, for fear it should get to the enemy."

"What a winter is this!" writes Colonel Wadsworth from Hartford. "The sound all frozen up; nothing can come into New London; the ice reaches out to sea at Rhode Island."[1] And Washington writing to Lafayette says: "The severity of the frost exceeds anything of the kind that had ever been experienced in this country before."[2] Well might he say, "We have had the virtue of the army put to the severest test."

Meanwhile the men were working upon their huts as hard as the weather would permit; but with such obstacles to contend against, it was not till the middle of February that the work was completed. Then, as they found themselves once more with solid log walls between them and the biting wind, and a cheerful fire-place to gather

[1] Greene's Papers. MSS.　　[2] Sparks, *Writings of Washington,* vol. vi. p. 487.

round, they could listen to the storm outside, and feel that one of their ills had ' been overcome. But all the others remained in full force.

Badly fed, badly clothed,[1] with present starvation before them, and nothing to guard them or theirs against future want, what could hold the troops together? The errors of former years had borne their fruit. Depreciation had almost reached its lowest point, and the money was little better than waste paper. And as if the natural depreciation were not sufficient of itself to destroy the public credit, the enmity of the Tories gave it a new impulse by stealthily introducing a large amount of forged money.[2] The want of means to fill up the army in the name of Congress, compelled Congress to call upon the States to fill their quotas in their own names. Had all the States been equally able and equally well disposed, these State establishments would still have been a fatal blow to the yet incomplete confederation. But some States could provide well for their troops, others could not; and when the men thus unequally provided for were called to fight

[1] A year before it had been reported to Colonel Lamb, "The distressed situation of the men for want of clothes is deplorable. There are sixteen of them almost naked and barefooted. I had only one pair of shoes to forty-five men at the last drawing. There are three or four coats in the company, and about as many shoes and stockings." This was October, 1779, and things were unchanged in January, 1780. — Life of Lamb, p. 229. The manner in which the soldiers bore these trials is spoken of feelingly by Knox in a letter of January 6, 1780, to Lamb, ut sup. 234.

[2] The quantity also would seem to have been increased by singular irregularities in the emission of it. In the accounts for 1779 it was found that over five millions and a half more than Congress had authorized was in circulation. Gordon, vol. iii. p. 346. Sparks, Writings of Washington, vol. vi. p. 413.

side by side in the same cause, the ill-provided could not but envy their more fortunate comrades, and feel that something was wanting in the government which permitted equal services to be so unequally rewarded.[1]

Great discontent arose also from the "original dissimilarity of the terms of enlistment," those who had enlisted for the war, finding themselves deprived of the bounties which were offered to those who had engaged for limited terms, in order to induce them to engage anew.[2] At Washington's suggestion, a gratuity of $100 was given to all who had "enlisted for the war previous to the 23d of January, 1779. Still, many denied or evaded their engagements in the hope of securing the State bounties, and some went so far as to appeal to the civil authorities for protection. Judge Symmes, of the Supreme Court of New Jersey, took their case in hand, and addressed the Assembly upon the subject in a letter of which he sent a copy to Washington. Washington, with his usual temperate firmness, explained the matter to Governor Livingston, and there it ended.[2] "Certain I am," wrote Washington to Joseph Jones, on the 31st of May, "unless Congress speak in a more decisive tone, unless they are vested with powers by the several States competent to the great purposes of war, or assume them as matter of right, and they and the States respectively act with more energy than they hith-

---

[1] Gordon, vol. iii. p. 362.

[2] Sparks, Writings of Washington, vol. vi. pp. 470, 471.

erto have done, that our cause is lost." [1]   I shall return to this subject presently, for it is intimately connected with the history of the Quartermaster-general's department.

Great as the sufferings were which the cold weather brought with it, it offered one chance of which Washington longed to take advantage. The rivers and bay were frozen, and the ice soon became so thick that the heaviest cannon could be carried over it without danger.[2] " A detachment of cavalry marched from New York to Staten Island on the ice." New York city was no longer an island. " All is continent," wrote Knyphausen.[3] The ships which had been the protection of its double water front, were frozen in at their moorings, and in the apprehension of a sudden attack upon the city, parts of their crews were drawn from them to serve on shore.[4] The garrison, reduced by large detachments to the South, was too feeble to hold its ground long against a vigorous attack. The refugees and Tory militia were called in to the aid of the regular troops. " Nature," writes Greene, " has given us a fine bridge of communication with the enemy, but we are too weak to take advantage of it." Washington was compelled to content himself with an unsuccessful attempt to surprise the posts on Staten Island. The enemy retaliated

[1] Sparks, *Writings of Washington,* vol. vii. p. 67.

[2] Six feet thick, says DeKalb, *loc. cit.,* and Major-general Pattison to Lord George Germaine in Almon's *Remembrancer,* vol. ix. p. 368.

[3] Almon's *Remembrancer,* vol ix. p. 367.

[4] Duer's *Stirling,* p. 206. Sparks, *Writings of Washington,* vol. vi. p. 447. A very interesting account of the Staten Island expedition is given

by a bold and successful raid on the neutral ground.[1]

Winter wore slowly away amid anxious cares and fallacious hopes. Mrs. Washington, Mrs. Greene, and Mrs. Knox were again with their husbands. An assembly was formed by subscription to give something of the air of organization to the amusements of the long evenings. Washington's name heads the subscription.

For Greene the winter gave a tenderer association to Morristown, for his second son, Nathanael Ray, my father, was born there on the 29th of January, and he enjoyed for the first time, though thrice a father, the rapture of holding his infant babe in his arms. The other three were born in Rhode Island.

In April Lafayette arrived from France with the promise of an army as well as a fleet. The tidings were not equally welcome to all. "As an American citizen," wrote Major Shaw, an aid of General Knox, when they were actually arrived, " I rejoice in the prospect of so speedy, and I hope, effectual an aid; but *as a soldier*, I am dissatisfied. . . . 'Tis really abominable that we should send to France for soldiers, when there are so many sons of America idle."[1] Meanwhile the question was, " What shall we do to make the most of this timely succor?" The

by a Rhode Island soldier, William Allen, in a letter to Theodore Foster, *Revolutionary Correspondence*, p. 257, Publications of Rhode Island Historical Society ; and of the raid, in Matthew's narrative, *Historical Magazine*, vol. i. p. 104.

[1] General Pattison to Lord George Germaine. Almon's *Remembrancer*, vol. ix. p. 369.

[2] *Life of Lamb*, p. 243.

hope which had flashed upon the mind of Washington on the first arrival of D'Estaing two years before, revived as he thought over all the chances of the hazardous game. "If we can take New York, we shall put an end to the war."

But now a new danger arose. Desperate from present suffering, two Connecticut regiments clubbed their arms, and declared that they would either return home or feed themselves at the point of the bayonet.[1] The exertions of their officers, supported by a brigade of Pennsylvanians under Colonel Stewart, brought them back to duty. But the rest of the army had looked on with sympathy, and how deep that sympathy was, the revolt of the Pennsylvanians themselves, on the first of the following January, clearly showed. The welcome tidings were quickly carried to Knyphausen, the British commander of New York. It was an event which the Tories had long foretold, and the English, both at home and with the army, looked forward to with confidence. Nothing less than a general dissolution of the army was expected.[2] A body of five thousand men was promptly thrown over from Staten Island, and on the morning of the 6th of June, advanced full of hope from Elizabethtown point on the road to Springfield. But their hopes were quickly dashed.[3] The barbarities of the November and December of 1776 had sunk deep into the hearts of the people. The "mud rounds"[4] were still fresh in the

---

[1] Marshall, vol. i. p. 359.

[2] Gordon, vol. iii. p. 370.

[3] Marshall, vol. i. p. 360.

[4] The "mud rounds" was the name given by the army to the muddy marches of the retreat

memories and the traditions of the soldiers. The country rose on all sides. Small bodies of Continentals patrolled and watched the roads. It was but five miles to Connecticut Farms, but before they had marched those five miles the British soldiers were exasperated by the fire that met them from behind the fences on the wayside and at every turn of the road. The officers saw that they had miscalculated their chances in counting upon the discontent of the Americans. In brutal revenge they set fire to the helpless village; and for years after, men told with a shudder, how one in the garb of a British soldier had shot the wife of a beloved clergyman, as she sat in the midst of her children, with an infant in her arms. Even to this day the name of Hannah Caldwell awakens bitter recollections.[1]

Disappointed though not disheartened, Knyphausen pressed forward towards Springfield. Maxwell, a gallant officer, had thrown himself in front with the Jersey Brigade and a small party of militia. With these he made a resolute stand at a "defile near the Farm Meeting House," and when compelled to retreat, still continued to dispute the ground step by step, "harassing the enemy right and left," and regaining at Springfield, by a desperate charge, the ground which he had lost in another. Meanwhile the militia came flocking in from all quarters.[2] The smoke that

---

through the Jerseys. *Vide* a very able essay on "Washington at Morristown," in *Harper's Monthly* for February, 1851.

[1] Marshall, vol. i. p. 360.

[2] I follow Maxwell's letter of June 14 to Gov. Livingston, which I find printed in a New York paper as a

floated over Connecticut Farms was a sure guide
to the enemy's track. Washington, too, was at
hand, and taking post at the Short Hills, just behind the village, was preparing to give battle.
But night came on before the armies met, a dark
and stormy night. The Americans lay on their
arms, expecting to fight the next day. The British, also, divided their ground and sent out their
pickets. Weary men and weary officers laid
themselves down on the bare earth to sleep. But
at ten came the order to retreat. Knyphausen
was dissatisfied with his situation, and anxious to
get back within reach of his shipping. It was
very dark, the clouds of a rising thunder-storm
deepening the obscurity of the hour. The orders
were passed from regiment to regiment, and each
moved off so silently that one company of the
Grenadier guards did not hear when the other
went. In the midst of their retreat, the storm
burst upon them. The rain fell in torrents. The
thunder deafened them. The lightning flashed in
the faces of the bewildered men, blinding them
with its brightness. " Once or twice" the whole
army was compelled to halt. The horses in their
terror reared and plunged, and Knyphausen's
threw his rider. As they passed Connecticut
Farms, some of the houses which they had set fire
to in their advance were still burning, and by the

specimen of a collection of papers in
the hands of C. B. Norton of that
city. Sparks, *Writings of Washington*, vol. vii. pp. 75, 76 and note, and
Marshall, vol. i. p. 360, and Gordon,
vol. iii. p. 368, mention circumstances
omitted by Maxwell. The Tory view
of this incursion and the murder of
Mrs. Caldwell may be gathered from
the extracts from Rivington in
Moore's *Diary of the Revolution*, vol.
ii. p. 289.

mingled glare of the flames and the lightning they saw "now and then" the body of some human victim of the merciless work of the morning lying stark and stiff by the roadside. In the intervals of the thunder peals they listened breathlessly for the Americans, expecting every moment that the roar of their muskets would break upon them from the surrounding darkness.[1]

Meanwhile Washington had called his generals together in council. "The enemy outnumbers us by half; what shall we do?"

"When I compare their strength and ours," said Greene, "I am in favor of a retreat. If Knyphausen, as is probable, is making a feigned movement in this direction, and really aiming at the heights of the North River, our retreat will be merely a change of position."

Some one proposed a night attack. Steuben caught eagerly at the suggestion, and "solicited a command." The bold counsel was accepted, and the time fixed for midnight.[2] It was well for Knyphausen that he began his retreat early. A delay of two hours might have been disastrous to the British, who would have fought under great disadvantages with an enemy familiar with the ground. When the retreat of the English was discovered, a detachment was sent out in pursuit; but it mistook the road, and Knyphausen reached

[1] The storm, which is not mentioned by the American writers quoted above, forms the subject of a long paragraph in Matthews' narrative, *Hist. Mag.* vol. i. pp. 104, 105.

Matthews differs from the American writers in saying that Connecticut Farms was burnt on the retreat.

[2] Gordon, vol. iii. p. 370.

Elizabethtown Point unmolested but somewhat "in confusion." Once more the invasion of the Jerseys had ended in disappointment and shame. Washington in general orders bestowed great encomiums upon all the troops, both regulars and militia, adding, " Colonel Dayton merits particular thanks." [1]

In February Major-general Pattison had written to Lord George Germaine, "We already learn that the recent display of loyalty here, with the great acquisition of force it produced, has had effects upon the friends of government without the lines as well as upon the enemy, who have been apprehensive of an attack being intended upon their main force at Morristown. It has probably too, contributed to the great defection which has lately prevailed amongst their troops in the Jerseys." [2] In August Sir Henry Clinton wrote, "The revolution fondly looked for by means of friends to the British Government, I must represent as visionary." [3]

Still Knyphausen lingered at Elizabethtown Point, and Washington, when he remembered that Sir Henry Clinton was on his way northward with troops fresh from the successful siege of Charleston, grew anxious for the passes of the Highlands. What would the victorious general do? To seize West Point was to seize the key of the line of the Hudson. A rapid march and impetuous onset might give him Morristown with

---

[1] Gordon to Greene, Aug. 27 and Sept. 12, 1785, and Greene's reply, without date. Greene Papers.

[2] Almon's *Remembrancer*, vol. ix. p. 369.

[3] Mahon's *England*, vol. vii. Appendix, p. 6.

the strong mountain passes which had protected the American army through two winters. He decided to strike a sudden blow for them, still taking care to keep Washington in suspense.[1]

Washington was at Springfield, watching the movements of his adversary. But on the 21st of June he became so certain of the enemy's intentions that he resolved to move his main body cautiously northward, leaving Greene with Maxwell's and Stark's brigades, Lee's corps, and the militia, "to cover the country and the public stores." "The dispositions for this purpose," say the orders to Greene, "are left entirely at your discretion, with this recommendation only, that you use every precaution in your power to avoid a surprise and provide for the security of your corps."[2] Particular attention was called also to the gathering and transmission of intelligence. It was pleasant for Greene to escape from the annoyances of the Quartermaster's department, now very near their culmination, and find himself at the head of a little army.

The next day at five in the afternoon he wrote, "Mr. P——l has this moment returned from Elizabethtown. He says that General Clinton with the whole British army will be in motion this evening." Their intention, according to this account, was to cut Washington off from the entrance of the Clove.

"It is probable they are about to move," adds Greene,

---

[1] Washington's letters from 1st to 26th June. Sparks, *Writings of Washington*, vol. vii. pp. 69 *et seq.*

[2] Sparks, *Writings of Washington*, vol. vii. p. 83

" but I think their route and object very uncertain. I shall watch their motions and give them all the trouble in my power, and will duly advertise you of everything necessary for your information.

" I have ordered the troops to be in readiness to move at a moment's warning, and sent for the general officers to fix upon our plan. The enemy sent a small party out this afternoon about two miles. They were drove' back with the loss of two or three killed and two prisoners."

And again at ten at night, —

" I have been impatiently waiting in consequence of the intelligence received this afternoon from Mr. P——l to hear of the enemy's beginning their march. It is now ten o'clock, and no accounts received from the lines of the least appearance of a movement. The positive manner in which the intelligence came and the other circumstances mentioned by Major Lee, induced me to believe that the enemy were about to make some movement, and they may still get in motion before morning; but I begin to have some apprehension whether this movement to the northward may not be given out with a view of forcing your Excellency as far towards the North River as possible in order to leave an open passage to Trenton.

" I do not know what kind of credit is to be given to this Mr. P. but he says he is employed by your Excellency, and that he is willing to forfeit his life if everything he tells is not strictly true as far as he can determine from the appearance of things. May not the enemy be apprized of his being a double spy and endeavor to play him off accordingly in order to mislead our attention? I told him the consequence of deceiving us would be nothing less than a forfeiture of his life. He really appears to be sincere, but I begin to doubt his intelligence. Colonel Dayton is gone down to the lines to get intelligence; but whether he will succeed I know not.

" The two prisoners mentioned in my last have since come in, but both so drunk and sulky that they cannot or will not give the least information. . . . . The troops and militia are all ordered to lay upon their arms. I am in hopes to give a good account of them if they come out."

And thus in watchfulness and preparation he passed the day and night before his first battle — the first, I mean, of independent command.

At six the next morning he wrote : —

" The enemy are out on their march towards this place in full force, having received a considerable reinforcement last night."

And again at eleven, from " Near Bryant's Tavern " : —

" I informed your Excellency this morning that the enemy were on the advance in force. I now acquaint you that they proceeded with vigor until they had gained Connecticut Farms. They then were checked by Colonel Dayton's regiment. They have since advanced in two formidable columns on the Springfield and Vauxhall roads. After very obstinate resistance they are now in possession of Springfield with one column. With the other they are advanced near the bridge leading to Vauxhall where Angell's pickets lay. From present prospects they are directing their force against this post, which I am determined to dispute so far as I am capable. They are pushing a column to our left, perhaps to gain the pass in our rear towards Chatham. If they pursue this object we must abandon our present position. The militia to our aid are few, and that few are so divided as to render little or no support. They advance with seven pieces of artillery in front and appear not disposed to risque much."

A fresh report comes in, and when he resumes his pen, he adds : " The militia are collecting, and I hope to derive support from them."

At five in the afternoon of the same day he writes to Lord Stirling from Connecticut Farms: —

"The enemy advanced this morning and forced their way into Springfield; they were warmly opposed by several corps of the army, and after burning almost every house in the town, they retreated. We are now pressing their rear, but the principal part of their army has reached Elizabethtown.

"I wish you to countermand your orders to the militia. Their service may not be wanted at this time."

How the day passed he tells more at length in a letter of the 24th to Washington, whom, meanwhile, he had already advised of the later movements and supposed designs of the enemy: —

"I have been too busily employed until the present moment to lay before your Excellency the transactions of yesterday.

"The enemy advanced from Elizabethtown about five o'clock in the morning, said to be about five thousand infantry, with a large body of cavalry and fifteen or twenty pieces of artillery. Their march was rapid and compact. They moved in two columns, one on the main road leading to Springfield, the other on the Vauxhall road. Major Lee with the horse and pickets opposed the right column, and Colonel Dayton with his regiment the left, and both gave as much opposition as could have been expected from so small a force. Our troops were so extended, in order to guard the different roads leading to the several passes over the mountains, that I had scarcely time to collect them at Springfield, and make the necessary dispositions, before the enemy appeared before the town; when a cannonade commenced between their advance and our artillery posted for the defense of the bridge.

"The enemy continued manœuvering in our front for

upwards of two hours, which induced me to believe they were attempting to gain our flanks. My force was small, and from the direction of the roads my situation was critical. I disposed of the troops in the best manner I could to guard our flanks, secure a retreat, and oppose the advance of their columns. Colonel Angell, with his regiment and several small detachments and one piece of artillery, was posted to secure the bridge in front of the town. Colonel Shreve's regiment was drawn up at the second bridge to cover the retreat of those posted at the first. Major Lee with his dragoons and the pickets commanded by Captain Walker, was posted at Little's[1] Bridge on the Vauxhall road; and Colonel Ogden was detached to support him. The remainder of General Maxwell's and General Starke's brigades was drawn up on the high grounds at the Mill. The militia were on the flanks. Those under the command of General Dickinson made a spirited attack upon one of the enemy's flanking parties, but his force was too small to push the advantage he had gained.

"While the enemy were making demonstrations to their left, their right column advanced on Major Lee. The bridge was disputed with great obstinacy, and the enemy must have received very considerable injury; but by fording the river and gaining the point of the hill, they obliged the Major with his party to give up the pass. At this instant of time their left column began the attack on Colonel Angell. The action was severe and lasted about forty minutes, when superior numbers overcame obstinate bravery, and forced our troops to retire over the second bridge. Here the enemy were warmly received by Colonel Shreve's regiment; but as they advanced in great force with a large train of artillery, he had orders to join the brigade. ·

[1] The real name is *Littell*, as I am advised by J. S. Littell, Esq. of Germantown, editor of Graydon's *Memoirs*; to whose courtesy I am indebted for the knowledge of some very important letters.

" As the enemy continued to press our left on the Vaux-hall road, which led directly into our rear, and would have given them the most important pass, and finding our front too extensive to be effectually secured by so small a body of troops, I thought it advisable to take post upon the first range of hills in the rear of Bryant's Tavern, where the roads are brought so near to a point that succor might readily be given from one to the other. This enabled me to detach Colonel Webb's regiment commanded by Lieu-tenant-colonel Huntington, and Colonel Jackson's regiment with one piece of artillery, which entirely checked the ad-vance of the enemy on our left and secured that pass.

" Being thus advantageously posted I was in hopes the enemy would attempt to gain the heights, but dis-covered no disposition in them for attacking us ; and seeing them begin to fire the houses in town, detachments were ordered out on every quarter to prevent them burning any buildings not immediately under the command of their cannon and musketry. In a few minutes they had set fire to almost every house in town and begun their retreat. Captain Davis with a detachment of one hundred and twenty men in several small parties and a large body of militia, fell upon their rear and flanks, and kept up a con-tinual fire upon them till they entered Elizabethtown, which place they reached about sunset. Starke's brigade was immediately put in motion on the first appearance of a retreat, which was so precipitate that they were not able to overtake them.

" The enemy continued at Elizabethtown Point until twelve o'clock at night, and then began to send their troops across to Staten Island. By six this morning they had totally evacuated the point and removed their bridge. Major Lee fell in with their rear guard ; but they were so covered by their works that little or no injury could be done them. He made some refugee prisoners, and took some stores which they abandoned to expedite their re-treat.

. " I have the pleasure to inform your Excellency that the troops who were engaged behaved with great coolness and intrepidity, and the whole of them discovered an impatience to be brought into action. The good order and discipline which they exhibited in all their movements do them the highest honor. The artillery under the command of Lieutenant-colonel Forest was well served. I have only to regret the loss of Captain-lieutenant Thompson, who fell at the side of his piece by a cannon-ball. It is impossible to fix with certainty the enemy's loss ; but as there was much close firing, and our troops were advantageously posted, they must have suffered very considerably.

" I herewith inclose to your Excellency a return of our killed, wounded, and missing, which I am happy to find is much less than I had reason to expect from the heavy fire they sustained.[1] I am at a loss to determine what was the object of the enemy's expedition. If it was to injure the troops under my command, or to penetrate further into the country, they were frustrated. If it was the destruction of this place, it was a disgraceful one.[2] I lament that our force was too small to save the town from ruin. I wish every American could have been a spectator ; he would have felt for the sufferers and joined to revenge the injury.

[1] Thirteen killed, and forty-nine wounded, and nine missing.

[2] From a letter of Clinton of which Mr. Sparks has published an extract (*Writings of Washington*, vol. vii. p. 86), it appears that he had no positive design against West Point, but was looking out for an opportunity to strike a blow somewhere. The object assigned in Matthews' narrative is the most reasonable one : " Here we endeavored, as we had done before, to bring on a general action, but to no purpose." He adds that " The burning of Springfield was against the positive orders of the commanding officers ; but they found it impossible to keep the soldiers from setting fire to the houses. Indeed it is not to be wondered at that the soldiers should have wished to fire the houses from which the rebels had fired on them." *Hist. Mag.*, vol. i. p. 104. The same reason was assigned for burning Charlestown : but why burn Connecticut Farms ? Clinton is silent about both.

"I cannot close this letter without acknowledging the particular service of Lieutenant-colonel Barber, who acted as deputy adjutant-general, and distinguished himself by his activity in assisting to make the necessary dispositions."

Greene and his officers were thanked in general orders, and Angell's brilliant stand at the first bridge mentioned with special commendation.[1]

On receiving Greene's first letter of the 23d, Washington had immediately detached a brigade to act on the enemy's flank, and retraced his steps with his main body to the support of the little army at Springfield.[2] The next few days were passed in uncertainty, although the conviction was gradually gaining ground that West Point would not be attacked, or if attacked, would be able to defend itself.[3]

Then came tidings that on the evening of the 10th of July, the first division of the French fleet, seven ships of the line and two frigates, bringing six thousand troops under Count Rochambeau, had arrived at Newport. Had Washington's counsels been followed, the Americans would have been prepared to act with them.[4] But they had not been followed, and before any decisive step could be taken, the English were reinforced, and the French fleet blockaded in Newport harbor. Clinton resolved to take advantage of his superiority in numbers, and attack the French by

[1] An interesting account of this battle is given by Colonel Angell in the *Providence Gazette*.

[2] Marshall, vol. i. p. 363.

[3] Sparks, *Writings of Washington*, vol. vii. p. 94.

[4] Sparks, *Writings of Washington*, vol. vii. p. 80.

sea and land. Eight thousand men were embarked, and for a few days Huntington Bay, the gathering place on Long Island, swarmed with ships and transports, and resounded with the notes of preparation. To capture or destroy the fleet and army of this division would be a deadly blow to the alliance.

But Washington too was on the alert, and calling upon the militia for aid to his thin ranks, he crossed the Hudson and directed his march towards King's Bridge. This bold manœuvre, which threatened the weakened garrison of New York, recalled the British General in all haste, though the British fleet still continued to lie in wait off Block Island. Rochambeau was left at leisure to attend to his sick, and strengthen his position by new fortifications.[1]

Greene, upon whom the laborious duty of providing the means of transportation and securing the supplies of the army which had been thus suddenly put in motion devolved, felt when he reflected upon the aim and the success of the movement, that this was one of the occasions in which a General might add to his moral strength by explaining his conduct and motives to his army. And therefore on the 3d of August he wrote to Washington from Verplanck's Point: —

" The more I have thought upon the subject of explaining the reasons and causes of our movements to the army and through them to the country, the more I am confirmed in my opinion of the propriety and necessity for it.

[1] Sparks, *Writings of Washington*, vol. vii. pp. 128, 129, and Sir Henry Clinton in Appendix to Mahon's *England*, vol. vii. p. 4.

"Your Excellency will consider this is a great movement, and has been very rapid. The march of the army has been very fatiguing. The teams of the country have been impressed, and every kind of property laid hold on to pave the way to a certain plan of operations. If it is all relinquished without any explanation, the natural reflections that will arise upon the occasion will be, Why has the army been harassed without an object, why has the people been dragged from their homes with their teams, and the public subjected to a most enormous expense, and why has the property of the people been laid hold on by the hand of power, when there appears nothing to warrant these extravagant measures?

"Without some explanation we shall not do justice to ourselves, nor will your Excellency to your own military character. The enterprise was great, the object noble, and the end for which it was undertaken appears to have been partly answered if not fully so. To explain the reasons of the movement will give the army a high opinion of the confidence you have in their spirit and enterprise, and perfectly reconcile them to all the past fatigues and to those which may follow in regaining our former position. It will strike the enemy with the boldness of the design. It will be pleasing to the French army as a measure calculated to give the most speedy relief. It will reconcile the county to all the inconveniences they have felt, and prepare their minds for future exertions of a similar nature in full confidence that the object is worthy the preparations.

"Though I am no advocate in common for giving reasons either to the army or the community for our movements, yet there are cases when substantial advantages can be drawn from it, and even the people's curiosity can be gratified and the public be benefited at the same time. I think it will be justifiable to adopt the measure.

"It is unnecessary to gasconade highly upon the occasion, but I think we may with great reason suppose the enemy's return to be in consequence of our movements, and that gives us the reputation of having saved our allies from an injury, and subjected the enemy to the mortification of having been obliged to relinquish their object.

"If the explanation takes place there will be no inconvenience in our recrossing the river; without it I think there will; for both the army and the country will think all is given up, and there will be no preparations proportionable to the business in contemplation. Your Excellency may remember that Sir Henry Clinton explained his movement up to Stony Point last summer after General Wayne took that place. He had not half the reasons for that explanation as you have for this.

"I wish your Excellency to determine upon future operations as soon as possible, as boards and teams are impressing, collecting, and coming to camp as fast as possible. If the teams are not likely to be wanted immediately, they had better be discharged without loss of time, as it will save a great expense and free the people from no small inconvenience.

"Colonel Hay has sent down a considerable number of boards to King's Ferry, and more are coming. Mr. Clarke of Dansbury writes me he has got an account of 100,000 feet, which may be had, but not without great inconvenience to the inhabitants, as they were got to rebuild the houses burnt by the enemy last campaign. There is a great number of impressed teams at King's Ferry on the other side, which I wish to dismiss if there is not an immediate necessity for them."

Deep was Washington's regret when he saw the chances of an attack upon New York and a decisive campaign slipping from his grasp. It was not his fault that no adequate preparations had been made in time to turn the cooperation of our allies to the best account. His busy pen had respectfully reminded some and considerately admonished others of their duty, but no satisfactory response had come from Congress or the States. Greene felt that in the actual situation of things there was something Quixotic in the idea of an enterprise that demanded men, money, and supplies; and he had the more reason for feeling so, as it was on his department that the chief burden of preparation fell. To know what they could, and what they could not do, Washington and Rochambeau decided to meet at Hartford, and discuss their plans and resources in a personal interview.

Meanwhile on the 24th of August Greene had been sent out upon a foraging expedition to Bergen and the English neighborhood. " Such are the necessities of the army, and such the situation of the inhabitants," says Washington in his instructions, " being all within the power of the enemy, that you will make the forage as extensive as possible in the articles of hay and grain, as well as in cattle, hogs, and sheep fit for slaughter, and horses fit for the use of the army. All the articles are to be receipted for by the respective departments to which they belong. . . . Should the enemy attempt to interrupt you in the business, you must govern yourself according to circumstances. I leave you at liberty either to attack or retire, as you may think prudent, from the force in which they may appear." [1]

[1] Sparks, *Writings of Washington*, vol. vii. p. 173.

On receiving his orders, Greene immediately wrote to Colonel Biddle :—

"A detachment of the army under my command being directed down to Bergen to cover a foraging party, you will give the necessary instructions for having all the wagons loaded under the direction of the Quartermaster-general, who follows the army with a large number for the purpose ; you will appoint such and so many forage officers as you may think necessary to give the greatest despatch to the business, and as it is a critical movement, I wish you to go with the party yourself and to have the business conducted with the greatest regularity and despatch possible, taking care to have the most valuable forage taken first."

The expedition was successful, and some necessary supplies were secured. But it brought into painful light the demoralization which had crept into the army under the influence of hunger, nakedness, and a worthless currency.

On the 26th Greene wrote to Washington from the Three Pigeons : —

"There has been committed some of the most horrid acts of plunder by some of the Pennsylvania line that has disgraced the American arms during the war. The instances of plunder and violence is equal to anything committed by the Hessians.

"Two soldiers were taken that were out upon the business, both of which fired upon the inhabitants to prevent their giving intelligence. I think it would have a good effect to hang one of these fellows in the face of the troops, without the form of a trial. It is absolutely necessary to give a check to the licentious spirit which increases amazingly. The impudence of the soldiers is intolerable. A party plundered a house yesterday in

sight of a number of officers, and even threatened the
officers if they offered to interfere. It is the opinion of
most of the officers that it is absolutely necessary for the
good of the service that one of these fellows should be
made an example of, and if your Excellency will give
permission, I will have one hung up this afternoon when
the army are ready to march by.

"There is also a deserter taken three-quarters of the
way over to New York, belonging to the 7th Pennsylvania regiment, which the officers not only of the regiment,
but several others, wish may be executed in the same way
that I propose to execute the other in. Several deserters
are gone off yesterday and last evening.

"The light infantry have fallen back to this place, and
I propose to march back to camp at five o'clock this
evening, unless collecting the stock upon Seacanaus (sic)
should detain us longer.

"The enemy have made no movement except in their
shipping ; a few more transports have fallen down to the
watering place, and a few have hauled off in the road.

"I wish your Excellency's answer respecting the two
culprits, as we shall march at five this evening."

And in a postscript he adds : —

"More complaints have this moment come in of a more
shocking nature than those related."

"I am this moment favored with your letter of this
day," writes Washington in answer. "I need scarcely
inform you of the extreme pain and anxiety which the
licentiousness of some of the soldiery has given me.
Something must and shall be done, if possible, to put an
effectual check to it. I entirely approve of the prompt
punishment which you propose to have inflicted on the
culprits in question. You will, therefore, please to order
one of the soldiers detected in plundering, and also the
deserters you mention, to be immediately executed."

Soon after Greene's return to camp, Washington, who was preparing for his interview with the French General, called a council of war, in order to collect the opinions of his officers upon a plan of operations. After laying the subject before them, he asked them to give him their sentiments in writing. It was the last time that Benedict Arnold — who, however, was not present at the council — was called upon to give his views upon the situation and prospects of the American army.

" I have taken into consideration," Greene wrote on the 11th of September, " as far as my health would permit, the several matters submitted to the general officers in the council held the 6th instant, and am of opinion that as the second division of the French fleet has not arrived, and there being little probability that it will be here in season to attempt anything to the northward, it would be a folly to persevere further upon our original plan of operations laid down for the campaign.

" The very great deficiency in our own preparation of men, provisions, and stores of every kind, for an attempt upon New York, furnish a stronger argument for changing our plan of operations. It is unnecessary to search for the cause of these deficiencies; whether they originate from a want of ability or inclination, the effect is the same. It is sufficient that we know that more powerful arguments cannot be offered to the people than has been, to draw forth either men or supplies of any kind. Nevertheless, should a large reinforcement arrive immediately from the West Indies, it would be our duty to attempt a coöperation, but I confess I doubt of its success while the business of finance and the supplies of provisions are upon so disagreeable a footing. Three objects claim our attention in the state of our affairs, which your Excellency has laid before us. The force necessary to be kept in this quarter, the expedition into Canada, and the situation of the southern States. The first is the great object, and the other two are to be considered only as appendages. It is a difficult point to determine how to employ our force, their time of service is so short and their future establishment so uncertain. Our prospects of provision and pay are still more distressing and disagreeable. Our present collective strength here, upon a Continental establishment, is equal to that of the enemy, but will be soon rendered greatly inferior by the expiration of the time of service for which the troops are engaged. Was the whole to be continued through the winter if the enemy's force remains the same that it is in New York, divided as ours must be for the winter cantonments, it would be barely sufficient for their own safety, for the security of the fortifications in the Highlands, and for covering the country and protecting the inhabitants against the ravages of small parties of the enemy. But as this force will be diminished near or quite one half by and by, detaching from it for any purpose will be hazardous, and may be ruinous, except such a small party as Major Lee's horse and foot. They may be detached to the south and would be useful.

"Could there be a junction formed of a part or the whole of the French forces at Newport, and measures taken to recruit this army for the war, detachments might be made with a degree of safety and not without, unless the enemy detach before us. Whether there is a possibility of the French forces forming a junction with us, or whether there are any measures likely to take place for recruiting this army, your Excellency can best judge. The French fleet might be safe in Boston harbor without their land force, and I believe they also might be safe up Providence River; but they are the best judges of what force and what place is necessary for their own security. Should the enemy detach largely from New York to the southward, it may lay us under the necessity of detaching also, or it may open new prospects with respect to prosecuting our original plan of operations, especially if a reinforcement should arrive from the West Indies to join the French army.

" From all the intelligence coming from Canada there appears a favorable disposition among the inhabitants for our undertaking an expedition into that country. But to undertake it with troops whose time of service will expire before the business is completed, will be a folly ; and besides this objection, we have not provisions and stores necessary for such an attempt. However, if there should be no offensive operations to the southward, an expedition might be made into Canada in the winter, and for this purpose I would direct magazines of provisions and forage to be laid up at Albany and Cohoes.

" What I would recommend with respect to our southern affairs would be to levy an army in that country, for the war if possible, of regular troops. My plan would be to act upon the defensive. If great bodies of militia are kept in the field, the country will soon become incapable of making any opposition. I would not employ a larger force than is necessary to secure great objects, and though this may not be so popular for the General, it will be more salutary for the people.

" When any offensive operations are undertaken for the reduction of Charleston, there must be a naval force to give it success. To attempt anything before, will only be attended with disappointment and disgrace ; every account agreeing that the country, from its own resources, is unequal to the support of an army sufficient for the reduction of Charleston and the expulsion of the enemy. Nor can I persuade myself that the same people who could not protect themselves, after having sufficient time to collect their force, can ever bring into the field an army sufficient to expel the enemy, unless the enemy should greatly diminish their strength, which is by no means the case in that quarter.

" When our allies furnish a naval force, and we are in a condition to furnish a land force to act in conjunction with those of our ally, which, joined by those in the southern States, will be sufficient to reduce the garrison of Charleston, then I would undertake offensive operations, and not before. Provisions and stores sufficient for the support of the army may go under convoy of the fleet. Until then I am persuaded all our efforts to regain possession of that country will be fruitless and ineffectual, and the more we attempt it the greater will be our distress in that quarter. Nothing but regular troops should be employed in a country where provisions and stores are so difficult to provide as they are to the southward, and as double their number of militia will not give equal security to the country."

CHAPTER VIII.

I HAVE already said that Washington was to meet Rochambeau at Hartford. On the 17th of September he set out for his interview. "In my absence," he had written to Greene on the 16th, " the command of the army devolves upon you. I have such entire confidence in your prudence and abilities, that I leave the conduct of it to your discretion, with only one observation; that, with our present prospects, it is not our business to seek an action, nor to accept one, but upon advantageous terms." The morning orders of the 17th were issued in the name of the Commander-in-chief. Greene added in after-orders: —

"His Excellency the Commander-in-chief, going to be absent from the army for a few days, the knowledge of which may possibly reach the enemy and encourage them to make some movement in consequence thereof, the General desires officers of all ranks to be in perfect readiness to meet them on the shortest notice; and recommends to the outguards to be very vigilant and attentive, and the patrols to be watchful and active." [1]

On the very next day he found himself compelled to have recourse to stringent measures for supplying the army with food.

"You will take the command," he writes to Colonel Butler on the 18th, " of a party of horse and foot, detached this morning, and march them to the neighborhood of Newark mountain Meeting-house. The object of the detachment is to assist the civil magistrate in collecting a number of cattle in that country for the use of the army. Dr. Burnet, one of the civil magistrates, and Mr. Daniel March, the county contractor, are both written to on the subject, setting forth our situation and the necessity for the measure. The letters will be delivered by yourself or Colonel Stewart. It is intended the whole shall be conducted under the auspices of the civil magistrate. But you must urge our necessity, and favor the collection all in your power, and execute all such orders as you may receive from the Doctor or Mr. March for this purpose.

" I have entire confidence in your discretion and prudence that no insult or injury will be offered the people but what cannot be avoided from the nature of the service.

" I recommend secrecy and dispatch."

The letter to Dr. Burnet enters more fully into the reasons of the measure.

" The scanty supplies of provisions we have on hand, and the ravages that have taken place in the neighborhood of camp in consequence thereof, makes me dread another event of the kind. Our present stock of provision will last only to-morrow and it is very uncertain whether a further supply will come seasonably ; nor is the whole we have any account of, more than sufficient to last us five

<hr />

[1] Whiting, *Revolutionary Orders*, p. 105.

days. To prevent similiar ravages with those which have taken place about camp or close on, as well as to prevent the fatal effects of having the troops without provision, as there will be great danger of their disbanding, I have sent a party of horse and foot commanded by Colonel Butler to receive your orders, and to assist in collecting and bringing to camp the cattle you mentioned to Colonel Dayton, who informed me that you told him several hundred head might be got in the neighborhood of Newark mountains. I beg you to make your collection as large as you can without oppressing the people too much. I am sorry that necessity renders this measure necessary, but it is the only way of avoiding a worse evil. The Commander-in-chief is gone to Hartford, and will not return under a week or a fortnight. This circumstance renders it more necessary that the troops should not be without provisions.

" Colonel Dayton thinks a number of cattle may be got in and about Elizabethtown. I have written to Mr. Marsh to request his attendance to receipt for the cattle as they are collected, and I trust both of you will spare no pains to satisfy the people of the absolute necessity of the measure."

To Mr. Marsh he writes in the same strain, adding that " in the late scarcity the soldiers had threatened to disband," and he " fears they will put it in execution in the next instance."

This expedition, like his own foraging expedition, would have appeared much like a failure in happier times; but now, accustomed as he was to see the army live from hand to mouth, it was with a feeling of real satisfaction that he wrote to Washington on the 21st, " We are pretty well supplied with provisions for five or six days to come, with what is in camp and on the road from the eastward and the westward."

If we want a closer view of Greene's daily life at this moment, we shall find something of it in an order of the day of the 18th : "The General desires the old officers of the day to favor him with their company at dinner during the absence of the Commander-in-chief."

Before Washington left, it had been decided to bring the army forward to Tappan, a spot soon to become sadly famous in the history of the war.

On the 19th the orders for marching were issued.

"At seven o'clock to-morrow morning the general will beat, the assembly at nine, and the army will march at ten. The baggage will precede the army and begin to file off precisely at eight, agreeably to the order of march to be given for that purpose. The baggage that is not ready to fall in agreeably to the order, will be thrown out of the line and left in the rear of the troops ; it is expected, therefore, that the officers will be punctual in having their baggage ready at the time appointed. The General desires the march may be conducted agreeably to the regulations, and with the greatest regularity ; for this purpose every officer is requested to attend to his particular command. Before the march commences, the soldiers are to fill their canteens with water and the roll is to be called about one quarter of an hour before the line of march is taken up. The officer who leads the column will take care to regulate the motion of the troops so as not to injure them by too rapid a march, and will order proper halts at about five miles' distance, and if possible, at such places as to give the men an opportunity to replenish their canteens with water. The invalids are to precede the baggage, and the officer commanding the baggage escort will take care and provide for those who shall fail on the march. He is to allow no women to ride in the wagons unless their peculiar circum-

stances require it.   The sick of the light infantry and of
the right wing, who are unable to march, are to be collected near General Patterson's brigade in the second line ;
those of the left wing and park of artillery, at the road
leading to Paramus, near Lord Stirling's quarters.   The
whole to be collected at 3 o'clock this afternoon." [1]

One of the most serious consequences of the
demoralization of the army was desertion, and it
was in changing camp and on marches that desertion was most to be apprehended.

"As the army is to march in the morning," Greene
writes to Major Pace, " it is not improbable there will be
a number of deserters attempt to get in to the enemy.
You will, therefore, in order to intercept them, march your
riflemen down the road towards Bergen, and take post a
little this side of the road leading to Fort Lee, and there
establish the proper patrols for your own security, and
make the best disposition you can for intercepting the deserters.   You will continue in that position until Thursday
morning unless you should see or hear of any motions of
the enemy which will expose you ; in that case you will
send word to me of what you have discovered and take
steps for your own security.   The army will take their old
ground at Tappan."

It was on these marching days as well as on field
days and parades, that the value of Steuben's les-
sons was seen.   The orders passed regularly from
brigade to brigade and regiment to regiment.
Every drum-beat and bugle-call had its meaning,
and was understood by all.   Every man and every
horse knew his place, and while all seemed to be
moving at once, and each attending to his own
work, there was no confusion.   Then at a signal

1 Whiting's *Revolutionary Orders*, p. 106.

from drum and fife, the men struck their tents and threw them into the wagons, and the long line of march began, every subordinate following his leader, and the leader himself guiding his movements by orders that came to him in regular gradation from the leader of all, till the whole body from front to rear seemed to obey the impulse of a single will.[1]

This march was but a day's march, and by nightfall the army was once more close to the banks of the Hudson. It was here on one of these days that Greene first met Joel Barlow, not yet as a poet, but as " a young clergyman from Connecticut," whose prayers, it is recorded, showed so little of the fervor of religious inspiration that his friends were glad to defend him by saying that he was better " calculated " for a poet than for a parson. His friend Humphreys had already written warmly in his favor to Greene, holding out great expectations from the " Vision of Columbus."[2]

One of Greene's first cares on reaching Tappan was to report to Washington what he had done.

" Agreeably to your Excellency's directions of the 18th, I have taken our old camp at this place. We marched yesterday, and Megg's regiment for West Point the day before.

" Colonel Tilghman communicated the last intelligence we have from New York. Since that I have not been able to obtain the least information of what is going on there, though we have people in from three different quarters; none of them returning makes me suspect some secret ex-

---

[1] Thacher, p. 202.

[2] Thacher's *Military Journal*, p. 209.   Greene Papers.

pedition is in contemplation, the success of which depends altogether upon its being kept a secret. Colonel Dayton is gone to Elizabethtown and Major Burnet to Newark to see if anything can be learned from those places. . . . . Nothing material has happened in the army since your Excellency left camp."

We have seen how carefully Greene provided for the army ; he took equal thought of the protection of the people.

"The burning of fences and breaking up of enclosures," he says, in his first orders of the day from the new camp, " is so distressing to the inhabitants, as well as disgraceful to an army that has the least pretension to discipline and order, that the General earnestly exhorts the officers of all ranks, but more particularly the commanding officers of regiments, to take all possible care to prevent it ; and, for this, the camp and quarter guards are to confine every person detected either in moving or burning fencing stuff ; and as it frequently happens that there are a number of soldiers standing round a fire made of fencing stuff, none of whom will acknowledge or inform who made it, all such persons shall be considered as the authors unless they point out those who really are, and shall be confined and punished accordingly.

" As it is much better to prevent crimes than to punish them, the General desires the commanding officers of regiments to pick out proper places for kitchens, that the cooking of provisions for the regiments may be done as much together as possible, and that the police officers may visit them during the cooking hours as well to see that the cooking is properly performed as that the fires are not made of fencing stuff."

I add the rest of the order as an illustration of the difficulties that arose between officers, all of which, it will be remembered, came to the commander for final decision.

"At a general court-martial, whereof Colonel Jackson is president, 16th instant, Major Newman of the Engineers was tried for unofficer and ungentlemanlike behavior, in taking possession of the quarters of the Reverend David Jones in his absence, and for similar behavior to him in quarters.

"The court are of opinion that Major Newman having a right to take possession of the quarters which Mr. Jones calls his, is not guilty of unofficer and ungentlemanlike behavior in taking possession of them. The court acquit Major Newman of the last part of the charge against him.

"Major-general Greene confirms the opinion of the court. Major Newman is released from his arrest."[1]

Meanwhile Rodney had arrived at New York with ten ships of the line, and ten more were said to be on the way. "This confirms," writes Greene to Reed, "the report concerning the Count de Guichen's coming upon the coast, as it is not probable that Rodney would leave such a naval force behind as the combined fleets would form."

Conjecture was busy at the American headquarters. What will Rodney do? "Reports from New York say," writes Greene to Reed, "that Rodney is going to join Arburthnot, and that an attack is intended upon the fleet and army at Newport. I think this is possible but not probable. Preparations for a considerable embarkation has been making for some time in New York. The destination of the troops is unknown. But from a combination of circumstances I am led to believe

[1] Whiting, *Revolutionary Orders*, p. 107.

they are going to Virginia; the refugees of that country being invited to engage in it." "Another account," he writes to the President of Congress, (says) "the rescue of the convention troops is in contemplation. . . . . These may be blinds," he adds, "but I have thought it my duty to communicate matters as I receive them." That they were blinds, and of what menacing significance, we shall presently see.

Nothing further was known when he wrote to Washington on the 23d : —

"Colonel Dayton and Major Burnet are still at Elizabethtown and New York. No intelligence can be got by the way of Paulus Hook. I am afraid the great difficulty is the want of encouragement to run the hazard.

"The minister of France stole a march upon us in camp. He came incog., and is on his way to Newport to pay a visit to the French army.

"Colonel Pickering arrived yesterday, and takes up the business of the department to-day or to-morrow. He is in a bad state of health and has come to camp empty-handed. The block-house is going on very well and will be completed in four or five days, and I think will be a very strong place. The minister was down to visit it yesterday.

"The army is without rum ; can there be no measures taken to get on the rum at Springfield ? I have been obliged to make a seizure of some among the sutlers and followers of the army."

And while these thoughts were pressing upon him, it was impossible that the thought of what could yet be done for the rescue of the South should not press upon him too : —

"What measures are taking with respect to our southern

affairs?" he wrote to Reed on the 19th of September. "The plan of calling out great bodies of militia must be destructive in the end. The resources of the country cannot support it, and though at first it may afford a seeming security, yet it in time will really weaken the opposition by wasting the strength of the country to little purpose. What is wanting in that quarter is a good regular army, not large, yet sufficiently strong to confine the enemy from overrunning the country. To attempt the expulsion of the enemy out of the southern States before we have a navy to aid our operations will be a folly and end in disgrace and disappointment. The general that commands there ought to act altogether upon the defensive.

"This plan will not be agreeable to the inhabitants of that country, who are impatient under their sufferings, and are anxious to make every exertion to recover the southern States. But the more we waste our strength in such a fruitless attempt, the less we shall be able to give protection to the rest of the southern States not yet in the enemy's power."

The defeat of Gates at Camden was already known, and there is a deep interest in this paragraph, when we remember that before another month was passed, the question of offensive or defensive, and the fate of the South, rested upon Greene.[1] Very interesting too, is the paragraph that follows; and as we read it we should bear in

[1] Greene's first impressions upon this subject are given in a letter to Governor Greene, September 5, 1780. The closing paragraph is particularly deserving of attention : —

"It is high time for America to raise an army for the war, and not distress the country by short enlistments, and hazard the liberties of the States with an order of men, whose feelings, let their principles be ever so good, cannot be like those who have been long in the field. — *Collection of Rhode Island Historical Society*, vol. vi. p. 266.

mind that thus far Greene's relations with Gates had been almost hostile : —

" General Gates's late misfortune will sink his consequence and lessen his military character. He is bandied about and subject to many remarks, the common fate of the unfortunate. Whether he has been to blame or not, I cannot pretend to judge, and shall leave those who were nearer at hand to fix the common opinion."

The same subject recurs in a letter of the 22d to Governor Greene, introducing the French minister, whose " zeal for our cause and the attachment he has manifested for our interest, entitles him to every mark of public respect and private esteem : " —

" The affairs to the southward," he goes on to say, " are still more agreeable than the account I mentioned in my last. Most of the prisoners taken in the action at Camden were rescued by Colonel Marion as they were on their march to Charleston. Upon the whole the British have got little to brag of. General Gates's first account was shocking and very premature."

Then the chief anxiety of the hour comes out. Reports are in New York that an expedition is planning there against Wilmington in North Carolina, and another against Portsmouth in Virginia. " But some people think the whole is intended against Newport."

Clinton had scattered his doubts broadcast, and spread his snares with a skillful hand ; but the fate of a great nation was at stake, and God's shield was over it : —

" There has been some firing on the east side of the

North River at the shipping which lay near Tellard's Point, but I have no account of what effect it had more than to make the shipping move a little further from the shore."

Little did he dream what that firing meant. Other ears were drinking it eagerly in from an old house that still stands, as it stood then, on the shores of Haverstraw Bay, and one heart at least, beat fast as the fatal sounds boomed ominously over the waters. Two days more were to pass before their full meaning in the world's history was known.

Meanwhile Greene sends to the President of Congress the best information he can collect : —

" Your Excellency's favor of the 18th instant, with a copy of a letter from General Gates to Governor Jefferson I have had the honor to receive, and immediately transmitted copies thereof to his Excellency the Commander-in-chief.

" By intelligence from New York it appears that the enemy continue their preparation for a very extensive embarkation ; they are collecting their force on Long Island for the purpose of embarking them at White Stone, and at the same time a number of transports have fallen down to the watering place to prepare for sea. Admiral Rodney has detached five ships of the line to join Admiral Arburthnot, who is said to be off Block Island. The remainder of his fleet, consisting of the *Sandwich* of ninety guns, the *Alcides, Terrible, Triumph,* of seventy four guns each, and the *Yarmouth,* of sixty-four guns, remain at the watering place and have been joined by the *Rainbow* of fifty, and the *Romulus* of forty-four guns. They are repairing and taking in their stores with all possible expedition. The enemy have detached near five hundred of the best men from the new corps in garrison at New York, Paulus Hook, and

Staten Island, with orders to join the main army near White Stone ; they have laid a general embargo on all shipping, and continue to impress men for their fleet.

" The reports in the city of New York are alternately that they are intended for Rhode Island and Virginia.

" I hope to be able to forward for the satisfaction of Congress in a few days some intelligence which will enable them to determine on their intended operations with more certainty. I have, however, thought proper to communicate what has come to hand for their consideration."

The closing paragraph is the most significant of all, and shows how jealously he watched events and how justly he reasoned from them.

" By the New York paper of the 21st instant, which I have the honor to inclose for your Excellency's perusal, I find Sir Henry Clinton has removed General Robertson from the duties of commandant of the city, which is no doubt to answer some very particular purpose."

The same subject fills his letter of the same day to Washington : —

" Since I wrote last, Major Burnet has returned from Newark, and brings intelligence that the enemy continued their preparations for a very extensive embarkation. They are collecting their force on Long Island, while a number of transports have fallen down to the watering place and are preparing for sea. They have detached near five hundred of the best men from the new levies in garrison at New York, Paulus Hook, and Staten Island, with orders to join the main army on Long Island, near White Stone.

" The Guards 57th and 80th regiment have been relieved from near Fort Knyphausen by the Anspach regiment, and have marched from New York to embark. Admiral Rodney has detached five ships to join Admiral Arbuthnot off Block Island ; the remainder, consisting of the

Sandwich, Alcides, Terrible, Triumphant, and *Yarmouth,* remain at the watering place and have been joined by the *Rainbow* and *Romulus.* They are repairing the ships and taking in stores with all possible expedition, and it is reported they will be ready for sea by the 27th instant They continue to impress men for their fleet. . . .

" By the New York papers of the 22d instant, which I have the pleasure to inclose for your Excellency's perusal, it appears they have laid a general embargo on all shipping, and have placed Lieutenant-colonel Brich in the command of the city, which I think indicates but a small garrison to be left. These accounts are generally confirmed by several deserters from the fleet and army, the examination of which I have inclosed.

I have transmitted the accounts to Congress as they have come to hand.

" The enemy landed a small party at Nyack this morning, from one of their ships, and attempted to fire the houses. I had detached a guard to that place last evening, which compelled them to retire immediately after having set fire to the house of Major Smith, which was consumed."

The next was one of Steuben's days ; an inspection and general exercise of the troops.

" The truly martial appearance of the troops yesterday," say the orders of the 26th, " the order and regularity with which they made the different marches, and the facility with which they performed the several manœuvres, do them the greatest credit, and open the most flattering prospects of substantial service to the country and military glory to the army.

" Nothing can be more pleasing to the officers who feel for the honor of the army and the independence of America, than to see the rapid progress which has been made by the troops in military discipline. The good conduct of all the officers yesterday gave the General the highest satisfaction, and the particular service of the Inspector-general and those in that line deserve his especial thanks."

The cares of the day were over. It was nearly eleven o'clock, and Greene must have been almost ready to lay down his pen and take up the volume with which he was accustomed to calm his mind for sleep, when an orderly entered with a letter. He recognized the hand of Hamilton, and read : —

"There has just been unfolded at this place a scene of the blackest treason. Arnold has fled to the enemy. André, the British Adjutant-general, is in our possession as a spy. His capture unraveled the mystery. West Point was to have been the sacrifice. All the dispositions have been made for the purpose, and 'tis possible, though not probable, to-night may see the execution.

"The wind is fair. I came here in pursuit of Arnold, but was too late. I advise you putting the army under marching orders, and detaching a brigade immediately this way."

How Greene felt as he read these lines we shall see presently; but now he instantly issued the orders Hamilton advised, and then taking his pen wrote to the President of Congress : —

"Enclosed I send a copy of a letter which this moment came to hand from Colonel Hamilton, communicating a discovery of the blackest treason that ever disgraced human nature.

"I have thought it advisable to forward your Excellency this intelligence that you may take measures to search for his papers in Philadelphia, and those of the family with whom he is connected. Perhaps some discovery may be made which may lead to further scenes of villainy."

Then giving the army part of the night to rest in, he roused them at three, ordered two regiments of the Pennsylvania line to set out immediately for West Point, and the rest to hold themselves in readiness to start at a moment's warning. At a quarter past three another express arrived with a letter from Washington. Its instructions were already anticipated, and Greene immediately answered : —

"Your Excellency's letter dated at Robinson's house 7 o'clock last evening came to hand 1-4 past three this morning; before the receipt of which I had put the first Pennsylvania brigade in motion, and put the whole army under marching orders, in consequence of a letter received from Colonel Hamilton, dated at Verplanck's Point. As the first brigade had marched I thought it most advisable to let the second follow it rather than break a division in the left wing. The troops marched without their baggage, which is to follow them this morning. The rest of the army is in perfect readiness to move at the shortest notice.

"I beg leave to congratulate your Excellency on this happy discovery, but am struck with astonishment at the horrid treason.

"The plot being laid open, I think the enemy will be altogether disconcerted for some days to come, and give you full time to make such dispositions for the better security of West Point as you may think necessary."

At the usual hour the troops were mustered for parade. They had been roused by the night alarm; they had heard the movements of the two regiments as they set forth on their early march, and every eye in every regiment was fixed anxiously on the Adjutant as he read : —

" Treason of the blackest dye was yesterday discovered. General Arnold who commanded at West Point, lost to every sentiment of honor, of private and public obligation, was about to deliver up that important post into the hands of the enemy. Such an event must have given the American cause a dangerous if not a fatal wound ; happily the treason has been timely discovered to prevent the fatal misfortune. The providential train of circumstances which led to it, affords the most convincing proof that the liberties of America are the object of Divine protection. At the same time that the treason is to be regretted, the General cannot help congratulating the army on the happy discovery. Our enemies despairing of carrying their point by force, are practicing every base art to effect by bribery and corruption what they cannot accomplish in a manly way. Great honor is due to the American army, that this is the first instance of treason of the kind, where many were to be expected from the nature of our dispute ; the brightest ornament in the character of the American soldiers is their having been proof against all the arts and seductions of an insidious enemy. Arnold has made his escape to the enemy, but Major André, the Adjutant-general in the British army, who came out as a spy to negotiate the business, is our prisoner."

What would come next it was impossible to tell, or in what direction the army might move ; but to be prepared for a sudden march Greene resolved to send the sick to a place of greater comfort and security.

" The situation of Paramus," he writes to Dr. Tilton on the 27th, " and the uncertainty of our armies continuing at this place, induces me to think it will be for the interest of the service to send the sick to the huts at Morris. You will therefore take measures for their immediate removal, having regard to the weather, so as not to expose the sick more than what is necessary, as we are not yet pressed in point of time.

"Application must be made to the magistrates for wagons, and for fear it should not be in their power to procure them agreeable to the forms of law, I have sent you a party of light-horse and a press warrant to impress such a number as shall be competent to the service. Such of the sick whose cases are very bad, and when there will be danger in moving them, may be left at Paramus, and a surgeon remain with them. All convalescents not fit to join the army and yet able to march, should travel on foot to Morris in order to ease the transportation.

"Dr. Cutting will move his hospital stores up towards the mouth of the Clove, somewhere in Ramapaugh."

Then came another letter from Washington, dated from that little, low-studded house, opposite West Point — Robinson's house — which still nestles unchanged in the heart of the Highlands: —

"I have concluded to send to camp to-morrow Major André of the British army, and Mr. Joshua H. Smith, who has had a great hand in carrying on the business between him and Arnold. They will be under an escort of horse, and I wish you to have separate houses in camp ready for their reception, in which they may be kept perfectly secure ; and also strong, trusty guards, trebly officered, that a part may be constantly in the room with them. They have not been permitted to be kept together, and must be still kept apart. I would wish the room for Mr. André to be a decent one, and that he may be treated with civility; but that he may be so guarded as to preclude a possibility of his escaping, which he will certainly attempt to effect, if it shall seem practicable in the most distant degree. Smith must also be carefully secured and not treated with asperity. I intend to return to-morrow morning, and hope to have the pleasure of seeing you in the course of the day,

You may keep these several matters secret. I write to Mr. Tilghman." [1]

It was not till the 28th that Greene found time to write the story to his wife : —

" I have only a moment to inform you by the post that General Arnold has fled to the enemy. He was about delivering the fortifications of West Point into the hands of the enemy. Happily for this country the treason was discovered before the plan was ripe for execution. Major André, the British Adjutant-general, who had been with Arnold settling the plan, was taken on his return to New York, which brought out the whole scene of villainy. Arnold got intelligence of André's being taken just time enough to make his escape. General Washington was on his return from Hartford (to whom the capture of André was reported) and arrived at West Point a few minutes after Arnold got off. Half an hour's stay longer would have prevented his escape and subjected him to the punishment due to his crimes. His escape was so sudden that he had only time to say to Mrs. Arnold, who had arrived in camp but a few days before, ' I have this moment received two letters which oblige me to leave you and my country forever.' After making this dreadful declaration, he rode off and left her in the most awful situation that imagination can form. Two days she was raving distracted.

" I expect the General into camp to-day and Major André with him in close confinement. Joshua Smith, where you lodged on your return home, near King's Ferry, is concerned in the treason and will be hung accordingly. His wife, poor woman, in a strange land and among a new people, without friend or relation. Her case must be distressing indeed, to have her husband torn from her arms and exposed to an ignominious death, and she left without

---

[1] Sparks, *Writings of Washington*, vol. vii. p. 221.

support. But this is her fate, miserable as it is. To lose
a friend is nothing in an honorable way to what it is when
accompanied by such disagreeable and disgraceful circumstances. Hug thyself, Caty, in thine own felicity, and
thank heaven that thou art connected with a man whose
soul abhors such crimes, and who loves you too dearly to
expose you to such disgrace, ruin, and reproach.

" The discovery appears to have been providential, and
convinces me that the liberties of America are the object
of divine protection. God grant that all such perfidy may
come to light and the [torn] meet with their just desert.

" You shall have a more full account of this matter in
a day or two. I would have written to the Governor, but
am not yet possessed of all the particulars necessary to give
a full and satisfactory account. If you please you may
give the Governor this short account until I can send him
a more perfect one."

The next day he resumes his narrative : —

" I wrote you a letter by the post yesterday respecting
General Arnold. Since writing that letter General Washington is arrived in camp, and the British Adjutant-general
and Joshua Smith, both of which are kept under strong
guards. They are to be tried this day, and doubtless will
be hung to-morrow. Mr. André is a very accomplished
character, and while we abhor the act we cannot help
pitying the man. From his apparent cheerfulness he little
expects his approaching fate."

" His Excellency says Arnold has been guilty of the
greatest meanness imaginable, such as cheating the sutlers
of the garrison and selling the public stores. From all I
can learn Arnold is the greatest villain that ever disgraced
human nature. I had but a few minutes conversation
with the General, the marquee being crowded with people
of all characters. To-day I expect to learn more. I expect it will fall to my lot to sit as president of the court

which will decide upon the crimes of Smith and André. It will be a disagreeable business, but it must be done.

" I am very apprehensive the people will be fired with jealousy from this instance of treason, and that it will be productive of mischievous consequences. God grant it may not. My pride and feelings are greatly hurt at the infamy of this man's conduct. Arnold being an American and a New Englander, and of the rank of Major-general, are all mortifying circumstances. The event will be a reproach to us to the latest posterity. Curse on his folly and perfidy.

" Colonel Duer is talking to me, therefore you will have an incorrect letter. General Putnam is here talking as usual, and telling his old stories, which prevents my writing more. The old gentleman, notwithstanding the late paralytical shock, is very cheerful and social."

Washington now resumed the immediate command. In his first orders after announcing the appointment of Colonel Pickering as Quartermaster-general, he adds : —

" The Commander-in-chief takes this occasion to thank General Greene for the able and satisfactory manner in which he has discharged the duties of the Quartermaster-general's department during his continuance in that office, and also to express his approbation of Major-general Greene's conduct and orders during his absence." [1]

On the same day the Board of Inquiry into the nature of André's case was organized, and meeting in the old Dutch church at Tappan, no longer standing, they read Washington's letter of instructions, and entered at once upon their painful duty. Greene was president, as he had expected ; and few men in any army could have brought higher qualifications to the discussion of a question of

[1] Whiting, *Revolutionary Orders,* vol. iii.

military law, even if there had been any grounds
for doubt. With the common law he was familiar
as far as an attentive study of Jacobs and Black-
stone could make him familiar with it, and the law
of nations he had studied in Vattel, the leading authority of the day.[1] But André's case was too
plain a one to require a reference to authorities, and none who knew the circumstances of his
capture, doubted the result of his trial. We can
easily conceive that as the graceful young man came
forward and bowed to the court a sad silence fell
upon it, and all felt as if they would gladly have
turned away from the painful duty. "It is not
possible to save him," said Steuben to North; and
yet he would gladly have saved him.[2]

"Read the names of the members," said Greene,
"and let the prisoner say if he has anything to
object to any of them."

"Nothing," was the reply.

"You will be asked various questions," Greene
continued, "but we wish you to feel perfectly at
liberty to answer them or not as you choose.
Take your own time for recollection and weigh
well what you say."

André told his story, and presented a written
statement of it to the court. This we have; but
our knowledge of the oral interrogatory is frag-
mentary.

"Did you consider yourself under the protection of a flag?" was one of the questions.

---

[1] I am thus minute in order to
meet the erroneous statement in Lord
Mahon's (Earl Stanhope) *History of*
England from the peace of Utrecht, vol
vii. p. 70.

[2] Kapp's *Steuben,* p. 289.

" Certainly not; if I had I might have returned under it," was the unhesitating answer.

" You say that you proceeded to Smith's house?" asked Greene.

" I said a house, but not whose house," he replied.

" True," said Greene, " nor have we any right to ask this of you after the terms we have allowed."

" Have you any remarks to make upon the statements you have presented ? "

" None. I leave them to operate with the Board."

The guard and prisoner withdrew. The court remained alone ; and never had the consecrated walls of the old church, which had witnessed so many solemn moments, witnessed a moment more solemn than this. Greene broke the silence.

" You have heard the prisoner's statements and the documents that have been laid before you by order of the Commander-in-chief. What is your opinion ? "

" That he is to be considered as a spy, and according to the laws and usages of nations ought to suffer death," answered each in turn.

The opinion of the court was drawn up in full and handed to Greene for signature. A tear, say our family traditions, dimmed his eye as he set his name to the fatal scroll, but the hand and the will were unshaken.

The report was laid before the Commander-in-chief. He too was deeply agitated. Hamilton's quick sympathies had been enlisted for André, and he had not concealed them from Washington. Not rashly, but after mature deliberation, Washington wrote on the following day : —

"The Commander-in-chief approves of the opinion of the board of general officers respecting Major André, and orders that the execution of Major André take place to-morrow, at five o'clock P. M."

Meanwhile Clinton had written to claim the surrender of his adjutant, and Washington in answering him, inclosed him the opinion of the board. The English General, who was warmly attached to André, resolved to make one more effort to save him. Assuming that the board could not have been rightly informed of all the circumstances essential to the formation of a correct opinion, he announced his intention of sending Lieutenant-general Robertson and two other gentlemen to give a true state of facts and to declare (his) sentiments and resolutions. On receiving this letter, Washington postponed the execution, and ordered Greene to repair to Dobbs' Ferry and meet the English deputies.

Greene was already on the spot when the *Greyhound*, with the white flag at her mast-head, cast anchor off the ferry. A boat was quickly lowered, and quickly rowed to the shore, and in a few moments an officer stood before him with a request for permission for Lieutenant-general Robertson, Hon. Andrew Elliot, Lieutenant-governor, and Hon. Wm. Smith, Chief Justice of the Province of New York, to land. It was a dexterous attempt to take the question out of the hands of the military

authorities and transform it into a question of civil
law. " No one but General Robertson can be allowed to land," was Greene's reply; and the two
civilians were compelled to wait on board for the
result of the conference. Robertson immediately
landed. And there they stood, face to face, Americans by birth, both of them, but one a general in
the service of the king and the other in the service of his country. Robertson and Washington
had been acquaintances, but Greene and Robertson, I believe, had never met before. The English
general must have looked curiously upon the Quaker general, whom report, even among the English themselves, had already singled out as the
possible successor of Washington.[1] But the occasion was too grave a one for curiosity. Robertson
began by a compliment to Greene : " It is a great
satisfaction to meet you upon an occasion so interesting to the army and to humanity."

It was a dexterous assumption that the question
was still an open one. " We must understand
from the outset," Greene replied, " the ground we
stand upon. I do not meet you as an officer, but
as a private gentleman. It is in this quality alone
that General Washington allows me to meet you.

---

[1] " And what if Washington should close his scene.
Who would succeed him ? Have we not a Greene ? "

These lines are found in the *American Times*, a very rare satirical poem in three parts. " In which are delineated the characters of the leaders of the American Rebellion — by Camillo Querno — poet-laureate to the Congress." It was published first in London in 1780, and republished by Rivington in the same volume with the *Cow Chase*. The supposed author was Jonathan Odell. This, however, the learned and accurate librarian of the New York Historical Society regards as uncertain ; and there is no higher authority.

The case of an acknowledged spy does not admit of discussion."

"I come to state facts," said Robertson, "and whatever character I may be supposed to speak in, I trust they will have their own weight."

He then attempted to prove that André was under the protection of a flag, and acted wholly by Arnold's directions.

"These questions have already been examined by the Board," said Greene, "and I find nothing in what you have said to change my opinion."

"But Arnold also asserts that he was under a flag."

"We believe André rather than Arnold."

Failing to make any impression upon the mind of the American general, Robertson proposed that the question should be referred to Rochambeau and Knyphausen as disinterested men, familiar with European usage. But this, too, could not be done without impugning the deliberate decision of a competent tribunal. The same objection lay against an appeal to Congress. And then as a last resort an open letter from Arnold to Washington was introduced. Greene read it, according to Marbois, and threw it contemptuously at Robertson's feet.[1] Sometime in the course of the conference, and most probably after all the appeals to argument had been exhausted, an appeal was made to feeling. Humanity and the consideration which Clinton, as it was asserted, had shown to persons in whom Washington had taken interest, were urged.

---

[1] Marbois, *Complot d'Arnold*, p. 149.

"If we give up André we shall expect you to give up Arnold," Greene is made to say in Robertson's report to Clinton. And he adds that he only answered by a look of indignant reproof.

As they were parting, Robertson added: "I shall trust to your candor to represent my arguments to General Washington in the fairest light." He announced also his intention of waiting till next morning in the expectation of taking either André himself, or at least an assurance of his safety, back with him to New York.

Upon what his hope was founded it is impossible to conjecture, for surely it was not authorized by anything that Geene had said. Instead of this assurance he received a note from Greene, saying : —

"Agreeably to your request I communicated to General Washington the substance of your conversation in all the particulars, so far as my memory served me. It made no alteration in his opinion and determination. I need say no more after what you have already been informed."

There was still another question to decide. André in a letter of the 1st of October had asked "not to die on a gibbet."[1] Washington consulted his officers, and it has been asserted, though not that I am aware with the confirmation of contemporary evidence, that six were for and six against granting his prayer, and that Greene as president of the board cast his deciding vote against it.[2] It is certain that believing André to be a spy, he held

---

[1] I hardly need remind the reader of Willis's beautiful poem upon this subject.

[2] I find this statement in the *Memoir of Gen. Starke*, by C. Starke, p. 83, but have not been able to verify it.

that if punished at all he must be punished as spies are punished by the laws of war. "Any other mode," tradition makes him say, "would, in the actual state of our relations with England, throw a doubt upon our conviction of his crime."

One more stern duty was to be performed. To give greater solemnity to the occasion, it had been decided that the principal officers of the army should be present. Washington and his staff were not there; but Greene was there on horseback, and received and returned André's salute as he passed to the gallows. And this is all concerning André that belongs to my story.[1]

[1] The chief authorities for the principal subject of this chapter are Sparks, *Life of Arnold*, and the appendix upon it in the 7th vol. of his *Washington*, Greene's letters, Thacher's *Military Journal*, and Mr. Biddle's admirable monograph, which exhausts the legal aspects of the subject. Marbois, *Complot d'Arnold*, is neither so accurate nor so complete as might have been expected from a writer of his talent and opportunities. The love of fine writing misled him. Several attempts have been made to weave the poetical elements of this story into a drama. But the only one that deserves mention is Mr. Calvert's *Arnold*, in which skillful dramatic development is combined with true perception of character and much good poetry. Earl Stanhope's (Lord Mahon's) view is fully met by Mr. Biddle, in every particular.

CHAPTER IX.

I RETURN for the last time to the Quartermaster's department, first gathering together at the risk of an occasional repetition, the facts scattered through the foregoing chapters.

The difficulties and embarrassments of this department may be traced to four concurring causes.

1st. The condition of the finances.

2d. Congressional delays.

3d. The increased expenditure caused by the frequent calling out of the militia and the annual raising of a new army.

4th. A decrease of interest in the war.

1st. The war of independence was so connected in form with the question of taxation, that Congress did not dare to begin its financial action by imposing taxes.   Unconscious of its real power, which, founded on opinion, was absolute, so long as that opinion retained its force, it hesitated where it should have acted, and waited for the public sentiment which it should have formed and led.   Hence when war came and money was required for the support of an army, instead of calling upon the people by direct taxation, the amount of which can always be estimated, it called upon them by indirect taxation, the amount of which always outruns the estimate.   Money was scarce, credit abundant, and Congress, forgetting that between credit and money there is a certain proportion which cannot be passed, drew solely upon credit without making the corresponding provision of money.   The enthusiasm which raised the first army sustained the first issues of Continental bills; but, obeying the natural law of human passion, grew cool and languished as the progress of the war, imposing new sacrifices, brought into play in its full proportions, the question of personal interest.   Depreciation began with the first questioning of the ultimate relation of the dollar in paper to the dollar in silver, and men having once ceased to measure their loyalty to the cause by their faith in its pecuniary representative, the promise of Congress to pay was received and discounted like the note of hand of a common merchant.   We shall presently see how disastrous the moral and financial effects of this depreciation were both upon the people and upon the army.

The first issue of Continental bills was decided

in June, 1775, and limited to two millions of dollars. A third million was called for in July; three more in November; five in February, 1776, five in May and five in July. By the end of 1778 the issues were over a hundred millions; by September, 1779, over a hundred and sixty millions. It was evident that this course could not be continued much longer, and Congress, in an eloquent and elaborate appeal to the people, pledged itself not to exceed the two hundred millions which it had already so nearly reached. But when the summing up day came, it was found, that what with forgery and what with negligence, the limit had been exceeded by a whole million.

It was not till the issues had reached nine millions that a sensible depreciation began; and even then, it has been questioned, whether the depreciation as manifested by the prices of goods was owing to a loss of credit or to an excess of the paper money. In January, 1777, it was only one and a quarter for one. But in January, 1778, it was four for one. Through 1778 it oscillated between four and six, passing rapidly in the following January from seven to eight and nine. Then moving in April with a rapid downward impulse from twelve and a half to twenty-two, it vacillated again through the summer and autumn, touched forty-five in November, returned to thirty-five in December, and at last, after holding its ground at sixty through April, May, June, and a part of July, 1780, moved swiftly towards the precipice through August, September, and October, and never rose again above one hundred, after it had once reached it in November. In May, 1781, it ceased to circulate as money, although it was still bought up for awhile by speculators at four hundred and even one thousand for one.

Various attempts were made to arrest the progress of depreciation and give stability to the Continental bills. From very near their first issue a brand was set upon the refusal to receive them, and the recusant noted with infamy as the enemy of his country. This proving insufficient, they were made a legal tender, and passed swiftly from eager into reluctant hands in the nominal payment of debts; the statute sanctioning what equity condemned, and legislation compelling men to accept as legal what their reason refused as unjust.

Equally unjust was the attempt to regulate prices. Conventions met, examined the state of the market, and fixing prices by their own estimate of values, required everybody to accept the regulated price for all articles needed by the army and not actually required for domestic use. But the natural law of demand and supply refuses the control of human enactments. Much injustice was committed, many wrongs and losses were suffered; yet the attempt to regulate prices, like the attempt to create values, failed.

At last an effort was made, in 1779, to form a sinking fund by calling upon the States for their quota of fifteen millions for that year and six millions annually for the eighteen years that followed. But the day of enthusiasm was passed, and the day of confidence was not yet come. The States answered very imperfectly to the call.

There was still one resource left. Over two hundred millions of bills were in circulation. It was useless to think of redeeming them at their full nominal value. But it was resolved to call them in by taxes at the ratio of forty for one; cancel them, and issue a new paper, one of the new for every twenty of the old, the whole redeemable in specie at the end of six years, and till redeemed, bearing an interest of five per cent. Of this new issue six millions were to be divided between the States, four millions to be subject to the order of Congress, and the final payment to be made by the States in due proportion, under the guarantee of the United States. Some hopes were excited, and much curiosity. Men had come to look with great doubt upon the financial skill of Congress; and few were surprised when the trial showed that this, like every other attempt to give life to the discredited currency, had failed.[1]

---

[1] How far this attempt was from awakening confidence may be seen by the following extract of a letter of Col. E. Bowen to General Greene : " Since the resolution of Congress to call in the present money in circulation, and redeem it at forty for one, it has depreciated near half, and hardly anything is to be purchased without hard money or some exchange of goods." — *Revolutionary Corr. Collections of the Rhode Island Historical Society*, vol. vi. p. 261.

Colonel Pettit also writes to Greene on the 17th of March, 1780 : " Two days ago a grand and deep scheme passed in committee of the whole, and this day I expect it will be tried in the house. The outlines of it are, to issue new money at an equality with specie, and call on the different States to fund it. Of this a proportion, say six tenths, is to be paid to the States for the supplies they furnish, the other four tenths to be in the disposition of Congress for contingencies. Reckoning (*sic*) the present two hundred millions at forty for one, five millions would redeem it. The States are to go on taxing and pay the money into the Continental treasury, for which they are to have credit at the rate of

Meanwhile some money had been raised by domestic loans, through loan offices, which were opened for this purpose in the different States; some by the sale of bills drawn on Dr. Franklin and other diplomatic agents in Europe, in anticipation or realization of foreign loans; some by lottery, some by taxes, and some by the sale of confiscated estates. But none of these resources was sufficient, either by itself or in conjunction with the others. The expenses of the government were constantly in advance of the receipts ; and even the most zealous patriots felt that if they would make provision for their wives and children, they must not entrust their money to the keeping of Congress.[1]

Congress, which seems to have been painfully haunted by the consciousness of its want of real power, sought to throw, as far as it could, the responsibility of action upon the States. The States brought in slowly and reluctantly their quota of taxes. To lighten their task while it made the accomplishment of it sure, recourse was had to

forty for one, or to receive new money in lieu of it at the same rate. Funds are to be opened for ten millions, so that there will be five millions of solid money to furnish supplies with besides redeeming the present two hundred millions. These I understand to be the principles. . . . I have an ill opinion of the scheme, but supposing it to answer to the wishes of the framers of it, so much time must necessarily be lost before it takes effect that I fear the worst of consequences by the delay. Till all the States have adopted it and provided the funds, it will not be safe to issue the money, and that cannot be expected under six months with the utmost approbation that can be hoped for ; but my opinion is, that the scheme will be so much reprobated as to either take more time or be rejected as impracticable. It appears to me to be an unnecessary and wanton sporting with the public credit, and that it will in its course have a great tendency to destroy it." — Greene MSS.

[1] For Washington's opinion *Vide* Sparks, *Writings of Washington*, vol. vii. p. 67.

payments in kind, as tobacco had long been used in Virginia, Maryland, and North Carolina, for money, and corn and cattle in New England, for the payment of taxes and public contracts. An elaborate table of the wants of the army was prepared, and each State called upon for its proportion of the necessary supplies.

The inherent defects of this system were quickly made manifest. Disputes arose between State officers and the officers of the United States. Questions concerning transportation gave rise to innumerable difficulties and delays; and when these had been overcome and the articles reached camp, they were often found deficient in quantity and kind.

" Every day's experience," wrote Washington after a full and fair trial, " proves more and more, that the present mode of obtaining supplies is the most uncertain, expensive, and injurious that could be devised." [1]

Upon none did the burden of depreciation fall so heavily as upon those who were dependent upon salaries and stipulated pay. The clergy were great sufferers ; and in most cases their parishioners shared too largely in the loss to be able to apply the only effectual remedy, an increase of salary, which should keep pace with the increase

[1] Sparks, *Writings of Washington,* vol. vii. p. 158. This was in August. In October he writes, " The army, if it is to depend upon State supplies, must disband or starve." *Ut sup.* p. 230. *Vide* also Rives's *Madison*, vol. i. pp. 227, 228. For illustration of the quality of supplies, *vide* Gordon, vol. iii. p. 495, note. And for a defense of the system, a letter of J. Armstrong to Washington, January 12, 1780. — *Correspondence of the Revolution,* vol. ii. p. 377.

of depreciation. If we turn to the army, we shall find that in 1780, the pay of a Major-general would not hire an express rider, nor that of a Captain buy him a pair of shoes.[1] If we follow the inquiry into civil life, we are told that a hat cost four hundred dollars and a suit of clothes sixteen hundred.[2]

Discontented citizens and discontented soldiers were the inevitable consequences of this unnatural state of the currency. Citizens would ask, "What compensation have we for our goods and labor?" Soldiers would ask, "What have we with nakedness and starvation in the present, to guard us against nakedness and starvation in the future?" It is evident that with such means the task of a quartermaster-general must have been very difficult, and his relations to the army and to the public very painful.

When Greene took the office, every part of it, as we have already seen, was in the utmost confusion; the public stores wasted, articles essential to the comfort and protection of the troops scat-

---

[1] Marshall, vol. i. p. 357.

[2] *Life of Samuel Adams*, vol. iii. p. 51. *Vide* also for some details, Curwen's *Journal*, p. 234.

The depreciation for 1779, 1780, 1781 was : —

	1779.	1780.
Jan.,	7, 8, 9.	40, 45.
Feb.,	10.	45, 55.
March,	10, 11.	60, 65.
April,	$12\frac{1}{2}$, 14, 16, 22.	60.
May,	22, 24.	60.
June,	22, 20, 18.	60.
July	18, 19, 20.	60, 65.

	1179.	1780.
August,	26.	65, 75.
Sept.,	20, 28.	75.
October,	30.	75, 80.
Nov.,	32–45.	80, 100.
Dec.,	45, 38.	100.

For 1781.

Jan.,	100.
Feb.,	100, 120.
March,	120, 135.
April,	135, 200.
May,	200, 500.

On May 31, Continental **bills** ceased to circulate

tered along all the roads over which they had passed, debts accumulated, and accounts neglected. To meet the demands of his situation, he was compelled to make constant calls upon Congress and the Board of War for authority, for explanations, and for money. This dependence brought him into conflict with the second cause of his embarrassments, Congressional delays.

2. It was one of the chief misfortunes of the Congress of the Revolution that it was both a legislative and an executive body. The laws which it made as a whole it administered by committees and boards. The habits of careful examination and exhaustive discussion which were required for the making of a law, were fatally opposed to the habits of prompt decision and vigorous enforcement which were required for the execution of a law. The habit of discussion naturally became the predominant habit. Both Washington and Greene found it impossible to bring Congress to look at questions from the same point of view with themselves, the point of view of action; and hence month after month was lost in debate, where debate had no power to enlighten, but a fatal power to delay. Washington's letters are filled with humiliating illustrations of this truth. We find it constantly forcing itself upon attention in Greene's letters also.

3. Underlying all those causes and acting with a diffusive power through them all, was the want of an army enlisted for the war. I have already told how the necessity of preparing year by year

the materials by which the war of the year was to be carried on, was felt among the common soldiers by imperfect discipline; among the officers by the want of a personal knowledge of their men; in the finances by the annual calls for bounties, and the reckless waste and consumption of stores by militiamen and raw-recruits; in the health of the army by ignorance of camp life; and in the country by the periodical recurrence of difficulties which were constantly reviving doubts, appealing to selfish and ignoble passions, and undermining the moral sense of the community. To this cause also the letters of Washington and Greene bear constant witness.

4. And lastly, the great body of the people was tired of the war. The errors and dissensions of Congress had destroyed the confidence which that body had once inspired. The judicious veil of secrecy, which had given its early acts the appearance of unanimity, had been withdrawn, and men knew that almost every day bitter words were uttered and bitter feelings displayed in Independence Hall. Efforts which had seemed the natural tribute of a good citizen in the first year of the contest, seemed questionable sacrifices in the fourth. The enthusiasm which had once made them easy was gone; and although the conviction which still made them possible remained, it remained buried in depths hidden from the common eye, and untouched by common causes. A sudden invasion, like Knyphausen's invasion of New Jersey, called out an energy equally surprising to

friends and to foes.   But no sooner was the occasion passed than men relapsed into their torpidity, and supplies were as hard to procure, taxes as hard to collect, and the ranks of the regular army as hard to fill, as ever.   "We have now obtained military knowledge in an eminent degree," writes Duane to Washington in September, 1780, " we have internal resources and reputation abroad; we have a great and respectable ally; of what then are we destitute but vigor and confidence in government, and public spirit in individuals?"[1]

The reader will remember how reluctantly Greene had accepted the office of quartermaster-general, and how burdensome he had found its duties through 1778 and 1779.   There was not a day in either of these years on which he would not have gladly transferred his commission to any one whom Washington would have accepted in his stead.   But the reasons which had originally led to his acceptance still existed in full force.   It was necessary that the man upon whose provident energy the power to subsist and move the army depended, should possess the full confidence of the Commander-in-chief.   And no one possessed Washington's confidence as Greene possessed it.

But as the winter of 1779 and 1780 wore on, it became evident that a change must be made in the powers of the Quartermaster-general, and in his relations to Congress.   The true position of the department was not understood, either by the people or by their rulers.   Men were ready to

[1] Sparks, *Correspondence of the Revolution*, vol. iii. p. 92.

complain that it was conducted upon a scale of
dangerous extravagance ; but they were not prepared to show that with prices at their actual scale,
and with a currency daily sinking in value, though
still unchanged in name, its necessary work could
be done for less.   Few indeed knew what the nature and extent of that work was ; that it embraced all " the details of the movements of troops,"
and all the details of encampment and quarters ;
that it extended to a thorough exploration of the
field of operations ; the opening and repairing of
all the roads on the line of advance and retreat ;
the choice of proper points for bridges ; the examination of fords ; the facilities afforded by the
country for obtaining the means of transportation
by land and water ; the extent to which it could
be counted upon for forage and supplies ; every
provision, indeed, which made it possible for an
army to march with ease, or to encamp with convenience and safety.   It should have been evident
to every thinking man that such duties could not
be performed long with such means.[1]

Various attempts were made by Congress to
correct the errors of their system.   As early as
November, 1778, it had been resolved in consequence of a letter from Greene, that

" *Whereas*, It has become necessary not only that speedy
and vigorous measures should be taken to regulate the
Commissary's and Quartermaster's departments but also
that a constant attention should be paid to those departments :

[1] *Vide* Macdougall's *Theory of War*, p..27,

" *Resolved*, That Mr. Scudder, Mr. G. Morris, and Mr. Whipple be a committee to superintend the same departments, and that they or any two of them, be empowered to take such steps relating to the same as they shall think most for the public service." [1]

In May, 1779, the Board of Treasury reported—

" That in their opinion it will be impracticable to carry on the war by paper emissions at the present enormous expenses of the Commissary-general's, Quartermaster-general's, and medical departments ; that it appears to them that a general opinion prevails that one cause of the alarming expense in these departments arises from allowing commissions to the numerous persons employed in purchasing for the army, and that a very general dissatisfaction has taken place on that account among the citizens of these United States ; and that in their opinion it is necessary to put these departments on a different footing with regard to the expenditure of public money.

" *Resolved*, That the same be referred to a committee of three, and that they be directed to report a plan for the purpose. The members chosen, Mr. Dickinson, Mr. Huntington, and Mr. Burke." [2]

On the 9th of July this committee brought in their report, and Congress resolved to " earnestly request . . . . the executive powers of each State to make the strictest inquiry into the conduct of every person within such State respectively employed, either in the Quartermaster-general's or purchasing or issuing Commissary-general's departments " in order to " remove or suspend . . . . in case of any kind of misbehavior or strong sus-

[1] Journals of Congress, Nov. 10, 1778. In August 1779, two other members, Mr. Root and Mr. Scudder, were added to the committee. Journals, August 17, 1779.

[2] Journals of Congress, May 28, 1779.

picion thereof," appoint new officers in their stead, and discharge such persons in the employment of those departments as they should "judge unnecessary."[1]

It was not by means like these that money was to be produced and credit restored. If there was some ground on the part of the people for objecting to compensation by commissions, there was at least equal ground on the part of the officers and men, for objecting to fixed pay in a constantly changing currency. Like all men who buy upon credit, the men who supplied the army had to pay for the privilege of deferring payment, for the bills and certificates which they gave in exchange for provisions and stores were little else than the acknowledgment of services performed. Whether that acknowledgment would ever be confirmed by actual payment in coin, was one of the elements of doubt which entered into the price and raised it so far above its natural standard. The striking of a few names from the list of officials was a very inadequate remedy for doubts confirmed by the daily depreciation of the currency, and which, springing from that diffusive source, had reached every walk of life and every class of society. This attempt also failed.

The next attempt was made in January, 1780, when it was resolved that "three commissioners, one of whom was to be a member of Congress," be appointed with ample powers to inquire into the condition of the staff, and with the approbation

---

[1] Journals of Congress, July 9, 1779.

of General Washington, introduce such reforms as they might deem necessary. Schuyler and Pickering were chosen on the 21st, and on the following day the number was completed by the addition of Mifflin. To Schuyler and Pickering no objection could be made, for their talents and information were beyond question, and their characters above reproach. But Mifflin's name looks strangely in this connection ; and when we recall his conduct as quartermaster-general in 1777, and his personal relations both to Washington and to Greene, it is impossible not to believe, with Greene, that the spirit of the " cabal " was not laid.

And thus another winter wore away and another campaign drew nigh, and no preparations were yet made. But in April Congress was startled into sudden action by a letter of Washington. " There never has been a stage of the war in which the dissatisfaction has been so general or alarming." And then, tracing the evil to its source, he added, " It were devoutly to be wished that a plan could be devised by which everything relating to the army could be conducted on a general principle under the direction of Congress." [1]

On hearing these grave words, the necessity of immediate action was acknowledged. " But how shall we act ? " A member moved " that a committee of three be appointed to proceed to head-quarters, to confer with the Commander-in-chief on the subject of his letter of the third instant, together with a report of the Board of War, and

[1] Sparks, *Writings of Washington*, vol. vii. pp. 13, 14.

the letter from Baron Steuben on the subject of a reduction of the regiments, and the report of the commissioners on the arrangement of the staff departments of the army." [1]

And here again we meet the spirit of the cabal face to face.

"Warm debates ensued," writes the French minister, M. de la Luzerne, to Count Vergennes. "It was said that this would be putting too much power in a few hands, and especially in those of the Commander-in-chief; that his influence was already too great; that even his virtues afforded motives for alarm; that the enthusiasm of the army, joined to the kind of dictatorship already confided to him, put Congress and the United States at his mercy; that it was not expedient to expose a man of the highest virtues to such temptations.

"It was then proposed that the committee should consist of one member from each State. This proposition also failed, on the ground that the operations of so large a number would be subject to all the delays which had been complained of in Congress. After a long and animated debate, the motion for a committee of three prevailed." [2]

Schuyler of New York,[3] Matthews of South Carolina, and Peabody of New Hampshire, were appointed. Matthews was known to have imbibed the most unfavorable opinion of Greene.

[1] Journals of Congress, April 6, 1780.

[2] MS. letter quoted by Sparks, *Writings of Washington*, vol. vii. p. 15.

[3] Schuyler had declined to serve on the commission for the staff departments, and shared fully Washington and Greene's interpretation of the appointment of Mifflin. *Vide* the letter to Washington already quoted, and a letter of March 22, to Greene.

Greene MSS. Upon Schuyler's refusal to sit upon the commission it was resolved," "That a committee of three be appointed to confer with the said commissioners, and with them devise the best ways and means of carrying their commission into effect; the members chosen, Mr. Sherman, Mr. Jones, and Mr. Schuyler." Journals, March 10, 1780.

Pickering and Mifflin were thanked in set terms for " their attention to the business committed to them, manifested in their plan for the arrangement of the staff department ; " and "informed that the remainder of the business referred to them must, from the necessity of adapting it to such plans as may finally be concluded on, be referred to the committee who are to proceed to head-quarters."[1]

This plan, according to Schuyler, was not the work of Pickering and Mifflin alone.

" Mifflin, Pickering, Jones, and General Sherman have furnished the first part of a voluminous system for the Quartermaster's department. The second part is to direct the Commissary-general of issues in the discharge of his duty, and the third will point at the regulations for the hospital. I do not mention the purchasing department, because that is to be abolished ; the States are to do all. As General Sherman roundly asserts, that system will strike off four thousand officers from the civil departments. As it is replete with absurdity it will pass into a law unless it should be thought proper to confer with the Commander-in-chief on the subject. There has been some wicked work respecting a certain appointment, which General Greene will advise you of verbally."[2]

" The new system I mentioned in my last," writes Greene to Washington on the 31st of March, "is yet undecided on. The more I view it the less I like it, and the stronger my conviction is that it is calculated not less to embarrass your Excellency than to disgrace and injure me. Mifflin and Pickering are gone to Reading ; and Mifflin

[1] Journals of Congress, April 14, 1780.

[2] Schuyler to Washington, April 5, 1780. *Correspondence of the Revolution*, vol. ii. p. 427.

has got the Massachusetts delegates into his house in town, upon very moderate terms and, it is said, with a view of strengthening himself in that quarter. Depend upon it, he has a scheme in concert with others.

"Public business is in a wretched train. All things at a stand ; and I don't believe the great departments of the army will be organized for a month to come unless the new system is adopted, which will starve and disband the army in half the time."

To this system the committee were instructed to "pay particular attention."[1]

They set themselves promptly to their task in an earnest and manly spirit. But the very first steps showed the necessity of Greene's coöperation.

"You did me the honor yesterday," Greene writes to them on the 3d of May, "to consult me upon the subject of the Quartermaster's department, and to ask my opinion respecting the most proper mode for accommodating it to the new plan for obtaining supplies for the army. I think it my duty to inform the committee that I cannot venture to offer my sentiments upon the matter until they have made such inquiry into the management and order of the business heretofore, as to enable them to judge whether it has been conducted properly or not. When the inquiry shall be made, and it shall be found that it has been conducted with as much economy and order as the nature of the business and the demands of the service would admit, and the committee shall satisfy Congress thereof, I shall most cheerfully give any assistance in my power for changing the present plan for conducting the business in every branch of the department where it shall be found necessary to accommodate it more effectually to the proposed plan for

[1] Instructions to the committee appointed to go to camp, No. 4. Journals of Congress, April 12, 1780.

obtaining supplies.   But if it shall be found that there have been those abuses prevailing in the department which have been represented, and that the reports have not originated from the arts of some and ignorance of others, delicacy would forbid the committee of either advising with or adopting the opinion of a person who had betrayed a want of capacity to arrange, or attention and industry to execute the business committed to his care.

"I pretend not to say that there may not have been instances of personal abuse of public trust, though I know of none; and upon every inquiry that has ever been made, they have been found to be the offspring of private spleen or public prejudice.   And I cannot help thinking that the public business of this department has been as faithfully and honestly executed as the nature of the service and the circumstances of the times would admit.   If my past conduct is not satisfactory both to Congress and the army, I should not have the least hopes of rendering it more so was I to serve the time over again ; nor do I choose to stem the current of prejudices any longer, or continue in an employment which is so ungrateful to my feelings."

To feel the full force of this letter, we must recall to mind what Greene had written to the President of Congress on the 12th of the preceding December : —

"It has been my wish for a long time to relinquish the office of Quartermaster-general.   This is the close of the second campaign since I engaged in the duties of this office, and I feel a degree of happiness in having it in my power to say with confidence that every military operation, whether in the main army or in any detachment, has been promoted and supported, as far as it depends upon this department.   The Commander-in-chief has given me the most ample testimony of his approbation ; [1] and the success

1 When Greene wrote this he had in his portfolio these words from

in every other quarter sufficiently evinces the ample provision that has been made.

" Having gone through the laborious duties of this employment successfully two campaigns, and having engaged originally in the business from necessity and not of choice, I am desirous of returning to the line of the army, which is more grateful to my feelings and consistent with my military pursuits. It has ever been· my study since I have been in the public service to serve my country in that capacity in which I could be most useful. And on these occasions I have frequently sacrificed my own private wishes to the calls of the public utility. It was well known to the Congress of that day in which I accepted my appointment, the necessity which urged a compliance, and the reluctance with which I agreed to hold the office. It was also well known to the committee of Congress who was delegated to negotiate this business that I claimed no extraordinary emoluments, but offered my services upon the same conditions on which they could engage my colleagues. I mention these things to show I took no advan-

Washington's pen : " You ask several questions respecting your conduct in your present department, your manner of entering it, and the services you have rendered. I remember that the proposal for your appointment originated with . the committee of arrangement, and was first suggested to me by them ; that in the conversations I had with you upon the subject, you appeared reluctantly to undertake the office, and in one of them offered to discharge the military duties of it without compensation for the space of a year; and I verily believe that a regard to the service, not pecuniary emolument, was the prevailing motive to your acceptance. In my opinion you have executed the trust with ability and fidelity.

" The services you have rendered the army have been important, and such as have gained my entire approbation, which I have not failed to express on more than one occasion to Congress, in strong and explicit terms. The sense of the army on this head, concurs, I believe, with mine. I think it not more than justice to you to say that I am persuaded you have uniformly exerted yourself to second my measures and our operations in general, in the most effectual manner which the public resources and the circumstances of the times would permit." Washington to Greene, 3d. September, 1799. Sparks, *Writings of Washington*, vol. vi. p. 337.

tage of the public necessity, or made the profits of office the conditions of my acceptance. I readily confess the appointment has been made somewhat flattering to my fortune; but in a very small proportion to what some people out of envy, through mistake, ignorance, or design, have represented. Though the perplexities incident to the business are infinitely superior to the benefits accompanying it, yet I do not mean to complain, nor do I wish further compensation. I am not desirous of leaving the department from a dislike to the term of service, but from the employment being injurious to my health, harassing to my mind, and opposed to my military pursuits. As interest was not the object which induced me first to accept the appointment, it would be my wish to resign, even if the emoluments could be made five times as large as they are, provided I could retire with the approbation of Congress, and without injuring the public service. These are the two only conditions which will determine my conduct in this affair; and it is on this account that I take this early opportunity at the close of the campaign, of laying my wishes before them."

He then enters into a minute exposition of the state and prospects of the department, calling the attention of Congress to the present difficulty and future danger.

"There are many things in holding this office," he says, "which wound my feelings as a military man; and many others in the execution thereof, from the complication of the business, which are perplexing and vexatious. But the principal source of all difficulties is the state of our money, the depreciation of which locks up almost every species of supplies, deprives us of the opportunities of making contracts or of gaining credit, and obliges us to employ innumerable agents to collect from the people what they would be glad to furnish was the representative of property upon a more stable footing. Here one evil arises out of another ; for (by) the great number of agents found necessary to procure the supplies for the army, the public expenditure is considerably increased, suitable agents more difficult to be got, and the detail of the business rendered more complex and subject to imposition. From this unfortunate circumstance great murmurings have prevailed, and innumerable inconveniences have arisen, suspicions of want of economy have crept in, and distrust and jealousies have prevailed on every side. The staff officers could only conduct the business by such means as they were provided with ; and the value of these depending so much upon opinion has given birth to great dissatisfaction from the different estimations which have prevailed at different times and in different places. The losses sustained by those individuals and the different districts which have been most forward to supply the public on credit and in the greatest plenty, have taught others to be more wary ; and this disposition has now grown to a most formidable height, not only among individuals, but in town, country, and even among most of the States, in all of which a spirit of competition prevails for the benefit of their own inhabitants which [is painful] to behold as well as destructive to the public interest ; and whenever the law of any State obliges the people to part with their property for the use of the army, the magistrates will not put it in execution unless the public agents are possessed of money to pay for the same. Had the currency any permanent footing or fixed value, such are the characters of many of the public agents, large supplies might be had upon their credit ; but the unsettled state of the money and the sufferings of those who have sold upon credit heretofore, as well as the heavy demands now against the department, leave us nothing further to hope from this source.

" In this distressing situation, without money and without credit, necessity obliges me to give Congress information, and to ask their advice what we are to do? Here is an expensive army to support, and the difficulty hourly increasing; besides, the preparations necessary for another campaign is fast approaching, while we are without the means either to defray the current expenses or discharge our past contracts, which are now very great, owing to the poverty of the treasury for some months past. And so dissatisfied are the people at being kept out of their money that they have begun to sue the public agents; the consequence of which will be an accumulated expense to the department, as well as a total loss of confidence in the public officers. So strict are the laws of some States, and so attentive are the magistrates to guard the people's property, that the forage officers have been prosecuted and heavily fined for presuming to take forage on the march of the army (to save the public cattle from starving) by virtue of a press-warrant granted by the Commander-in-chief."

After other important details, and the wish that Congress will take early measures to fill his place, he adds, that, —

" A new arrangement of the staff on salary is instantly required," for " so great has been their disgust and distress that it has been with the utmost difficulty and persuasion that they could be prevailed on to stay for this six months past, and nothing but personal influence and the fullest assurance that a more ample provision would be made for their support at the close of the campaign, has kept them in service. This is a matter of such importance, and the consequences of a delay so much to be dreaded, that I trust it will obtain the earliest notice. I shall be happy to give every information in this and all other regulations (which are not a few) that may be found necessary for the government of this department."

A letter like this, it might be supposed, would receive immediate attention. But on the 13th of January he writes again : —

" I did myself the honor to address Congress the 12th
ultimo on the subject of my resigning the Quartermaster's
department, as well as upon many other matters respecting
the same.   A whole month is now elapsed since I wrote,
and I have not been favored with a reply.   If I did not
conceive that the public interest suffers from a delay, I
should feel less anxiety upon the occasion ; but when I
view the alarming crisis to which things are drawing, and
the necessity there is of applying a remedy before the evil
becomes incurable, I cannot help pressing an answer.

" From the numerous complaints and the growing discontents of the agents in the departments, and the measures adopting by the different States which interfere with
the present system, it is indispensably necessary that some
new regulation should immediately take place to prevent
the business from running into confusion.

" I am sensible there are many weighty matters before
Congress, but the affairs of this department are so important, both to the public and the army, that I cannot help
thinking it claims their earliest attention."

The earliest attention given to the subject was
the appointment on the 20th of the commission
mentioned above, and on the 22d, of Mifflin as a
member of it.   To Greene's letter no answer was
returned.   He is still left in the dark, while embarrassments, faithfully detailed in his letters to
Washington, still thicken around him.   He turns
to another quarter for information, and on the 9th
of February writes to President Reed : —

" You was kind enough, when you was at camp, to
promise to give me full information what measures were
adopting by Congress respecting the Quartermaster's department.   I have been impatiently waiting the arrival of
a letter from you ; if there is no new objection to my receiv-

ing this necessary information through your means, you
will do me the favor of preserving your first intention, as
the intelligence you give can be more depended upon
than from any other quarter.

"I suppose you have seen the late extraordinary appointment of General Mifflin to superintend the staff department. This is the more extraordinary as he is still
under an impeachment for misconduct in this very business. If the institution is proper, some of the characters
to act under it are not so. It has the appearance, therefore, of a design rather to embarrass than facilitate the
public business. I cannot help thinking the Commander-
in-chief will feel himself hurt by this step, and consider it
as a new clog to encumber his military operations."

Reed answers on the 14th : —

"Your favor of the 9th instant is now before me. I
had neither forgot nor neglected my promise, when I had
the pleasure of seeing you, but was prevented by two
reasons ; first, that I really could not find out what was
doing at the civil head-quarters with sufficient certainty,
and secondly, that I expected you daily in town. I am
almost afraid to commit to paper my real and undisguised
sentiments on the present state of affairs with which you
are so specially connected. So many accidents have in
the course of this war happened from epistolary freedoms,
that I have grown very fearful of trusting anything in so
hazardous a channel. However, I will venture to tell you
that you have nothing to expect from public gratitude or
personal attention, and that you will do well to prepare
yourself at all points for events. General Mifflin's appointment to his present office, without including the heads of
the department, is a sufficient comment on my text, and by
your letter I find you understand it as I do. I have had
some experience of that body with whom your principal
concerns lay, and am clearly of opinion that more is to be

done by resolution and firmness, than temporizing. All public bodies seem to me to act in a manner which, if they were individuals, they would be kicked out of company for, and the higher they are the greater liberties they take. In my opinion you ought not to delay an explanation on your affairs; if a tub is wanted to the whale you are as likely to be it as any. A torrent of abuse was poured on Wadsworth, but that has all died away, as all ill-grounded and unjust calumny ever will. I think he was a valuable officer, and wish they may not feel his loss. Your particular situation will enable you to leave the department not only without discredit, but your station in the line will preserve a certain respect which in other circumstances might be wanting. Whoever is quartermaster this year must work, if not miracles, at least something very near it, for I verily believe there will not be shillings where pounds are wanted. In all my acquaintance of public affairs I never saw so complete a mystery; a vigorous campaign to be undertaken, an army of 35,000 men to be raised, fed, etc., and not one single step taken that I can learn which will raise our drooping credit, gratify the people, or conciliate a common confidence. A new arrangement of the army and reduction of the officers is now talked of with as much composure as if it was a common business. Little do they know the delicacy and difficulty of such a work. Nothing can rouse us from this lethargy but some signal stroke of the enemy; and I shall not be sorry to see them set about it, as I am persuaded we are sliding into ruin much faster than we ever rose from its borders. Whatever you do or resolve must be done soon or you will be plunged in another campaign without any possibility of retreat, and though the circumstance I have above alluded to is a favorable one, it is impossible to envy your situation; for whether you move or stand still, it may be improved to your disadvantage. If you quit, they will say that having made a large fortune you quit the department·

in distress when you could be of most service to your country. If you stand fast, you become responsible for measures and events morally impracticable. If an honorable retreat can be effected, it is beyond doubt your wisest and safest course; but I am not certain that this can be done even now, and every hour adds to the difficulty. Your department, as I have ever told Mr. Pettit, must bear some just censure for the appointments in this State, and they are now used as I expected they some day would be, to its prejudice. When such men as Hooper, Ross, Mitchell, etc., make display of fortune, it is impossible to help looking back, and equally impossible for a people soured by taxes and a continuance of the war, to help fretting ; and the general ill temper gives great latitude to thought and speech. When things go wrong, no matter where the wrong bias is given, every one concerned finds a pleasure in shifting the blame on his neighbor, or at least to divide it. 'It would never surprise me, therefore, to see a quartermaster or commissary-general made a political scapegoat, and carry off the sins, if not of the people, of those who represent them. Upon the whole I still retain my opinion of the propriety of your being here as soon as possible, and in the meantime, I can only inform you of two things with certainty. 1st. That the plan of the department will be altered as to commissions. 2d. That nothing but necessity will induce them to continue the present department, for though it may have a great deal of the utile it has little of the dulce on the palate of Congress. But you will be drilled on till the campaign opens, and if they cannot do better, they may keep you. In this as well as everything else much will be left to the chapter of accidents."

A letter of Mr. Pettit's, written the day after, gives a more favorable view of the intentions of Congress : —

" I have lately had some conversation with some members of Congress whom I esteem free from intrigue, and who, I believe, are our friends respecting your resignation, — the commissioners, etc. They seem to think that if Congress accept your resignation it will be merely to gratify your desires, but that they really wish you to continue, and so of your assistants ; that the commission was not intended to offend either you or the General, and they were told (when exceptions were made to a particular person) that some causes of exception had once existed, but that they were now entirely done away with, and that he would be acceptable and pleasing at head-quarters. As to the scheme of an entire change and bringing in Mr. D. as quartermaster-general, which Colonel Cox seemed confident was the case, they assured me that whatever individuals in the house or out of doors might have in view, such a scheme was not even thought of by the bulk of the members, and they thought Mr. D. was too well known among them to get above three votes."

But plausible as this interpretation seemed, Pettit did not accept it.

" You will have received before this reaches you," he writes in the same letter, " my opinion of your address to the General on the subject of public affairs, and in the undisguised manner you desire, though written before you expressed such desire. I also acquiesce fully in the scheme for calling on our people for a settlement. I like the advertisement in substance, especially that part of it that points at changes already made, or expected to be made, in the modes of doing business ; and had you not a resignation lying before Congress, I should recommend that you make a remonstrance directly to them on the subject, telling them directly and plainly of the embarrassments they are laying on the business, and the impossibility of proceeding in it the way they are proceeding, and showing

the absolute necessity their servants are under of quitting
their stations if they mean to preserve either reputation or
property.   For my part I am sick of it ; I wish sincerely
to be quit of it, gather up my crumbs and live a quiet life.
I am trying to prepare for leaving the public service this
spring if I can do it without evident impropriety.   As to
the manner of doing it I agree with you that under present appearances, it is better to wait events, and rather
ground my conduct on the measures of Congress, than
give them ground from mine to do what might eventually
be hurtful to me.   If I see a plan formed that appears to
me feasible, and my assistance should be thought necessary
to carry it into execution, I will not forswear the service,
provided they make the terms decent and create no obstacles by appointing me improper associates ; but in my
present view of the matter I would seriously rather quit
altogether, as I see nothing but expedients and whimsical
experiments in the schemes likely to be adopted."

Nor, with his views of the manner in which
Congress treated that grave question of finance
on which the existence of the department depended, could he feel any strong hopes of an
adequate reform.

"Congress, I am told, have appointed another committee on finance.   But in all matters of this sort the
members themselves have such scattered and heterogeneous ideas that none of them can form a tolerable judgment beforehand what will be the result of any motion
or measure set on foot.   I have been duped a thousand
times by the intelligence I have received from Congress
on this subject, though it came from gentlemen who I
believe told me sincerely all they knew of the matter,
or at least told me the truth so far as they went.   When
necessity presses so hard that something or other *must* be
done, they will then, and not before, take some course by

way of temporary expedient, trusting as usual to accident for the rest." [1]

A Rhode Island delegate, John Collins, writes on the 22d, in nearly the same strain. "I have not heard any mention of your resignation since my return to Congress. Neither have I heard of any new arrangement in your department; neither do I think there will be any soon."

Congress still continuing silent, some of Greene's friends urged him to go to Philadelphia and try the effect of a personal application. He hesitated, and among his grounds of hesitation acknowledged that he feared such a step might be construed into a wish to retain his office.

"I must confess," Colonel Pettit writes on the 5th of

[1] In a letter of March 5th, 1780, Colonel Pettit writes : "Whether it be that the leading members of Congress as well as myself are otherwise too fully employed, or whether it be pride or jealousy (in which I include suspicion) or too much self-conceit, or from what other cause I cannot absolutely determine, but so is the fact, that there is not that free communication of sentiments and opinions between them and me which might be useful to both, and I am sure might be conducive to the public good. I have to several of them and at divers times intimated a desire of these conferences, but I have generally found such a shyness and supercilious contempt for out-of-doors opinions, and such evident marks of a suspicion of interested and sinister motives, that I have been discouraged from further advances." Greene MSS.

[2] This letter gives us also an interesting glimpse of the questions of foreign policy which at that time occupied public attention : "European news we have none; and as to peace I can only give you my opinion, which is we shall have no peace this year, and my reasons for it is Spain is not yet ready for a peace. They will conquer the Floridas and the eastern banks of the Mississippi, and will have to settle with Congress how far they shall extend east. This is only my opinion, and the idea I have of what Spain will claim. They undoubtedly will take special care to keep the United States from their Mexican dominions, and shut all the world but themselves out of the Bay of Mexico, and leave the Floridas and what they may obtain east of the Mississippi a wilderness, to prevent the United States from getting too near their strong box." Greene MSS.

March, " I do not think the objection you suggested entitled to much weight, as your whole conduct lately has and probably will manifest a real desire to quit the department whenever you can do it without injury to the public; they cannot, therefore, find any ground to charge you with intriguing to keep in in opposition to your professions. On the other hand I think you might the more readily bring the matter to a determination by being on the spot and conferring with the committee of Congress, and conversing in a friendly way with members without doors; and it is really high time that the plan for future business should be decidedly established." [1]

Greene's position daily became more embarassing, and injurious reports began to circulate freely under the influence of personal enmity in some quarters and misrepresentations in others.

"MORRISTOWN, *February* 29, 1780.

" To HIS EXCELLENCY GOVERNOR REED : —

" DEAR SIR, — I thank you kindly for your letter of the 14th. It was my intention at the time you left camp to have been in Philadelphia before this, but Colonel Cox on his arrival there wrote me word that a new system was certainly fixed upon and new agents to fill it, which was all I wished for, as that would give me a fair opening to retire without censure; and should I go to Philadelphia I might be suspected of coming with a view of soliciting a continuance. As nothing was farther from my thoughts, so I was unwilling to give ground for the suspicion. You are perfectly right in your sentiments that I have nothing to expect from public gratitude; and I am the more convinced of this from what I have seen in camp. For if individuals can so easily forget their former distress and personal obligations, it is no wonder that changeable bodies ignorant of the circumstances should be ungrateful. I am

---

[1] Greene MSS.

placed in a delicate situation, and must move with great circumspection. Honest intentions and faithful services are but a poor shield against the secret machinations of men without principle, honor, or honesty; and therefore I have but little consolation for having served the public with fidelity, or little security from persecution from that consideration. But I will ever have an approving conscience, if I am not blessed with an applauding country. The one depends upon my own conduct, the other upon accidents.

" The advice of a friend in an hour of difficulty is worth a kingdom in a critical situation. I am more obliged to you therefore for your information and sentiments of the course I ought to pursue. But from Colonel Cox's positive manner of writing, I thought I should rather expose myself than serve the department if I went to Philadelphia. However, from letters I have since received from members of Congress whose interest it is not to deceive me, I am apt to think your advice was salutary. I shall wait a few days longer, and if nothing turns up that forbids my coming forward, I am rather inclined to think I shall set out for the city.

" I have been expecting the commissioners for superintending the staff for a fortnight past; this was one objection to leaving camp, lest I should be suspected of avoiding an inquiry. General Schuyler is expected in town this week. Perhaps the other commissioners mean to meet him here. I have had little conversation with the Commander-in-chief upon Mifflin's being appointed, but sufficent to convince me he is not pleased with the compliment.[1]

" Colonel Butler wrote me a few days since from Carlisle, that it was currently reported there that I had refused to serve in the Quartermaster's department any longer unless the Congress would give me three thousand guineas

---

[1] *Vide* letter from Colonel Pettit, February 16, 1780. — Greene MSS.

a year. I suppose this is the beginning of Mifflin's super-intendence, and I dare say the whole of his conduct will tend to embarrass the service and blacken characters.

" The king's speech and the debates in the British Par-liament has arrived, and seem to confirm what you con-jectured, that there would be another campaign. How are we to carry it on? We are without money, credit, or means of obtaining one or the other. Never was a nation in such a situation; and yet I am told Congress thinks all things are going smooth and easy. It is astonishing how they can be so indifferent to the approaching crisis; for a convulsion there must and will be in their affairs.

" We have opened an assembly at camp. From this apparent ease, I suppose it is thought we must be in happy circumstances. I wish it was so, but alas it is not. Our provisions are in a manner gone; we have not a ton of hay at command, nor magazines to draw from. The peo-ple that have the public horses to winter demand immedi-ate payment for the time past, and refuse to keep them any longer without it. If they persist, as I expect they will, I see nothing but we shall be obliged to sell the pub-lic cattle to keep them from starving. The inhabitants will not trust as they have done, while depreciation contin-ues to rage.

" Money is extreme scarce, and worth little when we get it. We have been so poor in camp for a fortnight that we could not forward the public dispatches for want of cash to support the expresses. Has this the appearance of a vigorous campaign?

" Colonel Biddle is now gone to Trenton, by order of the General, to represent to the Assembly the alarming sit-uation we are in with respect to forage.

" The new system recommended by Congress I fear will not be productive of all the good consequences ex-pected from it. On the contrary, I fear it will introduce much disorder and numerous complaints.

" I thank you kindly for your congratulations upon the increase of my family. Mrs. Greene joins me in kind compliments to you and Mrs. Reed.

" I am, with esteem and affection,

" Your most obedient humble servant,

" NATH. GREENE."

While Greene was still deliberating, he received a letter from Schuyler, which confirmed his views of the intentions of Congress. It was evident that no immediate answer to his letter on resignation was to be expected, although a draft of an answer had been reported, and the intention of requesting him to withdraw his resignation avowed. But this draft had been referred to the commission, and when they would act upon it it was impossible to foresee. He resolved, therefore, though with great reluctance, to try what personal representations would do.

" I shall set out early in the morning for Philadelphia," he writes to Washington on the 22d of March, " but can plainly see little is to be expected from it, unless it is dismissing myself from the department, which I devoutly wish, as well from what I discover from General Schuyler's letter to your Excellency, and from what he relates to Dr. Cochran.

" I am very confident there is a party business going on again, and as Mifflin is connected with it, doubt nothing of its being a renewal of the old scheme ; and the measures now taking is to be prepared to take advantage of any opening the distresses of the army may introduce. I wish I may be mistaken, but symptoms strongly indicate such a disposition.

" From the present temper of Congress I don't think it will be worth while to mention the matter of wagons, as there is not the least probability of obtaining an order for the purpose ; and if I should I have not the means to execute the business.

" I propose to take Colonel Biddle to Philadelphia with me, that a clear, full, and particular representation may be made of every branch of the Quartermaster's department, and the whole be brought to a speedy issue."

These lines were written on Thursday evening. On Wednesday the 28th he wrote to Washington from Philadelphia : —

" I got into town on Saturday night, but too late to do any business.   On Sunday nothing was to be done.   Yesterday I had a conference with a committee of Congress.   The public is insolvent to all intents and purposes.   The treasury is without money, and the Congress are without credit. There seems to be so many difficulties laid in the way of settling accounts, that people begin to be afraid to extend their credit who are in office.   I can see no opening through which the supplies for taking the field are to be obtained.

" The best people who are in Congress think the new system for drawing supplies from the States, will be found totally incompetent to the business.

" There is a new arrangement of the Quartermaster's department made by Mifflin and others, and now under consideration before Congress for adoption.   The scheme is too complex and tedious for such heavy and pressing demands as are frequently made on the department.   I am told it is to be confirmed without alteration.   General Schuyler and others think it will starve the army in ten days.   Some parts of it are the very alterations and plans I was mentioning to your Excellency.   It adds greatly to your Excellency's load of business and reduces the duties of the Quartermaster-general to almost nothing.   The Board of War are to appoint all officers except those serving with the army.   All payments with the army are to be drawn in detail by warrants and pass your Excellency's hands.

" General Schuyler and others consider it a plan of Mifflin's to injure your Excellency's operations.[1]

" Mr. Sherman and Mifflin are in close league in the business. I am now fully convinced of the reality of what I suggested to your Excellency before I came away. I shall take no hasty steps in the business of the Department, as I think myself in a disagreeable situation."

The days passed wearily and painfully at Philadelphia. His health was seriously impaired by anxiety and labor. On the 31st he wrote earnestly to President Reed upon the evils already caused, and the still greater evils to be feared, from the new law of the State which forbade the purchase of forage by the officers of the department. On one of these days, also, he enters for Washington into a minute examination of the law of Congress for supporting the army by specific supplies, pointing out its evils and dangers, and with what true perception and sound judgment, its total failure soon showed. On the same day in which he had written to Reed he writes again to Washington, going over the whole ground of the department, of Congress, and of the general state of public affairs. On the next day, in a long letter to Roger Sherman, he gives a full exposition of the principles upon which the system of transportation was founded; and in another confesses to Washington the impossibility of providing for the march of troops

[1] It is to this revival of the cabal that Lafayette alludes : " Cet esprit de parti fut tel, que trois ans après le Congrès s'en ressentait encore." *Mem.* vol. i. p. 37.

to the southward.   On the 3d, in another letter to
Washington, he returns briefly to the subject of
his difficulties, and says that in conversations with
members of Congress he has insisted upon the
necessity of sending a committee to head-quarters
to study and judge on the spot the questions at
which they were all halting with such injury to the
public service.[1]   And then addressing another full
and thoughtful letter to Congress, writes under a
separate cover : —

" Immediately on the close of the last campaign I communicated to Congress my inclination to decline the management of the Quartermaster's department, and at the
same time made a pretty full representation of some new
regulations necessary to take place for the well conducting
of the department.

" Several other letters to the same purpose were written in the course of the winter, all which remained unanswered until I set out for this city.   The business by this
had got so deranged, and the opening of the campaign so
near at hand, that his Excellency the Commander-in-chief
urged the necessity of my repairing immediately to Congress, and to endeavor to bring the several subject-matters
which had been laid before them respecting the department
to a full explanation and conclusion.

" On my arrival in this city I requested a conference
with a committee, to whom I communicated the injury
I felt by the late appointment of superintendents of the
staff departments ; and requested to know whether there
was the real want of confidence either in my integrity or
ability which those appointments but too strongly indicated, and urged this as a necessary step to a further
explanation.

[1] In a letter of the 14th May to James Duane, Washington enforces
the same idea.

" I have been waiting a whole week for an answer, but
as I find I am not likely to obtain one, and as I conceive
my attendance is no longer necessary here, I propose to
set out for camp the next day after to-morrow and there
await the issue of the business."

When this letter was read there were some who
felt the force of the grave and dignified remonstrance : —

" A resolution was proposed," Schuyler writes to Washington on the 5th of April, " that Congress had full confidence in his (Greene's) integrity and ability, and requesting his future exertions. This brought on much debate ;
amendments were moved, and the House got into heats ;
and an adjournment was deemed necessary to give the
members time to cool. A member, more zealous for the
General's reputation than prudent, observed that he was
an officer in whom the Commander-in-chief had the highest confidence ; that he was the first of all the subordinate
generals in point of military knowledge and ability ; that
in case of an accident happening to General Washington,
he would be the properest person to command the army ;
and that General Washington thought so too. Another observed that he had a very high opinion of General Greene's
military abilities ; that he believed the General had too ;
but that he believed no person on earth was authorized to
say as much as the words, above scored, implied.[1]

<hr>

[1] Colonel Pettit, on the authority
of Gen. J. M. Scott, writes to Greene
on the 18th of April : " A resolution
had been moved in Congress expressive of their high sense of the integrity
and abilities of the Quartermaster-
general, which was intended to plas-
ter the sore it was observed he felt on
the appointment of the late commissioners, which would have been carried had it not been conceived in too
high terms. It was observed in opposition that this would be a premature
contradiction of their own acts ; that
there were certainly wrongs in the
department somewhere, that was
too evident to be denied; that a
commission of inspection had been
appointed ; and to pass such a resolution before it was known where those
wrongs originated, whatever might
be the private opinion of each mem-

"I have entreated General Greene," Schuyler adds, "to remain a day or two longer in town, that I may be able to advise with him on the measures necessary to be pursued to prevent the ill consequences of his being driven to the necessity of a resignation, which, I conceive, would be an event much to be lamented, but in the present conjuncture, ruinous."

On the 5th Greene writes one more letter to Congress, proposing a method for settling the accounts of the department, in such a way as to meet the difficulties arising from the new method of supply. And then with strong feelings of dissatisfaction returns to Morristown. Of the difficulties that await him there, we find a faithful picture in a letter of the 17th to Washington : —

" The inclosed extract of a letter from Colonel Hooper, points out the difficulty of getting on the forage from Bucks County in Pennsylvania, on which we principally depend for the support of the cattle of this army.

ber, would in a manner be precluding further inquiry respecting the Quartermaster-general. The motion was therefore lost. However, he said, another motion would be made, declaring that Congress had not the least intention to impeach the conduct or character of the Quartermaster-general by that appointment, which he thought would be carried, and that it would be satisfactory to you. He argued that Congress, though a continually existing body, was composed of parts frequently changing, and that it behooved them to be exceedingly cautious in justifying an officer before full inquiry had been made into his conduct, however highly each individual of them might, in his private capacity, think of him. I agreed with him in that sentiment abstractedly considered; but told him I thought there was the stronger reason that they should also be exceedingly cautious that their public acts should not either directly or impliedly impute blame to an officer, especially one of high trust, before they had made such full inquiry into his conduct, and especially before they had made any at all. That setting aside his own feelings on such an occasion, it had a natural tendency to weaken and perhaps destroy his usefulness, and that having unwarily put an officer in so improper a situation, it were but justice to replace him on the ground he occupied before they shook his standing by any act of theirs." — Greene MSS.

" The Board of War have ordered the issue of provisions to cease at a number of posts where issues in the present state of things are unavoidably necessary. It is unfortunate that the stock of provisions is such as to stop all issues before a substitute is provided. We have not the power of saying let a thing be done and it is done; but we are obliged to pursue the ordinary modes by which men are influenced and business effected. To embarrass the affairs of transportation will as effectually ruin the army as if they were cut off from receiving provisions in the first instance, though by a more slow and less summary way. I believe there have been and still may be a great number of issuing posts that may be dispensed with; but before an order passes for stopping all issues at such places, time ought to be given to alter the channel of business, and inquiry made upon the spot whether greater injury will not arise from breaking up a post than continuing the issues.

" In the present case I would beg leave to suggest to your Excellency a remedy; that is, tell Mr. Wright, who has charge of the forage, to draw provisions from Trenton and deal it out to such persons as he finds necessary on the forage, and to such wagoners as are employed in the transportation, in both cases endeavoring to engage as many people to find their own provisions as possible.

" If your Excellency approves of this method, your order will be necessary to sanctify the measure; without this, or a similar expedient, I see no way we can get forward the forage."

" Last evening," says Hooper's letter to Greene, " I returned from Coryell's and MacCalla's. At Coryell's there is about five thousand bushels of oats and Indian corn, and at McCalla's three thousand bushels of oats, all of which I owe for. This grain can be sent on to you, but Mr. Wright says he cannot subsist the teamster and about six people that he must necessarily employ at that post, for the issuing commissary at Coryell's is dismissed. You'll please to give the necessary orders about the business."

" Order given to supply the provision," is Washington's endorsement on Greene's letter.

Under the same cover Greene had inclosed a letter from J. Bruen, major of artificers :—

" I have just received a note from Major Burnet (Greene's aid) requesting me to have a gallery built for the reception of the ambassador from France ; it is not in my power to do it for the want of boards. There is plenty in this county and not far from this, but they cannot be had without cash to purchase them."

On the 25th Greene writes to Reed :—

" My situation is peculiarly disagreeable, and I have a most delicate and critical part to act. If I force myself out of the department, and any great misfortune happens, no matter from what cause, it will be chargeable to my account. If I stay in it, and things go wrong, or any failure happens, I stand responsible. What to do or how to act I am at a loss. I think upon the whole your advice is prudent, and on the safer side of the question. And therefore I determine to seek all opportunities to get out of the business.[1]

" I feel myself so soured and hurt at the ungenerous as well as illiberal treatment of Congress and the different Boards, that it will be impossible for me to do business with them with proper temper, and besides I have lost all confidence in the rectitude and justice of their intentions. The Board of Treasury have written me one of the most insulting letters I have ever received either from a public or a private hand. I shall write them as tart an answer, and as I expect it will bring on a quarrel, I shall have oc-

[1] Reed had written him on the 17th of April : " No compensation you can expect to receive is or will be adequate to your labor and responsibility. And as to honorable notice and attention, which is the soldier's reward, a quartermaster is not to expect it, be his sacrifices what they may. My sincere and earnest advice, therefore, is to quit; seek the occasion if it does not present itself." — Greene MSS.

casion to call upon you and others to certify the manner of my engaging in this business, the circumstances it was under, and all other matters that may be necessary to give the public a proper idea of the part I have acted should I be obliged to publish anything in my own justification. Nothing will be more disagreeable to me, but necessity may drive me to it.

"With respect to the committee that is coming up I fear more is expected from them than they will be able to perform. I think, however, they ought to have been men intimately acquainted with the great seat of the business."

CHAPTER X.

IT could hardly be expected that whatever Greene's feelings toward the members of the committee might be, he should be willing to act with them as the representatives of a Congress which had treated him with injustice and indignity, without some assurance that the injustice and indignity were not the deliberate expression of their sentiments. But the moment was critical, delay had been extended to a perilous extreme, prompt decision and prompt action were demanded. The committee, after carefully considering his letter of the 3d of May,[1] replied on the 5th : —

"Your favor of the 3d instant has been received and claimed our serious attention.

"It is the wish as well as the inclination of this committee to give you every satisfaction as far as their power extends. But to undertake an investigation into the state and conduct of your department at this moment, the business being of so diffuse and complex a nature, we conceive would be highly inconsistent with the public welfare,

[1] *Vide.* p. 258.

as the consequent delay attending such an inquiry would evidently tend to defeat the great object we have primarily in view, — the immediate supply of the army.

"We feel great anxiety, sir, at your seeming determination not to enter into business with us until such inquiry shall have been previously made. We cannot, however, but flatter ourselves, that on mature reflection, taking in view the great object by us alluded to, on the immediate execution of which you well know so much depends, you will waive the application, and with that zeal and alacrity which have hitherto distinguished you in the service of your country, afford that aid which your abilities and experience enable you so effectually to give, and which we had in charge from Congress to require of you."

But Greene's feelings had been too deeply wounded to admit of his accepting this interpretation without a remonstrance, and his judgment confirmed the suggestions of his feelings : —

"Your favor of yesterday in answer to mine of the 3d has been received.

"I am very sorry to find the committee averse to making an inquiry into the order and arrangement of the Quartermaster's department ; nor can I conceive how they can execute their commission without it. On what ground can they make any alterations to confirm any part of the present plan without such an investigation ? I did not expect the committee to go into the details of the business, but to examine the plan and general principles upon which it has been conducted, and see how far the service has been supported. Nor do I wish or desire that this should operate to exculpate any person from any misconduct, or to prevent any after inquiry which Government may think proper to make into the conduct of all or any part of the staff officers in the Quartermaster's department. I mean that the committee should satisfy themselves with respect to the great lines of the business and the general conduct of the principal agents, and if they find them just and proper to report accordingly to Congress, that every improper suspicion that may operate to the prejudice of the public service may be removed. My own honor obliges me to insist upon this; and I believe the committee will ágree with me in sentiment when they read the inclosed copy of my letter to Congress and also one from the Board of Treasury to me.

" If my further services are wanted by the public in the Quartermaster's department, I conceive it highly reasonable and absolutely necessary to remove every shadow of imputation which may affect my character or standing with Congress. Nor will I agree to conduct the business where so much is left to be governed by discretion, unless there is the most unlimited confidence in my integrity and ability. Neither will I serve under the direction of any other superintending Board than that of the Board of War, unless they belong to Congress.

" I shall be always happy to render the public every service in my power either with or without reward more than a necessary support, though my fortune is small and a growing family dependent upon me, when I can do it not subject to personal indignity or to certain loss of reputation. Under such circumstances I hope it will not be expected that I either accept or continue in an employment.

" I am afraid the public will feel the bad effects of that policy which has been directed to excite jealousy and distrust in the people respecting the civil staff of the army. One indiscriminate load of censure has been poured out upon every order without regard to their merit or services, or without fixing a single crime upon an individual. The business has been rendered by this policy so odious that every man is determined to quit it, and could they be prevailed on to continue, a great part of their usefulness is lost for the want of a proper confidence of the people. Neither do I see but very little prospect of engaging others in so disagreeable an employment in which those who have gone before him have been treated more like galley-slaves and public pickpockets than faithful agents."

Disagreeable as in many respects Greene's situation was, it was still a very strong one. He had neglected no duty toward Congress. When accused by implication, he had courted prompt and full investigation. He was esteemed and respected by the army, and enjoyed the full confidence of the Commander-in-chief. As soon, therefore, as he became convinced that the committee were sincerely anxious to begin the work of reform, he began to give them a sincere and strenuous coöperation. His personal relations with the members soon became intimate. Schuyler he had long known and esteemed, and he consulted him with confidence in his sincerity and reliance upon his judgment. What his early relations to Peabody had been I have no means of knowing, but from this time forward they became intimate and confidential. Matthews, as I have already said, had brought with him to camp the prejudices of the hostile faction in Congress. But when he found himself in daily relations with Greene, saw his independence, earnestness, exact and accurate information, sound judgment, prompt decision and untiring industry; saw too how the army loved him, how his brother officers respected him, and how constantly and confidingly Washington leaned upon him, he laid his prejudices aside, and became Greene's firm and zealous friend.

While Greene was forming these pleasant relations with the committee of Congress, and both were exerting themselves to bring the general system of the staff into a form better adapted to the demands of the service and the condition of the country, he received a letter from the Treasury Board, calling for his accounts in terms which implied insulting suspicions of his integrity. It was some time before he could command himself enough to reply, and then before he sent his answer, he communicated it to Hamilton with a request for his advice.

" When you ask my advice as a friend," writes that wise and sincere one, " I must always act the part of a true friend, however frequently the advice I give may happen to clash with your feelings, justly irritated by injuries you have not merited. Considering the Board of Treasury as so many individuals, the complexion of their letter to you would abundantly justify the asperity of your reply; but considering them as a public body, one of the first in the State, policy pronounces it to be too great. We are entered deeply into a contest upon which our all depends. We must endeavor to rub through it sometimes even at the expense of our feelings. The treasury will always be essential to your department. The board conducting it will necessarily have no small influence. You may continue at the head of the department. I should think it imprudent to push differences to extremity, or to convert the airs of official consequence and the temporary work of popular prejudice into rooted personal resentment. This appears to me to be the tendency of the present letter. The Board, from the necessity of our affairs, may sue for peace, but they will hate you for the humiliation you bring upon them, and they may have it in their power to embarrass your operations.

"I would have you show a sensibility of injury, but I would wish you to do it in milder terms." [1]

"I thank you kindly for your candid reply," Greene answers on the same day, "I confess myself unable to write a milder letter upon this subject than this I send you. My feelings are so irritated that the moment I begin to write my passions take the lead in the sentiment and mingle in such a manner as you see by my composition. I strove as much as ever mortal did to keep down my resentment, but I found it impossible, and was in doubt with respect to the propriety of what I had written.

"I send you herewith the letter of the Treasury and my answer, and if you are at leisure and will write your sentiments upon the subject in the manner you think I ought to answer, keeping in mind the charge and insult, and that too tame submission will confirm them in the truth of the charge, I shall be much obliged to you. One thing more I would have you keep your eye upon, which is, I intend to get out of the department the moment I can do it without certain ruin to myself."

In June another question came to embitter his relations to the Treasury Board : —

"I do myself the honor," he writes to the President of Congress on the 19th of June, "to inclose to your Excellency copies of several letters which have passed between Mr. Pettit, one of my assistants, and the Treasury Board.

"The letters seem to be hinting at so strange, new, and unexpected a doctrine, that I think it requires some immediate explanation; they imply a responsibility in me, for the expenditure of public money by persons of my appointing, that neither law nor reason will warrant; and

[1] Greene MSS. Neither Hamilton's letter nor Greene's draft of his answer, has any but the file date, which makes Hamilton's the 16th of May, and Greene's the 15th. One of these is evidently wrong. Both were probably written on the same day.

such as neither the Committee of Congress, the Commander-in-chief, or myself ever had in contemplation at the time of my appointment.

" I never considered myself responsible for persons appointed in the different branches of the department any further than to show that the appointment was necessary, and that at the time it was made the person was deserving of the trust. I think it my duty to call every person to account for public money delivered him for the public service ; but if he should fail to give a satisfactory account, after I have used my best endeavors to effect it, the public must suffer the loss. This was my idea of the matter, nor did I think any other construction could be put upon it.

" A greater responsibility than this would deter any man from holding the office, or making a single appointment, however necessary for the public service. Nor could it be consistent with the public interest that there should be a greater responsibility, for if the principal was made responsible in the last resort, he would become interested in concealing frauds and misconduct instead of assisting in bringing delinquents to justice.

" I have ever considered the office of Quartermaster-general as a place of great trust, with latitude to act at discretion for the interest of the public ; and that he stands between the subordinate agents and the public ; not accountable for their conduct but to judge of it as the only person having that intimate acquaintance with the nature and circumstances of the business which can make him capable of determining rightly between them and the public.

" I always supposed the appointment of a subordinate officer was given to the principal not with a view of creating greater responsibility in him, but to establish a necessary dependence and to give despatch to business. The power of appointing is essential to the public interest in every point of view.

"Somebody must make the appointments, and who is so proper as he who is to govern the business under the ties of honor and the solemnity of an oath, and subject to disgrace and the loss of reputation from improper appointments? As the Quartermaster-general derives no benefit from the appointment of subordinate officers, why then should he be made to suffer for their misconduct?

"No man can with safety to himself be subject to a greater degree of responsibility than that of calling the under-agents to account, but not to be accountable for them, nor would I hold the office a moment upon any other footing. What advantage could the public desire from a greater responsibility? It is true they might have it in their power to ruin an individual, but at the same time they make it that individual's interest and lay him under a sort of necessity to conceal as much as possible every abuse of public trust. If this is either just or necessary, I am a stranger to the laws of one or the reasons of the other.

"The very nature of the trust reposed in the Quartermaster-general requires the greatest confidence, and government should be very careful not to lodge the power where they have not the confidence.

"I pretend not to great abilities, nor was it my wish to have engaged in the business of this department; on the contrary, I did everything in my power to excuse myself, but the Committee of Congress and the Commander-in-chief would not be refused. I have done my best to serve the public, and notwithstanding popular clamor and vulgar prejudices it will be found by after experience that the public business has generally been both faithfully and prudently conducted. If I have ever betrayed my trust let me suffer.

"The demands of the service, like the wants of human nature, cannot be dispensed with, and can only be known by experience and observation. Neither law nor systems can change the nature of business. Orders may bind men but cannot alter the nature of things. The best way of guarding against public impositions is to employ only men of principle and virtue and reward them generously for their service. From such you have a right to expect fidelity, and are rarely ever deceived.

"The Treasury Board appears in a great measure strangers to the nature of this business. Their ideas of keeping accounts and making returns are totally inadmissible. Could the affairs of the department be conducted like the plain business of a common storekeeper, their orders might be reduced to practice; but a business so various and extended, subject to so many accidents, obliged to be executed in the midst of hurry and confusion, and the proper agents properly instructed in all the forms of business difficult to be got, nay, impossible to be found; the orders of the Board can never be reduced to practice, nor would the Board think of such a measure had they an opportunity to see the business in its true point of light.

"It is vain to impose conditions that cannot be complied with; the business must stop or the orders be disregarded. The first is ruinous to the public, the last may be to the agents. I wish to do everything in my power to give the Board and the public every satisfaction that the nature of the business will admit; but it is not in my power to change the great governing principles of it, and to attempt it will only bring ruin on myself and distress upon my country.

"The duties of this office are very complex, extensive, and extremely disagreeable in the best state of things, from the great variety of tempers, characters, and applications attending it; but when these are multiplied by improper restriction, accompanied with orders from different boards, which in the nature of things cannot be conformed to, the business becomes intolerable, nor do I choose to contend with such a complication of difficulties.

"I hold the office of Quartermaster-general not of

choice but with a view of obliging the public, and I cannot
think of exposing myself to so many unnecessary embarrassments and mortifications as beset me in my present
standing.

"I beg Congress to give me their sense of the matter,
without which I cannot proceed further in the business."

These just reclamations did not fall on willing
ears. Two members of the Board were also members of Congress, and it could hardly be expected
that they would listen silently as delegates, to this
strong condemnation of their acts as commissioners. Of the debates that arose we have no record.
Greene's letter was referred to a committee of three,
composed of Ellsworth, Duane, and Madison. They
reported on the 24th of July, confirming the decision of the Board, with the softening but unsatisfactory clause, that when "abuses and frauds"
occurred in spite of the "customary precautions"
they would determine on the circumstances as they
arise and make such favorable allowances as circumstances may require."[1]   It is not probable
that Greene would have consented to continue in
so unwelcome an office with such a sword of Dam-
ocles constantly suspended over his head. But
when the resolution of the 24th reached him his
letter of resignation was already written.

The committee, as I have said, had promptly set
themselves to their task. Their first consultations
with Washington and Greene had convinced them
of the necessity of forming a thorough system for
the staff, without confining themselves to the plan

---

[1] Journals, July 24, 1780.

proposed by the commissioners, and which the instructions of Congress authorized them to "adopt, amend, or alter," as they might think best.[1] The details of their progress are not known, but about the middle of June Schuyler repaired to Congress to lay the result of their labors before that body and consult them upon the subject. But while

[1] Instructions, Art. 4. Journals, April 12, 1780. Of the Treasury Board Pettit writes, July 28 : —

"I have reason to believe the Treasury Board are tottering. They have attempted to spin their thread finer than they had skill to manage it. They have singed their wings, and will either fall to the ground or pitch to a more moderate height. It seems now to be the general opinion, that however necessary and proper the office may be, the men are not equal to it." —

He had already written on the 2d of July : "On my return I met your favor of the 29th June inclosing copies of your letter to Congress and of that to the Board of Treasury. The latter appears to have been written with less leisure than the former, though substantially good. Indeed, I like the substance of both; they contain excellent observations, and will probably bring about useful reflections. I wish the great men to whom they are addressed had sufficient knowledge of the business to give those observations the proper effect. I had before heard of your letter to Congress, which has been a subject of debate. The point of responsibility has raised a question which has its partisans on both sides and divers corps de reserve, which wait for further information. It is a question I could wish there had been no occasion for agitating, as I have great hopes there will be no occasion for its application; but since so much occasion has been given for suspecting an improper intention, I am glad you have thus put it in motion. The Board I expect will bounce on the occasion, but they have in other instances so overdone their part that they would not be destitute of opponents if we were silenced. Even their own household (the chambers of accounts) are at war with them and have appealed to Congress on some points of punctilio as well as on some more substantial. They have given cause of complaint to so many people, that some from one attachment and some from another, the members of Congress have pretty generally let in an idea that they are not perfectly right in all things, and you know that when once men cease to believe the Pope infallible they are apt to cease to be papists. It has been my hope from the beginning of our difference that they would overshoot their mark. I have seen it working for some time, and believe I have before hinted it to you. My fear is now that either from a cringing disposition, or the advice of some of their friends, they may grow more prudent as to other matters so as to regain influence enough to keep us under their clutches." — Greene MSS.

he and his colleagues were elaborating one plan, Congress was equally busy with another ; and how such a course could be reconciled with custom or duty it is difficult to see. The duty of Congress was plain. If the committee was not competent to the service required of it, it should have been instantly recalled. If competent it should have been left free to follow its instructions and do its work. But Congress followed neither of these obvious courses. They had twice refused to call Washington and Greene to Philadelphia for consultation.[1] They still continued to spend "their time in debate, or small matters of form to the neglect of the substance."[2] And in this instance going still farther they seem to have taken an unworthy pleasure in counteracting the endeavors of their own agents. Schuyler returned to camp, and the committee, receiving no intimation that they were no longer expected to do the work which had been entrusted to them, continued their labors with zeal, and in daily consultation with Washington and Greene.

Another important part of their duty was to assist the Commander-in-chief and the Quartermaster-general in preparing the means for coöperation with the French fleet and army which were daily expected on the coast. Greene, whose experience led him to look with doubt upon the measure, wrote to Washington on the 23d of May : —

"I have had a long conversation with General Schuyler

---

[1] Schuyler to Greene, March 22, 1780.

[2] McDougal to Greene, 29th May, 1780.

this morning, and have seen the powers and appointments upon the present business entrusted to the direction of the committee, as well as their powers to act under. From all which I am fully of opinion, that the plan is altogether incompetent to the purpose and end proposed. Time will not permit me to enter into the detail of objections, nor perhaps would their force appear in the same point of light to another, who has less experience in the difficulties attending the business than I have.

" It is my opinion that your Excellency ought to ask the decided opinion of the committee in writing, whether they think their powers are competent to the business expected of them. If they say not, as I am sure they must, then I would require of them the powers and the plan they conceive necessary to support the enterprise; the whole of which I would state to Congress, supported with my own sentiments, as well with respect to the defects of the present plan, as the plan necessary for the business. Nothing but some such decisive measure as this, will put the business on a proper footing. The measure will at least put your conduct in the fairest point of light. It will free the committee from their present embarrassments and place the laboring oar where it ought to be. If you undertake the business upon the present footing, and exercise powers beyond the present scheme, it will be asked why you did not ask for an enlargement of the committee's powers, if you deemed them inadequate. And if you engage and fail for want of support, it will be asked why you embarked in such a business, without being fully persuaded that the means were adequate to the end. In whatever point of view I consider the subject, I see the greatest propriety in your Excellency's stating to the committee this quere, whether it is their opinion they can give you such support as will warrant your engaging in a coöperation with the French forces for the redemption of New York.

"I have just seen Colonel Hamilton, who says your Excellency desires my opinion upon the position the fleet off the Hook ought to take, upon the supposition it is a French fleet, and come with a view of coöperating with us. It is my opinion if your Excellency intends to support the expedition against New York at all events, without regard to the powers or plan laid down by Congress, (if that should fail or appear inadequate to the end,) then the fleet and forces ought to be immediately brought into the Hook, and the troops landed upon Staten Island, where our army ought to reinforce them at the same instant of time. But if your Excellency is determined to depend upon civil government for support altogether, without any exertions of your own, and you think the present plan and powers of the committee defective, it is my advice to let the fleet and forces go into Rhode Island; unless you should think it advisable to put one thousand or fifteen hundred men on board and push on the fleet, without loss of time, to the southward.

" To bring the fleet into the Hook without having taken some decisive resolution upon the line of conduct you mean to pursue, may tend to embarrass you and injure our ally. We ought carefully to avoid bringing our friends into distress and disgrace, if we cannot avail ourselves of the benefit intended us.

" I shall be at head-quarters, in a few minutes, and will give your Excellency my further sentiments on the matter."

Greene's private feelings at this time are strongly expressed in a letter of June 29th to his cousin, Griffin Greene : —

"I beg you to write to me by every opportunity, as nothing is more agreeable than domestic matters in this bustle of life. You cannot imagine what pleasures letters from our friends afford. You are at home among all your connections, and think less of us who are absent, than we of you. You are happy in your circle, we are not so, and, therefore, want something to entertain us. No pleasure is equal to domestic happiness. This mode of life is living for ourselves, every other is living for other people. I wish the war was over, that I might return to my dear fireside. I can say with Solomon, ' all is vanity and vexation of spirit.' The world is full of folly, superstition, and ignorance, and overrun with malice, prejudices, and detraction. Good intentions are no security against abuse, especially when ambition is to be gratified by prostituting honor and justice. Little did I think when I first engaged in the public service, it was such a slippery, thorny path. My heart was honestly devoted to the public interest, and I expected to feel myself rewarded according to the merit of my actions. But what a novice did I find myself. The black passion of jealousy, and the cankering spirit of envy, had well-nigh worked my overthrow, before I had the least idea that I had an enemy in the world. I was an enemy to no man, and could not see why they should be to me. But so it was, and so it will be to the end of the world, in political life.

Meanwhile Congress was busy with the new system.

" The system for the Quartermaster's department," Pettit writes from Philadelphia on the 2d of July," has been under consideration. I am told it is the idea of Congress that it is only intended as a temporary business for the residue of this campaign, and therefore they do not see the necessity of two additional assistants. Neither, indeed, do I if that is to be the case ; but I had imagined this plan looked forward to the end of the war. One great complaint against the system is that it is too long, and the members cannot understand it ; and yet General Cornell tells me five or six pages have been lately added to it . . . .

I am told they have agreed to allow the Quartermaster-general and his assistants 166 dollars each per month, so that you may look on your fortune as made."

But during the next twenty-four hours a change took place in his sentiments, and he writes on the 3d : —

" This plan of Congress appears to me much better than I had expected. . . . The inferior objections to it are fewer than I had supposed would arise in my mind, and such as might perhaps be removed without great difficulty if the department were well supported with money."

Still nothing definite, had been decided upon, even ten days later.

" A few days since," Pettit writes on the 13th, " General Cornell dined with me, when he showed me a plan comprised in fewer words than are already in this letter, which he told me would probably be substituted in lieu of the system. As well as I remember — for I read it hastily in the midst of conversation, — it leaves the whole arrangement to the Quartermaster-general. He is to be responsible for the appointments he makes, that is, that they are men of sufficient abilities and character, and for the orders he gives them ; they to be answerable for the execution of the orders they receive. . . . ."

And returning to the subject in the same letter, he adds : —

" A day or two ago a member of Congress wrote me a note as a friend, requesting my opinion of the draught shown me by General Cornell, and that I should communicate any plan I might have in my thoughts. . . . The gentleman also asked what sum would be satisfactory to you, in answer to which I gave him the following paragraph.

" ' With respect to the sum that would be satisfactory to
General Greene as Quartermaster-general, I cannot pretend to ascertain it.   Were he looking to this office as
one he would wish to continue in, I have reason to believe
he would not accept of less than £5,000 currency per
annum, and perhaps he might demand £3,000 sterling ; but
as I am confident he now continues in from other motives
than a view of gain, and wishes to leave it whenever he
can consistently with the public good and his own honor,
I believe he will neither demand nor accept of more than
an indemnification for his expenses.   I ground this opinion
as well on what I have heard him say on the subject as on
my own feelings, being actuated by the same motives as to
continuance in office as I suppose him to be.   Whether
he means to admit the pay he receives as Major-general
as a deduction or not, I cannot say, but I should suppose
that ought not to be the case.' "

The substitute was not accepted.   A member
of Congress writes him on the 21st : —

" The system for the Quartermaster's department I
mentioned in my last, metamorphosed as it is, passed Congress a few days since, and is ordered to take place immediately.   As it is now in the press and will be sent you,
I shall say no more on that subject."

The same letter gives us a glimpse of the in-
terior of Congress Hall, which, at this moment, we
greatly need : —

" Mr. Elsworth, who is gone home to Connecticut, was
your fast friend and his country's friend.   Mr. Sherman —
he is full in the faith that no more expense ought to be
created, than the people will annually pay by taxes.   Yet
I believe you may set the State of Connecticut down as
your friend, if that can be determined by the majority of
their delegates.   Mr. Ingersoll hath prejudiced me much

in his favor; he appears at all times to be governed by principles of the strictest honor and justice. Mr. Matlack is a strange mortal for a man of sense. I never know one day where to find him the next. He hath a great notion of being a courtier; perhaps in some countries he would appear a coarse courtier. As for Livingston, Scott, and Duane, they were for curtailing every salary fixed in the Quartermaster's system; they have something in view; what I am not certain; they make me think of the snake in the grass. It is often thrown out in Congress as a burlesque, that who can ask such and such things of you when you had the modesty to write Congress you would serve them for three thousand a year sterling. Perhaps more of this in my next.

"Congress are very sanguine in their expectations on the intended offensive operations. It is not popular even to suppose a miscarriage, in case any unforeseen accident should happen, much less to mention any of those difficulties that at present to me appear almost insurmountable.

"Congress in general appear exceeding easy in the present situation of affairs. There doth not appear the most distant wish for more powers, but rather on the contrary, a wish to see their States without control (as the term is) free, sovereign, and independent. If anything appears difficult in regard to supply, etc., what can we do? Why, we can do nothing; the States must exert themselves; if they will not, they must suffer the consequences.

"For my own part I have been exceedingly disappointed in my expectations in regard to Congress, and am still at a loss as to their motives and views, *if they have any.* There appears to be a languor that attends all our conduct, want of decision and spirited measures. The greatest part of our time is taken up in disputes about diction, commas, colons, consonants, vowels, etc. More in my next."[1]

[1] General Cornell to General Greene, Philadelphia, July 21, 1780. — Greene MSS.

For a full understanding of Greene's conduct at this time, we need a correct view of his relations to Congress; and such a view can only be obtained from a careful study of the opinions and character of that body. What some of their members and some who lived in daily intercourse with their members thought of them, we have already seen. I will add a few side lights from other sources. " Congress," writes Varnum, in March, 1780, — no longer a soldier, and in the December of this year about to become a member of the body he judges so severely : —

" Congress, I fully agree, seem totally inadequate to the great concerns of their appointment. When they demand the different contingents of men or money or other supplies, they do it in so formal, so indifferent, and so careless a manner, that the respective legislatures are led to imagine they intend only to be refused. The vigor of exertion ever lessens from the source to the remotest branches ; and if Congress only exhibits an empty parade, an imaginary, deceitful show, to obtain better terms of peace without expecting repeated campaigns, well may the States individually recline at ease, resolve to comply with their requisitions, and in resolving, resolve themselves into perfect nullity.

" This State have voted to furnish their quota of troops and proportion of supplies, and have opened the treasury. An airy phantom, the mere reverberation of a greater echo ! " [1]

The popular feeling towards Congress Mr. Madison has painted by a single touch : " Congress

[1] Varnum to Greene, 26 March, 1780. Greene MSS. Compare also among many others a letter of Joseph Jones to Washington, June 19, 1780. *Correspondence of the Revolution*, vol. ii. p. 476.

complaining of the extortion of the people : the people of the improvidence of Congress." [1]

In this Congress Greene had some firm friends and some bitter enemies.

Meanwhile summer was wearing away. Lafayette had arrived from France on the 27th of April, with the promise of a French army and a French fleet. After a careful examination, it had been decided to lay siege to New York. The decisive moment was come. Five thousand French soldiers, thoroughly disciplined and perfectly equipped, were ready to range themselves under Washington's command. Where were the stores and supplies and means of transportation of the Americans ? Greene had tendered his resignation in December. Congress had begun to take the condition of the department into consideration in January. July was half gone, and no decision had been reached. Washington could wait no longer.

"I have determined upon a plan of operations," he writes to Greene on the 14th of July, " for the reduction of the city and garrison of New York, which is to be pursued in conjunction with the French forces daily expected from France. The number of troops to be employed upon this occasion may be about forty thousand men. You are hereby directed, therefore, to make every arrangement and provision in your department for carrying the plan of operations into execution. You will apply to the States for what they are bound to furnish, agreeably to the several requisitions of Congress and their committee at camp. All such articles as the States are not bound to furnish, which will be necessary for conducting the operations, you will

[1] Madison to Jefferson, March 27, 1780. Rives' *Madison*, vol. i. p. 219.

provide ; and for this purpose you will apply to the Treasury Board for the requisite supplies of cash.

" I have been in anxious expectation that some plan would be determined upon for your department ; but as it has not hitherto taken place, and as it is impossible to delay its operations a moment longer, I have to desire that you will yourself arrange it in some effectual manner, to give dispatch and efficacy to your measures equal to the exigency. Your knowledge and experience in the business will be sufficient to direct your conduct without my going into more particular instructions. It is my wish that your provisions should be ample, as nothing is more fatal to military operations than a deficiency in the great departments of the army, and particularly in yours, which will be the hinge on which the whole enterprise must turn. The committee of Congress, in their applications to the States, have requested them to deliver the supplies raised at such places as the Quastermaster-general and the Commissary-general should point out for the articles in their respective departments. The committee informed me that they had given you and Colonel Blaine information on this head. But if anything remains to be done, you will immediately do it ; and I should be glad that you would see the Commissary, Mr. Blaine, if present ; if not, Mr. Stewart, to concert the arrangement with him.

" I am informed that there is at Albany a quantity of plank and timber sufficient for constructing about forty batteaux, which may be procured. If you have not a sufficiency of boats, you will endeavor to procure the above mentioned plank and timber. General Schuyler will give you more particular information." [1]

Greene's position was difficult. He had received no answer to his letter to Congress asking their view of the interpretation which the Treasury

[1] Sparks, *Writings of Washington*, vol. vii. p. 106.

Board had put upon his responsibility in appointments; and without some assurance upon this he felt that it would be unsafe to make them. If Congress delayed now as it had delayed heretofore, the coöperation and siege must fail. There was but one resource. The committee were the representatives of Congress, and in their pledge he could put trust.

"CAMP AT PRECANESS, 14*th July*, 1780.

"THE HONORABLE COMMITTEE OF CONGRESS: —

"GENTLEMEN, — I inclose you a copy of an order, No. —, received this day from the Commander-in-chief, directing me to arrange the Quartermaster-general's department, and to put everything in a proper train to enable him to coöperate with the French fleet, which arrived at Newport on the 10th of this instant.

"I should cheerfully comply with his Excellency's order, but the Treasury Board in their correspondence with Mr. Pettit upon the subject of accounts, Nos. 2, 3, 4, 5, 6, seem disposed to hold me responsible for persons of my appointing, in a very different manner from which I ever conceived myself bound. Nor would I hold the office upon such a footing for any consideration that could be offered me. I have written to Congress upon the subject, the inclosed, No. 7, is a copy of my letter, to know whether their ideas of responsibility are similar to those of the Treasury Board; to which I have received no answer. In my letter, I have stated the degree of responsibility incumbent upon me; nor shall I agree to make a single appointment upon any other footing. If the committee agree with me in sentiment upon this subject, and will signify the same, I shall proceed in the business; but if they are of a contrary opinion, I must beg them to make the necessary appointments, as I will not take upon me such a responsibility.

"I shall wait their answer before I proceed further.

"The committee will observe that the Commander-in-chief directs me to apply to the Treasury Board for such sums of money for contingent expenses, and to provide such further supplies as the States are not requested to furnish. But the Treasury Board have a standing order of the 23d of March on No. 9, requiring estimates to be laid before them of such a nature as is not in my power to comply with, and consequently I cannot carry the General's orders into execution. I have endeavored to convince them of the impracticability of the thing, as well as of the inutility of the measure, but without effect, as you will see by the letters Nos. 8, 9, 10, 11, passing between us upon the occasion. Was I to employ my whole time in framing estimates, it would not be in my power to conform to their order, without a foreknowledge of future events ; and no person the least acquainted with the nature of the business would have thought of such a measure. I have been always ready to show the general uses of all the moneys applied for, as well as the appropriation of it ; but it is out of my power to point out the particular application. If this is necessary, I am unable to conduct the business ; nor will I deceive the Commander-in-chief, or disappoint the people in what they will have a just right to expect from me.

"I have for a long time felt myself exceedingly hurt to see the pains that has been taken to draw into discredit the conduct of the staff officers ; nor can I see the object of this measure, unless it is with a view to ruin individuals. Public prejudices, where people are unwilling to meet conviction, soon become insupportable. I regard not the idle opinion of those who are unacquainted with the business ; but if national policy is be governed by common prejudices, it is not difficult to foresee that disgrace and ruin is not far distant. Whatever may be the sentiments of administration with respect to the economy and order of the business under my direction, I am confident, while the war continues upon the present scale, they will not have it done with either more method or less expense than it has been. Those who have not an intimate acquaintance with it can no more judge of the difficulty and expense attending it than youth can of the feelings of old age.

"The business may be divided under various forms, and supplies drawn from different quarters, which may seem to lessen the expense, but collectively you will find it far greater.

"The American [war] is upon a wide extended scale, and will admit of little or no contraction. We are vulnerable upon the whole sea-coast, and we are equally exposed upon our frontiers, — one from the shipping, the other from the savages, — and not a measure is taken for the security of either but proves a tax upon the Quartermaster's department.

"The oblong figure of the thirteen United States, and the vast extent of country over which the inhabitants are spread, adds infinitely to the expense of this business from the manner in which we are obliged to collect and support our forces. The chain of communication which is necessary to be kept up throughout the States, the posts upon the frontiers and those upon the sea-coast, together with such other establishments as are requisite for supplying the army and to organize it for motion, create an expensive and extensive arrangement; nor will it be in the power of government to lessen them, unless they sacrifice greater objects to lesser considerations.

"There can be no possible situation more disagreeable than to be placed where you can give satisfaction to no parties. If the army is not supplied with everything necessary to its convenience and operations, censure and reproach follows; but if the provision is made, the expense gives national disgust. Could I have foreseen the em-

barrassments incident to this employment, no money would
have induced me to engage in it, nor any other consideration but that of saving my country from the loss of
liberty, and a disgraceful servitude.

"To convince you that emoluments were not the motives
which induced me to engage in the Quartermaster's department, I inclose you an extract of a letter from his
Excellency General Washington, No. 12. And to convince you that I am still not more influenced by motives
of interest than formerly, I inclose you a copy of my letter to him, No 13.

"It is true I am not in circumstances to act altogether
regardless of interest. My fortune is small, and I have a
growing family whose welfare it would be criminal to
neglect. Nor can I persuade myself that impoverishing
individuals is the best way of promoting the public good.
The fortunes of the most active citizens may give a
momentary relief to government, but this advantage is
purchased by the loss of the best men in the community.

"The committee have an opportunity since they have
been in camp to look into the history of this business, and
to judge of the expenses from the estimates which I have
laid before them, as well as hearing the numerous complaints and seeing the many embarrassments attending our
affairs. I appeal to them whether I can or ought to do
more than I have done.

"It has been my wish to adopt a new mode of employing
the deputies; which is, to give salaries instead of commissions; not that I think it will lessen the public [expense],
but because it seems to correspond more with the views and
wishes of administration. Without men of interest and
influence are employed, the public business must fail, and
you cannot engage such without some very handsome consideration. To expect more of men than reason and experience warrants, is only depending upon a baseless fabric,

and must end in disappointment. I have taken unwearied
pains to conciliate the minds of the officers in this department to their present situation ; and constant oppression,
where there is no hope of redress, will make men regardless of the public interest. I wish this may not be our
situation from the measures which have been pursued ; as
you as well as I have seen symptoms of this kind arising
in different quarters.

"The subject of responsibility being explained, and the
proper supplies of money furnished, my best endeavors
shall not be wanting to promote the public service in the
business of the Quartermaster's department during the
operations of this campaign.

" I have the honor to be,

With great respect.

Your most obedient humble servant,

NATH. GREENE, Q. M. G.''

But without waiting for the answer, Greene instantly began his preparations.

" CAMP PRECANESS, *July* 15, 1780.

"SIR, — The Commander-in-chief has given me directions
to make the necessary provision in the Quartermaster's department for a coöperation with the French forces which are
now at Newport, for the reduction of New York. I am to
request, therefore, that your Excellency will give orders
for such sums of money on the treasury of the State in
favor of Mr. Bowen, Deputy Quartermaster-general, from
time to time as the service may require ; without this it will
be *impossible* to go on with the business. Mr. Bowen has
had orders to collect the flat-bottomed boats in the State,
which he could not effect for want of money. He has instructions now to forward them to Connecticut River, which
I fear cannot be done unless the State can supply money
for the purpose. I shall be exceedingly obliged by the
friendly offices of the State in promoting at this critical

time the necessary preparations in the Quartermaster-general's department, for carrying into execution the General's plan of operations.

In military operations one thing depends so much upon another, and the success of the whole upon the provision of each part, that nothing is more common than for great events to depend upon little things. Therefore what may appear a trifling consideration, often involves important consequences. •

" I beg my compliments to your family.

" I have the honor to be,

Your Excellency's most obed't humble servant,

NATH. GREENE,

" His Excellency Governor GREENE."   *Quartermaster-general.*

He writes to President Reed on the same day : —

" CAMP PRECAMP, 15th *July*, 1780.

" TO HIS EXCELLENCY GOVERNOR REED : —

" SIR, — His Excellency General Washington has determined upon a plan of operations for the reduction of New York, in conjunction with the French forces who arrived at Newport, Rhode Island, on the 10th, and he has given me orders to make every preparation in the Quartermaster's department for carrying his plan into execution. The committee of Congress have also furnished me with an estimate of a variety of articles which they have required of your State, to be furnished for the use of the army in the Quartermaster-general's department. I am to request that your Excellency will please to inform me in the most particular manner the nature of the thing will admit, what measures are taken to provide the articles, when they will be ready, and where they are to be collected in the first instance. Forage horses and wagons are the principal articles in my department, and they are matters of the highest importance to the success of the expedition. Indeed nothing

can be undertaken without them, nor ought we to proceed
in the preparations unless we have the fullest assurances
from each and every of the States that the requisitions
will be complied with, and in due season. No time is to
be lost in the preparations, and therefore your Excellency's
answer will be absolutely necessary to enable us to know
how to govern ourselves.

"I am persuaded it is unnecessary for me to use any arguments to urge the State to any further exertions than
their own good sense will impel them to. Nor can I say
anything that your Excellency don't fully comprehend the
necessity for, having long experience in military matters,
and knowing the connection and dependencies of one
branch of business upon another."

The committee answered without delay : —

"In Committee of Congress, Precaness, *July* 16, 1780.

"Sir, — Your letter of the 14th ultimo, with the several papers inclosed, was delivered us this morning.

"We observe in your letter of the 19th ultimo to Congress, that you have stated the degree of responsibility
which you think ought to be required of you on the expenditure of moneys in the Quartermaster-general's department,
and that you have requested the sense of Congress on that
subject. As you have not obtained their determination ; as
the system for conducting your department reported by
this committee has not to our knowledge been decided
upon ; as the Commander-in-chief, impelled by necessity,
has directed you to arrange it in some effectual manner to
give dispatch and efficacy to your measures equal to the
present exigency ; and as you decline making the necessary
appointments until this committee afford you their opinion
on the degree of responsibility by which you ought to be
held, as Quartermaster-general, in the expenditure of public
money, they conceive it incumbent on them in order to
prevent the evils which may arise to the public from a dis-

solution of the department before the sense of Congress can be obtained, to give you their opinion on the subject: We have maturely considered the reasons which you assigned in your letter to Congress in support of your proposition, and we assure you they appear so cogent to us that we do not hesitate to declare our sentiments generally coincident with those you have stated on the third paragraph of the letter to which we have alluded.

" With respect to the resolution of the Treasury Board of the 23d March last, requiring estimates approved of by the Board of War to accompany every application for money to prosecute the business of the department, we must suppose it to have originated from a want of the necessary information, or it would have occurred that a strict adherence to the order in your department, under our circumstances, must of necessity in some cases involve the army in great difficulties and in others prove absolutely ruinous. It would be easy to state a variety of instances which, from the nature of things, must occur in every campaign in support of this opinion, but we decline giving them, as it would, we conceive, be like demonstrating a self-evident proposition.

" In justice to you, sir, we embrace this occasion to declare that after having examined your arrangement of the Quartermaster-general's department, we are convinced the measures you have adopted and the principles on which these measures were founded, were well calculated to promote the service, whilst they fully evinced your attention to the public interest; how far your arrangements have been complied with by your subordinate officers; whether these have appointed more assistants than what were absolutely necessary properly to conduct the business; whether they have adopted the most prudent measures in the purchases, and expended the public property with a proper degree of economy, are questions we are not

in a situation to determine, nor does it appear necessary we
should on this occasion.

"We have the honor to be,
With great respect and esteem, sir,
Your most humble servants,
PHILIP SCHUYLER,
NATH'L PEABODY.

"General GREENE, *Quartermaster-general.*"

These were encouraging words, and Greene set
himself strenuously to his task.

"CAMP AT PRECANESS, 16th *July*, 1780.

"SIR, — In answer to your letter of this date covering
an estimate for teams to bring forward the ordnance from
Easton and the shells and shot from, Mount Hope and
Pompton, I can only say it is my opinion the only practicable mode is to send out a party of light horse to impress the teams for the purpose. The inhabitants are busy
in getting in their harvest, and we have no money to pay
the people ; therefore they cannot be got out, nor is the
civil magistrates able to bring them out without money.
Two attempts have been made lately without success, one
at Sussex and one at Pompton, and I am confident that
will be the fate of every future attempt without force.
Mr. Howe has just returned from Pompton, and says it is
impossible to get the teams without a military party, the
justices having done all in their power to little effect.

"I am fully with you in opinion that the ordnance and
stores from the eastward must come from Providence by
water, if not directly from Boston. The transportation
will be too great to bring them all the way by land."

"To THE HONORABLE COMMITTEE OF CONGRESS IN CAMP, 17th *July*, 1780.

"GENTLEMEN, — I do myself the honor to inclose you
an extract of a letter from Mr. Charles Pettit, one of my
assistants, respecting our prospects of a supply of cash.

" The committee must be convinced from this state of
things, that the manner of obtaining as well as the matter
to be obtained from the Treasury is so illy suited to the
emergencies of service, as well as incompetent to the demands of it in common, much less upon this present pressing occasion which requires every exertion and dispatch,
that it is highly necessary to think of some other mode
of supply. I would beg leave, therefore, to propose to
the committee the propriety of addressing the different
States, especially those to the eastward, — there is less necessity for those to the southward, — requesting them to
furnish such supplies of cash for the use of my department
as I may point out to be necessary to promote the public service ; and that such advances shall be considered
to the State advancing it as so much towards their proportion of the taxes.

" The committee are fully informed of the General's intentions, the great exertions that will be required upon
the occasion, the necessity for a large supply of cash,
as well as the impossibility of prosecuting the business
to effect without it, that it is unnecessary for me to
use any arguments to induce them to take a measure
so indispensably requisite to promote the public service." [1]

[1] Extract of a letter from Charles
Pettit, Esq., acting Quartermaster-
general, dated Philadelphia, July 13,
1780 : —

" The new money of this State cir-
culates but slowly, and as yet heavily,
but it is working its way and gaining
some strength. Tradesmen and common people are shy and fearful of it,
and therefore it does not obtain so
ready a currency in small affairs as
was expected. Were it ever so flip-
pant in its passage, the whole amount
is far short of the supplies expected
from this State, and the money aris-

ing from taxes has so many other
pores to supply that we are hardly
sensible of any benefit from it.

" The Continental Treasury is
wretchedly poor, and affords so little,
or at least so little comes from it to
me, that I have no money at command on the most pressing emergencies. I am obliged for every demand
upon me, however trifling, to frame an
estimate and make a special application ; and sometimes, though not commonly, I get some kind of answer in
the course of two or three weeks after
applying. The 21st of June I sent

While Washington and Greene and the committee were exerting themselves to make up for lost time, Congress brought its long labors upon the Quartermaster's department to a close. On the 15th of July the new system was approved. On the 26th, Greene received it from Washington in the camp of Preakness. He had thought and felt too much upon the subject to hesitate a moment about his course of action. His views, Washington's views, had been freely communicated to Congress; and this was the reward of two and a half years' devotion to a laborious and uncongenial office. He instantly wrote to the President of Congress as follows : —

" His Excellency General Washington has just transmitted to me a plan for conducting the Quartermaster's department agreed to in Congress on the 15th instant, wherein I am continued as Quartermaster-general, and directed to make the necessary appointments and arrangements in the department agreeably thereto as soon as possible.

" It was my intention from the peculiar circumstances of our affairs, and I have long since communicated it to the Commander-in-chief and the committee of Congress, to continue to exercise the office of Quartermaster-general during the active part of this campaign, provided matters were left upon such a footing as to enable me to conduct

an application on the estimate of Colonel Cox for drawing from the tradesmen and equipping the new wagons he had ordered in this State; about ten days afterwards I got a warrant for the sum; yesterday I got a letter of advice from the Board to the treasurer, and to-day I have got near one fifth of the money. This movement, slow as it may seem to you, has been pushed with uncommon assiduity and with more than common success; it is therefore one of the most favorable specimens I can give you of the course of business."

the business to satisfaction; and in order to remove every shadow of suspicion that might induce a belief that I was induced by interested motives to make more extensive arrangements than were necessary, I voluntarily relinquished every kind of emolument for conducting the business, save my family expenses.

" But however willing I might have been before to subject myself to the fatigue and difficulties attending the duties of this office, justice to myself as well as to the public constrains me positively to decline it under the present arrangement, as I do not choose to attempt an experiment of so dangerous a nature where I see a physical impossibility of performing the duties that will be required of me. Wherefore I request that Congress will appoint another Quartermaster-general without loss of time, as I shall give no order in the business further than to acquaint the deputies with the new system, and direct them to close their accounts up to the first of August coming.

" It is unnecessary for me to go into the general objections I have to this plan. It is sufficient to say that my feelings are injured, and that the officers necessary to conduct the business are not allowed; nor is proper provision made for some of those that are. There is but one assistant quartermaster-general, who is to reside near Congress, and one deputy for the main army allowed in the system. Whoever has the least knowledge of the business in this office, and the field duty which is to be done, must be fully convinced that it is impossible to perform it without much more assistance than is allowed in the present arrangement. Whether the army is large or small, there is no difference in the plan, though the business may be occasionally multiplied threefold.

" The two principal characters on whom I depended for support, and whose appointment under the former arrangement I made an express condition of my accepting the office, are now left out; and both have advertised me

that they will take no further charge of the business; and
I am apprehensive that many others who have been held
by necessity, and not by choice, will avail themselves of
this opportunity to leave an employment which is not only
unprofitable but rendered dishonorable. Systems without
agents are useless things, and the probability of getting
the one should be taken into consideration in framing the
other. Administration seem to think it far less important
to the public interest to have this department well filled
and properly arranged than it really is, and as they will
find it by future experience.

"My best endeavors have not been wanting to give success to the business committed to my care, and I leave the
merit of my services to be determined hereafter by the
future management of it under the direction of another
hand.

"My rank is high in the line of the army, and the sacrifices I have made on this account, together with the
fatigue and anxiety I have undergone, far overbalance all
the emoluments I have derived from the appointment.
Nor would double the consideration induce me to tread
the same path over again, unless I saw it necessary to preserve my country from utter ruin and a disgraceful servitude."

The committee were the representatives of
Congress in camp.

"I do myself the honor," he writes them on the following day, "to inclose you a copy of the letter of resignation
I am sending to Congress. I think it my duty to give
you the earliest information of everything that concerns
the interest and well-being of the army, and therefore take
the liberty to trouble you on this occasion.

"I shall make no comments on the measures of administration, further than to remark that to introduce a new
system in the middle of a campaign is a bold and danger-

ous experiment, and such a one, I believe, as never was attempted by any nation upon earth. I wish it may succeed agreeable to their expectations; but I cannot think of making myself responsible by attempting the execution when I see so little probability of succeeding. My inclinations and intentions have been so fully explained to the committee that it is unnecessary to be more particular on this occasion. Whatever may be the consequences of the present plan of administration, I flatter myself I shall stand fully acquitted, having given seasonably the necessary information to Congress and the committee to put this business on a proper footing, and offered my services from a desire to promote the public interest under our present embarrassments, without fee or reward save my family expenses."

To Washington also, he wrote on the same day, although delicacy forbade him to take counsel upon such an occasion with either the Commander-in-chief or the friend. But he wrote thus, and with a thorough knowledge of Washington's opinion.

"I do myself the honor to inclose your Excellency a copy of a letter of resignation as Quartermaster-general to Congress, and another on the same subject to the committee in camp.

"I have only to regret that the measures of administration have laid me under the necessity at this critical moment. It is true it has been my wish for a long time to get out of the department; but as our political affairs were in so disagreeable a train I was willing to submit to many inconveniences in order to promote the public welfare, while I had a prospect of conducting the business to answer the expectations of the public and to the satisfaction of the army. But a new system of Congress has cut off all prospect, and left me without the shadow of hope.

"The principal characters on whom I depended are left out, and many parts of the plan it is impossible to reduce to practice. Under this view of things I found myself constrained to quit the department, and leave those to answer for the consequences who have reduced matters to this extremity.

"When I take a view of the religious and political prejudices that have frequently influenced public bodies at different periods to adopt the most ruinous measures, I am not surprised to see an attempt to change a system of one of the most important departments of the army in the most critical and interesting season of the campaign, and when every exertion under the best direction is incompetent to the demands of the service.

"Was measures of this kind new in the history of mankind, I should be led to apprehend that more was intended than a change of modes for conducting business.

"I am persuaded that your Excellency will approve my conduct, however inconvenient it may be to the service, as I am confident you would not wish me to attempt what there is a physical impossibility of accomplishing; and more especially when the attempt will only tend to deceive you and the public in your expectations from me.

"Since the commencement of this war I have ever made the good of the service the rule of my conduct, and in no instance have I deviated from this line; and where there has been a seeming variation, it has been only in such cases where I could not render my services without forfeiting my reputation."

Matthews was absent when Greene's letter of the 27th was delivered to the committee, but Schuyler and Peabody wrote the next day in reply: —

"Your letter of yesterday's date, covering copy of yours to Congress of the 26th instant, has been duly received.

"Persuaded that a change of officers in your depart-

ment at this advanced stage of the campaign, of which
the business is so very extensive and complicated, must be
attended with the most ruinous consequences, we have
thought it our duty to express our apprehensions to Congress on the subject, and have since had a conference on it
with the Commander-in-chief; and we are perfectly in
sentiment with him, ' that your declining to act at present,
will be productive of such a scene of confusion and distress that it will be impossible to remedy the evil or to
reduce the business to a proper channel during the remainder of the campaign ; ' we have therefore most earnestly
to entreat that you will continue to direct the department
until the sense of Congress can be obtained on your letter
of the 26th and on ours of yesterday ; but as you positively
decline acting under the plan established by Congress on
the 15th instant, which has been officially handed to you
by the Commander-in-chief, and as the consequences which
we have stated must inevitably follow, and probably be
extended to eradicate every hope which the country entertains of an efficient operation against the enemy in conjunction with the force of our ally, we conceive it indispensably our duty from these considerations to require of
you to continue the direction of the Quartermaster-general's
department under the order of the Commander-in-chief, as
signified in his order to you of the 13th instant, and on the
conditions stated in our letter of the 16th instant, until the
further pleasure of Congress can be known ; and we undertake to justify you for acting in consequence of this requisition, and will submit our conduct on this occasion to the
judgment of Congress." [1]

Greene replied on the same day : —

"I am honored with yours of this day, requesting me still
to take the direction of the Quartermaster's department
until the sense of Congress can be known upon my letter

[1] Records of the Committee, MSS. Department of State.

of resignation ; and as I have already refused to conduct it under the plan of the 15th instant, you advise me to take it upon the order of the General of the 14th. But this cannot be done, as the General has already recalled that order by his letter of the 26th, a copy of which I inclose you.

"If the General will give a new order authorizing me, notwithstanding the new system, to proceed in the business independent of it, and as it is the request of the committee that I should continue till the sense of Congress is known, I will agree to conduct the business for ten days."

Meanwhile Greene's letter of resignation had reached Congress : —

"Your letter," . . . . General Cornell writes on the 29th, "was this day read in Congress containing your determination not to act in the Quartermaster's department; some warmth appeared on the occasion. For my own part, I must confess it would have given me pleasure if you could have reconciled yourself so far as to have superintended the department until the end of the present campaign, as you would thereby kept out of the power of your enemies, at least so far as to prevent their tantalizing over you, to the great mortification of your friends, of which you have a number in Congress who I believe are unanimous in opinion that your resignation at this time is attended with many delicate circumstances. When I pay the greatest deference to your wisdom and prudence, I cannot but believe it is in the power of Congress to hurt your feelings more sensibly than they yet have done, which I am ready to believe some of them would be happy in showing an instance of, and that soon. Your letter is committed; the committee are Mr. Ward, McKean, and Henry, from Maryland. I suppose they will report on Monday next ; the measures that will be taken I will not undertake to say, but I expect debate will run high.

" I wrote you a letter sometime since. I fear it is mislaid, as I have no answer. I cannot take my leave of you without saying that I never approved of the plan as adopted by Congress for regulating the Quartermaster's department. My greatest objection was, that many of the salaries were, as I thought, insufficient, and by that means the public would suffer for want of men of ability to act in the several departments, which I expected they would soon be sensible of ; and had you continued, Congress must have taken all that blame to themselves, which by the steps you have taken they will endeavor to lay at your door with too much success. I hope I may be mistaken. I suppose there is not a set of men on earth more fond of charging their blunders to other people's fault than we are. As I conceive the great clamor against the staff departments to be first raised in order to charge the depreciation of the currency to their account by the Board of Treasury and by them spread like other infections." [1]

This letter was written Saturday. On Monday, when Congress met again, two other letters upon the same subject were laid before them, — a letter from Washington, and a letter from the committee in camp.

" I think it my duty to assure Congress," writes Washington, " that I entirely agree with the committee in opinion, and that unless effectual measures are immediately taken to induce General Greene and the other principal officers of that department to continue their services, there must of necessity be a total stagnation of military business. We not only must cease from the preparations for the campaign, but in all probability shall be obliged to disperse if not disband the army for want of subsistence." [2]

[1] General Cornell to General Greene. Philadelphia, July 29, 1780. — Greene MSS.

[2] Sparks, *Writings of Washington,* vol. vii. p. 126.

The language of the committee was equally strong. Congress was very indignant. The fire that had burnt so fiercely at the reading of Greene's letter, blazed up afresh at the sound of these unwelcome words. The committee's letter in particular gave great offense, members seeming to forget that the members of the committee were like themselves members of Congress. "I have not seen that letter," writes Pettit, "and therefore can only judge of it by its effects and from select expressions which have been retailed to me, and in which you are charged with dictating terms and conditions in a manner which they deem highly offensive." [1]

"If I can judge from information and from my own observation," writes Cornell, "I shall be happy if the dispute shall terminate more favorable to you than the passing a resolution ordering the Commander-in-chief to excuse you from all further command in the line of the army until you shall have fully settled all your accounts in the Quartermaster-general's department. In a word, I believe it is the wish of some that the suspension may finally operate as a final discharge. I am convinced your conduct is considered in a different point of view from what you expected." [2]

The new letters were referred; Greene's recommitted.

There was no delay now. The report was brought in the very next day: —

"That General Greene's refusal," it ran, "be accepted.

[1] Pettit to Greene, August 11.   [2] General Cornell to General
— Greene, MSS.   Greene, August 1, 1780.

" That General Washington be impowered and directed to appoint a Quartermaster-general.

" That General Greene be acquainted that Congress have no further service for him."

" That report," writes General Cornell, " was taken up every day for a week, but nothing determined. At length it was agreed to postpone the report for the present. Congress then agreed to make choice of a Quartermaster-general. Colonel Pickering was chosen, with the rank of Colonel and pay of Brigadier-general. There the matter rests at present, and I think will, unless some other evil spirit should get among us.

" I can assure you Mr. Sherman hath been your fast friend in the whole of this affair, as well as every member from that State. And among your friends you may reckon New Hampshire, Rhode Island, Pennsylvania, and some members from some of the other States. Your enemies are, or pretend to be, exceeding sanguine in their expectations of Colonel Pickering's conducting the department with economy. I must confess I more fear his want of ability than the want of economy. At the same time I wish him success.

" Before this will reach you it is more than probable you will hear that Congress have recalled their committee from head-quarters. The measure was become necessary for several reasons. Some States were dissatisfied, many members of Congress were displeased with the letters they wrote.

" The situation of our finances is such as to make every thinking man shudder. The new money ordered into circulation by the resolution of the 18th of March meets with so many obstructions I almost despair of the credit it will have in the States that comply with the resolution. If that should fail, good God, what will be our fate, without money or credit at home or abroad ? We have not one farthing of money in the treasury, and I know of no quarter from which we have a right to expect any. Yet we go on contented, pleasing ourselves with the sanguine hopes of reducing New York. I have seen many new scenes before I came to this place. But what I have experienced since, exceeds anything I have ever seen before. I never before saw a set of men that could quietly submit to every kind of difficulty that tended to the ruin of their country, without endeavoring to make one effort to remove the obstruction. I believe they wish their country well, but suffer their time almost wholly to be taken up in business of no consequence." [1]

The word in Greene's letter which Congress found it hardest to bear was the word " administration."

" I am informed," writes Colonel Cox, " that the word *administration*, in your letter of resignation, was so *highly* offensive to Congress, that some of the worthy members immediately on the letter being read, moved the House instantly to disrobe you of all military rank at the same time that they accepted your resignation as Quartermaster-general. Others more moderate, though not at bottom more friendly, objected to a measure so violent, but at the same time proposed that Congress should immediately desire the Commander-in-chief to signify to you that your future services in the line would be dispensed with until your accounts in the Quartermaster's department were settled ; neither of which proposals, though warmly urged by your enemies, were carried into resolves ; nor do I believe they dare, great as they are, seriously to attempt anything of the kind, though some of your friends have been not a little alarmed on the occasion." [2]

---

[1] General Cornell to General Greene, August 13, 1780. — Greene MSS.

[2] Colonel John Cox to General Greene, August 7, 1780. — Greene MSS.

While Congress, although upon the eve of a great operation, were thus wasting precious time in acrimonious debate, their committee in camp, and Washington and Greene with them, were strenuously urging their preparations for early action.

"I wish your Excellency," Greene writes to Washington from Verplanck's Point on the 3d of August, "to determine upon your further operations as soon as possible, as boards and teams are impressing, collecting, and coming to camp as fast as possible. If the teams are not likely to be wanted immediately, they had better be discharged without loss of time, as it will save a great expense, and free the people from no small inconveniences.

"Colonel Hay has sent down a considerable quantity of boards to King's Ferry, and more are coming. Mr. Clarke of Danbury writes me that he has got an account of one hundred thousand feet which may be had, but not without great inconvenience to the inhabitants, as they were got to rebuild the houses burnt by the enemy last campaign. There is a great number of impressed teams at King's Ferry, on the other side, which I wish to dismiss if there is not an immediate necessity for them."

Meanwhile the ten days for which Greene had consented to remain in office were rapidly passing.

"The time for which I engaged to act in the Quartermaster's department, at the request of the committee of Congress, for coöperation," he writes to Washington on the 5th, "is almost expired; and as I cannot exercise the office any longer consistent with my own safety, I am to request your Excellency will take measures for relieving me as soon as possible from the disagreeable predicament I am in. In the meantime I shall be exceedingly obliged to your Excellency for the sense you entertain of my conduct and services since I have been in the department, as you alone are the best judge of the propriety of one and the merit of the other. The business is truly disagreeable and distressing, and has been so for a long time ; notwithstanding, if it had been possible for me to have got through this campaign consistently with my own safety and the public good, upon the plan which Congress proposed, I would readily have done it. But from the knowledge I have of the department, I know it is utterly impossible to follow the system and answer the demands of the service ; and to attempt it at this critical season, will most assuredly defeat our plan of operations, and bring the army into the greatest distress.

" It would be a folly for me to attempt to combat the prejudices of public bodies with hopes of success. Time alone can convince them that their measures are destructive of their true interest, as well as highly injurious to some of their most faithful servants.

" I am sensible my conduct has been viewed by many in a very improper light ; and I am persuaded many think the business can be done with more method and at a less expense than it has been. I wish it may be the case ; but am much mistaken if the nature of the business is capable of more system, or will admit of less expense, if the plan of the war continues on its present scale and the army on its present footing.

" I have endeavored to the utmost of my power to enter into the spirit and intention of your Excellency's measures ; and if my conduct has not been satisfactory to government and to yourself, it has been owing to a want of abilities, and not inclination."

" I have received your letter of yesterday," Washington answers from Peekskill on the 6th. " When you quit the department, I shall be happy to give you my sense of your conduct ; and I am persuaded it will be such as will be entirely satisfactory. I cannot, however, forbear thinking that it would be unadvisable for you to leave the department before the success of the letters written from Paramus by the committee and myself to Congress, is known, and I entreat you to wait the issue of the application." [1]

The success of those letters was very different from what either Washington or Greene or the committee had expected. Of the members of Congress who had taken up a prejudice against Greene, no one seems to have taken it up more strongly than Joseph Jones of Virginia, an active member of the committee of three which had been appointed on the 10th of March, to confer with the commissioners appointed on the 20th of January to inquire into the expenses of the staff departments. In this capacity he had taken part in the formation of the new system, and his feelings were naturally enlisted in the support of it.[2] It was from him that Washington received his first intimation of the intentions of Congress.

" We have been greatly perplexed the last week," he writes to Washington on the 7th of August, " with General Greene's refusal to act in the office of quartermaster-general, unless the new system was totally repealed, and he was allowed to conduct it, under your direction, in such manner as he thought most conducive to the public service. Besides, Congress were to request Pettit and Cox to resume their offices. If General Greene thought the new system wanted amendment, and had pointed out the defect, Congress would have considered the matter, and I doubt not would have made the necessary alteration. But the manner of these demands, made in such peremptory terms,

[1] Sparks, *Writings of Washington*, vol. vii. p. 144.

[2] *Vide* Journals of Congress, January 20, March 10, 1780, and Schuyler's letter to Greene, *supra*.

at the moment of action, when the campaign was opened, the enemy in the field, and our ally waiting for coöperation, has lessened General Greene not only in the opinion of Congress, but I think of the public; and I question whether it will terminate with the acceptance of his refusal only.

"On Saturday Colonel Pickering was appointed to the office of quartermaster-general, with the rank of colonel and the pay and rations of a brigadier-general, and to hold his place at the Board of War without pay or right to act while in the office of quartermaster-general. This gentleman's integrity, ability, and attention to business will, I hope, not only prevent the evils to be apprehended from a change in so important a department at this time, but will, I hope, be able to reform some of the abuses crept into that business, and lessen the amazing expenditures of the department. He must, if he accepts, have a disagreeable office in the present state of our finance; but we must support him all we can."[1]

Washington's answer was prompt and decisive: —

"The subject of this letter will be confined to a single point. I shall make it as short as possible, and write it with frankness. If any sentiment, therefore, is delivered which might be displeasing to you as a member of Congress, ascribe it to the freedom which is taken with you by a friend who has nothing in view but the public good.

"In your letter without date, but which came to hand yesterday, an idea is held up as if the acceptance of General Greene's resignation of the Quartermaster's department was not all that Congress meant to do with him. If by this it is in contemplation to suspend him from his com-

[1] *Correspondence of the Revolution,* vol. iii. p. 51. The date of this letter is conjectural Mr. Sparks affixes an interrogation point to the –7–, which it bears in his work. But as it speaks of Pickering's acceptance as not yet received, and the journals for the 6th announce it, I should say that Sunday the 6th was probably the true date.

mand in the line, of which he made an express reservation at the time of entering on the other duty, and if it is not
already enacted, let me beseech you to consider well what
you are about before you resolve. I shall neither condemn
nor acquit General Greene's conduct for the act of resignation, because all the antecedent correspondence is necessary
to form a right judgment of the matters, and possibly if
the affair is ever brought before the public, you may find
him treading on better ground than you seem to imagine ;
but this by the by.   My sole aim at present is to advertise
you of what I think would be the consequences of suspend-
ing him from his command in the line (a matter distinct
from the other) without a proper trial.   A procedure of
this kind must touch the feelings of every officer.   It will
show in a conspicuous point of view the uncertain tenure
by which they hold their commissions.   In a word, it will
exhibit such a specimen of power, that I question much
if there is an officer in the whole line that will hold a commission beyond the end of the campaign, if he does till then.
Such an act in the most despotic government would be attended at least with loud complaints.

"It does not require with you, I am sure, at this time
of day, arguments to prove that there is no set of men in
the United States, considered as a body, that have made
the same sacrifices of their interest in support of the
common cause, as the officers of the American army ; that
nothing but love of their country, of honor, and a desire
of seeing their labors crowned with success, could possibly
induce them to continue one moment in service ; that no
officer can live upon his pay ; that hundreds having spent
their little all in addition to their scanty public allowance,
have resigned because they could no longer support themselves as officers; that numbers are at this moment rendered unfit for duty for want of clothing, while the rest
are wasting their property, and some of them verging fast
to the gulf of poverty and distress.

"Can it be supposed that men under these circumstances, who can derive at best, if the contest ends
happily, only the advantages which accrue in equal proportion to others, will sit patient under such a precedent?
Surely they will not ; for the measure, not the man, will
be the subject of consideration, and each will ask himself
this question: If Congress by its mere fiat, without inquiry and without trial, will suspend an officer to-day, and
an officer of such high rank, may it not be my turn to-
morrow, and ought I to put it in the power of any man or
any body of men to sport with my commission and character, and lay me under the necessity of tamely acquiescing,
or by an appeal to the public, exposing matters which
must be injurious to its interests? The suspension of
generals Schuyler and St. Clair, though it was preceded
by the loss of Ticonderoga, which contributed not a little
for the moment to excite prejudices against them, was by
no means viewed with a satisfactory eye by many discerning men, though it was in a manner supported by the public clamor ; and the one in contemplation, I am almost
certain, will be generally reprobated by the army.

"Suffer not, my friend, if it is within the compass of
your abilities to prevent it, so disagreeable an event to
take place. I do not mean to justify, to countenance or excuse, in the most distant degree, any expressions of disrespect which the gentleman in question, if he has used
any, may have offered to Congress, no more than I do
any unreasonable matters he may have required respecting the Quartermaster-general's department ; but as I
have already observed, my letter is to prevent his suspension, because I fear, because I feel it must lead to very
disagreeable and injurious consequences. General Greene
has his numerous friends as well out of the army as in it ;
and from his character and consideration in the world, he
might not, when he felt himself wounded in so summary
a way, withhold himself from a discussion that could not

at best promote the public cause.[1] As a military officer
he stands very fair, and very deservedly so, in the opinion
of all his acquaintance. These sentiments are the result
of my own reflections, and I hasten to inform you of them.
I do not know that General Greene has ever heard of the
matter, and I hope he never may ; nor am I acquainted
with the opinion of a single officer in the whole army
upon the subject, nor will any tone be given by me. It is
my wish to prevent the proceeding ; for sure I am, that it
cannot be brought to a happy issue if it takes place." [2]

Two days after these words of grave admoni-
tion were written, he wrote again to Greene : —

" As you are retiring from the office of Quartermaster-
general, and have requested my sense of your conduct and
services while you acted in it, I shall give it to you with
the greatest cheerfulness and pleasure. You have conducted the various duties of it with capacity and diligence,
entirely to my satisfaction, and, as far as I have had an opportunity of knowing, with the strictest integrity. When
you were prevailed on to take the office, in March, 1778, it
was in great disorder and confusion ; and by extraordinary
exertions you so arranged it as to enable the army to take
the field the moment it was necessary, and to move with
rapidity after the enemy when they left Philadelphia.
From that period to the present time your exertions have
been equally great. They have appeared to me to be the
result of system, and to have been well calculated to promote the interest and honor of your country." [3]

1 " You mention something of
publishing, and it is just, it is a duty
you will one day owe to yourself and
to your country." Nathaniel Peabody to General Greene, Sept. 18,
1780. — Greene MSS.

2 Sparks, *Writings of Washington*,
vol. vii. p. 149. In the wide range
of Washington's letters there is not

one superior to this ; not only for
judgment, sense, and feeling, but for
the skill with which it is composed ;
and that he wrote it, — not one of
his aids, — is evident from the closing sentences.

3 Sparks, *Writings of Washington*,
vol. vii. p. 153.

And now, too, it was known that the letter of
the committee also had given great offense. The
first indication of it was a resolution of the 2d of
August on their letter to Greene of the 16th. No
mention is made, indeed, of the letter of the 27th,
but the spirit which was warring against Greene
makes itself plainly manifest in the explicit condemnation of the interpretation which the committee had put upon the question of responsibility.

" The subject-matter of the Quartermaster-general's letter to the said committee in camp," says the resolution;
" so far as it regards his responsibility, has been already
determined by Congress ; and as the committee knew that
the Quartermaster-general had requested the sense of Congress on so important a subject, they ought not to have interfered therein." [1]

Of the fatal delay in carrying out the orders of
the Commander-in-chief, which the refusal of the
committee to express an opinion would have
caused, not a word is said. Nine days pass, and
the meagre and unsatisfactory journals make no
further mention of the committee. How little
effect their letter of the 27th July had produced
is shown, indeed, by a resolve of the 5th of
August —

" That the absolute refusal of Major-general Greene, at
this important crisis, to act under the new arrangement
of the Quartermaster-general's department, has made it
necessary that the office of Quartermaster-general be immediately filled." [2]

[1] Journals of Congress, August   [2] Journals, August 5, 1780.
2, 1780.

Another week passes, and it is

"*Ordered*, that the committee appointed on the 13th day of April last, to repair to head-quarters, be discharged from further attendance there, and that they report their proceedings to Congress." [1]

" By the inclosed letter," Cornell writes to Greene on the 15th, " you will be informed the committee are recalled. It is there mentioned as a necessary measure. I believe it to be so, to keep harmony among ourselves. Some members were against their appointment; they have never failed to blow the coals on all occasions. The committee have at some times wrote plainly to us and pressed our difficulties close upon us, which is another matter many of us cannot bear, although founded on the greatest truths. For my own part, I see nothing to charge the committee with in point of conduct; some of their letters were in a style rather warm, but that I imputed to Schuyler's zeal and the warm climate of Matthews' nativity." [2]

[1] Journals, August 11, 1780.

[2] General Cornell to General Greene, Philadelphia, August 15, 1780. The opinion of the army upon the recall of the committee is strongly expressed by Colonel Scammell in a letter to Colonel Peabody, September 5, 1780: —

" The army regrets the recalling decree of Congress, and that your committee should be absent from the army at this critical juncture, when famine daily extends her threatening, baleful sceptre." Scammell's position as Adjutant-general gives great weight to his words. What Washington thought of him may be seen by his letter to the President of Congress announcing Scammell's wish to resign. — Sparks, vol. vii. p. 314. Scammell's letter is published in *Farmer and Moore's Historical Collection*, vol. iii. p. 286.

Greene writes of them to Peabody, September 6 : " You have had your day of difficulty as well as I. Congress seems to have got more out of temper with the committee than with me ; and I am told, charge great part of the difficulties on the committee, that have taken place between the committee and me. However, of this I suppose you are better informed than I am. It appears to me, that Congress were apprehensive some disagreeable consequences might take place from the measures they have been pursuing, contrary to the advice of the committee, and therefore they took the earliest opportunity to bring them into disgrace to lessen their influence The committee stand fair with the army, and I believe with the public at large ; and bad as our condition is, I believe we are altogether indebted to the committee for the tolerable state we are in."

If it fared thus with Greene's friends at a distance, it may well be supposed that his friends near at hand were not smiled upon.

" The zeal I shew against adopting the new plan for regulating the Quartermaster-general's department," writes Cornell, in the letter already quoted, " caused the majority of Congress to treat me with great coolness for a considerable time. It hath now entirely subsided. I am now treated with the greatest politeness, and enjoy as great a share of their confidence as I can expect ; which leads me to believe they are sorry they have carried the matter so far, but their pride will not permit them to retract. I can say no more than that it hath appeared to me from the first that some thought it necessary to sacrifice one for the salvation of the whole. But upon the whole it is my opinion, some particular pique and prejudices excepted, Congress, that is, every member, wish well to their country. But there being so many members, and so many different sentiments, and to that may be added want of ability or general knowledge, and inattention to business, that it cannot be wondered at if difficulties arise in carrying on our public affairs." [1]

Pettit also writes that at first he had found the torrent too strong to be stemmed. Towards the middle of August, however, it began to subside ; and on the 20th he says : —

" The fever in a certain house is much abated, and I believe the rash step proposed in the beginning and revived with redoubled fury on the letters from the committee shortly after your letter of refusal came, is laid aside. Other objects have taken up their attention and afford exercise for their various passions which have been lately so much awakened. The time will probably come when

1 Cornell to Greene. — Greene MSS.

some of them will see their own folly in the transactions
of some months past.　Certain notions of dignity will prevent any direct acknowledgment of conviction, though it
may and I hope will have an influence on their future
conduct."

" I observe in a letter to Mr. Cox this morning," writes
Reed on the 19th, " you mention the design of superseding
you in command is not laid aside.　I assure you it never
was seriously entertained by a great majority of Congress.
One hot member dropped it in a speech, another afterwards moved it with some more formality ; but it was
scouted, and respect paid to your military character at the
time that your freedom as a Quartermaster gave um-
brage." [1]

Greene's answer contains a summary of the
whole subject : —

" Your obliging letter of the 19th I have had the pleasure to receive.　I should have been happy to have had
your advice and opinion before I sent in my resignation to
Congress.　But I thought then, and cannot help thinking
still, that the measures pursued in Congress were calculated
to compel me to quit the department.　This might not be
the design of the greater part ; but I am persuaded it was
the plan of a few, who influenced others to adopt their
measures upon different principles than governed themselves.

" You know I had got sick of the department long since,
not less from the treatment I met with in Congress than
with the army, and was desirous of resigning ; but I should
not have ventured upon the measure this campaign, if I
could possibly have conceived I could have got through the
business upon the new system.　But it appears to me that
Congress intended to tie up my hands in such a way that
I should either fail in the business or depart from the plan.

[1] Joseph Reed to Greene. — Greene MSS.

In either case I should have been ruined. If I had not answered the demands of the service, I should have fallen into disgrace with the army ; and if to answer the demands of the service I had departed from the system, I laid myself liable for the consequences, which, to be judged of hereafter by persons altogether strangers to the circumstances, could not fail of being censured, if not subjected to heavy losses. Upon the whole, I considered myself as cruelly and oppressively treated. I did not wish to desert the business at a critical hour, nor did I wish to go into a quarrel with Congress. My letter of resignation may have more tartness in it than was prudent ; but I am far from thinking it merited the severity with which they were about to treat it. For I am well informed it was seven days in agitation to dismiss me the service altogether. This they may do whenever they please. I am not anxious to continue a moment longer than I am thought useful to the community.

"If I have many friends in Congress at this time, my enemies have the art of moulding them to their views. Leaving out Mr. Cox and Mr. Pettit served to convince me that the measure was more personal than political.

" What served to fix my determination for quitting the department was, just about the same time that I received the new system, I received a resolution of Congress that the principals of the departments which handled public money, however different, should be held responsible for all the subordinate agents. This appeared to me so unreasonable as well as unjust, that the whole complexion of the business had something so cruel and at the same time so personal in it, that I was determined to leave it, be the consequence what it might.

" As to public gratitude, I expected none, especially in so changeable a body as that of Congress. For the members this year cannot know the merit of their servants last, and therefore not very likely to reward them for past services.

" All things considered, I am very glad I am out of the department, though I have run some risk in getting out, and perhaps lost some friends by it.

" I can assure you there are but few people here that are your enemies. If there are any freedoms taken with your character, it is unbeknown to me, except by Mr. Matthews, who said some bitter things, however, not altogether personal, as they regarded the policy of the State more than your personal conduct.

" This gentleman came to camp with all the prejudices imaginable about him respecting the Quartermaster's department, and he appeared to be afraid to make inquiry for fear of meeting conviction; but I believe none of the committee leave the army with more favorable sentiments respecting my conduct and the order and management of the business than he does. I believe him to be a well-meaning man, but a person of violent passions, great pride, and sudden prejudices. Under the influence of such a temper he may take a wrong bias with very honest intentions. However, this much may be said with certainty, you are not to number him among your particular friends.

" He and I have had several conversations respecting you, as I make it a rule in case, never to hear a friend of mine spoken injuriously of without endeavoring to defend his character and conduct. But they have never been attended with any heat, as it was only respecting the motives that led and governed your political conduct.

" I have no wish to go into any further disputes with him upon any matters, and therefore beg you to take no notice of this information.

" I wish you would come to camp once in a while; it serves to set many things to rights. There is a matter now in the Pennsylvania line which originated by the appointment of Major McPherson to the command of one of the light infantry battalions. That I fear will be attended with some serious and disagreeable consequences between

General St. Clair and General Wayne.   One time the matter got so high that I really apprehended the loss of your whole line.   The great difficulty is in part got over.   But there is a settled dislike taken place between the two generals.   Perhaps you may have some influence towards bringing about a reconciliation, though I confess I see but little prospect of so desirable an issue.   For this purpose and some other matters which are taking place in New England respecting a general convention of the States I should be happy to see you at camp.

" I have been on a command to Bergen after forage and cattle.   We gave the enemy a military insult, and our position here is nothing less than a challenge.   We got some grain and long forage, about two or three hundred head of cattle, and a few sheep.   The enemy gave us no disturbance, though we waited three days to give them an opportunity to come out if they thought proper.

" We are in a starving condition, not having an ounce of meat in camp, and very little coming in.

" I beg my compliments to Mrs. Reed, and am with perfect esteem, your" etc.

Reed and Pettit felt that Greene had been badly used, but Reed thought that he had " never had fewer enemies in Congress than" at that moment; and Pettit thought that the objections to the new system were not so insuperable as they appeared to Greene.   " If I have many friends in Congress at this time," Greene replies to Reed, " my enemies have the art of moulding them to their views." Moreover, Reed, who on the question of State supplies had been brought into something like a rough collision with the committee, seems to have thought that they had given Greene false ideas of the real feeling in Congress towards him and his department.   Pettit takes the same view in several letters, although both acknowledge that he had strong grounds for suspicion and even for actual complaint. " Our friends in camp," writes Pettit on the 20th of August, " see things through the same medium that you do.   Our friends here see them differently ; my vision partakes a little of both."   How Congress saw things, we have seen among other sources, by Jones's letter to Washington.   How the committee felt, we may learn from a letter of Peabody to Greene : " The whole of the late conduct of Congress," he writes from Morristown on the 18th of September, " relative to you, sir, and to the committee, had it appeared in any other age than the present, or in any other body of men than those who resort together in Chestnut Street, Philadelphia, it would have been a phenomenon astonishing to all who beheld it." [1] Pickering, as we have already seen, was appointed Quartermaster-general on the 5th of August.   In the interval between the receipt of Greene's resignation and that day, an attempt had been made to induce Pettit to accept the office ; but he declined.   He was then asked to remain in the office of assistant quartermaster-general.   It was a delicate and difficult question.   To consent might seem like an approval of the conduct of Congress.   To refuse might draw upon him the ill-will of that body, already so ill-disposed towards Greene and Cox.   The accounts of the department were not yet settled, and it was in the power of Congress

[1] Greene MSS.   *Vide* also a note of the judicious Sparks, *Writings of Washington*, vol. vii. p. 226.

and of the Treasury Board to double both the labor and the expense of settling them. His own interest, the interest of his colleagues and, what all three appear to have felt in an equal degree, the interest of the creditors of the department, required a prompt settlement of their numerous claims. Such a settlement he might hope to make if he remained in office; and with it he knew that the unjust accusations which had been brought against the department would of themselves fall to the ground. How could Congress believe him guilty of abuse of trust, and at the same time solicit him to retain that trust? After much and anxious deliberation, he resolved to remain. Greene and Cox approved his resolution.[1] The result demonstrated the wisdom of it. The examination of the accounts of Greene's administration must have convinced even his worst enemies that he had been a diligent and faithful servant.

Pickering was a man of fine parts, quickened and improved by generous culture, of great industry, great energy, and an integrity above reproach. He remained at the head of the department till the end of the war, doing all that zeal, judgment, and strenuous exertion could do to fulfill its arduous duties. But at every step he met the difficulties which Greene had met, repeated the complaints which Greene had made, found himself in the midst of starving and naked soldiers, and was compelled to bear the burden of unmerited reproach. On one occasion he was even arrested as

---

[1] These reasonings are taken from the letters of Pettit and Cox to Greene. — Greene MSS.

a private citizen for a debt which he had contracted as a public officer.[1]

But although Pickering had been appointed to the department on the 5th of August, it was not till the 30th of September that he had been able to enter upon its duties in camp. Those duties meanwhile had been performed by Greene, and the preparations for action virtually brought to an end under his direction. " You have had undue hardship imposed on you," writes Pettit, " in being kept so long in the toils after a new appointment: but you may be assured your perseverance will redound much to your honor." In the general orders of the 30th, announcing Pickering's appointment, Greene is thanked " for the able and satisfactory manner in which he had discharged the duties of the Quartermaster-general's department during his continuance in that office." [2]

Immediately after his resignation, he had begun to call in the accounts of the department by circular letters to his deputies.[3] In most instances he adds his thanks for the assistance which they had rendered, and expresses in warm terms his approbation of the manner in which they had performed their duties. The tone of his letters shows what a pleasant footing they had lived upon.

It was a happy moment when he found himself free from the unwelcome duty of providing for the

[1] Pickering's *Life of T. Pickering*, vol. i. p. 397. See also, among many others, a letter of Wayne to President Reed and one of Washington to Gouverneur Morris, in Reed's *Life of President Reed*, vol. ii. pp. 315–317.

[2] Whiting, *Washington's Revolutionary Orders*, order 79, p. 111. *Vide* also letter on p. 470.

[3] Greene MSS.

physical wants of an army instead of aiding in
the direction of its military operations. Every day
that he had passed in the laborious drudgery of the
staff had been a day of sacrifice and self-denial.
He could look back upon it without self-reproach,
for his work had been systematically and scrupu-
lously done. But he could not look upon it without regret, when he thought of the work that he
would have preferred to do. But the reward
came at last. The probation of the Quartermaster-general's department proved an instrument of
success, a completing of that severe and rigorous
discipline of mind and character by which he had
been prepared for the exercise of independent
command; and when at Charlotte he set himself to
the study of the condition and resources of his
army, he found that the period of his public life
which he regretted most had been fruitful of an
experience, and through experience of a knowledge, without which he would never have won the
proud name of Conqueror of the South.

CHAPTER XI.

In accepting the office of Quartermaster-general Greene had reserved, as will be remembered, his rights as a Major-general. His dislike of the duties of the staff, and his intention to return to the line at the first favorable moment, made him extremely sensitive to any attempt to call his right in question. Under the influence of this feeling, he wrote in September, 1779, to those of his fellow-officers whose claims would have been affected by his, to ask for a frank expression of their opinions. Most of them agreed with him in the interpretation which he put upon his reservation. Washington did not, and frankly told him so.[1]

Relieved from the burden of the staff, Greene was now free to direct his attention to the more congenial duties of the line. The cherished plan of the campaign had failed. The French fleet was shut up in the harbor of Newport by a superior force. The French army was for the moment compelled to remain inactive. There was no prospect of present movements, and the future looked

---

[1] Sparks, *Writings of Washington*, vol. vi. p. 337.

gloomy and uncertain. Congress indeed was earnestly engaged in forming a new system for the army; but they formed it without previous consultation with Washington, and thus fell into errors which it took much precious time to correct. Anxious forebodings darkened men's minds, and a vague surmise of something like treason, even before Arnold's treason became known, seems to have cast an ominous shadow over the land.

' The state of our public affairs," writes Reed in September, " now appears so problematical that I confess myself bewildered, and can hardly find a resting place for hope that some convulsion will not give the machine a new bias. Those who trace causes and effects, see nothing in our situation which might not be ascribed to the politics and measures of the summer of 1779, when the prospect of a winter's peace ardently pervaded all our public measures, and the landed men thought no risk of national honor or interest too great to turn off the weight of taxes. To these men, supposing no lurking treachery or wish to fall back to Great Britain, and to their measures, we owe our present distress. Hence has arose the absurd system of specific supplies, which in other words is a system to carry on war without money; hence the clamors against public officers, because otherwise those clamors would have fallen elsewhere. Perhaps it may be the crisis of our disorder, and we may find our political diseases less fatal than they appear in prospect. . . . The change of sentiment which has taken place in the army with respect to civil government has for the first time given me apprehensions. I am told that some officers of considerable rank have pressed the General to assume dictatorial authority. Is it so? Necessity may, perhaps, plead for such a measure; but certainly such power should be received from other hands. He, it is said, treated the proposition in a suitable manner. That necessity has ever been the tyrant's plea, and I prize his judgment and virtue too highly to believe he will contaminate a glorious and honorable life by this fatal mistake ; for however Congress may be depreciated, as well as their money, they are yet the supreme power of the country, and may be much easier appreciated than the public safety and honor after such an event." [1]

While the report that Washington had been urged by some of his officers to assume the dictatorship was spread in Philadelphia, an equally unfounded report that the eastern States were upon the point of forming a new confederacy, was spread in camp. [2] Both reports show the restlessness and anxiety of the public mind.

Arnold's treason had left the command of West Point vacant, and the certainty that the condition of this key of the Hudson was known to the English commander, made it necessary to take immediate steps for putting it in a state of defense. St. Clair was ordered there provisionally, but only till permanent arrangements could be made. Greene was anxious to obtain the command.

" A new disposition of the army going to be made," he writes to Washington on the 5th of October, "and an officer appointed to the command of West Point and the district on the east side of the North River, I take the liberty just to indicate my inclinations for the appointment. Your Excellency will judge of the propriety, and determine as the honor of the army and the good of the service may require.

" I hope there is nothing indelicate or improper in the application. I am prompted to the measure from the feel-

[1] Greene MSS.

[2] Letter of Royal Flint from Windham, October 6, 1780. — Greene MSS.

ings incident to the human heart, as well as encouraged in the hope that it would meet your approbation, from the flattering manner in which you have been pleased to speak of my conduct upon different occasions. I shall make use of no arguments, being persuaded my intentions and inclinations will have their full operation, and that nothing short of the public good and military propriety will contravene my wishes.

"My first object is the freedom and happiness of my country. With these, your Excellency's reputation and glory are inseparably connected; and as it has been my constant wish, so it shall be my future endeavor, to promote the establishment of both."

"There is no disposition that can be made of the army at this time, under our present uncertainties," writes Washington on the next day, "that may not be subjected to material change, as you will be convinced by recurring to the conversation which I held with you on Wednesday last. It is, as I observed to you on that occasion, a matter of great question with me, whether West Point will not become the head-quarters of the army, when we go into cantonments for the winter. I am very apprehensive that the diminution of our present force and the little prospect of recruiting the army in season, the importance of West Point, and economical motives, will compel us to concentre our forces on the North River, keeping light parties only on our flanks. If under this information you should incline to take the immediate command of the detachment which is about to march for West Point, and the general direction of matters on the east side of Hudson's River, it will be quite agreeable to me that you should do so. But candor has led me to a declaration of the uncertainty of that post's being long removed from my immediate command. The army will march and separate to-morrow. Your immediate determination is therefore necessary, that the orders may be prepared accordingly."[1]

[1] Sparks, *Writings of Washington*, vol. vii. p. 281.

Greene accepted, received his instructions the same day, and on the 7th his two divisions, composed of the Jersey and York brigades, with the brigades of Starke and Poor, began their march up the west bank of the Hudson. On the 8th he writes to Washington from Verplanck's Point : —

" The inclosed is an account given by a deserter just come to this post. It is probable, if the person is a spy, he will be in camp to-day, and probably to-morrow, as the army is on the move, and uncertain where it is marching to. To fix that, may detain him a day or two longer. I have thought it of sufficient importance to send an express, as the detection of spies is an interesting matter to the safety of an army, and the more hazardous the business is rendered the more difficult it will be for the enemy to obtain their intelligence.

" The troops under my command encamped last night at Haverstraw, and this morning marched for West Point. Part of the baggage is gone up the river, and the rest will go this evening. Most of the covered wagons are over the river, and by to-morrow morning the whole of the wagons will be over.

"General Wayne marched last evening from Haverstraw. General St. Clair, with the other brigade, will march in the morning, but perhaps not until late, as it will be difficult for me to give the orders this evening, not knowing with certainty whether the troops will arrive at West Point until the morning.

" Mr. Arthur Lee crossed King's Ferry last evening ; he purposes calling at head-quarters on his way to Philadelphia."

By evening he reached West Point, and immediately his observant eye and busy pen were at work.

" I am ordered here by the Commander-in-chief, with

four brigades to garrison this place," he writes to Governor Clinton on the 9th. " I got into garrison late last evening, and am sorry to find a place of such great importance is in such a miserable situation. The condition of the works, and the knowledge the enemy has of them from Arnold's late shameful and treasonable conduct, makes it necessary that every exertion should be made to complete them ; and I have it in charge from the Commander-in-chief to leave nothing unattempted to accomplish it.

"Though the force I command is but small, though the works are in such a bad condition, yet if the garrison is but furnished with provisions, wood, and forage, I have nothing to fear from the enemy, being persuaded the discipline and bravery of the troops will make up for the smallness of their numbers and the defects in the fortifications.

" The garrison is now upon half allowance of flour, and altogether unfurnished with wood, and but a trifling quantity of forage. While we remain in this situation, nothing can be done.

" The state of the treasury and the circumstances of the staff departments leave me little to hope without the helping hand of government. I therefore take the earliest opportunity to make your Excellency acquainted with the situation of the garrison, nothing doubting but that I shall receive every aid and support which the resources of the country, under the direction of legislators perfectly disposed to give it, can afford. Much is to be done and but little time to do it in. For this reason I wish I could have the honor of an interview with your Excellency ; and as it is impossible for me to be absent a night, if it should be inconvenient for you to visit this post I should be happy to meet you at Fishkill."

On the same day he detaches one hundred infantry and forty cavalry to collect cattle under the governor's warrant; and writes to call Colonel

Hughes to the Point to examine with him the question of supplies, "and many other matters too numerous to enter into the detail of." " In order to lessen the consumption of forage," he directs " all the officers' horses to be sent out into the country to be kept," and entering into detail, adds, " It will be best to agree with the farmers to keep them by the week, if possible, and to take the entire charge of them."

He had found his garrison upon a short allowance of provisions. " As you have been long in this place," he writes to Colonel Hay on the 10th, " and are perfectly acquainted with all the resources of every kind, as well as the most proper means of drawing them forth, I should be happy to see and consult with you on the subject." Thus his first step is to seek information from those whose experience qualified them to give it.

On the 10th he again writes to Colonel Hughes:

" His Excellency the Commander-in-chief is exceeding anxious to have the fortifications completed at this place, as well on account of Arnold's knowledge of them, and for the more certain security, should we at any time be obliged for want of provisions or other articles to reduce the garrison. A great quantity of lime will be wanted for this purpose, and the quartermaster here informs me there is very little on hand. I am therefore to request you will take the most effectual and speedy measures for furnishing us with an immediate supply. We cannot proceed in the works without it. Besides what will be wanted for the .fortifications, a considerable quantity will be wanted for the barracks of the men and officers."

The artillery comes next in order of preparation, and on the 11th he writes to Knox : —

" I have been here so little time that I have not had opportunity to examine fully into the state of the artillery, but
from the observations I have made, I see the gun-carriages
are in bad order. I am told there is no artificers in your
line, and by the return very few in the quartermaster's line,
and a prodigious deal of work to do in every line, particularly in yours and the engineer's. I beg you, therefore, to
order us a detachment of artificers from the main army,
without which I fear your department will be in a bad state,
as it is impossible to furnish artificers for that service from
the few that is in the quartermaster's line.

" Everything here is in a bad state. But the worst of
all is we have not a mouthful of flour in garrison except
the little lodged in the forts."

Another counsellor whom he calls to his aid is
McDougall, the commander of one of his divisions.
He has had McDougall under him before and
knows him to be firm and prompt in action. He
has letters of his too, in his portfolio, letters written during McDougall's long and efficient agency
as deputy of the general officers to represent their
claims to Congress, and he knows him to be wise
and judicious in council.

" I am ordered here with four brigades," Greene writes
him on the 11th, " to garrison this place, and to endeavor
to complete the fortifications. Your division is two of the
four brigades, which I was directed by the Commander-in-
chief to inform you of.

"I shall be happy to see and consult with you upon the
proper disposition to be made of the troops for the security
of the garrison as well as for covering the lower country.
To-morrow I propose to pay my compliments to the Governor at Poughkeepsie, as we are in a most wretched
situation for want of provisions, wood, and forage.

"I shall go to Fishkill Landing by water and then by land and intend to be back the same night. The day after to-morrow I could wish to see you here for one day. After which you will be at full liberty to attend to your domestic affairs.

"We have not an ounce of flour in the garrison, except the little deposited in the fortifications. This is not a little alarming. The main army was in the same situation when I left it."

The same day opens his official correspondence with his successor in the Quartermaster's department.

"On my arrival at this place, I found everything in so disagreeable a train, so much to do and so little time to do it in, that I have stopped Captain Seiger's company of artificers from marching, until I would have an opportunity to inform you of the situation of the garrison and the necessity for increasing the artificers here, without which it will be impossible to go on with the fortifications agreeable to the order of the Commander-in-chief. The engineer requires double the number now in employ here, and there is constant repairs of boats and so forth sufficient to employ fifty men, besides a great number of barracks to be built for the winter; and as they are all to be framed it will be a slow, tedious business without a great number of hands.

"Instead of decreasing our present number, we want large reinforcements either to put the garrison in a proper state of defense or comply with his Excellency's order.

"I shall wait your answer respecting Captain Seiger's company's marching."

Colonel Livingston, who still commands at Verplanck's Point, where his cannonade of the *Vulture* had led to such important results, writes to Greene for instructions upon several points.

"Your two letters of the 10th and 11th were duly received," Greene answers on the 11th.

"I have made particular inquiry respecting the whale-boats and can hear of none. I shall make further inquiry, and if I can find any will order a couple to your post.

"Never did I see such a gulf to swallow up men as this post. Such a detail of guards and fatigues as is called for astonishes me, and yet I cannot say but the whole appears necessary from the circumstances of the post and its appendages and the nature of the business which is carrried on of different kinds in the several departments.

"You must contrive to man your two boats (if possible) from your own people,[1] and if there are none that can perform the service you will please to inform me. The two other boats which I propose to send shall be manned from the garrison at this place.

"The deserters shall be tried as soon as they arrive, as we have a court in being to try all persons brought before them.

"I beg you will look over the issues of provision at your post, as Mr. Stephens returns a great quantity issued."

On the next day he goes to Poughkeepsie to consult with Governor Clinton. But Clinton had not received Greene's letter in season. "I should do myself the pleasure of waiting upon you at West Point," he writes, "but from the information contained in the papers inclosed in the letter to his Excellency General Washington (which I send under a flying seal for your perusal and to be forwarded by express), I find it absolutely necessary

---

[1] Colonel Livingston had written on the 11th of October, "I must beg you'll give your orders that no old countrymen are sent here for the guard boats, as they can by no means be depended upon." — Greene MSS.

to proceed to Albany, and intend to set out this evening or to-morrow morning. The total want of every species of supplies I fear will prove fatal to us." Greene's only reward for that day's exertions was a row in his barge through the beautiful Newburg Bay and the return by starlight under the shadow of the Storm King, into the wild gorge of the Highlands.

On the next day, the 13th, he begins to carry out his plan for the collection of supplies. " I have detached a party of two hundred men," he writes to the quartermaster of the post, Daniel Carthy, " for the purpose of assisting the Quartermaster's department in getting a supply of wood for the use of this garrison. I wish you to take measures immediately for employing them to the most advantage in this service. As the party is to be divided into four divisions it will be necessary for you to look out four places to employ them at. This is done that we may see which is the most faithful in executing the orders they may receive. You will provide tools and everything necessary for the service."

The reader will remember Greene's solicitude about the kind of food which his soldiers ate, and the strong ground which he takes about the necessity of an abundant supply of vegetables. Another order of the 13th shows that he still holds to his old opinion upon this subject. " You will immediately provide a sufficient quantity of roots and vegetables of different kinds for the troops of this garrison," he writes to Colonel Udney Hay.

The amount of the garrison is at present about three thousand men, and perhaps will continue so until the 1st of January, when it will be reduced to little more than two thousand. I will give the commissary instructions to furnish you with the necessary estimates, and beg your early attention to the business."

Then having fairly begun his work in all its departments, he takes his pen in hand to tell Washington what he has done thus far.

"I arrived at this place on the evening of the 8th. The troops got into garrison on the morning of the 9th.

" The works of the garrison are very incomplete ; indeed very little has been done to them this campaign. On my arrival I made the following disposition of the troops. New Jersey brigade to man the redoubts Nos. 1, 2, 3, and 4. New York brigade to man Fort Putnam, Webb's and Wyllis's redoubts. Stark's brigade Fort Clinton. Two regiments of the New Hampshire brigade are on Constitution Island and two regiments are on the east side of the river on the table of ground at the foot of the mountains on which the north and south redoubts are constructed. On all alarms the troops are to man the respective works assigned them.

" I have detailed one hundred men to join the horse under Colonel Jameson to cover the lower country, and intend to detach a party of fifty men more on purpose to follow what are called the Cow-boys. This party I mean to be at liberty to pursue thieves through all their turnings and windings, as I am persuaded five thousand men upon stationary guards would not prevent their inroads.[1]

[1] Colonel Jameson wrote from Bedford New Purchase on the 10th of October : "I give it as my opinion that not less than six hundred men are sufficient to give protection to the inhabitants in the lower part of the country. The Cow-boys are so well acquainted with the country that it

" Upon examining the post at King's Ferry I find too much ordnance and too many stores there to be held upon the footing your Excellency has directed, and yet I fear it will be attended with great jealousies to remove them at this time. I am persuaded the greatest part will fall into the enemy's hands, it being impossible to get them off in the time that will be given between the enemy's appearance and their being up with the works.

" It appears to me highly probable, if the enemy ever move up the river in force, with a view of attacking this place, that the transports will be preceded by three or four armed vessels, which will immediately pass the batteries and prevent the stores from going off by water; nor can they get them away by land unless teams are kept in constant waiting for the purpose. If a surprise is meant upon West Point, no regard will be paid to the works below, and then considerable ordnance will be necessary to annoy the shipping as they pass.

" If a surprise is not meant, measures will be taken to prevent the stores from being got off. A disposition, therefore, that will be necessary for one purpose will be a little dangerous for the other. To dismantle the works at this time will give great alarm to the country already full of jealousies and apprehensions. If the ordnance and stores are continued, the redoubts had best be sold as dear as possible and held to the last extremity. I suppose if fifty men and two or three officers, at most, were left in each of the works and all the other officers and men sent away on the appearance of the enemy in force, and those that are left behind to have directions to defend the redoubts as long as possible, perhaps the alarm by their fall will not be materially different from an alarm by evacuation, and

will be necessary to keep scouts on every road between North River and the Sound to keep them from driving off the cattle. They are so connected with the people through this country that they frequently pass within two hundred yards of our sentries without our getting the least intelligence of them." — Greene MSS.

it will give more time to call in the country for the defense of this place. However, I don't apprehend the least danger of an attack from the enemy this winter; nor could they carry their point by storm if attempted.

" I have been round and viewed the works with Colonel Gouvion, and am of opinion that a block-house is absolutely necessary to keep possession of the ground between the redoubts No. 3 and 4, and have given orders for the construction accordingly. If the enemy should possess that ground I am persuaded they could soon dispossess us of the redoubts No. 3 and 4. Number 1 and 2 would become useless; and artillery be immediately opened upon Fort Putnam and all the lower works, which could not fail of reducing them.

" The numerous guards and detachments which are necessary for the service of this department will leave but a small number of men to be employed upon the works. Nor is the Quartermaster's department in a condition to second the business, being altogether in a state of confusion and unprovided with the articles. However, this difficulty, I hope, will be soon removed.

" I have sent off all the horses, as well private as public property except one for the commanding officer of brigades and the engineers' horses, and shall take every step in my power to provide wood and forage for the winter. But such is the poverty of the public and the difficulty attending the business, I am afraid the utmost exertions will fall far short of the demands of the service.

" We have been out of flour most part of the time since I have been here, and the troops have suffered exceedingly. The want of water prevents the mills from supplying us. I went to Poughkeepsie yesterday to see the Governor upon the business, but he was gone to Esopus. On my return last evening was happy to find eighty barrels had arrived from the southward. We have been obliged to take some from the forts, after letting the troops be without two

days. Colonel Barber has forwarded the returns called
for in your Excellency's letter of the 10th.

" Captain Philips has just returned from New York,
and says that a body of troops sailed from that place on
Sunday last.

" I have been so busy since I have been here that I have
not had time to complete the calculations of the expense
of an army of 32,000 men ; but am in hopes of getting
through this evening, and if I should will forward them in
the morning.

" I am taking measures to obtain intelligence, but the
channel is not yet open.

" I wish to be informed whether Major Lee's party succeeded in the attack on Bergen, and whether there is any
news from the southward, where the troops that sailed from
New York are said to be going."

I have already said that the closing of Greene's
connection with the Quartermaster's department
still occupied a portion of his attention. Questions with regard to the mode of handing over
the public property to the new department, and
of the claims of the original owner upon stores
not yet paid for, arose from time to time and were
referred to him for decision.

" The letter I wrote you respecting the delivery of the
public stores," he writes to Colonel Hay on the 10th of
October, " was upon the presumption that the people who
had the mortgage would not insist upon the sale of them
to discharge their claims upon the public for supplies.
This was what I mentioned to Colonel Pickering and
Colonel Hughes; that I am confident the people would
relinquish this claim, and that you would not think yourself justifiable to withhold the public stores because you
stood responsible for the debts.

"I am still of opinion the inhabitants will give up their mortgage, and let their demands rest upon the general principles of public credit, notwithstanding it is not the best. I wish the people to have all the credit due to their merit, and only wish you to settle the matter as soon as possible that the public service may not suffer, and that we may not be suspected of embarrassing the affairs of the new department. These were my motives for waiting and these are my wishes for your compliance. I am sensible you are in a delicate situation, and that you have run every risk to support the army and the business of my department. It is foreign from my wishes to plunge you into new embarrassments. On the contrary I should be glad to give you every assistance and indulgence in my power to enable you to extricate yourself.

"I shall add nothing further upon this subject, as I hope the pleasure of seeing you in a day or two."

Some officers of the staff had supposed that they were authorized to retain unpaid public stores as a protection against creditors.

"It is not my opinion," Greene writes to Morgan Lewis on the 14th of October, "that you can retain any of the public stores belonging to the Quartermaster's department upon any pretense whatever; and as your character and conduct has hitherto been unexceptionable, I wish you to avoid giving the least pretense to any one to tax you with an impropriety.

"To attempt to discriminate between the stores that may or may not be wanted, will only bring on this question. We cannot know what operations are in contemplation, and therefore cannot tell what stores will be wanted. If the stores are not necessary for the department at all, how came they to be provided. Upon the whole I am of opinion it will be more for your interest to deliver all the stores than to attempt to retain any part.

" The resolution of Congress for discharging the debts of the department for supplies agreeable to the specie value at the time and place where the debts arose, I conceive comprehends all debts due, let them have originated for supplies, services, or incidental expenses, and that there will be some medium of discrimination to be formed for the government in the settlement of the accounts of the agents. I wish you to write Mr. Pettit for an explanation, and desire him to forward you your account and voucher, as they are lodged with him at Philadelphia."

Other questions too, arise, which give us interesting glimpses of things remote from our daily experience but of daily occurrence then. " One Kennicutt," Colonel Jameson had written him on the 10th, " is very desirous to have his family moved from below and has applied to me for assistance ; he informs me that most of his property is with the enemy, but that he is afraid to venture below our lines as Arnold is acquainted with his character. I should be happy to have your directions whether to assist him or not."

" From the account and character of Mr. Kennicutt," Greene replies, " I think he is entitled to some assistance, and therefore wish you to help his family and effects."

In the same letter he answers some questions concerning Cow-boys, which Jameson had asked him in a letter of the 12th : —

" I can give no reply at present to propositions for exchanging the Cow-boys, nor can I promise a pardon to those on the line until I write Governor Clinton on the subject. But you may inform them that there is not the least doubt of their obtaining a pardon if they leave the service they are in immediately."

And in the postscript comes a stern question of discipline : —

" Inclosed I send you warrants for executing (two) men of your dragoons, Greene and Wearing, tried and condemned by a court-martial. I have given warrants for both their executions, but if there is anything in either of their characters which entitles them to mercy, it is my wish that but one should be executed as a sacrifice, as one will serve for an example as well as both. But if you think neither of them objects of mercy, you will have both executed. On the contrary, if you spare one, I will forward you a pardon."

It is pleasant to meet such proof that familiarity with the idea and sight of violent death had not blunted his sense of the sacredness of human life. That where duty required its sacrifice he never shrank, we have already seen and shall see again.

Another kind of appeal reaches him on the 14th.

" Your letter of yesterday," he writes to Colonel Udney Hay, " stating the suffering of the troops to the northward and requesting the liberty to take fifty head of fat cattle from this department, has this moment come to hand. I believe our stock of cattle on hand is far from being great, but if you and the commissary on consulting together are of opinion there will be a plenty for the troops here and comply with the requisition, I most cheerfully give my consent. But, on the other hand, if taking from this post will only serve to bring us into the same disagreeable situation, I cannot agree to it, as this post is far the most important, and the want of provisions will entirely frustrate our winter preparations, which from the extent of business and approaching season requires the greatest despatch.

"You will acquaint the commissary with the substance of this letter and take your measures accordingly."

There are other appeals, too, which cannot be passed over in a picture of the times. Francis Gennings appeals to him for a discharge, asserting that he had enlisted for three years and was about to be kept for the war. "The cause of my country," he writes in a clear business hand, "I have as much at heart (perhaps) as any one of my abilities; but to be defrauded into its service is what I am convinced the freemen of America never designed." [1]

A sadder case is that of Captain Mills, and we know from abundant contemporary testimony that it was but one of many. "Necessity," he writes, "compels me to trouble your Honor with a disagreeable narrative of my circumstances. I have served my country as faithfully as my abilities would admit ever since the commencement of the war. And what little interest I had is exhausted and a chargeable family to maintain. They are now suffering from want of the necessaries of life. I have no more horses or cattle to sell, which obliges me to beg the favor of an order to the commissary for provisions at the Continental price, for I cannot purchase it in the country for want of money." [2]

[1] Greene MSS. The petition of Francis Gennings, soldier in Colonel H. Jackson's regiment, 12th October, 1780.

[2] D. Mills, Captain of Artificers, to General Greene. — Greene MSS.

Often, too, as he took up his pen he must have fancied himself back again in his old department.

" Inclosed I send you," he writes to Colonel Blaine on the 15th, " a copy of a letter from Colonel Hay, Deputy Commissary-general for this State. The object in its consequences is so important, and the business requires such dispatch, that Mr. Betts is sent on purpose to receive your instructions upon the subject. I beg you to give me full information on the business, and to take the most effectual steps for providing for this garrison. You know its importance, and therefore there needs no arguments to urge your exertions.

" If salt is to come from the eastward, let me know from whom and from what place, and I will add my influence to yours to get it on before the cold weather sets in.

" The frontiers of this State is attacked, therefore the greater attention to this department will be necessary.

" I want to have a general state of the arrangement of your department to the eastward, and the agents you employ, that I may communicate with them upon all emergencies. Such is the state of public business and the want of money, that every department as well civil as military, must unite their influence to supply this defect, and all will prove incompetent."

" P. S. — This place has been without flour the greater part of the time I have been here, and there is scarcely a hogshead of rum in garrison, and no prospect of a better supply."

Meanwhile he had found or made time for answering Washington's call for estimates of the expenses of the war. I give the whole letter, for there can be no better illustration of the relations between Washington and Greene than such calls and such answers to them.

"Inclosed I send your Excellency," Greene writes on the 14th, "the estimates of the annual expense of the war, and the amount of what each State can pay towards the charge. Nothing more can be expected from them than to prove that our income is not equal to our expense. They are calculated upon a low or lower scale than the neat cost will amount to.

"Besides these estimates there are several other matters not included in the bills, namely, the expenses of the navy, the charge of enlisting men, the support of our ministers abroad at foreign courts, the interest of our funded moneys, with a great variety of other matters, which can only be calculated upon under the head of contingencies, but will operate upon the people in the bills of general charges. On the other hand, the States are taxed as high as they can bear, and much higher I am afraid than will be paid, unless our governments are far more nervous than they have been.

"By the account current your Excellency will see that our expenses overrun our income near one half, and this is a fact that I have been a long time convinced of, though I did not think our arrearages had been as great as I now am persuaded they are.

"I wish my knowledge was more competent to the business, and that I had had more leisure to have done justice to the subject. I have devoted as much time, paid as much attention, and got as good information as my situation and circumstances would admit. If the calculations shall in any manner reflect any light upon the subject, or pave the way to further and more accurate estimates, I shall be amply rewarded."

It was to the power which Greene displayed in dealing with subjects like these that Hamilton alluded when he attributed to him an "universal and pervading genius, which qualified him not less for the Senate than for the field." [1]

And now active work seems to be preparing on the northern frontier.

"The letter from Governor Clinton which will accompany this," he writes to Washington on the 15th, "will give your Excellency an account of the inroads of the enemy upon our frontiers, of the surrender of Forts George and Ann, and that preparations are making for the investiture of Fort Schuyler.

"The inclosed paper, containing the examination of Sergeant Ceely, who came here last night, being forwarded by General Bayley, may give your Excellency some idea of the enemy's force.

"I think it will be important to give the enemy as early a check as possible, and for this purpose I have ordered Colonel Gansevort's regiment to embark immediately for Albany, and put Clinton's whole brigade under marching orders. I don't think myself at liberty to go further without your Excellency's directions, but hope the step I have taken will meet your approbation.

"Provisions are as scarce and difficult to be got to the northward as they are here. I was obliged to give an order last night that fifty head of cattle be sent from this place to prevent the forts to the northward from being evacuated for want of provisions. This was previous to my hearing of the incursions of the enemy, though I expected it from the preparations making in Canada.

"The propriety of detaching largely from this place will depend in a great degree upon the number of men that lately embarked at New York, of which your Excellency I hope is more fully informed than I am.

"I will have the transports in readiness to embark the remainder of Clinton's brigade, against the return of the express.

[1] Eulogium on General Greene. — Hamilton's *Works*, vol. ii. p. 482.

" Colonel Hay set out yesterday to the northward, to provide in that quarter ; and as Colonel Hughes begins to act in the Quartermaster's department, I hope the exertions here will be equal to the emergency of the occasion."

CHAPTER XII.

WHILE Greene was thus strenuously engaged in the duties of his new command, the conviction was gradually gaining ground that he would soon be called to a broader and more important field. As early as September it was forseeen that the friends of General Gates would be compelled by the general dissatisfaction which his conduct excited, to consent to his recall. On the 6th of September, almost as soon as the tidings of Gates' defeat reached head-quarters, Hamilton wrote to Duane : —

" Was there ever an instance of a general running away, as Gates has done from his whole army ? And was there ever so precipitous a flight ? One hundred and eighty miles in three days and a half ! It does admirable credit to the activity of a man at his time of life. But it disgraces the general and the soldier. I always believed him to be very far short of a Hector or a Ulysses. All the world, I think, will begin to agree with me. But what will be done by Congress ? Will he be changed or not ? If he is changed, for God's sake overcome prejudice, and send Greene. You know my opinion of him. I stake my reputation on the events, give him but fair play." [1]

[1] *History of the Republic of the United States of America*, as traced in the

" Should a Major-general be detached to relieve General Gates, which is not improbable," Cornell wrote on the 19th of that month, " I believe you would be the man." Greene remembered what Washington had written him before Gates had been appointed.

" I am sorry for the difficulties you have to encounter in the department of Quartermaster, especially as I have been instrumental in some degree in bringing you into it. Under these circumstances I cannot undertake to give advice, or even to hazard an opinion on the measures best for you to adopt. Your judgment must direct you ; if it points to a resignation of your present office, and your inclination leads you to the southward, my wish shall accompany it ; and if the appointment of a successor to General Lincoln is left to me, I shall not hesitate in preferring you to this command ; but I have little expectation of being consulted on the occasion."

He was not consulted ; and the favorite of Congress met a disastrous defeat. But there was reason to believe that " the spirit of party was now much abated," [1] and that the opinion of the Commander-in-chief would be listened to with the deference which his character and position demanded. What that opinion was no one could doubt.

" When the intelligence first came from the southward," writes Pettit on the 5th October, " it pressed hard upon the reputation of a certain general, even from his own account of the matter ; but when further explanations came, it seemed to kindle into a flame which could not be wholly suppressed, though most people seemed desirous

writings of Hamilton and some of his cotemporaries, by John C. Hamilton, vol. ii. p. 124.

[1] Joseph Jones to Washington. Correspondence of the Revolution, vol. iii. p. 103.

of keeping it secret, some from real regard to his fame, others from prudential motives, unwilling to be foremost in attacking so eminent a character (no matter how raised); and others again thought it might be injurious to the public to unhinge him at so critical a season, and under such difficult circumstances as the southern army, and indeed our affairs in general, are reduced to. The reasoning also run probably into smaller branches; but be that as it may, the matter seemed to cool and be skinned over in such a manner that many doubted whether it would not lie buried till the end of the campaign, or some more convenient season of inquiry. For my own part I thought it would depend much on the part the officers of the Maryland line should take; and thus it rested on my mind till I received your letter. On making some inquiry about it, I find the letters from the southward have expressed great dissatisfaction; that the North Carolina militia particularly are much hurt on the occasion, and charge their disgrace on the commander-in-chief, and that they refuse to serve under him again.[1] These things have been told me, and by the proceedings in Congress I suppose them to be true."

And continuing his letter the next day, he adds : —

" I have been obliged to break off till this morning. A member of Congress has just informed me that a Court of Inquiry is ordered on the conduct of General Gates, which clearly suspends his command; that Congress have desired General Washington to appoint a general to the command; that the southern gentlemen particularly seemed desirous that General Greene should be appointed; 'but,' added the gentleman, ' I hope he will not, because I know the fate of the officer who shall undertake it, especially if he be from the eastward; no eastern man can please

[1] *Vide* also a letter of Governor Nash of North Carolina to General Washington, dated Newbern, 6 October, 1780. *Correspondence of the Revolution*, vol. iii. p. 107.

those people, nor succeed in his command, unless he should be favored by circumstances which no man has a right to expect.' I asked who else they could get, or whether a southern general could be found fit for it; the answer was ' No; but (making use of pretty harsh epithets in expressing the sentiment) they understand one another best and are fittest to go together.' These orders, it seems, passed in Congress yesterday, and though they have not, that I can learn, pointed out any person to the General for the command, it has been talked of among them. General St. Clair has been mentioned (*an illegible line*)— was objected, and it went off, though I fancy that was not the real reason with them all; but the southern people are strongly prejudiced against a Caledonian, having an ugly nest of them in their own bounds in North Carolina. The general expectation here, so far as I have learned, is that General Greene ought to be and will be the man. My informant of this morning offered another reason in support of his wish to the contrary — that General Greene's presence to the eastward would be indispensably necessary. His particular meaning in this he did not explain." [1]

Colonel Biddle writes on the same day : —

" Yesterday Congress ordered that a court of inquiry should be held on General Gates, and I am told you were to be proposed this day for the southern command. Though you have warm and honest friends, you have your enemies also to oppose you. I shall hope that you may obtain this command, because I think you may serve your country and distinguish yourself." [2]

On the 10th Colonel Pettit returns again to the subject; for not only Greene's friends, but the country in general felt that this, at the moment, was the most important subject before them.

[1] Greene MSS.   [2] Greene MSS.

"In a letter I wrote to you five or six days since," he says, "and left at the deputy quartermaster's office to be forwarded (knowing of no earlier method), I mentioned to you all I could collect respecting the workings in Congress relative to the general to the southward. The substance and amount of which was, that General Gates was to be recalled and inquiry made into his conduct, and that his Excellency, the Commander-in-chief, was desired to appoint a general officer to take his place ; and that also by the particular desire of the southern representatives, that appointment would probably fall on General Greene ; that some of his friends here, so far as this distinction appears honorable, were pleased with it as an act of justice rather than as of favor, and considering some late transactions, they thought the honor the greater because — I need not say why. But at the same time these friends rather trembled for his fate unless he should be favored with greater success than circumstances, or rather appearances, at present allow us to expect on the scale of human probability. The general opinion supposes success more probable in the hands of General Greene than any other that has been named, and doubts not he would acquire it if it be attainable by any one ; but the prospect in that quarter (I mean chiefly as to our ability and means to furnish supplies) is rather gloomy. This circumstance, however, is in some respects favorable to the person who shall undertake the business. It will lessen the censure in case of failure, and if he succeeds his success will be the more brilliant. Some one must take the command, and the public good requires it should be him in whose hands success is most likely to happen." [1]

On the 13th the intelligence of Gates' recall reached camp, and Knox immediately wrote : —

"By this time, it is to be presumed, you are pretty well

[1] Greene MSS.

seated amidst the mountains of Hudson's River; but I pray you not to fix your affections too strongly on the craggy precipices that surround you; if you do, it is probable a separation might cause you much pain. I am informed (not from head-quarters) that General Gates is recalled to answer to Congress some matters respecting the geography of the Southern States, and that his Excellency is directed to send some general in his stead. Who will that person be? You may ask me the same question, but I protest I know not, for I have had no opportunity of deriving knowledge where it was to be found, since I heard of Gates' recall. Poor fellow! the heat of the southern climate has blasted the laurels which were thought from their splendor to be ever green!" [1]

I have said that the resolution of the 5th of October reached head-quarters at the Falls of the Passaic on the 13th, and with it a letter of the 6th from Mr. Matthews. "I am authorized," says this letter, "by the delegates of the three southern States to communicate to your Excellency their wish, that Major-general Greene may be the officer appointed to the southern department, if it would not be incompatible with the rules of the army." [2] Had there been any hesitation in Washington's mind, such a recommendation, under such circumstances, would have gone far towards removing it. But there was no hesitation. He still remembered what he had written in June; and since June, every occurrence in which Greene had borne a part had contributed to raise him still higher in public estimation. In what esteem the army held him everybody knew; and even with

[1] Greene MSS.   [2] Sparks, *Writings of Washington*, vol. vii. p. 259.

Congress he was thought to " stand foremost in the line of major-generals in their good graces." [1] Without delay, therefore, Washington wrote on the 14th of October : —

" By a letter received yesterday afternoon from his Excellency the President of Congress, dated the 6th instant, and inclosing a copy of a resolution of the preceding day, I find it has been their pleasure to order me to direct a court of inquiry to be held on the conduct of Major-general Gates, as commander of the southern army; and also to direct me to appoint an officer to command it in his room, till the inquiry shall be made. As Congress have been pleased to leave the officer who shall command on this occasion to my choice, it is my wish to appoint you ; and from the pressing situation of affairs in that quarter, of which you are not unapprised, that you should arrive there as soon as circumstances will possibly admit. Besides my own inclination to this choice, I have the satisfaction to inform you that from a letter I have received, it concurs with the wishes of the delegates from the three southern States most immediately interested in the present operations of the enemy ; and I have no doubt that it will be perfectly agreeable to the sentiments of the whole. Your ulterior instructions will be prepared when you arrive here.

" I suppose that General Heath, if not already at West Point, is on his way from Rhode Island. I write to him to take command of the post. If he is with you, be pleased to communicate to him your instructions with respect to it, and any other matters you may judge it to be material

---

[1] " Ever since the exceeding hard ride General Gates had between the 16th and 20th of August, which is a most mortifying stroke to the gentlemen from Massachusetts and some others, though I think they do not yet sufficiently realize their mortifi- cation. A proper opportunity is only waited for, when justice will be done, which never fails to make the tools of wickedness shudder." General Cornell to General Greene, Sept 19, 1880. — Greene MSS.

for him to know. If he has not arrived, General Mc-
Dougall will command till he comes; to whom I also write
for the purpose, and to whom you will make the communications I have requested, which he will transfer to
General Heath.

"I have only to add, that I wish for your earliest arrival, that there may be no circumstances to retard your
proceeding to the southward, and that the command may
be attended with the most interesting good consequences
to the States and the highest honor to yourself." [1]

It is easy to conceive the feelings with which
Washington traced these lines, and the responsive
feelings with which Greene read them. They
had both suffered much from the weak ambition
of Gates, his hostility to Greene having even
betrayed him into ungentlemanly rudeness to
Greene's wife.[2] Mortification and disgrace had
come upon him through his own folly. We shall
presently see how gently both of these injuried
men bore themselves towards him in the day of
his adversity. But their feelings towards each
other had never found such an occasion for mani-
festation before. Washington's appointment of
Greene was an open avowal of confidence at a
moment of peculiar delicacy. Greene's acceptance of it was a declaration that he felt himself
worthy of the trust. How fully that confidence
was justified and that declaration borne out, my
next volume will show.

"Your Excellency's letter of the 14th, appointing me to
the command of the southern army," Greene immediately
replied, " was delivered me last evening.

[1] Sparks, *Writings of Washington*,   [2] Greene MSS.
vol. vii. p. 257.

"I beg your Excellency to be persuaded that I am fully sensible of the honor you do me, and will endeavor to manifest my gratitude by a conduct that will not disgrace the appointment. I only lament that my abilities are not more competent to the duties that will be required of me, and that it will not be in my power on that account, to be as extensively useful as my inclination leads me to wish. But as far as zeal and attention can supply the defect, I flatter myself my country will have little cause to complain. I foresee the command will be accompanied with innumerable embarrassments. But the generous support which I expect from the partiality of the southern gentlemen, as well as the aid and assistance which I expect to derive from your Excellency's advice and extensive influence, affords me some consolation in contemplating the difficulties.

"I will prepare myself for the command as soon as I can. But as I have been five years and upwards in service, during which time I have paid no attention to the settlement of my domestic concerns (and many divisions of interest, and partitions of landed property between me and my brothers have taken place in the time, and now lie unfinished), if it was possible, I should be glad to spend a few days at home before I set out to the southward, especially as it is altogether uncertain how long my command may continue, or what deaths or accidents may happen during my absence to defeat the business. I beg your Excellency's opinion on the matter, by which I will regulate my conduct. However, it will not be possible for me to leave this place in several days, if I put my baggage in the least order, or my business in a proper train for such a long journey. Nor is my health in a condition to set out immediately, having had a considerable fever upon me for several days.

"General Heath arrived last evening, and will take the command this morning. I shall make him fully acquainted with all the dispositions I have made and steps taken which concern the post and its dependencies, and will give him my opinion what is best to be done to carry into execution your Excellency's instructions for putting the garrison in a proper state of defense, and prepare it for the approaching winter.

" General McDougall is also here, and I have the pleasure to inform you that he and I perfectly agree in sentiment in what concerns the garrison and its dependencies."

Greene's appointment was not long a secret.

" Colonel Peabody informs me," writes Richard Claiborne, from Morristown, the very day that it was made, " that General Gates is suspended, and that you have been solicited to take command of the southern army. The thing has got out, and every one wishes you may accept the appointment. . . . . I am happy to find that notwithstanding the unjust prejudices in Congress against you, they still acknowledge that this country is much indebted to you for your attention to its welfare, and that it must not want your further services.

" Colonel Peabody is anxious for you to take the command proposed, and Mr. Matthews, who was no great friend of yours when the committee first came to camp, acknowledges the importance you have been and can be to the public good." [1]

Pettit received the tidings with great joy. Greene's appointment to such a command at such a moment, was a public declaration that the charges against his administration of the Quartermaster's department were false. This implied declaration had been made when he was reappointed under the new system; but this new

---

[1] Major Claiborne to General Greene, from Morristown, 16th October 1780. — Greene MSS.

appointment left no pretext for malice to build
upon. Greene stood justified by the voice of his
country. Pettit writes in great glee : —

" General Greene's appointment to the command of the
southern army leads me to expect him here in a very few
days. I take it for granted he will occupy the quarters
he had when he was last in town, without the ceremony of
a formal invitation, or the compliments usually made to
great men on such occasions. I mention this, however,
rather to accommodate than embarrass him ; and my expectation rests on a supposition that it will be perfectly
convenient to him.

" The uncertainty of this letter's meeting you either at
camp or on the way hither, discourages me from making it
lengthy ; otherwise you would probably have had the
trouble of reading more pages than one, as my head is so
far recovered as to have collected a few ideas again, and it
is long since I have been able to write to you with the
wonted ease and freedom ; but what I write to you is intended for your own reading, and I would not willingly
give the person into whose hands it might fall, in case it
should miss you, the trouble of reading what might be
perfectly uninteresting to him.

" On recollection, my memory suggests (but it is yet
rather flimsy) that Major Burnet dropped some expressions that indicated Mrs. Greene's being expected at
camp ; in that case she will probably accompany you thus
far. I beg you to present to her the very respectful compliments of Mrs. Pettit, my daughters, and myself, and ask
her whether she would choose to alight at our door in the
first instance, or go to an Inn, in order to have the ceremony
of being waited on. If the latter be her choice, I beg she
would settle the form beforehand, and favor me with a
copy in writing. If she should have occasion for a precedent, one may be found in the proceedings of a certain

great assembly on the reception of a foreign minister, which were published in August, 1778."

Greene's appointment was received by the army with universal satisfaction. "General Greene is to go," writes Major Shaw to his brother William. "Let the people in that quarter furnish the men and the necessary supplies, and, if anything is to be expected from the abilities and exertion of a single person, I think no one will be more likely to answer every reasonable expectation than this amiable officer. There can be no better proof of his worth than the universal regret which all ranks among us feel at the idea of parting with him, although the good of our country calls loudly for the separation. A glorious tribute this, which can only be paid to true merit."[1]

Greene immediately began his preparations, numerous details of his past and present command crowding upon him together. A glance at those preparations will give us a nearer view of him. And first, with his habitual method and order, he provides for the Quartermaster's department by a circular to his former assistants. It is dated on the same day with his acceptance of his new command.

"Being appointed to the command of the southern army, I take the earliest opportunity to acquaint you therewith ; that if there arise any difficulties in the Quartermaster-general's department, that they must be referred to Mr. Pettit, as it will be impossible for me to pay the least attention thereto. I beg you'll favor Colonel Picker-

[1] *Life and Journals of Major Shaw*, p. 83.

ing, the present Quartermaster-general, with a return of all the stores you have to deliver over to the new department; and the sooner you can bring your accounts to a close the better. Nothing like the time present to settle disputable points. If the accounts are not brought to a close before the war ceases, and the circumstances should be forgot, and people to judge of the matter altogether unacquainted with the transactions, and thoroughly tinctured with prejudices, little justice is to be expected from people of this cast. The only way to avoid it is to push things to a close as soon as possible."

We have seen that Greene had asked for a few days at home, in order to arrange his private affairs. What the condition of these private affairs was we shall see by and by; but although the desire was natural and just, it could not be granted.

" Your letter of the 16th," Washington had answered on the 18th, " was delivered to me an hour since. I am aware that the command you are entering upon will be attended with peculiar difficulties and embarrassments; but the confidence I have in your abilities, which determined me to choose you for it, assures me you will do everything the means in your power will permit to surmount them, and stop the progress of the evils which have befallen and still menace the southern States. You may depend upon all the support I can give you, from the double motives of regard to you personally and to the public good.

" I wish that circumstances could be made to correspond with your wishes to spend a little time at home previously to your setting out; but your presence with your command as soon as possible is indispensable. The embarkation at New York sailed the 16th, and is in all probability destined to coöperate with Earl Cornwallis, who, by the last advices, was advanced as far as Charlotte. I hope to see you without delay, and that your health will be no obstacle to your commencing your journey." [1]

" Your Excellency's favor of the 18th," Greene replied the following day, " came to hand this afternoon. I had given over the thoughts of going home, even if I obtained your permission, before I received your pleasure upon the subject. My affairs require it ; but I am fully convinced that the time it will take, and the state of the southern department, will not admit of the indulgence. When I marched from Tappan, I wrote to Mrs. Greene to come to camp, and expect her here every hour. Should I set out before her arrival, the disappointment of not seeing me, added to the shock of my going to the southward, I am very apprehensive will have some disagreeable effect upon her health, especially as her apprehensions have been all alive respecting my going to the southward, before there was the least probability of it.

" My baggage sets out in the morning, if Colonel Hughes does not disappoint me about the horses; and my stay shall not be more than a day longer, whether Mrs. Greene arrives or not. Your Excellency cannot be more anxious to have me come on, than I am to comply with your orders, especially since the two last articles of intelligence, the sailing of the troops at New York, and the advance of Lord Cornwallis into the State of North Carolina." [2]

One of his last letters from the Point was addressed to his friend and kinsman, Governor William Greene. It is dated the 19th of October : —

" I was favored with your letter by General Heath, who arrived at this place three days since.   Just as he arrived

---

[1] Sparks, *Writings of Washington*, vol. vii. p. 263.

[2] As a proof of Greene's industry, I will add that this letter as originally drafted, differs materially from the copy sent to Washington. I give the original draft in the Appendix. To me it seems easier and stronger than the corrected copy.

I received a letter from the Commander-in-chief, informing me that General Gates was recalled from the command of the southern army, and that I was appointed to the command. The southern clime has blasted the northern laurels; and I wish I may not fall a sacrifice to the lukewarm measures pursuing in that quarter, to oppose a powerful enemy already there and now going there.

"A great man said it was not in the power of mortals to command success; but he would do more, he would endeavor to deserve it. My best endeavors shall not be wanting to serve my country; but I much doubt my abilities for such a difficult command, accompanied with so many embarrassments.

"I leave the northern world with a heavy heart, as it will be such a great remove from my nearest and dearest connections. Mrs. Greene will be made very miserable upon the occasion; and what will make it still more grievous is, its duration is altogether uncertain, and the distance is so great, and my fortune so small, that I shall have but little opportunity to see any part of my family until my return.

"This will be handed you by Colonel Sherburne, who is on his return home, his regiment having been reduced sometime since. A better officer the service don't afford; and perhaps few persons possess an equal share of good qualities to render domestic life agreeable, or to adorn a public station with more dignity.

"I shall not have time to write to the brothers at Potowomut; but I beg you'll remember me affectionately to all of them. Please also to make my most respectful compliments to Mrs. Greene and the young ladies.

"I could write you a volume upon politics, but time will not permit. I must beg leave to refer you to the Colonel, who, having been much in my family lately, has a perfect knowledge of my sentiments and those of the army in general, as well as many out of it."

CHAPTER XIII.

Influence of Domestic Feelings. — Greene's Letters to his Wife. — Expects her at Camp. — Correspondence. — Disappointment. — Sets out for Head-quarters. — Goes to Philadelphia.

BUT our picture of these last days on the banks of the Hudson would be incomplete without that home group of his wife and their four little children which his letters to her keep so constantly before us. I know that these things have little to do with the external manifestations of the statesman and the soldier, but they often have much to do with the spirit which makes those manifestations possible. And in Greene's character, as in Washington's, they impose sacrifices and self-denials, little heeded in the common summary of events, but which deserve to be carefully considered if we would paint men and things as they really were. Washington, in announcing to his wife his appointment to the command of the army, assures her that he would " enjoy more real happiness in one month with (her) at home, than (he) had the most distant prospect of finding abroad, if his stay were to be seven times seven years." [1]   Greene, on the point of first setting " off for camp," writes, " I have not so much in my mind that wounds my

[1] Sparks, *Writings of Washington,* vol. iii. p. 2.

peace as the separation from you." [1] As they felt
when they wrote those words, they felt to the last.
The longing for home went with them wherever
they went. It finds expression in long letters,
written late in the night, after a toilsome day. It
suggests hasty lines, written in the saddle, when
the last sounds of battle are dying away. And
when winter comes, and the marching and fighting
cease for a while, the first thought of these true men
is to call their wives to them, and make for themselves a family fireside within the narrow walls of
their log huts. If we would tell their story truly,
we must not leave out these feelings and their constant and earnest expression of them.

On the 16th of September, Greene wrote to his
wife from the camp near Hackensack : —

" The express which went eastward with the circular
letters of the first of this month, has returned, and brought
me your letters of the 6th and 7th, with three shirts.
You mention six having been sent. I beg you will be kind
enough in your next to inform me by whom the other
three were forwarded, as they have not come to hand, and
I am afraid will not.

" As I shall have an opportunity to write you by a safer
conveyance than the post in a few days, I shall not enter
upon several points mentioned in your letters, but beg you
to rest perfectly satisfied that all is harmony and gentle-
ness, perfectly to your wishes.

" General Gates's defeat to the southward, and the report prevailing of a French fleet's being upon the coast
from the West Indies, prevents my being explicit upon the
subject of your coming to camp.

---

[1] Greene to his wife, vol. i. p. 83.

"I am sorry to hear Nat is unwell, but am glad he is getting better. It gives me the most sensible pain to find your health is on the decline. I am happy the rest of the little flock are in good health, knowing from your sensibility your health in a great degree depends on theirs.

"I have been a little unwell for some days; but am now in good spirits, and perfectly recovered, except my old complaint of the asthma, which is troublesome o' nights."

One of the subjects of Mrs. Greene's letters was the prospect of a visit to camp.

"Your letter of the 2d of this month," Greene writes on the 22d of September, "with the three shirts by the wagoner, came safe to hand.

"Your poetry is both agreeable and distressing. It is true my benevolence feels sensibly for you, but my love and affection much more. What can I do, or how shall I act? If I grant your wishes, perhaps I shall involve you in greater difficulties. Nothing is determined with respect to the issue of the campaign; and our affairs to the southward leave me much in the dark what turn things will take with respect to myself. I long to see you, yet fear to meet in the army. Everything here is disagreeable, and there is little prospect of things mending soon.

"Your hopes cannot be stronger than my wishes; and still I hesitate to indulge one and gratify the other. You shall not be kept, my dear, in a moment's suspense after I can determine what is best for our mutual happiness.

"You mention the black eyes of Mrs. —— and Mrs. ——. Let me ask you soberly whether you estimate yourself below either of these ladies. You will answer me No, if you speak as you think. I declare upon my sacred honor, independent of the partiality I ought to feel, I think they possess far less accomplishments than you; and as much as I respect them as friends, I should never be happy with them in a more intimate connection.

will leave you so to-morrow as well as to-day. If I err, it is from the best of motives. I am not willing you should become like the spring flowers, engaging only for a day. I want to render your happiness permanent and lasting; and though it may vary like the seasons, will nevertheless be agreeable through the whole.

" The minister of France is on his way to Newport. He dined with me to-day; and says he intends to go by the way of Providence. If so, it is probable he will call on you at Coventry. For this reason I have set down to write you this letter, though late in the night, as the minister goes early in the morning.

" His Excellency is from camp, and I have the command of the army. This makes a great man of me for a few days. What puppies and pygmies men are. You say we are the lords of creation. Many of us are the dupes of knaves and the tools of folly. O this war! I would to God it was over! But alas, I fear this is but the middle of the horrid scene; and yet I cannot help flattering myself with more agreeable things.

" How and where is Polly? You don't mention her in your letters. Is she yet on Block Island, or at Coventry? Have you got your carriage painted? Pray get it done before you think of coming from home with it, for the reasons I have mentioned before in a former letter." [1]

In October things seemed to have taken a more decided turn, and for the moment a turn favorable to Mrs. Greene's wishes. " I am this moment going to begin my march for West Point," her husband writes on the 7th of October, " which place, and the troops on the east side of the North River, I am to have command of. This is only a temporary disposition for the fall. It is yet uncertain what dis-

---

[1] The arms of the former owner, a Tory.

position will be made for the winter. Perhaps I may spend the winter there, and perhaps not. The situation is not much to my liking, there being little prospect of glory or comfort; and therefore I am almost afraid to give you an invitation to come and see me." He gives it, however, adding, " When I wrote you before respecting the children, I thought it was your wish to bring George with you. The situation and many circumstances are against it; nevertheless I leave it altogether with you. Mrs. Knox too hopes to pass the winter there, and Mrs. Hagen will be with them."

This was an uncertain prospect, but still there was promise in it. Mr. Hubbard goes as a special messenger to attend Mrs. Greene on her journey. Greene counts the days, gives Mr. Hubbard four to reach Coventry, Mrs. Greene four to prepare and six to come in. In fourteen days she would be with him, and wild and craggy West Point would begin to look like home.

Then came Washington's letter of the 16th, and all was changed. Another express was dispatched, " with orders to ride night and day," in order to give Mrs. Greene time to reach the Point before her husband left. But neither letter nor express came; and late in the evening of the 20th, Greene retraces his steps by starlight from Fishkill, whither he had ridden to meet her, to the house of Mr. Mandervill, opposite West Point, where he was to pass the night, and taking up his pen with a heavy heart, writes his farewell words.

"I am rendered unhappy beyond expression," he begins, "that fatal necessity obliges me to take my leave of you in this way. I have waited until the last moment, in hopes of your arrival, and have just returned from Fishkill, where I went this afternoon, in hopes of meeting you. But alas, I was obliged to return with bitter disappointment. My longing eyes looked for you in all directions, and I felt my heart leap for joy at the sound of every carriage. O Caty, how much I suffer, and how much more will you. Could I have seen you, it would have given my bosom great relief." He had so much to tell her; she was dissatisfied with Coventry, and he wished to assure her that she must consult her own feelings alone in the choice of a new home. She would naturally wish to go to the South; he wished to tell her why it would not be wise to attempt it now. There were business details too, into which he had intended to enter, and important business papers to give her, the memoranda of his small fortune.

"As we shall be separated by a great distance," he concludes, "and all our letters subject to be opened, you must be very careful what you write, and not to write anything that will give the enemy a triumph, even if it should fall into their hands. My letters will be written with equal caution; therefore don't conclude that they contain a true index of my heart, or speak as I feel."

From Fishkill he had written a few lines to Colonel Hughes; for he felt that there was still a hope, though a faint one, and to this he clung with all the tenacity of his nature. " I set out in the morning for the southward, having waited one day in hopes of seeing Mrs. Greene, who I have been expecting the arrival of for two days past. Should she arrive any time this evening, or early in the morning, beg you'll dispatch an express to me with the intelligence, as I could wish to see her before I go."

Morning comes, and that last hope vanishes. He writes one more adieu, the last words that he ever wrote on the banks of the noble river, around which the memories of these days cluster so thickly.

" I am this moment setting off for the southward, having kept expresses flying all night to see if I could hear anything of you. But as there is not the least intelligence of your being upon the road, necessity obliges me to depart. I have written you largely by Colonel Sherburne last evening, and to him I must refer you for further particulars respecting the necessity of my setting out. As I shall ride very fast on to the southward, and make a stop only of one or two days at camp, and about the same time at Philadelphia, it will be impossible for you to get up with me. Therefore I recommend your immediate return home, wherever this reaches you. What things you have for me, you will please to forward by the express that will deliver you this.

" I have been almost distracted, I wanted to see you so much before I set out. My fears of being ordered to the southward, though there was scarcely a possibility of the thing taking place, was what made me hurry away Hubbard at such an early hour. God grant you patience and fortitude to bear the disappointment. My apprehensions for your safety distresses me exceedingly. If Heaven preserves us until we meet, our felicity will repay all the painful moments of a long separation. I am forever and ever yours most sincerely and most affectionately."

"I beg you will forward the letter which accompanies this to Mrs. Greene as soon as possible," he writes to Colonel Hughes. "It is to advertise her of my setting out, and to advise her to return home, as there is but a bare probability of her overtaking me ; and to attempt it and be disappointed, and then have to return a much greater distance over this rough country, will only add to her affliction, already too great for her delicate constitution."

"Give me leave for once," Colonel Hughes replies on the same day, "to say that your lady, *if possible without injury to herself*, must see you. My God! She will suffer a thousand times as much by a disappointment, as she can by going ten times the distance.

"I shall accompany her out of danger, myself, you may rely. I ordered the person that went to Danbury to caution her not by any means to go by the way of Peekskill."

This letter found Greene in camp. What should he do? It revived a lingering hope. Should he yield to the temptation?

"Your favor of yesterday has this moment come to hand," he writes to Colonel Hughes on the 22d. "The friendly manner in which you interest yourself in Mrs. Greene's happiness, and the feeling manner that you speak upon the subject, deserves my particular thanks.

"I am greatly perplexed, and know not how to act. I wish to gratify Mrs. Greene; but I am afraid my stay will be so short at this place and at Philadelphia that it will not be possible for her to overtake me.

"However, as you have detained the letters, and as she must be far on her way by this time, I think it will be best for her to proceed on until she hears further from me. My motives for stopping her was to save her a long and disagreeable ride for uncertain advantages. If I shall find it impossible to wait for her to come up to me, she shall hear of it by a flying express.

" I thank you kindly for the hint you have given Mrs. Greene to avoid Peekskill route from Danbury, as it is at all times dangerous, but more particularly so at this time, as appears by a letter just come to hand from General Heath.

" I shall be exceedingly obliged to you to see Mrs. Greene safe across the North River, and you will please to deliver her the letter that accompanies this."

" I wrote you yesterday by express," says this letter, the handwriting of which still bears witness to the haste with which it was penned, " and forwarded you a letter which I intended should have been delivered by Colonel Sherburne, both of which I desired Colonel Hughes, Deputy Quartermaster-general, to forward on to you to stop your coming forward, as I was obliged to set out for the southern army before you could possibly get up. But from motives of humanity, he writes me, he has retained the letter, and permitted you to pursue your journey. My motive for stopping you was an apprehension that you could not overtake me. My fears are still of the same kind. Our affairs are distressing to the southward, and the General pressing my departure. In this situation, I know not what advice to give. I want to see you before I go, and I know you are equally desirous of seeing me. In this state of perplexity, I have altered my first intention, and concluded to advise you to come on as far as Trenton, where I will endeavor to meet you. Colonel Cox will be very happy to see you. General Morris also insists upon your spending a few weeks with his family. I wish you would.

" Should anything turn up that will prevent my meeting

you, I will communicate it by express. God bless you with health to bear the fatigues of your journey."

And in a postscript, he adds : —

" You will please to thank Colonel Hughes very politely and kindly, as he has interested himself in your happiness exceedingly, and deserves both our thanks."

Two days pass, and another letter comes from Hughes : —

" This moment," it says, marking 8 o'clock of Tuesday evening as the moment, " I learn that your lady is at Litchfield, and does not expect to be in before Saturday. I shall send a messenger with your *last letter* to her in the morning. The others I shall deliver when I have the honor of waiting on her. My reasons I presume are obvious, as I suspect the two first are discouraging.

" I confess, General, that I have taken unwarrantable liberty with you on this occasion, and don't know but I may appear before a court-martial for my conduct. But if I do, I will plead *Mrs. General Greene.*

" I wish she was with you. I am told she intends making a tour to the southward. I am certain this will detain you, General, or I am an utter stranger to your humanity.

" I sent your rider off by the way of Danbury, as soon as he arrived, to prevent your lady taking the Peekskill route."

Meanwhile Greene is in the camp at Preakness, sitting for the last time with Washington at the council-board, looking for the last time with Hamilton into the dark and uncertain future, indulging for the last time with Knox in those expansions of the heart which gave such a charm to his intercourse with that true and genial friend. His instructions were prepared at length, and in such language as a confiding friend uses to the object of his confidence.

"Congress," they say, "having been pleased by their resolution of the 5th instant, to authorize me to appoint an officer to the command of the southern army, in the room of Major-general Gates, till an inquiry can be had into his conduct as therein directed, I have thought proper to choose you for this purpose. You will, therefore, proceed without delay to the southern army now in North Carolina, and take the command accordingly. Uninformed as I am of the enemy's force in that quarter, of our own or of the resources which it will be in our power to command for carrying on the war, I can give you no particular instructions, but must leave you to govern yourself entirely according to your own prudence and judgment, and the circumstances in which you find yourself. I am aware that the nature of the command will offer you embarrassments of a singular and complicated nature ; but I rely upon your abilities and exertions for everything your means will enable you to effect. I give you a letter to Congress, informing them of your appointment, and requesting them to give you such powers and such support as your situation and the good of the service demand. You will take their orders in your way to the southward.

"I propose to them to send Baron Steuben to the southward with you. His talents, knowledge of service, zeal, and activity, will make him very useful to you in all respects, and particularly in the formation and regulation of the raw troops who will principally compose the southern army. You will give him a command suited to his rank, besides employing him as inspector-general. If Congress approve it, he will take your orders at Philadelphia. I have put Major Lee's corps under marching orders, and so soon as he is ready, shall detach him to join you."

And then, with frequent glances behind him and anxious listenings for the hurried tread of the express that was to bring him tidings of his wife, he sets forth on his momentous journey. Friends were waiting for him in Trenton, so full of inspiring associations; friends were in waiting for him at Philadelphia also, that city visited on so many occasions of anxious deliberation, but never with such a sense of responsibility before. And there, as he sits in the midst of letters and reports, a last express, with a last letter from the kind-hearted Hughes, overtakes him.

"I am the most unfortunate fellow living," it ominously begins. "Mrs. Sterne, ten miles hence, told me when I sent the express to you that your lady was on the road, and had sent her word that she would be there by last night. I have had three expresses out, and all returned without any account of Mrs. General Greene; and what adds to my mortification greatly, is, that a traveller who left Providence last Tuesday tells me that your lady was not then set out, nor did not intend, as she thought it impracticable to overtake you before you got to Carolina. Though this is all report, or mere hearsay, yet I am afraid it is too true. Never did I experience greater anxiety than I have for these several days, both on your lady's and your own account, sir. If I was not riveted to this c——d post, I would wait on her at Providence and have the affair settled to her mind.

"I know I ought to do penance for imposing on you; but how could I help it? A lady of veracity told me what I mentioned, and she, poor creature, like the rest of her sex, was deceived.

"You may inflict what punishment you please. I will

submit, and avail myself of the mistake in future.   Most unfeignedly do I sympathize with you and your lady.

"Anything that comes to hand for you or your lady shall be forwarded with the utmost care and dispatch.

" P. S. — I shall send an express with your lady's letters to Providence, and copies of what has passed here, for her satisfaction, and to prevent my incurring censure."

And thus ends the hope of seeing his wife, and thus too he passes from the auxiliary light of biography to the full light of history; becoming the source and controller of the operations which redeemed the southern States, and made possible the establishment of a free and independent empire. The story of this redemption, and of the three hurried years that followed it, form the subject of my third and last volume.

APPENDIX.

The following letters are given in full, for those who wish to make a more thorough study of this important period: —

GENERAL GREENE TO HON. HENRY MARCHANT.

CAMP AT FREDERICKSBURG, *October* 15, 1788.

DEAR SIR, — Your favor of the 16th of September came to hand a few days since. I am very happy to hear you express yourself so favorably upon the subject of the Rhode Island expedition. I think the army did everything that could be rationally expected of them. But the issue was so different from the prospect that gave rise to the plan, and success so necessary to guard against reproach, that I did not expect to escape some degree of censure.

You mistake me, my dear sir, if you think I meant to complain of Congress or my friends in it, for not taking more particular notice of me. I freely confess I have ever had an honest ambition of meriting my country's approbation; but I flatter myself I have not been more solicitous to obtain it than studious of deserving it. However, people are very apt to be partial to themselves; but I have sometimes thought my services has deserved more honorable notice than they have met with, not from Congress, but the army.

I thank you kindly for your friendly hints upon the state of the Quartermaster's department. I am sensible of the difficulty of conducting such an extensive business without leaving some cause for complaints. But I cannot help think the agents employed are nearly in the same predicament that Lord Chesterfield says ministers of state are. They are not so good as they should be, and by no means as bad as they are thought to be. A charge against a quartermaster-general is most like the cry of a mad dog in England. Every one joins in the cry, and lends their assistance to pelt him to death. I foresee the amazing expenditure in our department will give rise to many suspicions; and I make no doubt there will be some impositions and many neglects; but the great evil does not originate either in the want of honesty or economy in the management of the business, but in the depreciation of the money and the growing extravagance of the people. I have taken all the pains in my power to fix upon the most deserving characters as agents to act under me, and always gave the most positive instructions to retrench every unnecessary expense.

It was with great reluctance that I engaged in this business. The committee of Congress and the Commander-in-chief urged it upon me contrary to my wishes. They painted the distress of the army and the ruin that must follow unless that I engaged in the business, as there was no other to be found who could remove the prejudices of the army and supply its wants. Before I would undertake it, both the committee and the General promised to give me all the aid and assistance in their power.

How far the business has been conducted to the public satisfaction I cannot pretend to say, but I am persuaded the successes of the campaign are owing to the extraordinary exertions made in this department to accelerate the motions of the army.

I readily agree with you that, so far as the commission allowed for doing the public business increases the expense, so far it is injurious (to) its interest; but I cannot suppose that I have given an appointment to one person who would wish to increase the public charge for the sake of enlarging his commission. However, I may be deceived. I wish it was possible for the public to get their business done without a commission; but I am persuaded it is not. Be that as it may, the evil, if it be one, did not originate with me. The commission given to most of the deputies in the western States under the former Quartermaster-general was much higher than is now given. The Board of War gave larger commissions for such persons as they employed in the department before I came in than I would give to the same persons afterwards. I have got people upon the best terms I could, and I hope there is few, if any, but what are men of principle, honor, and honesty. To the eastward I am confident there is no abuse of the public trust worthy notice. You may depend upon my keeping a watchful eye over all the branches of the department, and no impositions shall pass unnoticed. But as I am at so great a distance from many parts of the business, abuses may prevail for some time, unless my friends will be kind enough to give me seasonable information.

GENERAL GREENE TO GENERAL WASHINGTON.

FISHKILL, *October* 21, 1778.

SIR, — Upon examination into the state of the forage department, I find there is wanted two hundred men to man a number of batteaux which are to go up the river single, and then to be lashed together and come down double. Six tons of hay may be brought upon two batteaux in this way.

The weather is now good for the business, and the greater exertions are necessary as the time will be short. There is fifty fatigue men wanted also to assist in securing the hay. The whole of these will be wanted for some time; and as it will be constant duty, the men must have some extraordinary allowance. Besides the foregoing, there are twenty carpenters and twenty masons wanted to forward the barracks now on hand.

If there is a regular draft made from each brigade (that is, an equal number according to their strength), it will be very trifling. Your Excellency is sensible how much business an army creates, and how necessary it is to have that business done rapidly, to keep pace with the seasons. You are also sensible how difficult it is to get men, and what feeble influence money has to effect it. It would be my wish, if it was practicable, to transact all the business of my department independent of the army. But I believe it is the universal custom of all armies to give temporary aid to the great departments of provision and forage. If it was possible (which it is not) to procure men, it must be at an expense that would soon be too burdensome for the continent to support. To keep a great number of men always in pay, to be equal to all the emergencies of business, would often leave a considerable number idle upon our hands.

There is a great number of vessels employed in transporting flour, forage, wood, etc., etc., and the garrison at West Point takes up a great number of our artificers upon the works, which leaves us weaker than we shall be by and by. There is also a considerable number of batteaux men employed in furnishing the garrison with materials for the works and provisions for the troops. Upon the whole, our people are all employed, and all we can get we have engaged, without giving very extraordinary pay. Therefore necessity obliges me to solicit your Excellency for a further aid from the line of the army, that everything may be done that can be done to draw together a sufficiency of forage to supply the demands of the army. If your Excellency thinks proper to detach the men, let them be ordered to Colonel Hay, who will give them the proper instructions, and put them in the different branches of business. Both men and officers that are detached for the batteaux should be acquainted with that service, or with sea service, if such can be had; but if they cannot, we must take raw hands and learn them.

This will render it necessary to have no shift of men until the season of business is over.

GENERAL GREENE TO GENERAL VARNUM.

CAMP AT FREDERICKSBURG, October 24. 1778.

DEAR SIR, — When I left Rhode Island I directed Mr. Bowen to apply to you and General Glover to nominate some persons in your brigade to act as brigade quartermasters. I received a letter from him this day in which he says that Mr. Mitchel claims a promise to be continued, and that you confirmed it. I am fully persuaded both you and he are entirely mistaken in the matter. I remember a promise for a temporary continuance, and the grounds upon which it was made. The resolve of Congress was then in its infancy, and it was uncertain whether the establishment of the army would be gone into or not. While things remained in that situation, I was willing Mr. Mitchel should continue, because there was no other person that I should have wished to have taken his place but to comply with the orders of Congress. But the establishment is now gone into in all its forms, and necessity obliges me to a conformity in my department; or else I shall lay myself liable for all the extra pay and perhaps be impeached for contempt of authority. Mr. Mitchel's circumstances and fidelity would make me wish to continue him if I could consistently. But I cannot, and therefore must beg you to nominate some person belonging to the line to supply his place. I have wrote to Mr. Bowen that if there is any department that he can be usefully employed in to continue him in the public service.

A large part of the enemy at New York have embarked; their destination is unknown. Many conjecture they are bound to Boston. I am rather of an opinion they are going to the West Indies. Another embarkation is said to be getting in readiness. Most people are of an opinion there will be a total evacuation of New York, but I am not of the number. I think they will leave a garrison, if it is but a small one. General Gates and General McDougal have marched with six brigades towards Boston. Make my compliments agreeable to Mrs. Varnum and to the officers of your brigade.

N. B. — I was at Capt. Drake's a few days since. Hatty says you must come and fetch your slippers.

GENERAL GREENE TO COLONEL BOWEN, D. Q. M. G.

CAMP FREDERICKSBURG, *October* 24, 1778.

SIR, — Your favor of the 19th of this instant came to hand to-day. I observe what you mention respecting Mr. Mitchel. General Varnum is certainly mistaken. It is impossible that I should ever have made such a promise as that Mr. Mitchel should be continued, notwithstanding the resolve of Congress to the contrary. I remember telling the General that Mr. Mitchel should continue until the matter was more fully explained. When this conversation happened it was in the infancy of the affair, and while it remained uncertain whether the establishment would be fully adopted. But General Varnum can't suppose that I meant or intended to continue Mr. Mitchel in direct opposition to a resolve of Congress. If I was to do this I should be obliged to allow all the extra pay ; besides lay myself liable to be impeached for contempt of authority. There is nobody that would wish to oblige General Varnum sooner than I should, or that is more desirous of gratifying Mr. Mitchel. For two reasons ; first, because of his lameness ; and secondly, because I think him an honest, faithful officer. But the laws of Congress impose a conformity that I am not at liberty to dispense with. Therefore I must repeat the order of having brigade quartermasters appointed from the line of the army ; and here I would just observe to you that the resolve of Congress confines the appointment to the officers actually belonging to the line of the army at the time the appointment is made.

If there is any place in any branch of the Quartermaster's department that Mr. Mitchel can be employed consistent with his own interest and the public good, I wish you to give him an appointment.

GENERAL GREENE TO COL. C. STEWART.

CAMP FREDERICKSBURG, *October* 26, **1778.**

To Colonel CHARLES STEWART, *Commissioner of General Issues.*

This may certify that all the artificers, that is, the non-commissioned officers and privates, are to draw one pound and a half of bread, one pound and a half of beef, and one gill of rum, or spirits, for their daily allowance; but when the duty is exceeding hard, the men are to be allowed two gills a day. The officers draw the same rations as the officers of the line in all respects.

GENERAL GREENE TO HON. JOSEPH REED.

CAMP AT FREDERICKSBURG, *October* 26, 1778.

DEAR SIR, — Inclosed is the arrangement of Colonel Greene's battalion, which he desired me to forward to you for the approbation of Congress.

I have seen several paragraphs of letters from you to Mr. Pettit. I thank you kindly for the hints you give. What you recommend will take place. The change would have been long before this, had I not been detained to the Eastward longer than I expected. Mr. Pettit's prudence, knowledge of business, and constant attention, I hope will go a great way to silence all complaints. I never was more happy in my life at any circumstance than that Mr. Pettit belongs to the department. His knowledge, his manners, and attention to business, are all so well adapted to the duties of the office, that he is of the highest importance to me. I shall be always happy to receive your advice and information at all times, as well upon the business of my department as other matters that may affect my interest or reputation.

I am told General Mifflin is striving to get into the president's chair.[1] Every body wishes you to accept it, and no one more than myself, providing it was consistent with your views and interest. I am happy to hear the Rhode Island expedition is spoke of with some degree of approbation. General Sullivan is the most unlucky man in the world. I thought it almost impossible for him to fail in the object of the expedition. Indeed, I was dreaming of whole hosts of men and cargoes of generals to grace our triumph. But all at once the prospect fled like a shadow. I was very happy that the General and I had a good agreement during the siege. At my leaving Rhode Island, he wrote me one of the highest letters of thanks you

---

[1] Of Pennsylvania. General Reed was chosen.

ever saw penned. I have not time to add more at present. I will send you a journal kept by Major Gibbs, who was one of my family during the expedition.

GENERAL GREENE TO GENERAL WASHINGTON.
CAMP NEAR FREDERICKSBURG, *October* 27, 1778.

SIR, — The campaign being near a close, the cantoning of the troops for the winter is probably under your Excellency's consideration. In the choice of a position, I doubt not due regard will be paid to the practicability of obtaining supplies of provisions and forage. But as the means of furnishing these capital articles fall much within my department, and I am apprehensive of some difficulties which may not have occurred to your Excellency, I think it incumbent on me to lay before you the present state of our resources, and to suggest a plan which appears to me to afford a better prospect of insuring a supply of provisions for the army and eastern posts than that now in use.

The seat of war having continued for nearly three years in the States of New York, New Jersey, and Pennsylvania, the husbandmen of these States have been so much engaged in the public service as militiamen, teamsters, artificers, etc., and the country has been so much exposed to the depredations of the enemy, and no inconsiderable part of it at times in their actual possession, that a very large proportion of land has remained unimproved, and the residue has not been cultivated with the accustomed vigor. Hence the resources of these States for provisions and forage are greatly reduced; more especially in New York and New Jersey, where the ravages as well as the burden of the war have been peculiarly great and distressing. In proportion as the resources have become scanty the demand for land carriage has increased. The supplies for the army being necessarily drawn from greater distances, this in turn has increased the consumption of forage to so great a degree that the country on every side of the army, within a convenient distance of the lines of communication, is almost entirely exhausted. The quantity of flour necessary to supply the grand army, and the troops and prisoners in Massachusetts Bay and Rhode Island, is estimated at three hundred barrels per day. Of this, perhaps, no part can with propriety be drawn from the country eastward of Delaware. The quantity which can be procured in that region being not more that may be absolutely necessary for other purposes. The whole must, therefore, come from the west side of Delaware. I have already shown to your Excellency in a calculation delivered in a few days since, that to convey this daily supply from Trenton to King's Ferry only, would require the constant employment of 1,340 wagons, with about 5,500 horses, including the forage teams necessary to support those immediately transporting the flour. The Deputy Quartermaster-general for the State of New Jersey is a gentleman of great industry, well acquainted with business, and stands fair with the people. He has been engaged for several months past in forming magazines at different posts on the roads through his district. But the constant consumption has been so great, that with the aid of the grain he has received from westward, he has not been able to retain a single bushel in store, nor will the country he is in afford him any supply worth mentioning. As to hay, he has some collected at different magazines; but the whole he can procure will scarcely be sufficient to supply the estimated number of horses for two months. Instances have already been not unfrequent of teams being delayed several days, merely through want of forage to enable them to proceed; and in some cases the loads have been discharged by the way and the teams returned from the same cause. The forage to support the teams in New Jersey must, therefore, come chiefly from the west side of Delaware also, and the greater part of it from Chesapeake Bay. The distance it must travel is so great, that even while the rivers continue open, it is with difficulty a quantity equal to the current demand can be got forward, and the magazines are yet empty. So that on the least obstruction of the navigation, disappointment must ensue, and the land carriage through New Jersey in a great measure cease. This, however, is not the only way in which we may meet disappointment. Land carriage through so great an extent of country, abounding with mountains, rivers, and difficult passes, is liable to numerous accidents, delays, and obstructions of various kinds, which the utmost precaution cannot altogether avoid. If under the favorable circumstances of mild weather and good roads, we find it difficult to bring forward a bare sufficiency for a current supply, but cannot accumulate a stock to guard against any accidental delay, what must be our condition when the winter season arrives, in which the roads are commonly so bad as to render the passage of wagons most precarious, and the rivers impassable, perhaps for weeks together.

But supposing a sufficient quantity of forage to be attainable, and that no other obstacle should remain but the expense, this alone would be worthy of consideration. The hire of a team and driver fed by the public is now established at fifty-five shillings, Pennsylvania currency, per day. The driver's ration, with little allowances which must be made to such people, will not cost less than five shillings. The forage for each team will cost the public about six dollars per day. The daily expense for each team will therefore be fourteen dollars, which for 1,340 teams estimated for the transportation from the Delaware to Hudson's River, will amount to 18,760 dollars per day, equal to more than half a million per month for that distance only. The expense of transportation further eastward may be inferred. According to this estimate the land carriage of a barrel of flour will cost but little less than six dollars for every ten miles, which, extravagant as it may appear, and though more than it may have heretofore cost, will not be found far from the truth in future. If so great a quantity must be urged on in teams hired by the day, and the forage to support them imported from other States, the difficulty of transporting so great a distance by land the quantity of flour necessary for the current demand, would in common times, and in the summer season, render such a supply too precarious to be relied on without the previous establishment of magazines to guard against accidental delays. I therefore take it for granted that under the present circumstances the necessity of establishing magazines, as well in the neighborhood of Hudson's River, as within a convenient distance from Boston, must be too apparent to admit of doubt. To form such magazines by land carriage only, appears to me utterly impossible; and no expedient seems to be left but, at all hazards, to attempt by water. A sufficient quantity of flour, I am told, may readily be collected on Chesapeake Bay or the Delaware; I should therefore beg leave to suggest the propriety of purchasing or hiring a number of small vessels, carrying from two hundred to five hundred barrels each, and loading them with flour and other necessaries for Boston or such other port as may be proper. These may sail separately, which will make the risk the smaller, and they can occasionally run into harbors to avoid cruisers. If only one out of four of these vessels should arrive safely, it would afford a saving in point of expense; but with proper management I cannot but imagine the arrival of two out of four at least may be counted upon.

WEST POINT, *October* 27, 1778.

DEAR SIR, — Since I wrote you before, the enemy have evacuated Verplanck's and Stony Point, and taken themselves off to New York.

A few days since they landed a party at Amboy, consisting of about five thousand men. They marched up to Brunswick and Middle Brook, where they burnt a few public boats and a couple of small magazines of hay. On their return, a party of their light-horse fell in with a small party of militia, who killed six of the horses of the light-horse, took a lieutenant-colonel and five of the privates, and killed four more of the party. The whole body of the troops went down towards Monmouth, where it is said they have embarked and returned to New York. This is the best account we have yet obtained of Sir Harry Clinton's Jersey expedition.

We have no news from the southward respecting Count D'Estaing and the operations in that quarter. Neither have we any European intelligence but what comes from the eastward.

We have been hourly expecting the arrival of the account of the evacuation of Newport. I was glad to see your proclamation forbidding all kind of plundering. This line of conduct will do the State great credit. If delinquents are to be punished, let it be by due course of law. It is dangerous to let loose the rabble upon people by way of punishment. Nothing tends more to unhinge government and destroy the morals of society. Such as have behaved unfriendly, bring them to a legal trial. But if I was to advise in this business, I would recommend great moderation. Let none fall a sacrifice but such as may be dangerous hereafter, or are necessary to deter others from a similar conduct. Passion and resentment mix so freely in our politics in a state of civil war, that we often listen to the voice of resentment instead of reason, justice, and moderation. Proscription and confiscation are rather to be considered as misfortunes than benefits to government, although we may seem to gain by the measure. Industry and harmony should be the great objects of legislation. These produce plenty, and diffuse general happiness in society. I know your moderation and humanity, and therefore speak the more freely to you on this sub-. ject. When passion, rage, and public animosity have subsided, the events of these days will be viewed through a very different medium to what they are at this hour. The name of him who has wantonly sported with human creatures will be held up to after ages with horror and detestation. Those who are at the head of government generally stand responsible for all transactions during their administration. The love and friendship I feel for you, and the desire I have that your administration should be glorious to yourself and honorable to the name, makes me drop these hints.

I herewith inclose you some very agreeable and very interesting intelligence from the southward, which has this moment come to hand. I beg leave to congratulate your Excellency on the occasion. I cannot detain the express to write you further.

My respectful compliments to your lady and family. You will please to excuse haste and inaccuracies, as I have not time to correct what I write.

GENERAL GREENE TO GENERAL WASHINGTON.

CAMP FREDERICKSBURG, *October* 28, 1778.

SIR, — Inclosed is General Schuyler's letter, which I have read. The utility of the plan which he recommends being altogether dependent upon the Canadian expedition, and that being rather in contemplation than agreed upon, I think it will be necessary, before I give any orders upon the matter, to receive your Excellency's instructions upon that head.

Your Excellency expressed a desire to have all the batteaux collected and repaired that were not in actual service that are now upon the North River.

I could wish to know where you would have them collected, and how soon to have the repairs completed.

As soon as your Excellency has determined in your own mind the line of cantonment, I could wish to receive a private intimation of it, because it would enable me to make many previous necessary preparations, not explanatory of your Excellency's intentions.

GENERAL GREENE TO COLONEL BOWEN.

CAMP AT FREDERICKSBURG, *October* 29, 1778.

DEAR SIR, — Your favor of the 23d this moment came to hand. I am sorry it is not in my power to enable you to repay the money borrowed from the military chest. The first supply of money that comes to hand shall be appropriated to that purpose. General Sullivan was very obliging in lending the money, and I wish to repay it in any way agreeable to his wishes.

With respect to damage done by the troops, the common mode has been to get some good substantial freeholders to view the damages, make an account thereof, and certify it before some civil magistrate, and their accounts are transmitted to the Board of War, who will direct payment hereafter, so as to do equal justice to the inhabitants of the United States that have been injured by military operations.

With regard to the carts, cattle, yokes, chains, etc., that men lost upon the Rhode Island expedition, I am sensible it is a great hardship upon the people to lose their property and get no satisfaction. I think General Sullivan should give orders for payment after being acquainted fully with the circumstances. However, if he will not, such teams as were impressed into the service and sustained real losses, properly proved, you may make them satisfaction.

You must be very careful in the payment of these accounts, as there will be a critical examination. Reasons must appear clear, and the facts fully ascertained, that no doubt may remain of the losses sustained or of the justice of payment.

I intended to have ordered you a party of artificers, but at my return I found it impossible to spare them from the army without doing more injury here than they could be of service to you. You must therefore endeavor to do without them.

You will forward us a copy of your account as soon as you possibly can with convenience. We are anxious to lay a state of our expenditure before the Congress, lest they should think from the very great sums which have been granted us, there is some misapplication. I have forgot whether I told you that I was to pay for the horse Colonel Laurens had, he having given me an order on his father for the money at Philadelphia.

GENERAL GREENE TO COLONEL BOWEN.

CAMP FREDERICKSBURG, October 29, 1778.

SIR, — I have sent you $88,000 by Mr. Whitehead, which I wish safe to hand. Out of this you will repay the money borrowed of General Sullivan from the military chest. If I recollect right the sum was $50,000.

I have directed Mr. Nehemiah Hubbard, Deputy Quartermaster-general of Connecticut, to send you sixty portmanteaux and forty valises for such of the officers of General Glover's and General Varnum's brigades as are in want. I have also directed him to send the price of them, that you may let every officer know at the time of his supplying himself, what he will have to pay, if the Congress should finally refuse to give them to the officers. You will make a charge for all that are delivered, against each respective officer, and take a receipt for the delivery, and insert in the body of the receipt a promise to pay to the value of the thing received, if hereafter called upon by the Quartermaster-general or his assistants.

I wrote you a day or two since upon the subject of brigade quartermasters so fully that is unnecessary to add.

GENERAL GREENE TO COLONEL LEWIS.

CAMP AT FREDERICKSBURG, *October* 30, 1778.

DEAR SIR, — His Excellency gave me an order to have all the batteaux upon the North River collected, that were not in actual employ, and to have them secured against the ice; and if circumstances would admit, to have them repaired. The reasons for this order I am a stranger to. Whether the General had heard the batteaux were going to ruin, or whether he wants them for some particular purpose, remains to be explained hereafter. If any in your district falls within the description of this order, please to have it complied with.

His Excellency has fixed upon a conditional plan for cantoning the troops for the winter. It is probable one brigade may take a position at Albany; but this is dependent upon contingencies. However, you will make the necessary preparations for their reception, should they be sent there. My compliments to General Schuyler and his family.

GENERAL GREENE TO COLONEL BOWEN.

CAMP FREDERICKSBURG, *November*, 1778.

DEAR SIR, — The business of the Quartermaster-general's office in camp requires some person well acquainted with accounts, and who is a judge of the value of different kinds of service, to enable him to pass accounts to the pay office. Such a person I am in great want of. I only mean him to act in the state of an auditor, and to direct the under clerks how to methodize accounts.

This service will be easy, and he will live in the family with me. Will you be so good as to make inquiry in and about Providence whether such a person can be engaged or not. Mr. George Olney would be much to my liking, if it is possible to persuade him from home, and you can part with him without injuring the business of your district. Whoever you can engage for the service suitable for the purpose, shall be handsomely paid.

My best respects to Mrs. Bowen and Mrs. Olney.

N. B. — I have received your accounts.

GENERAL GREENE TO ROYAL FLINT.

CAMP AT FREDERICKSBURG, *November* 3, 1778.

SIR, — In a letter just received from Mr. Nehemiah Hubbart, Deputy Quartermaster-general at Hartford, is the following paragraph: "Brigadier-general Gates desires me to inform you that we have no flour at this port but what is taken from private people."

Hubbart then goes on and says, "I can furnish any number of teams to transport it to this place, if I was directed where to send them."

I wish to know whether you have any particular orders you would wish to be given, in consequence of the above information.

I shall wait an answer before I write to Mr. Hubbart.

GENERAL GREENE TO COLONEL BOWEN.

CAMP FREDERICKSBURG, *November* 4, 1778.

DEAR SIR, — I wish you would be kind enough in your next to inform me of the price of the cloth you sent me with the wagon. Please to get me a bill of the whole, and of a hat that Major Gibbs got for me from the clothier's store.

I wish you to forward your accounts as early as possible, as Congress are anxious to be made acquainted how their money is laid out. I am anxious for New England, that all my deputies in that quarter may appear faithful stewards.

Are the enemy going to leave Rhode Island or not? Most people's expectations are high here that they are going to quit New York; but for my own part I think it a very doubtful question. I am rather of a contrary opinion.

Please to forward the inclosed letters by express.

My compliments to Mrs. Bowen and Mrs Olney.

GENERAL GREENE TO MR. NEHEMIAH HUBBARD.

CAMP AT FREDERICKSBURG, *November* 6, 1778.

SIR, — The convention troops belonging to Burgoyne are on their march for Virginia. On their march they will want a good quartermaster-general to accompany them. Please to appoint one to come on with them as far as the North River. He must be a person acquainted with accounts, polite in his manners, and of a firm and resolute disposition, to be able to do justice to the department and honor to himself. However, you must abate something if you cannot find a person possessing all these requisites. The appointment must be made immediately, and you must furnish the person you appoint with money to pay the incidental expenses. He should set out as soon as he receives his appointment to meet the troops.

You will write to the commanding officer of the guards that accompany the British troops, acquainting him of the appointment.

You will write me an answer to this letter as soon as you have completed the business.

The letter accompanying this, directed to Mr. William Joyce, please to send to Middletown by express, and let the express wait for an answer.

GENERAL GREENE TO GENERAL WASHINGTON.

CAMP, *November* 11, 1788.

SIR, — We find ourselves exceedingly distressed for want of wagoners. Mr. Thomson, Wagonmaster-general, informs me there are a number of soldiers in the hospital that are incapable of doing the duty of soldiers any more, who are about to be discharged from the service.

Mr. Thomson thinks they may be usefully employed as wagoners, and as they are enlisted during the war, it will be a public loss to discharge them.

If your Excellency thinks well of the matter, I wish all such as have become incapable of doing soldier's duty and are about to be discharged from the service, may be turned over to the wagon department. There they may serve themselves and their country usefully.

CAMP FREDERICKSBURG, *November* 14, 1778.

SIR, — Your letter of the 7th instant, came safe to hand. You will please receive the duck from Major Bigelow, and have it made up into tents immediately, giving him a receipt for the same, and advertising me of the quantity you receive.

If the order from General Gates for paying the teamsters, who carted the flour seized by his directions, was general, you will pay the whole of them; otherwise, you can only pay for carting the flour after it became public property. All expenses that may arise in the Quartermaster's department from the convention troops while in your district, must be paid, and you will keep a separate account of them to deliver in when called for. You will reëngage your six months teamsters, at four dollars per day, if they cannot be engaged for less. The express riders are a set of troublesome fellows; you must manage them as well as you can; but at any rate you must not raise their wages, as that will oblige us to raise the pay of express through all the States. I shall inquire into the authenticity of Mr. Thrall's certificate immediately. I wish you to keep the horse until you hear from me again on that subject. You are not to pay General Gates' bill unless he gives you a written order for that purpose.

N. B. — I sent a letter to Mr. William Joyce, at Middletown a few days past; has it gone to him? I want him for a clerk. Pray write to him to know whether he will come, and whether he has received my letter. I wish you would please to give me his character. I am exceedingly in want of a good clerk. I am told he is a most accomplished one. He has kept Mr. Webb's books.

CAMP FREDERICKSBURG, *November* 14, 1778.

SIR, — As forage is very dear and difficult to be got, you had better sell off all such horses as have got poor and unfit for service, especially those that are old.

You must advertise the sale of the horses, sometime before it begins. If there are any wagons or carriages that appear unfit for the purpose of a campaign, let them be sold off also; but don't sell any that are fit for the service another campaign, as we shall have new ones to get in their stead.

You will call on Mr. Whittlesea, quartermaster to Glover's brigade, and Mr. Mitchell, quartermaster to General Varnum's brigade, for their accounts. Bring them to a settlement of the same as soon as possible.

Mr. Whittlesea you will dismiss from any further employment. Settle his accounts before you advertise him of this. He has been dabbling in politics and creating mischief.

Please to write me whether Mrs. Greene is gone eastward.

GENERAL GREENE TO GENERAL WASHINGTON.

CAMP FREDERICKSBURG, *November* 14, 1778.

SIR, — Inclosed is Colonel Biddle's letter to me upon the distressed state of the forage department. Our cattle for this ten days past have not had one half the necessary allowance of forage. The resolution of Congress prohibiting the use of wheat and restrictive laws in the several States, in the neighborhood of camp, renders it impossible to subsist the cattle, unless some further aid can be given to the Foragemaster-general and his deputies.

The law of this State, appointing certain persons in every town to collect forage, and to say how much every farmer shall spare, is not attended with that advantage that the legislature designed in passing the law.

Men judge so differently from one another, and many, from motives of tenderness to their neighbors, take so sparing from the people, that our supplies are very deficient, notwithstanding we see the country full of forage. I am therefore under the necessity to call upon your Excellency for a warrant to impress such quantities of forage from time to time as we find ourselves deficient in obtaining in the regular modes pointed out by law.

GENERAL GREENE TO COLONEL C. PETTIT.

CAMP FREDERICKSBURG, *November* 16, 1778.

DEAR SIR, — We are preparing with all imaginable diligence to move the army into winter quarters. Our stoves are on their way to Middle Brook. I have seen Colonel Wadsworth, and had a long conversation with him on the subject of forage and the late resolution of Congress, prohibiting the use of wheat. The Colonel says he is perfectly disposed to concur with every measure that shall appear to be calculated to promote the joint interest of the commissary and forage department. He has no wish to engross grain or flour to form magazines that cannot be removed to the army for want of forage. But he thinks, such is the scarcity of wheat, that every measure should be taken to forage the army without the use of it. I inquired after the subject of dispute between him and Mr. Wade. He says Mr. Wade wrote something to some person in Philadelphia reflecting upon the conduct of the commisary's department that was not true. He also says there is one O'Hara, an assistant to Mr. Wade, either on the Quartermaster's or forage department, who there has been a complaint entered against for selling flour that should have been delivered over to the commissary. Dr. Scudder is possessed of the papers. The charge has been mentioned to some members of Congress. I wish the matter to be diligently inquired into ; this will be necessary to secure Mr. Wade from any unjust imputations, otherwise as it happened in his district the charge will naturally be levelled on the head. Colonel Wordsworth says Mr. Calhoun is one of the best deputies he ever saw. He does his business very silently and expeditiously. I wish the affair of Mr. Baty may not take place without first consulting him upon the subject. I am out of money, and obliged to stop payment. You know I cannot bear dunning, and therefore must beg you to forward me a supply. From several circumstances I foresee it will be necessary for us to see each other very soon. When I arrive at Middle Brook I will advertise you to meet me at Trenton. Colonel Cox has already agreed to be there. I shall have a double motive for coming, both business and pleasure.

My best respects to Colonel Cox and his family, to your family, Mr. Mitchel and his family.

GENERAL GREENE TO GENERAL WASHINGTON.

CAMP AT FREDERICKSBURG, *November* 16, 1778.

SIR, — The repeated instances of violence committed by officers of inferior rank in the line, upon wagonmasters, in direct violation of your Excellency's orders, render it necessary that some check should be given this unwarrantable practice.

The warrant officers begin to think their situation so very disagreeable that they are determined, one and all, to quit the service, unless they can find some freedom from such acts of oppression and injustice.

Wagonmasters have repeatedly been put under guard for the most trifling offenses, notwithstanding your Excellency hath again and again directed that they should only be subject to the same modes of trial and arrest for misconduct which officers in the line were.

There is now a regular complaint made to me by Mr. Byers, wagonmaster for the 2d Pennsylvania brigade, against Mr. Knox, quartermaster of the ninth Pennsylvania Regiment. The wagonmaster was in the line of his duty agreeable to the orders he had received from the commanding officer of the brigade, when the quartermaster interfered, and prevented him from pursuing his orders. This the wagonmaster took as an injury, and wrote him a note not the most polite, nor yet very insolent. The quartermaster no sooner received the note than he sent a file of men, took the wagonmaster prisoner, and confined him in the quarter guard all night.

I wish not to urge this complaint. I am sensible of the danger of opening disputes between the commissioned and warrant officers ; but the latter declare they will leave the service unless they can find some protection from the violence of the former.

What I have to request of your Excellency upon this occasion is, that you would be pleased to repeat your former orders, upon this subject, for the protection of warrant officers, forbidding the officers of the line, in the most pointed terms, under the severest penalties, from presuming to confine them otherwise than by arrest, for any offense whatever.

I hope such a declaration will check the evil and justify the party who brings forward the complaint. If your Excellency approves of the proposition, please to found the order upon a representation made by the Quartermaster-general of the great injury done to the public service by the violence offered by some indiscreet commissioned officers to warrant officers in the wagon department.

GENERAL GREENE TO GENERAL WASHINGTON.

CAMP FREDERICKSBURG, *November* 16, 1778.

SIR, — I wish, when your Excellency gives your orders for the troops to march from Fishkills, that those employed in transporting forage may continue in the service until the troops that are to winter there arrive, and furnish a party to receive them.

There are also a few masons now employed in building chimneys to the barracks. These I wish may be left for about a fortnight.

There will be wanted for a few days about forty men, to

facilitate the armies crossing the river; they should be good oarsmen, if to be got. Great part of our water men are employed in the forage business, and cannot be called off without great injury to that service. We have only about thirty men at King's Ferry to man the boats. These will be found insufficient to cross with as much expedition as I could wish.

Will your Excellency be so kind as to furnish me with a clue to find out the person in the forage department who you hinted to me the other day had betrayed his trust. No person in any branch of my department shall escape with impunity, if it is possible to detect him, who either neglects his duty or misapplies the public money.

GENERAL GREENE TO GENERAL WASHINGTON.

CAMP FREDERICKSBURG *November,* 20, 1778.

SIR, — Inclosed is Colonel Biddle's letter to me upon the subject of forage. I shall only add that a great number of our horses for ten days past have been falling away to such a degree for the want of a sufficient supply, that those which were in good order then are now almost unfit for duty.

I am persuaded that it will be impossible to subsist the cattle belonging to the army here, unless there is a press warrant granted to aid the Foragemaster. I shall take great care that no improper use is made of the warrant.

GENERAL GREENE TO COLONEL CHARLES PETTIT.

CAMP FREDERICKSBURG, *November* 23, 1778.

DEAR SIR, — I waited upon his Excellency immediately on the receipt of yours of the 15th at Elizabeth. He consented that Colonel White should go to Baltimore, but not without some difficulty; for he is apprehensive they will run mad with pleasure, as the situation will be favorable for diversions of all kinds.

I expected to have left this ground some days since; but the General thinks it prudent to remain in our present situation until the convention troops have passed the North River. The first division I expect will cross next day after to-morrow.

We are more and more distressed for want of forage every day. The General has given us a press warrant to enable us to secure a present supply. Great exertions must be made to the westward, or ruin awaits us. The restrictive laws in the several States, the prohibition of Congress, the depreciation of money, and the avarice of the people, all seem to conspire to distress us. I am well convinced, without the helping hand of government, our utmost exertions will be ineffectual, unless we agree to give the most extravagant prices for things.

If the Congress has in contemplation any plan for restoring the credit of their currency, the sooner they give a check to the evil the better. The people must agree to submit to some seeming arbitrary edicts, or else diminish their army.

The President of Congress writes me the subject of my letter to them is referred to a committee with full power to act upon it as they shall think proper. Governor Morris, Dr. Skudder, and General Whipple, compose the committee. You will please to wait upon them and give them a full history of the forage department.

Colonel Bowen and Colonel Lewis's accounts will accompany this. Inclosed you have a copy of a letter from the Secretary of the Board of War, with sundry resolutions of Congress, by which you will see the demand. You will therefore give the necessary directions to all the deputies west of the North River for obtaining the proper returns. Agreeably to the resolution of Congress, our deputies for the future must make their assistants send in their accounts at the close of every month. This will enable them to send us monthly returns, which, by the by, I believe would be a very pleasing circumstance to the Congress, and go a great way towards reconciling them to the expense. The prejudices of a certain order of people are so deeply rooted respecting the misapplication of public money, that nothing short of occular demonstration can convince them to the contrary. I shall demand the returns to the eastward.

There have been more applications for money since you left me than there were all summer before. I hope there is some on the way, or the Lord knows how I shall reconcile the people to the disappointment. It is surprising to me that the people have such an avidity for what they seem to set so little store by.

Upon weighing the matter more fully, I am of opinion it will not be for the interest of the department to put the management of it to the westward under Colonel Finney.

The people to the southward have high notions, and it is not improbable but that the same men who would willingly hold the office under the principal, would refuse it from a deputy. I wish that appointment not to take place until you hear further from me upon the subject.

I think it will be necessary for you to consult freely with Mr. Biddle, and if there has been any misconduct of the deputies or agents employed under him, let them be treated as their conduct deserves. I am informed, from pretty good authority, there have been some regular complaints laid before Congress respecting our department. The person I wrote to in Connecticut, don't appear, upon further inquiry, to be altogether qualified for the office of auditor. He has a perfect knowledge of book-keeping, but don't seem to be acquainted with business. Besides which his terms are such as cannot be complied with. I must request you, therefore, to endeavor to engage one in Philadelphia. You know the necessity, and therefore I need not urge it.

The complaints are so loud and so numerous from New Jersey, that I am almost afraid to go there. Trenton must save us, as it has done once before, or else there will be an end of the poor Quartermaster.

Remember I have a draft upon you for one hour's writing every day; I don't intend to lose the pleasure of your conversation and not have some compensation for it.

My best respects to Colonel Cox.

NATHANAEL GREENE.

AN EXAMINATION OF SOME STATEMENTS CONCERNING MAJOR-GENERAL GREENE, IN THE NINTH VOLUME OF BANCROFT'S HISTORY OF THE UNITED STATES.

BY GEORGE WASHINGTON GREENE,

AUTHOR OF "HISTORICAL VIEW OF THE AMERICAN REVOLUTION," ETC., ETC.

PREFACE.

MR. BANCROFT'S ninth volume, covering the history of the War of Independence from the summer of 1776 to the spring of 1778, contains statements concerning General Greene which I believe to be at variance, both in the spirit and in the letter, with all the contemporary historians, and with all those documents from whence authentic history is drawn. I cannot allow them to pass without contradiction.

Questions like these can only be decided by an appeal to the original documents, and to the original documents I appeal. First among them are the letters of Washington; in using which I have chiefly relied upon the judicious selection of Mr. Sparks. Next to these in importance, and equal to them in authenticity, are the letters of General Greene; some of which have been published by Force, in his great national monument, the "American Archives," and some by Sparks in the "Correspondence of the Revolution." By far the greater part, however, unfortunately for the true understanding of this period of our history, are still in manuscript. After these come the contemporary historians of the war, of whom Gordon is the fullest, and in general the most trustworthy. No man ever had better opportunities of ascertaining the truth than he, nor, as I believe, a stronger desire to tell it. He formed the plan of his history at the first breaking out of the war, collected his materials while it was going on, had access to the papers of the leading characters, and took great pains to establish the truth both by oral and written inquiry. I have many letters of his to General Greene containing questions concerning particular events, and some of General Greene's answers. A single extract will show the character of these inquiries : —

"JAMAICA PLAINS, *April* 5, 1784.

"DEAR GENERAL, — . . . . I have a grateful sense of your kindness when I was at Newport, and that I believe in your professions shall convince you by these presents.

"Pray you to inform me, —

"Who accompanied you when reconnoitering for a position upon the landing of General Howe?

"How far the cross-roads were from him?

"What was the name of the place the army occupied at the back of Wilmington?

"What was the particular spot you would have chosen on the other side of the Schuylkill, instead of crossing it, in hopes that General Howe would have fought you ere he attempted passing it and going on for Philadelphia?"

Similar letters of this indefatigable inquirer are found among the Washington papers, and it is well known that he was a correspondent of Gates also. That he had his prejudices cannot be denied; nor that they sometimes led him into error; but that he industriously sought the truth, even Mr. Bancroft has conceded, although he has so boldly differed from him in all that relates to General Greene. Upon what authority he relies, in thus denying the authority of Gordon, he nowhere tells us.

In publishing Greene's letters, I have given them in full, that the reader might have no ground to suspect me of selecting only what told for my cause. And I have done this all the more freely, inasmuch as it affords Greene an opportunity of painting himself. Every stroke of his pen, if I do not greatly err, is a triumphant, although an unconscious, vindication from the aspersions which Mr. Bancroft has cast upon his name.

Frederick the Great was once told that a distinguished general had never made a mistake. "Then," said he, "he must have fought very few campaigns." That Greene made some mistakes I have no doubt; nor that Washington made some. No one will accuse me of undervaluing Greene. Should any one suspect me of wishing to defend him at Washington's expense, I would refer to the opinion of Washington, both as a statesman and as a general, which I have expressed in my "Historical View of the American Revolution." No writer, as far as I have seen, has placed him higher than I have done in the eighth lecture of that volume.

GEORGE WASHINGTON GREENE.

EAST GREENWICH, R. I., *November* 21, 1866.

NATHANAEL GREENE.

" It is not the least debt which we owe to history," says **Sir Walter Raleigh**, "that it hath made us acquainted with our dead ancestors, and out of the depth and darkness of the earth delivered us their memory and fame." Deeply impressed with this truth, I purpose to examine the statements which Mr. Bancroft makes in his ninth volume concerning my ancestor, General Greene; still bearing in mind that " the essence of history is to be true, ... the essence of political history is to be a register or record, including nothing false, and omitting nothing important with reference to its end." [1]

I. Greene despondent.

Gathering the substance of his chapters into an analytical table of contents, Mr. Bancroft writes, in the analysis of his first chapter, " *Greene despondent*." On turning to the page (40) I find : " Greene had once before warned John Adams of the hopelessness of the contest ; and again on the fourteenth he wrote, 'I still think you are playing a desperate game.' "

The nature and extent of Greene's despondency may be gathered from the three letters to which Mr. Bancroft, not citing, but probably drawing from, Mr. Charles Francis Adams's life of his grandfather, John Adams, alludes. But before we pass to these letters, I must call the reader's attention to the meaning of the word *desperate*, which Mr. Bancroft, deviating from the sounder modes of historical quotation, has transformed into *hopelessness*.

It can hardly be necessary to remind the reader of the rank held by Middleton among the writers of the last century as a master of pure and idiomatic English.[2] What he means by *desperate* may be seen from the following passage — I could add a dozen — in his " Life of Cicero ": " The obscurity of his extraction, which depressed him with the nobility, made him the greater favorite with the people, who, on all occasions of danger, thought him the only man fit to be trusted with their lives and fortunes, or to have the command of a difficult and

---

[1] Lewis on the *Methods of Observation and Reasoning in Politics*, ch. vii. §§ 1-25.

[2] " Middleton," says Dugald Stewart in his *Life of Robertson*, " was recommended to Scotchmen as the safest model for their imitation." — *Stewart's Works*, vol. vii. p. 169.

desperate war ; and, in truth, he twice delivered them from the most *desperate* with which they had ever been threatened by a foreign enemy." [1]   It is evident that in both these passages *desperate* means, not *hopeless*, but *exceedingly difficult*.   In this sense Washington also uses it, in a letter quoted by Mr. Bancroft, p. 220 :   " Desperate diseases require desperate remedies." And that this is the sense in which Greene uses it in the letters so inadequately represented by this insulated sentence, is evident from the firm and resolute tone which runs through them from beginning to end.   One more remark before I pass to them.   They were addressed to Adams, not as a personal friend, but as a member of Congress, upon whose sanguine mind Greene sought to impress the difficulties of the contest, and the danger of trusting to intentions and resolves.

" BROOKLINE, LONG ISLAND, *May* 24, 1776.

" SIR, — The peculiar situation of American affairs renders it necessary to adopt every measure that will engage people in in the service ; the danger and hardships that those are subject to who engage in the service more than those who do not, is obvious to every body which has the least acquaintance with service.   'Tis that which makes it so difficult to recruit.   The large force which is coming against America will make it necessary to augment our forces.   If I am to form a judgment of the success of recruiting from what is past, the time is too short to raise the troops and be in readiness to meet the enemy ; and as every argument has been made use of upon the present plan of recruiting to engage people in the service, there must be some new motives added to quicken the motions of the recruiting parties.

" From the approaching danger, recruiting will grow more and more difficult.   If the Congress was to fix a certain support upon every officer and soldier that got maimed in the service, or upon the families of those that were killed, it would have as happy an influence towards engaging people in the service, and inspire those engaged with as much courage, as any measure that can be fixt upon.   I think it is nothing more than common justice, neither ; it puts those in and out of the army upon a more equal footing than at present.   I have not time to add anything more, Major Frazier now waiting for this.   The desperate game you have got to play, and the uncer-

[1] Vol. i. p. 27.

tainty of war, may render every measure that will increase the force and strength of the American army worthy consideration. When I have more leisure time, I will presume so much upon your good nature as to write upon some other matters. Believe me to be, with great respect, yours.

"NATHANAEL GREENE."

It is difficult to discover any traces of despondency in this letter; but it certainly displays a very just sense of the dangers of the situation, and a very wise and statesmanlike suggestion of the remedy. Let us see what he writes from

"CAMP ON LONG ISLAND, *June* 2, 1776.

"SIR, — I have just received your favor of the 26th of May, in answer to mine of the 24th. You must not expect me to be a very exact correspondent; my circumstances will not always admit of it. When I have opportunity I will write you with freedom. If any information I can give you should be of service, I shall he amply paid. I know your time is too precious to be spent in answering letters; but a line from you at all times will be very acceptable, with such intelligence as you are at liberty to give.

"By your letter I have the happiness to find you agree with me in sentiment, for the establishing a support for those that get disabled in the army or militia; but I am sorry to find, at the same time, that you are very doubtful of its taking effect. I could wish the Congress to think seriously of the matter, both with respect to the justice and utility of the measure. Is it not inhuman to suffer those that have fought nobly in the cause to be reduced to the necessity of getting a support by common charity? Does not this militate with the free and independent principles which we are endeavoring to support? Is it not equitable that the State who receives the benefit should be at the expense? The community, collectively considered, pays nothing more for the establishing a support than if they do not; for those that get disabled must be supported by the continent in general, or the province in particular. If the continent establishes no support, by the fate of war some colonies might be grievously burdened. I cannot see upon what principle any *colony* can encourage the inhabitants to engage in the army when the *State* that employs them refuses a support to the unfortunate. I think it would be right and just for every government to furnish their equal proportion of the troops, or contribute to the support of those that are sent by other colonies.

" Can there be anything more humilitating than this consideration to those that are in the army or to those that have a mind to come in it? If I meet with a misfortune I shall be reduced to the necessity of begging my bread. Is not this degrading and distressing a part of the human species that deserves a better fate? On the other hand, if there was a support established, what confidence would it give to those engaged, what encouragement to those that are not. Good policy points out the measure; humanity calls for it; and justice claims it at your hands.

" I apprehend the dispute to be but in its infancy: nothing should be neglected to encourage people to engage, or to render those easy, contented, and happy that are engaged. Good covering is an object of the first consideration. I know of nothing that is more discouraging than the want of it: it renders the troops very uncomfortable and generally unhealthy. A few troops well accommodated, healthy and spirited, will do more service to the state that employs them, than a much larger number that are sickly, dispirited, and discontented. This is the unhappy state of the army at this time, arising from the badness of the tents. His Excellency has ordered everything to be done to remedy the evil that is in his power, but before the remedy can take place the health of the troops will receive a severe wound.

" From the nature of the dispute, and the manner of furnishing the state with troops, too much care cannot be taken of those that engage, otherwise some particular governments more public-spirited than others, may be depopulated.

" Good officers is the very soul of an army; the activity and zeal of the troops entirely depends upon the degree of animation given them by their officers. I think it was Sir William Pitt's maxim to pay well and hang well to have a good army. The field officers in general, and the colonels of regiments in particular, think themselves grievously burdened upon the present establishment: few, if any, of that rank that are worth retaining in service will continue if any dependence is to be made upon the discontent that appears. They say — and I believe with too much truth — that their pay and provision will not defray their expenses. Another great grievance they complain on is, they are obliged to act as factors for the regiment: subject to many losses without any extraordinary allowance for their trouble : drawing from the Continental stores by wholesale, and delivering out to the troops by retail. This business has been attended with much perplexity, and accompanied with very great losses where the colonels have not been good accountants. This is no part of the duty of the colonel of a regiment, and by the mode in which the business has been conducted, too much of their time has been engaged in that employment for the good of the service. There should be an agent with each regiment to provide the troops with clothing on the easiest terms, allowed to draw money for that purpose occasionally, to be stopped out of the pay abstract. Those agents could provide seasonably, fetch their goods from a distance, and prevent those local impositions that arise from every reverse of the army.

"The dispute begins to be reduced to a national principle, and the longer it continues the more that idea will prevail. People engaged in the service in the early part of the dispute without any consideration of pay reward ; few, if any, thought of its continuance ; but its duration will reduce all that have not independent fortunes to attend to their family concerns. And if the present pay of those in the service is insufficient for the support of them and their families, they must consequently quit it. The novelty of the army may engage others, but you cannot imagine the injury the army sustains by the loss of every good officer. A young officer without any experience in the military art or knowledge of mankind, unless he has a very uncommon genius, must be totally unfit to command a regiment.

" I observe in the resolves of Congress they have reserved to themselves the right of rewarding by promotion according to merit ; the reserve may be right, but the exercise will be dangerous, often injurious, and sometimes very unjust. (Of) two persons of very unequal merit, the inferior may get promoted over the superior, if a single instance of bravery is a sufficient reason for such a promotion. There is no doubt but that it is right and just to reward singular merit, but the public applause accompanying every brave action is a noble reward.

" Where one officer is promoted over the head of another, if he has spirit enough to be fit for service, it lays him under the necessity of quitting it. It is a public intimation that he is unfit for promotion, and consequently undeserving his present appointment. For my own part, I would never give any legislative body an opportunity to humiliate me but once. I should think the general's recommendation is necessary to warrant a promotion out of the regular channel. For rank is of such importance in the army, and so delicate are the sentiments respecting it, that very strong reasons ought to be given for going out of the proper channel, or else it will not be satisfactory to the army in general, or to the party in particular.

" The emission of such large sums of money increases the price in proportion to the sums emitted ; the money has but a nominal value. The evil does not arise from a depreciation altogether, but from there being larger sums emitted than is necessary for a circulating medium. If the evil increases it will starve the army, for the pay of the troops at the prices things are sold at will scarcely keep the troops decently clothed. Notwithstanding what I write, I will engage to keep the troops under my command as easy and contented as any in the army.

" I observe you don't think the game you are playing as desperate as I imagine. You doubtless are much better acquainted with the resources that are to be had in case of any misfortune than I am ; but I flatter myself I know the history, strength, and state of the army almost as well as any in it, both with respect to the goodness of the troops and the abilities of the officers. Don't be too confident ; the fate of war is very uncertain ; little incidents has given rise to great events. Suppose this army should be defeated, two or three of the leading generals killed, our stores and magazines all lost, I would not be answerable for the consequences that such a stroke might produce in American politics. You think the present army assisted by the militia is sufficient to oppose the force of Great Britain, formidable as it appears on paper. I can assure you it is necessary to make great allowances in the calculation of our strength from the establishment, or else you will be greatly deceived. I am confident the force of America, if properly exerted, will prove superior to all her enemies, but I would risk nothing to chance ; it is easy to disband when it is impossible to raise troops.

" I approve your plan of encouraging our own troops rather than reducing theirs ; let us fight and beat them fairly and free our country from oppression without departing from the principles of honor, truth, or justice. The conditions you propose are very honorable, but I fear whether they are altogether equal to the emergency of the times, for mankind being much more influenced by present profit than remote advantages, people will consider what benefit they are immediately to receive, and take their resolutions accordingly.

"If the force of Great Britain should prove near equal to what it has been represented, a large augmentation will be necessary; if the present offers should not be sufficient to induce people to engage in the army, you will be obliged to augment the army; and perhaps at a time when that order of people will have it in their power to make their own conditions or distress the state.

"As I have wrote a great deal, and the Doctor waiting, I shall add no more, only my hearty wishes for your health and happiness. Believe me to be, with great esteem, your most obedient and humble servant, N. GREENE."

Eleven days after this letter was written, John Adams was appointed President of the Board of War. On the 14th of July, Greene again writes him : —

"CAMP ON LONG ISLAND, *July* 14, 1776.

"DEAR SIR, — I received your letter of the 22d of June ; if it was necessary for you to apologize for not writing sooner, it is necessary also for me. But as the express condition of my corresponding with you was to write when I had time, and leave you to answer at your leisure, I think an apology is unnecessary on either side. But I can assure you, as you did me, that it is not for want of respect that your letter has been unanswered so long.

"I am glad to find you agree with me in the justice and propriety of establishing some provision for the unfortunate. I have not had time to fix upon any plan for that purpose, but I will write you more fully in my next. I have never mentioned the matter to but one or two particular friends, for fear the establishment should not take place. The troops' expectations being once raised, a disappointment must necessarily sour them. On the other hand, if Congress established a support for the unfortunate unsolicited, it must inspire the army with love and gratitude towards the Congress for so generous an act.

"You query whether there is not a want of economy in the army among the officers. I can assure you there is not among those of my acquaintance. The expenses of the officers runs very high, unless they dress, and live below the gentleman.

Few that have ever lived in character will be willing to descend to that. As long as they continue in service they will support their rank ; and if their pay is not sufficient they will draw on their private fortunes at home. The pay of the soldiers will scarcely keep them decently clothed. The troops are kept so much on fatigue that they wear out their clothing as fast as the officers can get it. The wages given to common soldiers is very high ; but everything is so dear that the purchase of a few articles takes their whole pay. This is a general complaint through the whole army.

"I am not against rewarding merit, or encouraging activity ; neither would I have promotions confined to a regular line of succession ; but every man that has spirit enough to be fit for an officer, will have too much to continue in service after another of inferior rank is put over his head. The power of rewarding merit should be lodged with the Congress ; but I should think the general's recommendation is the best testimonial of a person's deserving a reward that the Congress can have.

"Many of the New England colonels have let in a jealousy that the southern officers of that rank in the Continental establishment are treated with more respect and attention by the Congress than they are. They say several of the southern colonels have been promoted to the rank of brigadier-general, but not one New England colonel. Some of them appear not a little disgusted. I wish the officers in general were as studious to deserve promotion as they are anxious to obtain it.

" You cannot more sincerely lament the want of knowledge to execute the business that falls in your department than I do that which falls in mine ; and was I not kept in countenance by some of my superior officers" (Greene was yet only a brigadier), "I should be sincerely disposed to quit the command I hold in the army. But I will endeavor to supply the want of knowledge as much as possible by watchfulness and industry. In these respects I flatter myself I have never been faulty. I have never been one moment out of the service since I engaged in it. My interest has and will suffer greatly by my absence ; but I shall think that a small sacrifice if I can save my country from slavery.

" You have heard, long before this will reach you, of the arrival of General and Admiral Howe. The General's troops are encamped on Staten Island. The Admiral arrived on Friday last. A few hours before his arrival, two ships went up the North River amidst a most terrible fire from the different batteries. The Admiral sent up a flag to-day ; but as the letter was not properly addressed it was not received. The Admiral laments his not arriving a few days sooner. I suppose he alludes to the Declaration of Independence. It is said he has great powers to treat, as well as a strong army to execute.

" I wrote you some time past I thought you were playing a desperate game. I still think so. Here is Howe's army arrived, and the reinforcements hourly expected.

" The whole force we have to oppose them don't amount to much above nine thousand, if any. I could wish the troops had been drawn together a little earlier, that we might have had some opportunity of disciplining them. However, what falls to my lot I shall endeavor to execute to the best of my ability.

" I am, with the greatest respect, your most obedient humble servant, NATH. GREENE."

On September 28th, after the battle of Long Island, and the retreat from New York, he writes to a brother : —

" I apprehend the several retreats that have lately taken place begin to make you think all is lost. Don't be frightened ; our cause is not yet in a desperate state. The policy of Congress has been the most absurd and ridiculous imaginable, pouring in militiamen, who come and go every month. A military force established upon such principles defeats itself. People coming from home, with all the tender feelings of domestic life, are not sufficiently fortified with natural courage to stand the shocking scenes of war. To march over dead men, to hear without concern the groanings of the wounded, — I say few men can stand such scenes, unless steeled by habit or fortified by military pride.

" There must be a good army established ; men engaged for the war, a proper corps of officers, and then, after a proper time to discipline the men, everything is to be expected.

" The Congress goes upon a penurious plan. The present pay of the officers will not support them, and it is generally determined by the best officers to quit the service unless a more adequate provision is made for their support. The present establishment is not thought reputable.

" The Congress has never furnished the number of men voted by near one half, certainly by above a third. Had we had numbers we need not have retreated from Long Island or New York. But the extent of ground to guard, rendered the retreat necessary; otherwise the army would have been ruined by detachments. The enemy never could have driven us from Long Island and New York, if our rear had been secured. We must have an army to meet the enemy everywhere; to act offensively as well as defensively. Our soldiers are as good as ever were, and were the officers half as good as the men, they would beat any army on the globe of equal numbers."

These letters need no comment. How far, if indeed it be an office of history to record the growth of controlling ideas, the history of this period is correctly represented by Mr. Bancroft's " Greene had once before warned John Adams of the *hopelessness* of the contest; and again on the fourteenth he wrote, ' I still think you are playing a desperate game,' "— I leave to the reader to determine. Had an illustration of the anxiety with which thoughtful men looked forward to the menacing future of this decisive year been required, a still more striking illustration might have been found in Washington's letter of December 18th, to his brother. " In a word, if every nerve is not strained to recruit the new army with all possible expedition, *the game is nearly up*." Three days after these words were written Greene was writing to Governor Cooke of Rhode Island, " I think, notwithstanding the general disaffection of a certain order of people, the army will fill up; if that be the case, nothing is to be feared."

I cannot envy the filial heart or the historic eye that should find in these words a proof that, while Greene was full of hope, Washington despaired.

II.   Did Greene " reflect " upon Washington?

It is no part of my duty to discuss the question of Washington's demeanor at Kip's Bay, however doubtful I may feel of the success of Mr. Bancroft's effort to reduce the violent outbreak of Washington's violent passions to a calm resolve " to shame or inspirit his men by setting them an example of *desperate* courage." Nor should I have alluded to it if he had not taken occasion to make it the opportunity of an injurious insinuation against Greene. " Greene's words are," he says in the note on pages 122, 123, " Fellows's and Parsons's whole brigade ran away from about fifty men, and left his Excellency on the ground within eighty yards of the enemy, and so vexed at the infamous conduct of the troops, that he sought death rather than life."

" The embellishments of the narrative," says Mr. Bancroft, " which have been gradually wrought out till they have become self-contradictory and ludicrous, may be traced to the camp. A bitter and jealous rivalry, which the adjutant-general had assisted to foment, had grown up between the New England troops and those south of New England. Northern men very naturally found excuses for their brethren, and may have thought that Washington censured them too severely ; but while I have had in my hands very many contemporary letters written by New-Englanders on the events of this campaign, I have never found in any one of them the least reflection on Washington for his conduct in the field during any part of this day, unless the words of Greene are to be so interpreted."

By what principle of interpretation they could be so wrested from their evident meaning, it is difficult to see ; or even why such a conjecture should have been introduced except to cast a doubt upon Greene's love and reverence for Washington. That Washington's temper was violent, no one who has come to the study of his history with an earnest love of truth will deny. It will be time enough to blame him for a gift of nature, when it can be shown that he ever, either as general or as president, permitted it to lead him to a hasty or an inconsiderate act.

III. Expedition against Staten Island.

Continuing my examination, I find on page 176 : " In the following night, Mercer, at first accompanied by Greene, made a descent upon Staten Island." If it was necessary to mention Greene at all in this connection, would it not have been fair to add, that the reason of his not following up the expedition in person was a sudden summons to head-quarters at Harlem ? " On the night of the 15th," writes Mercer on the 17th of October, 1776, to the President of Congress,[1] " General Greene passed over with me to Staten Island, with part of the troops at this post. . . . . Orders from General Washington arrived at eleven at night, which made it necessary for General Greene to repair immediately to Harlem."

[1] Force, *American Archives*, Ser. V. ch. ii. 1093

IV. Greene's Illusions and Murmurs.

On page 180, I read: " Lasher on the next day obeyed orders sent from Washington's camp to quit Fort Independence, which was insulated and must have fallen before any considerable attack ; but Greene, under the *illusions of inexperience, complained* of the evacuation as premature and likely to damp the spirits of his troops, and wrote murmuringly to Washington that ' the fort might have kept the enemy at bay for several days.' " That the reader may have an opportunity of forming his own opinion of the nature of Greene's " illusions " and the tone of his " murmurs," I give the letter in full. He may, perhaps, be surprised to find that it contains no allusion to " the spirits of his (Greene's) troops," which, from Mr. Bancroft's mode of expression, he would, perhaps, have expected to find there. This allusion occurs in a letter to Mifflin, as we shall see by and by, and be able to judge how far it is a complaint, and how far a just apprehension.

Fort Lee, *October* 29, 1776.

" Dear Sir, — Colonel Lasher burnt the barracks yesterday morning at three o'clock ; he left all the cannon in the fort. I went out to examine the ground, and found between two and three hundred stand of small arms (that were out of repair) about two miles beyond King's Bridge ; a great number of spears, shot, shell, etc., too numerous to mention. I directed all the wagons on the other side to be employed in getting the stores away, and expect to get it completed this morning. I forgot to mention five tons of bar iron that was left. I am sorry the barracks were not left standing a few days longer ; it would have given us an opportunity to have got off some of the boards.

" I think that Fort Independence might have kept the enemy at bay for several days, but the troops here and on the other side are so much fatigued that it must have been a work of time.

" Colonel Magaw showed me a letter from Colonel Reed, ordering the Rangers to march and join the army. Major Coburn was wounded in the Sunday action. Colonel Magaw says the Rangers are the only security to his lines. By keeping. out constant patrols, their acquaintance with the ground enables them to discover the enemy's motions in every quarter. The

Colonel petitions very hard for their stay. I told him I would send an express to learn your Excellency's further pleasure. The Colonel thinks if the Rangers leave him he must draw the garrison in from the lines. That would be a pity, as the redoubt is not yet in any great forwardness. From the Sunday affair, I am more fully convinced that we can prevent any ships from stopping the communication.

"I have forwarded eighty thousand musket cartridges more under the care of a subaltern's guard, commanded by Lieutenant Pembleton of Colonel Ralling's (Rawlings) regiment.

"This moment heard of the action of yesterday" (battle of White Plains). "Can learn no particulars. God grant you protection and success. Colonel Crawford says he expects the action to be renewed this morning. I hope to be commanded wherever I can be the most useful.

"I am, dear General, your most obedient and very humble servant, N. GREENE."

V. FORT WASHINGTON.

The eleventh chapter is devoted to Fort Washington. The table of contents says, "Infatuation of Greene, 185 — Clear judgment of Washington, 185 — His instructions to Greene. 185 — Orders to prepare for evacuating Fort Lee, 186 — Greene disregards Washington's intentions, 188 — Grief of Washington, 189 — Want of vigilance in Greene, 189 — Disingenuousness of Greene, 193 — Magnanimity of Washington, 193."

To this formidable array of accusations the text fully corresponds. "Greene, whose command now extended to that fort" (Washington), had not *scrupled* to increase its garrison by sending over between two and three hundred men," p. 184. "On the last day of October Greene, who was as blindly confident as Putnam, wrote to Washington for instructions; but without waiting for them, he again reinforced Magaw with the rifle regiment of Rawlings," 184. "Greene was possessed with the same infatuation," 185. "Greene framed his measures on a system directly contrary to Washington's manifest intentions," 187, 188. "Before the end of the thirteenth, Washington arrived at Fort Lee, and to his great grief found what Greene had done. . . . . Greene, his best and most trusted officer, and the commander of the post, insisted that the evacuation was uncalled for, but would be attended with *disastrous* consequences," 188.

" On the night following the fourteenth, the vigilance of Greene so far slumbered that thirty flat-boats of the British passed his fort undiscovered," 189. " Greene, who was persuaded that he had sent over men 'enough to defend themselves against the whole British army,'" 189. " Greene would never assume his share of responsibility for the disaster, and would never confess his glaring errors of judgment; but wrongfully ascribed the defeat to a panic which had struck the men so 'that they fell a prey to their own fears,'" 193.

Whether Greene was right or wrong in his belief that Fort Washington ought to be held, I shall not take upon me to say. It is a military question, which none but military men are competent to decide. Some readers, however, may think it fair to afford him an opportunity of telling his reasons in his own words. They are given in the following letter to Washington:

" FORT LEE, *November* 9, 1776.

" DEAR SIR, — Your Excellency's letter of the 8th this moment came to hand. I shall forward the letter to General Stevens by express. The stores at Dobbs's Ferry, I had just given orders to the quartermaster to prepare wagons to remove them. I think the enemy will meet with some difficulty in crossing the river at Dobbs's Ferry; however, 'tis not safe to trust too much to the expected difficulties they may meet there.

" By the letter that will accompany this, and was to have gone last night by Major Mifflin, your Excellency will see what measures I took before your favor came to hand. The passing of the ships up the river is, to be sure, a full proof of the insufficiency of the obstructions in the river to stop the ships from going up; but that garrison employs double the number of men to invest it that we have to occupy it. They must keep troops at King's Bridge, to prevent a communication with the country; and they dare not leave a very small number, for fear our people should attack them. Upon the whole, I cannot help thinking the garrison is of advantage, and I cannot conceive the garrison to be in any great danger. The men can be brought off at any time; but the stores may not be so easily removed, yet I think they can be got off in spite of them, if matters grow desperate.

" This post is of no importance only in conjunction with Mount Washington. I was over there last evening: the enemy seems to be disposing matters to besiege the place; but Colonel

Magaw thinks it will take them till December expires before they can carry it. If the enemy don't find it an object of importance they won't trouble themselves about possessing it. Our giving it up will open a free communication with the country by the way of King's Bridge, that must be of great advantage to them and injury to us. If the enemy cross the river, I shall follow your Excellency's advice respecting the cattle and forage. These measures, however cruel in appearance, were ever my maxims of war in the defense of a country; in an attack they would be very improper.

"By this express several packets from Congress are forwarded to you. I shall collect our whole strength and watch the motions of the enemy, and pursue such measures for the future as circumstances render necessary.

"As I have your Excellency's permission, I shall order General Stevens on as far as Equacannock at least. That is an important pass; I am fortifying it as fast as possible.

"I am, dear sir, your most obedient and very humble servant,
N. GREENE."

It will hardly be denied that there is weight in these considerations; and it is impossible, as we follow the army in its painful retreat through the Jerseys, not to wish that Fort Washington could have been preserved, and the necessity of that retreat avoided. Neither will it be denied that the defense of a half-finished redoubt and a rail-fence covered with hay, at Bunker Hill, against the best troops of the British army, afforded some grounds for hoping that a post which nature had made so strong might be held against an enemy no stronger. That American yeomen had not lost their skill or their courage in acquiring the discipline of regular soldiers, was proved in the same month of the next year at Fort Mercer and Fort Mifflin. Greene may have been mistaken; the questionable logic of results is against him; but his matured judgment still continued to approve what his immature judgment had suggested, and the conqueror of the South, after the experience of five campaigns, still believed that the possession of Fort Washington was worth a struggle. Mr. Bancroft calls this adherence to his opinion a refusal to "*acknowledge his glaring errors of judgment.*" Strange that Washington should have continued to rely upon such a man! He finds *disingenuousness* in Greene's attributing the loss of the fort to a panic;

Magaw said the same thing. Still, the only question which a civilian can be held competent to decide is, first, how far, as a question of discipline, Greene was justified in reinforcing the garrison before the eighth of November, and, secondly, in continuing to hold the Fort after Washington's letter of that day. The first question has been answered by Mr. Sparks, who not only wrote with the documents before him, but who brought to the study of them a candor of spirit, a rectitude of intention, and a soundness of judgment which have secured him a place second only to that of Peter Force, if second to any, among the students of our Revolutionary annals.

"General Greene," says this excellent man, whose name I cannot write without a thrill of tenderness and gratitude, both for the services which he rendered the history of my country and the parental kindness with which he aided me in my study of it, "General Greene, who was now stationed at Fort Lee (formerly called Fort Constitution), gave notice, on the 31st of October, that the enemy had taken possession of Fort Independence, on the north side of Kingsbridge, having made their appearance in that quarter two days before ; that he had previously caused everything valuable to be removed, and the bridges to be cast down. 'I should be glad to know your Excellency's mind,' he adds, 'about holding all the ground from Kingsbridge to the lines. If we attempt to hold the ground, the garrison must be reinforced, but if the garrison is to be drawn into Fort Washington, and we only keep that, the number of troops on the island is too large.' In reply, the Commander-in-chief wrote, that the question could be answered only by being on the spot, and knowing all the circumstances, and that he should submit the whole to the judgment of General Greene, reminding him of the original design to garrison the works, and preserve the lower lines as long as they could be kept, and thus, by holding a communication across the river, to stop the enemy's ships from passing up and down."[1] Up to the end of October, then, Greene had done nothing to diminish the confidence which Washington placed in his judgment and sincerity. From the beginning of November to the eighth of it he had full authority to follow his own judgment. Up to the same day Washington himself believed that Fort Washington might be held.

On the eighth of November, Washington wrote: "The late

[1] Sparks, *Writings of Washington*, vol. iv. p. 158, note.

passage of three vessels up the North River, of which we have just received advice, is so plain a proof of the inefficiency of all the obstructions we have thrown into it, that I cannot but think it will fully justify *a change* in the disposition which has been made. If we cannot prevent vessels from passing up, and the enemy are possessed of the surrounding country, what valuable purpose can it answer to attempt to hold a post from which the expected benefit cannot be had? I am therefore *inclined to think* that it will not be prudent to hazard the men and stores at Mount Washington; *but as you are on the spot, I leave it to you to give such orders as to evacuating Mount Washington, as you may judge best, and so far revoking the order given to Colonel Magaw to defend it to the last.*"

If we weigh these expressions, and give them their true force, we shall see, first of all, that Washington, on the eighth, was *inclined to think*, — not that he positively thought; in other words, he was wavering in the opinion which he had previously held, and again authorized Greene to decide for him, because Greene was on the spot and he was not. Greene, for the reasons assigned in his letter of the ninth, which I have already laid before the reader, decided to strengthen the garrison and try to hold the fort. This Washington knew, at least, as early as the eleventh. On the thirteenth he reached Fort Lee, where he remained part, if not the whole of the next day, as his letter of that date to the President of Congress from "General Greene's Quarters" shows. For a part of two days, then, and three days before the attack, *he also was on the spot*, and the reason for intrusting the decision to Greene ceased. It was in his power at any time from the thirteenth to the morning of the sixteenth to have visited the garrison and examined for himself the question of evacuation. But was it in his power to remove the troops? If we take literally a passage in his letter of the 19th November to his brother, it was not. "I did not care," he says, "to give an absolute order for withdrawing the garrison till I could get round and see the situation of things, and then it became too late, as the fort was invested." But on the fourteenth, when he had already been part of a day if not a whole one at "General Greene's Quarters," he writes to the President of Congress, "I propose to stay in this neighborhood a few days, in which time I expect the designs of the enemy will be more disclosed, and their incursions be made in this quarter, *or their investiture of Fort Washington*, if they are intended." The earliest mention that I find of the investment is on the fifteenth. Might not the same energy and power of combination which, in twenty-four hours, prepared the means for removing " nine thousand men, ... with their provisions, military stores, field artillery and ordnance, except a few worthless iron cannon " (I use Mr. Bancroft's words, p. 105), " and transported them from within ear-shot of the enemy across the East River where it is broadest and swiftest, have removed two thousand six hundred men across the North River, where the breadth is less and the current not so strong, and from a position which made it difficult for the enemy to discover their movements? That this was possible, Greene always believed ; that it was not impossible, Washington must have believed when he wrote Magaw that if he would hold out till night he would try to get him off. In the opinion of Stedman, the best English military historian of the war, the " grand error was in not withdrawing the garrison the evening preceding the assault." [1] However this may be, the documents, fairly and candidly considered, admit of but one conclusion ; that Greene's responsibility ceased with Washington's arrival at Fort Lee on the thirteenth. When Greene's ceased, whose began ?

One more illustration of the style of Mr. Bancroft's censures upon Greene's part in the fall of Fort Washington : " Greene, whose command now extended to that fort, had not *scrupled* to increase its garrison." [2] Very true ; but if Mr. Bancroft had added the following sentence from Greene's letter of October 24th, the effect upon the reader's mind would have been somewhat modified. " General Putnam requested a party of men to reinforce them at Mount Washington. I sent between two and three hundred of Colonel Durkee's regiment. Please to inform me whether your Excellency approves thereof." If we bear in mind that at this time Washington himself was in favor of holding Fort Washington, it will be difficult to discover anything in Greene's conduct but an eager desire to do his duty. When, indeed, did any other desire ever find entrance into that pure and earnest mind ? And in the performance of that duty I have not found a single instance in which, acting before orders, he did not immediately communicate his action to Washington for approval.

" And again on the last day of October, Greene, who was as blindly confident as Putnam, wrote to Washington for instruc-

---

[1] Stedman's *History of the American War*, vol. i. p. 218, quarto ed.

[2] Page 184.

tions; but without waiting for them, he again reinforced Magaw with the rifle regiment of Rawlings."[1] Would it not be fairly inferred from this statement that Greene had said nothing to Washington about this reinforcement? Yet in the very letter in which he asks for instructions he writes, " I shall reinforce Colonel Magaw with Colonel Rawlings's regiment, until I hear from your Excellency respecting the matter." This "matter" was the "holding the ground from King's Bridge to the lower lines," which, as we have already seen (letter of October 31), implied a strengthening of the garrison. Greene probably thought himself entitled to the praise of forethought rather than to the blame of assumption. Remember, too, that Washington in his answer, as we have also seen, refers to the original motive for holding the lines in a manner to show that he was still in favor of holding them.

VI. Greene did not scruple, etc.

Of the manner in which Mr. Bancroft has invited censure of Greene even stronger than that which he has expressed; of the skillful selection of such terms as " *did not scruple,*" where history would have said *did not hesitate,* if the cautious muse of truth had deemed any qualification necessary in the statement of a simple fact; of the fidelity of quotation with which he transforms Greene's " *any great danger*" into *any conceivable danger* of the fairness of construction by which, in one of the most insidious sentences ever framed, coupling Greene's name with Lee's, he represents an honest act of judgment on a question referred to his decision as a resolute intention to disobey, for selfish ends, the orders of his superiors: of the insinuation that in holding — though with Washington's knowledge — a direct correspondence with Congress, he was trying to build up for himself a reputation independent of the Commander-in-chief; of the historic justice with which an officer, whose zeal, activity, and incessant watchfulness are placed beyond question by documentary evidence, and the unvarying testimony of all who knew him, is made personally responsible for the failure of imperfectly trained soldiers to distinguish flat-boats cautiously stealing at midnight up the Hudson, where the palisades on one side and Mount Washington on the other cast their deepest shadows on the waters of the broad river; of the

1 Page 184.

boldness with which the charge of *disingenuousness* is brought against the man whom Washington loved in life and wept for in death as "great and good," I have nothing to say. The question between Mr. Bancroft and me is not a personal, but a historical question; and I would wish to treat it with the sobriety and the exactness of history. But I may venture to remind him, that, while no historian can hope to escape all error, no one also can be said to have given satisfactory evidence of his love of truth who withholds from his readers the means of testing the justice of his judgments and the accuracy of his assertions.

VII. Greene's easy, sanguine Disposition.

In the 12th chapter, which is devoted to the retreat through the Jerseys, Mr. Bancroft continues his accusations. "His (Howe's) first object was Fort Lee, ... which was in the more danger, as Greene, indulging his easy, sanguine disposition, had neglected Washington's timely order to prepare for its evacuation by the removal of its stores." [1]

As usual, Mr. Bancroft gives no authority for attributing an "easy, sanguine disposition" to Greene. Henry Lee, who served under him and knew him well, ascribes to him a habit of mind which it is somewhat difficult to reconcile with such a disposition. "No man," says he, "was more familiarized to dispassionate and minute research than was General Greene. He was patient in hearing everything offered, never interrupting or slighting what was said; and having possessed himself of the subject fully, he would enter into a critical comparison of the opposite arguments, convincing his hearers, as he progressed, with the propriety of the decision he was about to pronounce." [2] But the accusation is of so grave a nature, that I purpose to give the reader an opportunity of forming his own opinion, by showing how this "easy, sanguine" man was employed during his command at Fort Lee.

"Fort Constitution, *October* 12, five o'clock, 1776.

"Dear General, — I am informed a large body of the enemy's troops have landed at Frogg's Point. If so, I suppose the troops here will be wanted there. I have three brigades in readiness to reinforce you. General Clinton's brigade will

---

[1] Page 184.   [2] Lee's *Memoirs*, vol. ii. p. 39.

march first, General Nixon's next, and then the troops under the command of General Roberdeau. I don't apprehend any danger from this quarter at present. If the forces on your side are not sufficient, I hope these three brigades may be ordered over, and I with them, and leave General Ewing's brigade to guard the post. If the troops are wanted on your side, or likely to be, in the morning, they should be got over in the latter part of the night, as the shipping may move up from below, and impede if not totally stop the troops from passing. I wait your Excellency's further commands. Should be glad to know where the enemy has landed, and their number.

"I am, etc.,
"N. GREENE.

"P. S. — The tents upon Staten Island have been all struck, as far as discovery has been made."

This may correspond to Mr. Bancroft's idea of an *easy, sanguine disposition*; although I think that most historians would find in it promptness, energy, and devotion to the cause. But let us take a few more specimens.

"CAMP AT FORT LEE (lately Fort Constitution),
"*October* 20, 1776.

"TO THE PRESIDENT OF CONGRESS : —

"SIR, — I was at head-quarters near King's Bridge, with his Excellency General Washington, last night, and on leaving him was desired to send by express to acquaint you that the army are in great want of a large supply of cartridges, which no person can be spared to make. Therefore he requests that you will order all that are now made up at Philadelphia to be sent forward in light wagons that can travel with great dispatch, as they are really much wanted; and as none can be made up here, that persons be employed at Philadelphia to continue at that business, to furnish a full supply for the army.

"Mr. Commissary Lowry is in great want of a supply of salt, which he begs may be sent to Trenton, to enable him to furnish provisions for the army at King's Bridge, which are much wanted, and the supply from Connecticut may be shortly cut off, and I have great reason to apprehend the evil will soon take place, if not wholly, in part. The article of salt is essentially necessary, and must be procured, if possible. Fresh provisions cannot be passed over without great difficulty; and the state of health of the troops from a laxed habit requires a supply of salt. Mr. Lowry mentions the Council of Safety of Pennsylvania having a quantity.

" I am, with great respect, your obedient servant,

" NATHANAEL GREENE."

"FORT LEE, *October* 24, 1776.

" To GENERAL WASHINGTON : —

" DEAR SIR, — Inclosed you have a copy of the letter in answer to mine to Congress, relative to cartridges. As soon as the cartridges come up they shall be forwarded. Colonel Biddle has written to Amboy for ninety thousand that are at that post.

" We have collected all the wagons in our power, and sent over. Our people have had extreme hard duty · the common guards, common fatigue, and the extraordinary guards, extraordinary fatigue ; for the removal of the stores, and forwarding the provisions has kept every man on duty.

" General Putnam requested a party of men to reinforce them at Mount Washington. I sent between two and three hundred of Colonel Durkee's regiment. Please to inform me whether your Excellency approves thereof.

" We shall get a sufficient quantity of provisions over to-day for the garrison at Fort Washington. General Mifflin thinks it not advisable to pull the barracks down yet. He has hopes of our army returning to that ground for winter quarters. I think this would be running too great a risk to leave them standing in expectation of such an event, there being several strong fortifications in and about King's Bridge. If the enemy should throw in a thousand or fifteen hundred men they could cut off our communications effectually, and, as the state of the barracks are, they would find exceedingly good cover for the men. But if we were to take the barracks down, if the boards were not removed, it would in a great measure deprive them of that advantage. However, I have not had it in my power to do either as yet.

"I have directed all the wagons that were on the other side to be employed in picking up the scattered boards about the encampment. I believe, from what I saw yesterday in riding over the ground, they will amount to many thousands. As soon as we have got these together I propose to begin upon the barracks. In the mean time should be glad to know if your Excellency has any further orders to give respecting the business.

" I have directed the Commissary and Quartermaster-general of this department to lay in provision and provender upon the back road to Philadelphia for twenty thousand men for three months. The principal magazine will be at Equacanack. I shall fortify it as soon as possible. and secure that post and the pass to the bridge. which is now repaired. and fit for an army to pass over with the baggage and artillery.

" I rejoice to hear of the defeat of that vile traitor Major Rogers, and his party of tories ; though I am exceeding sorry to hear it cost us so brave an officer as Major Greene.

" I am, with great respect, your Excellency's obedient servant, NATHANAEL GREENE."

"FORT LEE. October 27. 1776.

" To GENERAL MIFFLIN : —

" DEAR SIR. — By Major Howell you will receive one hundred and nineteen thousand musket cartridges. Part arrived to-day. and part last night. As soon as the remainder comes up from Amboy and Philadelphia. they shall be sent forward. I have been to view the roads again. and fixed upon Aquacanack, Springfield. Boundbrook. Princetown. and Trentown to establish the magazines at. Trentown and Aquacanack to be the principal ones. the others only to serve to support the troops in passing from one to the other. They are all inland posts, and I hope the stores will be secure. I have ordered all the cannon from Amboy except two eighteen-pounders and two field-pieces. I have directed them to be sent to Springfield. Boundbrook. and Aquacanack, to secure the stores.

" The people have been employed on the other side in getting the boards together at Fort Washington and the ferry. Some have been brought from King's Bridge. To-day I sent up to Colonel Lasher to know what assistance he could give towards taking down the barracks. and bringing off the boards. and had for answer that he had orders to burn the barracks. quit the post. and join the army, by the way of the North River, at the White Plains.

" We have had a considerable skirmish on York Island to-day. The cannonade began in the morning. and held until evening, with very short intermissions. A ship moved up opposite Fort No. 1. Colonel Magaw got down an eighteen-pounder and fired sixty shot at her, twenty-six of which went into her. She slipped her cable, and left her anchor, and was towed off by four boats. I think we must have killed a considerable number of her men, as the confusion and distress exceeded all description. Our artillery behaved incomparably well. Colonel Magaw is charmed at their conduct in firing at the ship, and in the fields. I left the island at three o'clock this afternoon. We had lost but one man: he was killed by a shell that fell upon his head. We have brought off some of the enemy from the field of battle, and more are still lying on the ground dead.

" I am anxious to know the state of the troops in the grand army : whether they are high or low spirited; whether well or ill posted ; whether a battle is expected or not. We must govern our operations by yours. The troops here and on the other side are in good spirits, but I fear quitting Fort Independence will oblige Magaw to draw in his forces into the garrison, as the enemy will have a passage open upon his back. I fear it will damp the spirits of his troops. He did not expect it so soon. If the barracks are not burnt in the morning, and the enemy don't press too hard upon us, we will try to get away some of the boards.

" I am, dear General, your obedient servant,

" NATH. GREENE."

This last paragraph contains, as will be seen, the " fear for the spirits of the troops," which, by an ingenious and most suggestive juxtaposition, Mr. Bancroft leads the reader to look upon as a part of the " murmuring " letter of the 29th to Washington.

" FORT LEE, NEW JERSEY, *October* 28, 1776.

" TO THE PRESIDENT OF CONGRESS : —

" SIR, — This being a critical hour, when the hopes and fears of the city and country are continually alarmed, and yesterday there being a considerable heavy cannonade most of the day, I have thought it advisable to forward an express with an account of the action of the day. The communication between this and the grand division of the army is in great measure cut off; therefore it will be some time before you have any account from his Excellency General Washington.

" A ship moved up the river early in the morning above our

lower line, right opposite to Fort No. 1, near old head-quarters at Morrisa's, she began a brisk cannonade upon the ships. Colonel Magaw, who commands at Fort Washington, got down an eighteen-pounder and fired sixty rounds at her: twenty-six went through her. The gun was mostly loaded with two balls. She was assisted considerably by two eighteen-pounders from the shore. The confusion and terror that appeared on board the ship exceeds all description. Without doubt she lost a great number of men. She was towed off by their boats sent from the other ships to her assistance; she slipped her cable and left her anchor. Had the tide run flood one half hour longer we should have sunk her. At the same time the fire from the ships began the enemy brought up their field-pieces and made a disposition to attack the lines; but Colonel Magaw had so happily disposed and arranged his men as to put them out of conceit of their manoeuvre.

"A cannonade and fire with small arms continued almost all day, with very little intermission. We lost one man only. Several of the enemy were killed; two or three of our people got and brought off the field, and several more were left there. The firing ceased last evening, and has not been renewed this morning.

"General Washington and General Howe are very near neighbors. Some decisive stroke is hourly expected. God grant it may be a happy one! The troops are in good spirits, and in every engagement since the retreat from New York have given the enemy a drubbing.

"I have the honor to be your most obedient humble servant.

"NATHANAEL GREENE."

If these letters fail to display Greene's vigilance and activity, the two last certainly display his modesty; for in his account of the affairs which he evidently considered a creditable one, he gives all the credit to Magaw. Even Mr. Bancroft has admitted "that Greene animated the defence by his presence." But let us see what else he was doing at this time:—

Fort Lee, October 29, 1776.

"To General Washington:—

"DEAR SIR:—Inclosed is an estimate made of the provisions and provender necessary to be laid in at the different posts between this and Philadelphia to form a communication and for the support of the troops passing and repassing from the different States.

"Your Excellency will please to examine it, and signify your pleasure. Should the estimate be larger than is necessary for the consumption of the army, very little or no loss can arise, as the articles will be laid in at a season when the prices of things are at the lowest rates, and the situation will admit of an easy transportation to market by water.

"The ships have fallen down the North River, and the troops which advanced upon Harlem Plains and on the hill where the Monday's action was, have drawn within their lines again.

"I received the prisoners taken and have forwarded them to Philadelphia. I inclose you a return of the troops at this post, who are chiefly raw and undisciplined.

"I am with great respect your Excellency's most obedient humble servant,

"NATHANAEL GREENE."

Another letter to Washington, of the same date, has already been given above. On the 31st Greene again writes : —

"FORT LEE, *October* 31, 1776.

"DEAR SIR, — The enemy have possession of Fort Independence on the heights above King's Bridge. They made their appearance the night before last. We had got everything of value away. The bridges are cut down, and I gave Colonel Magaw orders to stop the road between the mountains.

"I should be glad to know your Excellency's mind about holding all the ground from King's Bridge to the lower lines. If we attempt to hold the ground the garrison must still be reinforced ; but if the garrison is to draw into Mount Washington, and only keep that, the number of troops on the island is too large.

"We are not able to determine with any certainty whether the troops that have taken post above King's Bridge are the same troops or not that were in and about Harlem several days past. They disappeared from below all at once, and some time after about fifty boats full of men were seen going up towards Hunt's Point, and that evening the enemy were discovered at Fort Independence. We suspect them to be the same troops that were engaged in the Sunday skirmish.

" Six officers belonging to privateers that were taken by the enemy made their escape last night. They inform me that they were taken by the last fleet that came in. They had about six thousand foreign troops on board, one quarter of which had the black scurvy and died very fast.

" Seventy sail of transports and ships fell down to Red Hook. They were bound for Rhode Island; had on board about three thousand troops. They also inform that after the Sunday action an officer of distinction was brought into the city badly wounded.

" The ships have come up the river to their station again, a little below their lines. Several deserters from Powle's Hook have come over. They all report that General Howe is wounded, as did those from the fleet. It appears to be a prevailing opinion in the land and sea service.

" I forwarded your Excellency a return of the troops at this post, and a copy of a plan for establishing magazines. I could wish to know your pleasure as to the magazines as soon as possible.

" I shall reinforce Colonel Magaw with Colonel Rawlings's regiment until I hear from your Excellency respecting the matter.

" The motions of the grand army will best determine the propriety of endeavoring to hold all the ground from King's Bridge to the lower lines. I shall be as much on the Island of York as possible, so as not to neglect the duties of my own department.

" I can learn no satisfactory account of the action of the other day.

" I am, etc.,

" NATHANAEL GREENE."

Again, on the 5th of November, from —

"KING'S FERRY, *November* 5, 1776.

" DEAR SIR, — Colonel Harrison wrote me you were in great want of flour. It is attended with very great difficulty to bring it up from Fort Lee by land. Wagons can't be got to transport a sufficient supply for your army. At Dobbs's Ferry there are eight or nine hundred barrels brought from the other side. I have directed Colonel Tupper to load a number of the pettiaugers and flat-bottom boats and sent them up to

Peekskill. Our troops are so arranged along shore that I am in hopes to keep a passage open for this mode of conveyance. If it can be done it will save an amazing expense.

"I found everything in this place in the utmost confusion,— the wagons and flour detained for want of boats and assistance to transport them over. I shall send Captain Pond hither as soon as I get back, to take charge of the public stores here and to transport the things across. Colonel Tupper is to convey the pettiaugers by the ships, and if the barges are manned the boats are to be run on shore, and Major Clark, who commands a party opposite the ships, is to protect them.

"I shall attempt to transport public stores from Burdett's Ferry, if the enemy make no new disposition. The utmost care shall be taken that nothing falls into the enemy's hands.

"I am informed by Colonel Harrison that your Excellency approves of the plan for forming the magazines. I have directed the Commissaries of the department to lay in the provisions as far as possible, and the Quartermaster-general is exerting himself to lay in provender.

"Many of our people have got into huts. The tents are sent forward as fast as the people get their huts complete.

"Should this ferry be wanted through the winter the landing must be altered. I can, by altering the road, shorten the distance two miles, one by land, the other by water. Where it now is it freezes up very soon; where I propose it, it is open all winter.

"I am now in the State of New York, and am informed by Colonel Hawkes Hay that the militia which he commands refuse to do duty. They say that General Howe has promised them peace, liberty, and safety; and that is all they want. What is to be done with them? This spirit and temper should be checked in its infancy. I purpose to send the Colonel about fifty men, and have directed the Colonel to acquaint them, if they refuse to do duty agreeable to the orders of the State, that I will send up a regiment here and march them to Fort Lee, to do duty there. I beg your Excellency's further advice.

"I am informed the Virginia regiments are coming on. I wish I could form a party sufficiently strong to make a little diversion in the rear of the enemy by the way of King's Bridge. The Hessians have relaid the bridge, and been across; but yesterday morning I believe they all went back again. What does your Excellency think of such a manœuvre? Is it practicable? Has it the appearance of being successful if attempted and well conducted?

" We have a flying report that General Gates has defeated Burgoyne. We also hear that a party of Hessians had deserted over to us. I wish to know the truth of both reports.

" All things were quiet at Fort Lee and York Island yesterday at noon.

" The people seem to be much alarmed at Philadelphia at the success of the enemy. The country is greatly alarmed at having their grain and hay burnt; yet I believe it will answer a most valuable purpose. I wish it had been earlier agreed upon.

" I am informed Hugh Gaine, the printer, is gone into New York. I have ordered all the boats stove from Burdett's Ferry to Hobrock, and from Powley's Hook to Bergen Point, to stop the communication. There is a vile generation here as well as with you. The committee from Philadelphia for inquiring into the state of the army, complains that enlisting orders are not given out. Please to let me know your pleasure.

" I am, etc.,

" N. GREENE."

Two days after he writes again from Fort Lee : —

"FORT LEE, *November* 7, 1776.

" DEAR SIR, — By an express from Major Clark, stationed at Dobbs's Ferry, I find the enemy are encamped right opposite, to the number of between three and five thousand, and the Major adds, from their disposition and search after boats they design to cross the river. A frigate and two transports or provision boats passed the *chevaux de frise* night before last; they were prodigiously shattered from the fire of our cannon. The same evening Colonel Tupper attempted passing the ships with the pettiaugers loaded with flour. The enemy manned several barges, two tenders, and a row galley, and attacked them. Our people run the pettiaugers ashore and landed and defended them. The enemy attempted to land several times, but were repulsed. The fire lasted about an hour and a half, and the enemy moved off. Colonel Tupper still thinks he can transport the provisions in flat-boats. A second attempt shall be speedily made. We lost one man mortally wounded.

" General Mercer writes me the Virginia troops are coming

on. They are now at Trent Town. He proposes an attack on Staten Island ; but the motions of the enemy are such I think it necessary for them to come forward as fast as possible. On York Island the enemy have taken possession of the far hill next to Spiten Devil. I think they will not be able to penetrate any further. There appears to be about fifteen hundred of them. From the enemy's motions, I should be apt to suspect they were retreating from your army, or, at least, altering their operations.

"Mr. Lovell, who at last is enlarged from his confinement, reports that Colonel Allen, his fellow-prisoner, was informed that transports were getting in readiness to sail at a moment's warning sufficient to transport fifteen thousand men.

"The officers of Colonel Hand's regiment are here with enlisting orders. The officers of the Pennsylvania regiments think it a grievance (such of them as are commissioned for the new establishment) that the officers of other regiments should have the privilege of enlisting their men before they get orders. I have stopped it until I learn your Excellency's pleasure. General Ewing is very much opposed to it. You'll please to favor me with a line on the subject.

"I am, etc., etc.,

"NATHL. GREENE."

I add one more specimen of this "easy, sanguine disposition."

"FORT LEE, *November* 10, 1776.

"DEAR SIR : — Your Excellency's favor by Colonel Harrison of the 8th came to hand last evening. I am taking every measure in my power to oppose the enemy's landing, if they attempt crossing the river into the Jerseys. I have about five hundred men posted at the different passes in the mountains fortifying. About five hundred more are marching from Amboy directly for Dobbs's Ferry. General Mercer is with me now. I shall send him up to take the command of these immediately. I have directed the General to have everything removed out of the enemy's way, particularly cattle, carriages, hay and grain. The flour at Dobbs's Ferry is all moved from that place, and I have directed wagons to transport it to Clark's and Orange towns. I was at Dobbs's Ferry last night, left it at sundown ; saw no new movements of the enemy. The enemy landed from on board the ships many bales of goods supposed to be clothing. I am sure the enemy cannot land at Dobbs's Ferry, it will be so hedged up by night. The flats run off a great distance ; they, can't get near the shore with their ships. If the enemy attempts to effect a landing at all, they'll attempt it at Naiacks or Haverstraw Bay. I wish their intelligences may not be calculated to deceive us. Methinks if the enemy intended crossing the river they would not give us several days to prepare to oppose them. They might have prepared their measures, lain concealed until they had got everything in readiness to cross the river, and then effect it at once. It might have been so much easier accomplished that way than it can now, and so many more advantages obtained in getting possession of the grain, hay, cattle, wagons, and horses, that I cannot help suspecting it to be only a feint to lead our attention astray. I wish it may not turn out so. However, I shall exert myself as much to be in readiness as if they had actually landed, and make the same disposition to oppose them as if I was certain they intended to cross.

" I shall keep a good intelligent officer at Bergen and another at Ball's Ferry to watch the motions of the ships.

"Your Excellency's letter to General Putnam this moment came to hand. *I have ordered the Quartermaster-general to send off all the superfluous stores*, and the commissaries to hold themselves in readiness to provide for the troops at Dobbs's Ferry and Haverstraw Bay.

" I have written to Colonel Hawkes Hay to have the road altered at King's Ferry. I directed Colonel Tupper to send up to that ferry all the spare boats. I had given orders for collecting and scuttling all the boats before your Excellency's letter came to hand on the subject. Our numbers are small for the duties we have to go through, but I hope our exertions may be in some proportion to your Excellency's expectation. Sixty or seventy sail of shipping from Frogg's Point and Morrisania have fallen down the East River to New York. In my next I will inclose your Excellency a return of the stores of all kinds at this post, and take your further directions as to the disposition of them.

" Believe me, dear General, to be, etc.,
" NATHANAEL GREENE."

I have been thus profuse of illustration, because I was anxious to let Greene paint himself. How far the *easy* could be attributed to the author of such letters and the doer of such things I leave the reader to decide. Against the *sanguine* I have nothing to say.

VIII. NEGLECT OF ORDERS.

The accusation of neglect to obey " Washington's timely order to prepare for its (Fort Lee's) evacuation by the removal of *its stores*," would be more serious if it were not disproved by documents which are published by Force, in volumes cited by Mr. Bancroft. It would be an insult to the industry upon which he justly prides himself, to suppose he had not seen them. The order is given in Washington's letter of the 8th of November. " You will, therefore, immediately have all the stores removed which you do not deem necessary for your *defense.*" Mr. Bancroft's statement would have been more accurate if he had said *superfluous stores* instead of " *its stores* "; although this would not have been so easy to reconcile with the idea of *evacuation*, of which Washington says nothing, as with the idea of *defense*, to which he expressly refers. Greene's answer is given in his letter of the 10th, in which, after stating that " the flour at Dobbs's Ferry is all removed from that place, and I have directed wagons to transport it to Clarke's and Orange towns," he says, in another part and another connection, " *I have ordered the Quartermaster-general to send off all the superfluous stores,* and the commissaries to hold themselves in readiness to provide for the troops at Dobbs's Ferry and Haverstraw Bay." That these " *superfluous stores* " were the stores at Fort Lee would be evident from the closing paragraph of this letter, if it were not already evident from the connection in which it stands. " *In my next,*" that paragraph reads, " *I will inclose your Excellency a return of the stores of all kinds* " *at this post, and take your further directions as to the disposition of them.*" Why a return of " *the stores of all kinds* " in answer to an express order to " *remove the stores not necessary for defense,*" unless the " *stores not necessary* " had been removed or were about to be removed? Why " *further orders* " unless the orders already received had already been or were being obeyed? In historical evidence as in legal evidence the accused is entitled to the benefit of every doubt that arises from established character. Greene's letters, as we have seen, constantly refer every question to Washington for decision, and every act for approval. Can this uniform habit be reconciled with disobedience ; or was

Washington a man to accept professions for deeds, and give his confidence to an officer who virtually called his authority in question? When authorized to decide for himself, Greene does not *scruple* to accept the responsibility: witness the holding of Fort Washington from the 8th of November to the 13th; when circumstances call for immediate action, he acts and refers instantly to Washington for approval: witness the reinforcement of Fort Washington mentioned in the letter of the 24th October, and the prohibition for officers of one regiment to enlist men from another regiment, as stated in his letter of the 7th November; and indeed every one of his letters, without exception, where the occasion calls for it. Therefore, until some positive proof is brought forward, he must be supposed to have obeyed the authority whose guidance and approbation he so uniformly invoked. Mr. Bancroft does not seem to be aware that, in degrading Greene, he belittles Washington.

It must also be borne in mind that Greene's command extended up the river to Haverstraw Bay, and that it was his duty to provide for the security of the men and stores all along this line. The insufficiency of the means of transportation, not at this period only, but until Greene himself became Quartermaster-general, is a fact well known to the students of our Revolutionary history. How far, in spite of this insufficiency and in the face of great obstacles, he succeeded in transporting the stores intrusted to his charge to a place of safety, the contemporary documents show. "I am sending off the stores as fast as I can get wagons," he writes to Washington immediately after the fall of Fort Washington. "I have sent three expresses to Newark for boats, but can get no return of what boats we may expect from that place. The stores here are large and the transportation by land will be almost endless. The powder and fixed ammunition I have sent off first by land, as it is an article too valuable to trust upon the water." "Our ammunition, light artillery, and the best part of our stores had been removed, upon the apprehension that Howe would endeavor to penetrate the Jerseys, in which case Fort Lee could be of no great use to us," writes Paine, who was serving on the spot as volunteer aid to General Greene. [1] "This loss," says Washington, speaking of the stores which actually fell into the hands of the enemy, "*was inevitable. As many of the stores had been removed as circumstances and time would admit of.*" [2]

[1] *Crisis*, No. 1. Force, iii. 1291, 5th Series.

[2] Sparks, *Writings of Washington*, vol. iv. p. 188.

IX. Greene's Want of Vigilance; takes to Flight, etc.

Mr. Bancroft continues: " In the night of the nineteenth, two battalions of Hessian grenadiers, two companies of yagers, and the eight battalions of the English reserve, at least five thousand men, marched up the east side of the Hudson, and the next morning about daybreak crossed with their artillery to Closter landing, five miles above Fort Lee. The movement escaped Greene's attention; so that the nimble seamen were unmolested as they dragged the cannon for near half a mile up the narrow, steep, rocky road, to the top of the Palisades. Aroused from his bed by the report of a countryman, Greene sent an express to the Commander-in-chief, and having ordered his troops under arms, took to flight with more than two thousand men, leaving blankets and baggage, except what his few wagons could bear away, more than three months' provision for three thousand men, camp-kettles on the fire, above four hundred tents standing, and all the cannon except two twelve-pounders. With his utmost speed he barely escaped being cut off; but Washington, first ordering Grayson, his aid-de-camp, to renew the summons for Lee to cross the river, gained the bridge over the Hackensack by a rapid march, and covered the retreat of the garrison, so that less than ninety stragglers were taken prisoners." [1]

In this single paragraph Greene is again accused of negligence, his retreat called a flight, his successful exertions to preserve his men ignored, the loss of stores and cannon misrepresented by an artful enumeration, and the presence of mind and energy which excited the admiration of the best contemporary historian of the war converted into cowardice and imbecility. Mr. Bancroft might be asked whether he expected Greene to mount guard on the Palisades, or having taken the usual means of protection, place the usual confidence in them? [2] He might also be requested to say why he neglects to mention the " *very rainy night*," mentioned by Greene in his letter to Governor Cooke, and which must necessarily have increased the difficulty of detecting the enemy's movements? Or why, when Paine, who as Greene's aid may have received the report, and must

[1] Pages 195, 196.
[2] In the report of detachments and outguards for November 14, I find : " Outguards, Bergen, Hoebuck, Bull's Ferry, Hackensack, and opposite *Spiten Devil* : Captains, 1 ; First Lieutenants, 2 ; Second Lieutenants, 2 ; Ensigns, 2 ; Sergeants, 6 ; Drums and Fifes, 10 ; Privates, 145."

have known who brought it, asserts that it was brought by an *officer*, he should prefer the statement of the English commander, who had no especial means of knowing beyond conjecture or common hearsay? If it was brought by a countryman, as Howe says, Greene owed his safety to accident; if by an officer, to his own vigilance; and which of the two lights the historian of the United States wishes to place him in he has left us no reason to doubt.

Coming now to the substance and details of the narrative, we shall see that it is directly contradicted in every part by Washington's letter of the 21st of November to Lee, and Greene's letter of the 4th of December to Governor Cooke, and Paine's narrative in the first number of the " Crisis." " Yesterday morning," writes Washington, " the enemy landed a large body of troops below Dobbs's Ferry, and advanced very rapidly to the fort called by your name. I immediately went over, and, as the fort was not tenable on this side, and we were in a narrow neck of land, the passes from which the enemy were attempting to seize, I directed the troops, consisting of Beall's, Heard's, the remainder of Ewing's brigades, and some other parts of broken regiments, to move over to the west side of Hackensack River. A considerable quantity of stores and some artillery have fallen into the enemy's hands."

" The loss of Fort Washington," writes Greene to Governor Cooke on the 4th of December, " rendered Fort Lee useless; his Excellency ordered its evacuation accordingly; all the valuable stores accordingly were sent off. The enemy got intelligence of it, and as they were in possession of Harlem River, brought their boats through that pass without our notice. They crossed the river in a very rainy night, and landed, about five miles above the fort, about 6,000, some accounts say 8,000. We had then at Fort Lee only between two and three thousand effective men. His Excellency ordered a retreat immediately. We lost considerable baggage for want of wagons and a considerable quantity of stores; we had about ninety or a hundred prisoners taken: but these were a set of rascals that skulkt out of the way for fear of fighting. The troops at Fort Lee were mostly of the flying camp, irregular and undisciplined; had they obeyed orders, not a man would have been lost.

" I returned to the camp two hours after the troops marcht off. Colonel Cornell and myself got off several hundred; yet notwithstanding all our endeavors, still near a hundred remained hid in the woods."

Add to these the narrative of Paine, who was then acting as volunteer aid to Greene.

" As I was with the troops at *Fort Lee*, and marched with them to the edge of *Pennsylvania*, I am well acquainted with many circumstances which those who lived at a distance know but little or nothing of. Our situation there was exceedingly cramped, the place being on a narrow neck of land between the *North River* and the *Hackensack*. Our force was inconsiderable, being not one fourth as great as Howe could bring against us. We had no army at hand to have relieved the garrison, had we shut ourselves up and stood on the defense. Our ammunition, light artillery, and the best part of our stores had been removed, upon the apprehension that *Howe* would endeavor to penetrate the *Jerseys*, in which case *Fort Lee* could be of no great use to us. . . . . Such was our situation, and condition of *Fort Lee* on the 20th of November, when an officer arrived with information that the enemy, with two hundred boats, had landed about seven or eight miles above. Major-general *Greene*, who commanded the garrison, immediately ordered them under arms, and sent express to his Excellency General *Washington* at the town of *Hackensack*, distant, by the way of the ferry, six miles. Our first object was to secure the bridge over the *Hackensack*, which laid up the river, between the enemy and us, about six miles from us, and three from them. General *Washington* arrived in about three quarters of an hour, and marched at the head of the troops towards the bridge, which place I expected we should have a brush for; however they did not choose to dispute it with us, and the greatest part of our troops went over the bridge, the rest over the ferry, except some which passed at a mill, on a small creek between the bridge and the ferry, and made their way through some marshy grounds, up to the town of *Hackensack*, and there passed the river. We brought off as much baggage as the wagons would contain ; the rest was lost. The simple object was to bring off the garrison."

It certainly was not from this writer that Mr. Bancroft drew the materials for his elaborate picture of trepidation and flight. And with these unimpeachable documents before me, and Mr. Bancroft's narrative by their side, he must excuse me if I go to his own vocabulary for the epithets which the comparison demands ; and if the accusation of " invention " which he launched against the amiable and truth-loving Grahame should be thought too harsh, soften it as he did on that memorable occasion into "unwarrantable misapprehension."

But, the reader will naturally ask, had Mr. Bancroft no authority for his narrative? I know of but one other American contemporary authority. Let us see what Gordon says.

"The next object that engaged their attention was *Fort Lee*, situated upon a neck of land about ten miles long, running up the North River on the one side, and on the other bounded by the Hackensack and the English neighborhood, a branch of it, neither of which are fordable near the fort. The neck joins the mainland almost opposite to the communication between the North and East rivers at King's Bridge. On the 19th, in the morning, Lord *Cornwallis*, by means of boats which entered the North River through this communication, landed near Closter, only a mile and a half from the English neighborhood. His force consisted of the first and second battalions of light infantry, two companies of Chasseurs, two battalions of British, and two ditto of Hessian grenadiers, two battalions of guards, and the thirty-third and forty-second regiments. The account of this movement was brought to General *Greene* while in bed. Without waiting for General *Washington's* orders, he directed the troops to march immediately and secure their retreat by possessing themselves of the English neighborhood; he sent off at the same time information to General *Washington* at *Hackensack* town. Having gained the ground and drawn up the troops in face of the enemy, he left them under the command of General *Washington*, and returned to pick up the stragglers and others, whom, to the amount of about three hundred, he conveyed over the Hackensack to a place of safety. By this decided movement of General *Greene's*, three thousand Americans escaped, the capture of whom, at this period, must have proved ruinous. Lord Cornwallis's intent was evidently to form a line across from the place of landing to Hackensack bridge, and thereby to hem in the whole garrison between the north and Hackensack, but General *Greene* was too alert for him. His lordship had but a mile and a half to march, whereas it was four miles from Fort Lee to the road approaching the head of the English neighborhood, where the other amused his lordship till General Washington arrived, and by a well-concerted retreat secured the bridge over the Hackensack." [1]

This account differs, as it will be seen, from all the others, in

[1] Gordon, vol. ii. p. 352.

expressly claiming for Greene the merit of securing the road to
Hackensack Bridge. It would not be difficult to reconcile Gordon's narrative with the narratives of Washington, Greene, and
Paine, and General Greene has nothing to lose, and Mr. Bancroft nothing to gain, by this reconciliation. But for my present purpose it is not necessary. Gordon contradicts Mr. Bancroft even more pointedly than any of the other authorities
contradict him; and before he can ask to be believed, he must
bring witnesses superior to the Commander-in-chief, Washington, who tells us what he did; to the commander of the fort,
Greene, who tells us what he and Washington did; to the eye-
witness, Paine, who tells us what he saw; and to the contemporary historian, Gordon, who tells us what he gathered from
the letters and the mouths of the actors.

X. Trenton and Princeton. How Greene "reposed."

In the brilliant and daring conception of the attack upon
Trenton, the only part assigned by Mr. Bancroft to Greene
is, "The general officers, especially Stirling, Mercer, Sullivan,
and, above all, Greene, rendered the greatest aid in preparing
the expedition." [1] In the other still bolder, and still more
brilliant movements which closed the campaign, Mr. Bancroft
writes, "Washington lost no time in renewing his scheme for
driving the enemy to the extremity of New Jersey. . . . .
*While his companions in arms were reposing, he was indefatigable
in his preparations.*" [2] Of Greene's claim to have done something more than repose through these critical days, Hamilton,
who a few weeks later became Washington's confidential aid,
wrote in a discourse pronounced before the members of the
Cincinnati, — actors many of them in these events: " As long
as the measures which conducted us safely through the first and
most critical stages of the war shall be remembered with approbation; as long as the enterprises of Trenton and Princeton
shall be regarded as the dawnings of that bright day which
afterwards broke forth with such resplendent lustre; as long as
the almost magic operations of the remainder of that remarkable
winter, distinguished not more by these events than by the
extraordinary spectacle of a powerful army straitened within
narrow limits by the phantom of a military force, and never
permitted to transgress those limits with impunity, in which skill

[1] Page 224. [2] Page 239.

supplied the place of means and disposition was the substitute for an army ; as long, I say, as these operations shall continue to be the object of wonder, so long ought the name of Greene to be revered by a grateful country. To attribute to him a portion of the praise which is due as well to the *formation as to the execution* of the plans that effected these important ends can be no derogation from that wisdom and magnanimity which knew how to select and embrace counsels worthy of being pursued." [1] " It would seem," says the judicious and accurate Sparks, in citing this passage, " that General Greene had his full share in *lending efficient counsel* on the present occasion, as well as during the previous part of the campaign." [2]

Of Greene's method of " *reposing*," the following letters may perhaps be accepted as a suggestive illustration : —

"PRINCETON, *December* 7, 1776.

" DEAR SIR, — Lord Stirling will write by the same express that this comes by, and inclose your Excellency several pieces of intelligence obtained of different people yesterday. His Lordship thinks the enemy are making a disposition to advance. For my part, I am at a loss to determine whether their disposition is made to advance or for defense. The enemy have got a party advanced about seven miles this side Brunswick ; another at Boundbrook, with an advanced guard two miles this side of the town. 'Tis reported by some of the country people that the enemy intend to advance in two columns : one this, the other Boundbrook road. General Mercer advanced upon this road, and I should think the German battalion might be advantageously posted on the other road.

" Major Clarke reports General Lee is at the heels of the enemy. I should think he had better keep upon the flanks than the rear of the enemy, unless it were possible to concert an attack at the same instant of time in front and rear.

" Our retreat should not be neglected, for fear of consequences. The bottom of the river should be examined, and see if boats can be anchored in the ferry-way. If there is no anchor-ground, the bridge must be thrown over below. Colonel Biddle had better make a trial immediately, that we may not be in confusion. If a bridge cannot be thrown over, forty boats should be manned under the care of a good officer, and held in readiness. With these boats prudently managed, the

1 Hamilton's *Works*, vol. ii.   2 Sparks, *Writings of Washington*, vol. iv. p. 544.

troops could be thrown over in a very short time. Methinks all the cannon that don't come forward with the army might well be posted on the other side of the river to cover a retreat.

"I think General Lee must be confined within the lines of some general plan, or else his operations will be independent of yours. His own troops, General St. Clair's, and the militia must form a respectable body.

"If General Dickinson would engage the militia for some definite time, there might be some dependence upon them, but no operations can be safely planned wherein they are to act a part, unless they can be bound by some further tie than the common obligation of a militia-man. I think if the General was at length to engage his militia on some such plea, your Excellency might take your measures accordingly.

"This moment a captain has returned that went to reconnoitre last night, and it is beyond a doubt the enemy are advancing, and my Lord Stirling thinks they will be up here by twelve o'clock. I shall make the best disposition I can to oppose them.

"I am, etc.,

"NATHANAEL GREENE."

"CORYELL'S FERRY, DELAWARE, *December* 16, 1776.

"To the President of Congress :—

"Sir, — I take the liberty to recommend Dr. Warren to the Congress as a very suitable person to receive an appointment of a sub-director, which, I am informed, they are about to create a number of. Dr. Warren has given great satisfaction where he has the direction of business. He is a young gentleman of ability, humanity, and great application to business.

"I feel a degree of happiness that the Congress are going to put the hospital department upon a better establishment, for the sick, this campaign, have suffered beyond description, and shocking to humanity. For my own part, I have never felt any distress equal to what the sufferings of the sick have occasioned, and am confident that nothing will injure the recruiting service so much as the dissatisfaction arising upon that head.

"I am, etc.,

"NATHANAEL GREENE."

Surely activity, energy, a comprehensive view of the duties and questions of the moment, may be claimed for the author of these letters. Who but one with whom Washington freely and confidingly took council could have written the letter of the 7th December from Princeton.

If we compare Greene's letter of December 21st with Washington's letter of the 20th December, we shall find such a harmony of opinions in them as could only have been the result of a free interchange of opinion.[1] If we consider the gravity of the subject, and the cautious character of Washington, we shall see that he would never have entered into such a discussion with any man in whom he did not place the fullest confidence. All of Greene's contemporaries believed, and all historians, till Mr. Bancroft, have written, that this was Washington's relation to Greene. Every document that I have ever seen confirms this view. Mr. Bancroft does not tell us why he paints Greene in colors so irreconcilable with it.

Letters like these need no comment to establish the position of the writer.

XI. Red Clay Creek. What Gordon says, and what Mr. Bancroft does not say.

In his narrative of the events which preceded the Battle of the Brandywine, Gordon wrote,[2] "General Greene attended with General Weedon was sent to reconnoitre, and find out an eligible spot for the encampment. He pitched upon one at the cross-roads, near six miles distant from the royal army, which he judged suitable, as the Americans would then have an open country behind them, from whence they could draw assistance, and would have opportunities of skirmishing with the enemy before they were organized and provided with teams and horses etc., for marching; and as Howe's troops would be a long while camped before they could get what was wanting in order to their proceeding. He wrote to the Commander-in-chief acquainting him with the spot he had chosen; but the information was received too late. A council of war had determined the same day it was transmitted to take a position upon Red Clay Neck, about half way between Wilmington and Christiana, alias Christeen, with their left upon Christeen Neck, and their right extending towards Chadd's Ford. When the reason for it, that it would prevent the enemy's passing on for Philadelphia, was assigned to General Greene, he maintained that they

[1] Vol. i. p. 289. [2] Vol. ii. p. 494.

would not think of Philadelphia till they had beaten the American army ; and upon his observing the position that had been taken, he condemned it as being greatly hazardous, and such as must be abandoned should the enemy when organized advance toward them. The Americans, however, spent much time and labor in strengthening the post." Both time and labor were thrown away, for, as Greene had foretold, they were obliged to retreat the moment the enemy advanced. But as this does not agree with Mr. Bancroft's predetermination to ascribe a brilliant stroke of generalship to Washington, he passes over it in silence.

XII. GREENE AT THE BRANDYWINE.

Greene's part in the battle of the Brandywine is told in the following words : " Howe seemed likely to get in the rear of the Continental army and complete its overthrow. But at the sound of the cannon on the right, *taking with him Greene and the two brigades of Mühlenburg and Weedon*, which lay nearest the scene of action, Washington marched swiftly to the support of the wing that had been confided to Sullivan, and in about forty minutes met them in full retreat. *His approach checked the pursuit*. Cautiously making a new disposition of his forces, Howe again pushed forward, *driving the party with Greene till* they came upon a strong position, chosen by Washington, which completely commanded the road, and which a regiment of Virginians under Stevens, and another of Pennsylvanians under Stewart, were able to hold till nightfall." [1] Let us see how Gordon tells the story.

" Generals Washington and Greene being together, and hearing the firing, conclude that Sullivan is attacked. Greene immediately hastens his first brigade, commanded by General Weedon, toward the scene of action with such uncommon expedition that in forty and two minutes it advances near four miles. The second brigade is ordered by Washington to march a different route, as it cannot be up in time for service. . . . . Greene, as he approaches the scene of action, perceives that Sullivan's defeat is a perfect rout. A council of war is held upon the field, and it is agreed that Greene's brigade shall cover the retreat of the flying troops. Greene keeps firing his field-pieces in the rear as he retreats, and continues retreating half a

[1] Page 398.

mile till he comes to a narrow pass well secured on right and left by woods. Here he draws up his force, consisting of the Virginia troops and a regiment of Pennsylvanians commanded by Colonel Stewart; and sends his artillery on, that it may be safe in case of his being under the necessity of making a hasty retreat. A warm engagement commences, which lasts from the sun's being three quarters of an hour high till dark. The tenth Virginia regiment, commanded by Colonel Stevens, supports the attack of the British cannonade and musketry for fifteen minutes, though they had never before been engaged. The whole brigade exhibits such a degree of order, firmness, and resolution, and preserves such a countenance in extremely sharp service as would not discredit veterans. Wayne and the North Carolinians, with the artillery and light troops after their defeat by Knyphausen, pass the rear of it in their retreat. At dark that also is withdrawn by General Greene; the extreme fatigue of the royal troops, together with the lateness and darkness of the evening, prevents its being pursued."

According to Mr. Bancroft, "Washington took with him Greene," etc., thus claiming for Washington the rapid march of Weedon's brigade. Mühlenberg's, which Mr. Bancroft does not say, took another road. In advancing this claim he unconsciously advances also a grave accusation against the Commander-in-chief, whom he makes rein in his blooded horse to the slow step of a column of infantry, when it was in his power, by taking his way across the fields, to reach the scene of action in a few minutes. The place for Washington at that critical instant was with Sullivan and the broken troops of the right. That this was Washington's own view of his duty appears from the statement of Joseph Brown, who served him as guide. "General Washington's head-quarters," says Mr. Darlington, "were at Benjamin Bing's tavern, about three quarters of a mile east of Chad's Ford. He was there and thereabouts all the forepart of the day of the battle. When he ascertained that the main body of the enemy were at Birmingham Meeting-house, and engaged with our troops, he was anxious to proceed thither by the shortest and speediest route. He found a resident of the neighborhood, named Joseph Brown, and asked him to go as a guide. Brown was an elderly man and extremely loath to undertake that duty. He made many excuses, but the occasion was too urgent for ceremony. One of Washington's suite dismounted from a fine charger, and told Brown if he did not instantly get on his horse, and conduct the General by the nearest and best route to the place of action, he would run him through on the spot. Brown thereupon mounted and steered his course direct towards Birmingham Meeting-house, with all speed, — the General and his attendants being close at his heels. He said the horse leapt all the fences without difficulty, and was followed in like manner by the others. The head of General Washington's horse, he said, was constantly at the flank of the one on which he was mounted; and the General was constantly repeating to him, '*Push along, old man, — Push along, old man!*' When they reached the road, about half a mile west of Dilworth's town, Brown said the bullets were flying so thick that he felt very uncomfortable; and as Washington now no longer required nor paid attention to his guide, the latter embraced the first opportunity to dismount and make his escape. This anecdote I had from my father, who was well acquainted with Brown, and had often heard him relate the adventure." [1]

Greene's own view of the part he bore in this battle may be gathered from various passages in his letters, of which the following, from a letter of July 5, 1778, to Henry Marchant, delegate from Rhode Island, is the fullest: "In the action of Brandywine, last campaign, where, I think, both the General and the public were as much indebted to me for saving the army from ruin as they have ever been to any one officer in the course of the war; but I was never mentioned upon the occasion.

"I marched one brigade of my division," — Mr. Bancroft, contradicting Gordon and Greene, says both, — "being upon the left wing, between three and four miles in forty-five minutes. When I came upon the ground I found the whole of the troops routed, and retreating precipitately, and in the most broken and confused manner. I was ordered to cover the retreat, which I effected in such a manner as to save hundreds of our people from falling into the enemy's hands. Almost all the park of artillery had an opportunity to get off, which must have fallen into their hands; and the left wing, posted at Shadsford, got off by the seasonable check I gave the enemy. We were engaged an hour and a quarter, and lost upwards of an hundred men killed and wounded. I maintained the ground until dark, and then drew off the men in good order. We had the whole

[1] W. Darlington, in *Proceedings of Hist. Soc. of Penn.*, vol. i. pp. 18, 58, 59.

British force to contend with that had just before routed our whole right wing. This brigade was commanded by General Weedon, and, unfortunately for their own interest, happened to be all Virginians. They being the General's countrymen, and I thought to be one of his favorites, prevented his ever mentioning a single circumstance of the affair. . . . . However, as I said before, I trust history will do justice to the reputation of those who have made every sacrifice for the public service."

XIII. GERMANTOWN. " GREENE FELL UNDER THE FROWN OF THE COMMANDER-IN-CHIEF."

We come next to the battle of Germantown. "The plan was," says Mr. Bancroft, "to direct the chief attack upon its right, to which *the approach was easy ;* and for that purpose to Greene, in whom of all his generals he most confided, he gave the command of his left wing." [1] " Greene should by this time have engaged the British right, but nothing was heard from any part of his wing. . . . . And where was Greene ? "

That Greene came on the ground over half an hour later than Sullivan no one has ever denied. The contemporary explanations of this delay Mr. Bancroft has collected in a note in such a manner as to give them the air of contradiction, and consequent insufficiency. Let us examine them more closely, and see how far one excludes the other. "On account of the darkness of the night, and the badness of some roads," writes Walter Stewart to Gates. It is not unnatural to suppose that under such circumstances they should "have mistaken their way," as General Lacy says they did. Neither of these statements conflicts with McDougall's explanation — and he we must remember was in high command on the spot, — " owing to the great distance," any more than Heth's statement to Lamb, that " there was some mismanagement," contradicts Sullivan's to Weare, that Greene's march "was delayed much by his being obliged to countermarch one of his divisions." " Greene's letter to Marchant," says Mr. Bancroft, significantly, " gives no explanation." True ; but see what Greene does say : —

" The battle of Germantown has been as little understood as the other by the public at large, especially the conduct of the left wing of the army. Great pains has been taken to misrep-

[1] Page 424.

resent the transactions of that day. *I trust history will do justice to the reputations of individuals.* I have the satisfaction of an approving conscience, and the confirming voice of as able a general as any we have in service, namely, General McDougall, who knows the report the troops were delayed unnecessarily to be as infamous a falsehood as ever was reported. The troops were carried on to action as soon as it was possible, and in good order."

That at least part of the road was bad, even Mr. Bancroft — although he had just before asserted that the approach on the right "*was easy*," — bears witness to in the subsequent assertion that Greene "attempted to advance two miles or more through *marshes, thickets, and strong and numerous post and rail fences.*" It is undoubtedly much to be regretted that Greene's report of this battle should not have been preserved; but a large part of all his papers of this period have been lost. That his enemies should have seized upon this occasion to attack him will readily be conceived by all who remember that this was the period when the Conway cabal first began to raise its venomous head, and that every blow which was aimed at Washington was aimed also at Greene as his most trusted counsellor and friend. How these attacks were received Henry Lee tells us: "The left column was under the order of Major-general Greene. Some attempts were made at that time to censure that officer; but they were too feeble to attract notice when leveled at a general whose uniform conduct had already placed him high in the confidence of his chief and of the army." [1]

" Greene on that day," continues Mr. Bancroft, "'fell under the frown' of the Commander-in-chief" Greene, in a letter to Washington of November 24, 1777, says: " In some instances we have been unfortunate. In one I thought I felt the lower of your Excellency's countenance when I am sure I had no reason to expect it." I am not aware that there is any other authority for referring this expression of a sensitive apprehension to Germantown, although Mr. Bancroft's inverted commas would seem to intimate the existence of some direct and authoritative statement. If so, the Commander-in-chief must be praised rather for his magnanimity than for his discretion; for within six weeks from this very time, having already distinguished Greene " early in the war," Chief Justice Marshall tells us, " for the solidity of his judgment, and his military tal-

[1] Lee's *Memoirs*, vol. i. p. 27.

ents," he selected him to command, against Cornwallis, England's best general, an expedition which required the highest degree of both.[1]

XIV. Who covered the Retreat?

" At about half-past eight," continues Mr. Bancroft, Washington, who " in his anxiety exposed himself to the hottest fire," seeing that the day was lost, gave the word to retreat, and sent it to every division. Care was taken for the removal of every piece of artillery. " British officers of the first rank said that no retreat was ever conducted in better order." [2] By the juxtaposition of these sentences it seems to be implied that Washington saved the cannon and conducted the retreat. I once more compare Bancroft with Gordon, whose statements he should have held himself bound to disprove before he ventured to reject them.

" Greene, with his own and Stephens' division, happens to form the last column of the retreating Americans. Upon coming to two roads, and thinking it will be safest, and may prevent the enemy's advancing by either so as to get ahead of him, and that the divisions may aid each other upon occasion, he marches one division on the one road and the second on the other. While continuing his retreat, Pulaski's cavalry, who are in his rear, being fired upon by the enemy, ride over the second division, and throw them into the utmost disorder, as they know not at first but that they are the British dragoons. The men run and scatter, and the general is apprehensive that he shall lose his artillery. He cannot collect a party sufficient to form a rear guard till he hits upon the device of ordering the men to lay hold of each other's hands. This answers. He collects a number, and by the help of the artillery brings the enemy to give over the pursuit after having continued it near five miles." [3]

XV. Why Greene was made Quartermaster–General.

" Driven by necessity, Congress won slowly a partial victory over their pride and their fears ; and on the second of March they elected Greene Quartermaster-general, giving him two assistants that were acceptable to him, and the power of appointing all other officers in his department." [4]

1 Marshall's *Washington*, vol. i. p. 179.   2 Page 428.
3 Gordon, vol. i. p. 524.   4 Page 469.

Mr. Bancroft might have added, that Greene accepted this office with great reluctance; that he was urged to it by the committee of Congress and the solicitations of Washington, and yielded only from a sense of duty to his country, and personal devotion to the Commander-in-chief. "There is a great difference," he writes to Washington on the 24th of August, 1779, "between being raised to an office and descending to one. There is also a great difference between serving where you have a fair prospect of honor and laurels, and where you have no prospect of either, let you discharge your duty ever so well. Nobody ever heard of a quartermaster, as such, or in relating any brilliant expedition. I engaged in this business as well out of compassion to your Excellency as from a regard to the public. I thought your task too great to be Commander-in-chief and quartermaster at the same time." Surely facts and sentiments like these form a part of the true picture of a great national contest.

CONCLUSION.

I have now examined one by one the passages of Mr. Bancroft's volume which relate to General Greene, and compared them with authentic documents. I have shown, —

1. That the assertion that Greene was despondent in 1776 is not only unfounded, but irreconcilably at variance with the general tone of his letters at that period, and even with those upon which the charge is founded.

2. That Greene's account of the affair at Kip's Bay contains no "reflection" upon Washington.

3. That the manner in which the attempt upon Staten Island is related conveys, by the suppression of an important fact, a false idea of Greene.

4. That Greene's letter to Washington upon the evacuation of Fort Independence contains no *murmurs*, and no allusion to the "spirit of his troops;" although Mr. Bancroft by an unfortunate juxtaposition conveys the impression that a phrase which actually occurs in a letter to Mifflin forms part of a letter to Washington. Greene expressly declares that he did not believe Fort Independence could be held.

5. That Greene reported promptly to the Commander-in-chief every step he took for the reinforcement of Fort Washington. That till the 8th November Washington himself be-

lieved that post could be held. That the question of evacuation was referred to Greene on the 8th of November, *because he was on the spot.*[1] That on the 13th, Washington by coming *on the spot* became the responsible officer. That if the success of the retreat from Long Island can be taken as a test, the troops might have been removed between the evening of the 13th and the morning of the 16th, when the attack began. And that Stedman, an English officer who wrote a history of high authority, expressly blames Washington for not removing them even after the investment began.

6. That Mr. Bancroft misrepresents Greene by a curious selection of suggestive words, and by changing Greene's own words. Did not *scruple* for did not *hesitate*, is an example of the first; any *conceivable* danger for any *great* danger, of the second.

7. That the charge of *easy, sanguine disposition* is disproved by Greene's letters.

8. That the charge of *neglect* of orders is disproved by all the documents.

9. That Greene, having taken the usual means of guarding his post, could not be blamed for relying upon them. That Mr. Bancroft's account of the fall of Fort Lee is contradicted by Washington, Greene, Paine, and Gordon; and in language so precise and distinct as to make it a matter of wonder from whence he could have drawn it.

10. That at Trenton and Princeton Greene was not merely an agent, but a trusted counsellor of Washington.

11. That in the narrative of the movements after Howe's landing at the Head of Elk, Greene is injured by omission, although the principal contemporary historian bears full witness to his services.

12. That his part in the battle of the Brandywine is almost ignored, although there is abundant and authentic testimony of the extent and importance of it.

13. That his part in the battle of Germantown is misrepresented, and his great services passed over in silence.

And, lastly, that in relating the fact of Greene's appointment as Quartermaster-general, Mr. Bancroft has suppressed the fact

---

[1] " I wrote to General Greene, who had the command on the Jersey shore, directing him to govern himself by circumstances, and to retain or evacuate the post *as he should think best.*" — Washington to President of Congress, November 16, 1776.

of Greene's great reluctance to accept that office, and his consenting to it only from a sense of duty, and personal attachment to Washington.

Aux grands hommes la patrie reconnaissante is the inscription of the temple which grateful France has consecrated to those who served her with their swords, with their tongues, or with their pens. Illustrious deeds are the legacy of the past, and the seed of the future. From them spring generous emulations, earnest thoughts, noble desires, the self-denial that purifies, and the aspirations that exalt. Woe to the people who, either in the cares or in the pleasures of the present, forget what they owe to the past! Woe to the nation that has no rebuke for the rash hand or the irreverent tongue!

To this pamphlet Mr. Bancroft replied in a letter to the editors of the " North American Review."

LETTER OF THE HON. GEORGE BANCROFT.

[THE following letter from Mr. Bancroft is a reply to a recent pamphlet by Mr. G. W. Greene, rather than to the notice of the ninth volume of Mr. Bancroft's History in the January number of this Review.

One of the two points in the notice on which the letter touches is whether General Greene was solely responsible for the loss of Fort Washington. The Review asserted that he was not, and as Mr. Bancroft admits the discretionary character of the orders under which the General acted, he appears to agree with the Review. On the question of Greene's good or bad judgment in the case, the Review expressed no opinion. The passage from Mr. Sparks, of which Mr. Bancroft, in the following letter (p. 664), cites only the first part, may be given in full, as summing up the whole matter: " From these facts it seems plain that the loss of the garrison, in the manner it occurred, was in consequence of an erroneous judgment on the part of General Greene. How far the Commander-in-chief should have overruled his opinion, or whether, under the circumstances of the case, he ought to have given a peremptory order, it may perhaps be less easy to decide." (Life of Washington, p. 216.)

The only other point referred to in the notice upon which the letter remarks is the responsibility of Greene for the disaster at Germantown. To prove this responsibility, Mr. Bancroft relies principally upon Greene's late arrival on the field, — a fact which no one, not Greene himself, ever denied, but which has never been regarded as the cause of the defeat. — EDITORS.]

NEW YORK, *March* 6, 1867.

TO THE EDITORS OF THE " NORTH AMERICAN REVIEW " : —

The notice in the " North American Review " for January last of the volume I recently published, does great injustice to me, and through me to the character of Washington and to historic truth. Its strictures are accompanied by a reference to a pamphlet by a grandson of General Greene. The grandson's paper, in itself, does not merit my notice. It assumes the appearance of fairness by a parade of documents and authorities; but many of the documents are irrelevant, decisive ones are left out, and some of those which are confidently cited are unhistoric. Moreover, I had used in one sentence, fairly and without confusion, a letter of October 27, and another of October 29, 1776. The grandson does not affirm that what is said in the one is dishonestly imputed to the other; but he insinuates enough to mislead the unwary.

A special biography may include details and laudations that have no place in history. It would be wiser to print the writings of Greene, or the elaborate biography which has been talked about for nearly half a lifetime, rather than to tarnish his name by mixing it up with uncandid accusations and insidious cavils. My volumes prove how highly I rate his abilities and patriotism. I have named him as superior to any officer between himself and Washington, except Montgomery; and my account of the war in the South, where he exercised a separate command, and had the best opportunity to display his powers, has not yet been printed. My opinions throughout his career do not differ from those which Washington has expressed.

Many of the charges controverting my statements are trivial, and refute themselves, making a muddle only by their number. The first, which fills nearly a quarter of the whole pamphlet, is in part an argument to prove that *desperation*, and not hopelessness, is the noun corresponding to the adjective *desperate*, — in part to make known that Greene was of a sanguine and hopeful temperament, which has been, and is my own opinion. The second is a gross and plain perversion of my words and meaning. The third is a silly charge of omission, which could be scarcely urged against a biographer. The fourth explains itself. The sixth is a mere criticism on language. The seventh complains that Greene is described as sanguine, which he certainly was. The eighth gains what plausibility it has by a confusion of orders, places, and dates. The ninth, which relates to Greene's want of vigilance, is refuted by the grandson's pamphlet itself, which shows that Greene was blind to the approach of danger by way of Closter Landing; for when Washington warned him by letter, "The enemy must design a penetration into Jersey, and to fall down upon your post," he answered, on the 10th of November : "If the enemy attempt to effect a landing at all, they'll attempt it at Naiack's or Haverstraw Bay ; " and the manner of his surprise proves that he remained of that opinion. The tenth is disposed of by the citation of my own language. At the same time it must be borne in mind, that Hamilton's eulogium on Greene is, like most other productions of that class, very far from being a safe historical authority ; that no letter of Washington, or any officer then present in the camp, has come to light, in which any one measure or merit or act in relation to Trenton is specially ascribed to Greene ; and that he himself, in an enumeration of his claims to praise, pretends to no more than that he was in the battle. The eleventh belongs at best to biography, and, in my opinion, not even there. The fourteenth complains of my narrative where it is but the reproduction of the statement, and almost the words, of eye-witnesses who were the most competent to give evidence.

From these multitudinous accusations I have reserved for fuller discussion the fifth and the thirteenth, as relating to topics noticed in the "Review," and the twelfth and the fifteenth, which are likewise of importance ; for to a public whose good opinion I value, and whose judgment I respect, I will cheerfully explain the authorities on which I relied, and, after reëxamination, still rely.

The fifth topic is THE LOSS OF FORT WASHINGTON ; and it has the intensest interest, because it opens to our view the inmost soul of Washington, like that cleft in the Jura which Agassiz speaks of as revealing at one glance all the great processes of nature. No incident in the war more clearly illustrates the soundness of Washington's judgment, his modesty, his respect for Congress, his deference to his instructions, his magnanimity towards an erring subordinate, and the exquisite pain which he silently suffered from the disasters that befell his army. I have studied the subject most carefully, having been upon Fort Washington and the adjacent ground on foot and on horseback, alone and in company with the well-informed, times without number.

And here I will premise, that if Sparks were still living, and still editor of the "Review," I should not now be put upon the defense ; for he too, drawing water from the well-head, has written : "It seems plain that the loss of the garrison, in the manner it occurred, was the consequence of an erroneous judgment on the part of General Greene." [1]

Congress, from the first, was jealous of the military power. The instructions which accompanied the commission of the Commander-in-chief directed him, upon any occasions that might happen, to advise with his council of war, and left it unsettled whether he was to be controlled by its decision. Congress had also, on the 11th of October, 1776, directly interposed with a resolution, which will be given below, and which induced the council of war and Washington to give an order to defend Fort Washington to the last. Early in November, experience proved clearly to the mind of Washington that Fort Washington ought to be evacuated; and knowing from the reports of Greene the different opinion of that officer, he embodied in his order for preparing for the evacuation the reasoning on which the order was founded, as follows: "The late passage of three vessels up the North River, of which we have just received advice, is so plain a proof of the inefficacy of all the obstructions we have thrown into it, that I cannot but think it will fully justify a change in the disposition which has been made. If we cannot prevent vessels from passing up, and the enemy are possessed of the surrounding country, what valuable purpose can it answer to attempt to hold a post from which the expected benefit cannot be had? I am therefore inclined to think that it will not be prudent to hazard the men and stores at Mount Washington; but as you are on the spot, I leave it to you to give such orders as to evacuating Mount Washington as you may judge best, and so far revoking the order given to Colonel Magaw to defend it to the last." [2] This order is given in full in Bancroft, vol. ix. pp. 185, 186; and when it is compared with Greene's conduct on receiving it, no room is left for doubt how that conduct is to be judged.

First, it was not modest for the inferior officer, who had already had occasion to explain his opinion, to thwart the system of his superior. Secondly, the Commander-in-chief had not only to take care of that part of his lines under the command of Greene, but to look after a distance of many miles on each side of the Hudson, and to gain one purpose by combining many movements. If every general had, like Greene, substituted a plan of his own, instead of unity and order, there would have been a chaos. Thirdly, the order to defend Fort Washington

[1] Sparks's *Washington*, vol. i. p. 216. [2] *Ibid.* vol. iv. pp. 164, 165.

to the last, was explicitly and unequivocally revoked, yet Greene thought proper to reinforce it with some of the best troops and arms. Washington would not risk twelve hundred men, and Greene chose to risk two thousand, which, according to the opinions of military men whom I have consulted, was not justifiable, and was rightly censured by Washington as " a noncompliance with an order." Lastly, a considerable discretion was left to Greene, and he used that discretion in the most injudicious manner.

As to what happened after Washington had completed his tour and reached Hackensack, I followed in my narrative his own accounts, addressed to Reed, a most intimate friend of Greene, and to Gordon the historian. They are as follows : —

WASHINGTON TO J. REED, 22 AUGUST, 1779.

" The loss of Fort Washington, simply abstracted from the circumstances which attended it, was an event that gave me much pain, because it deprived the army of the services of many valuable men at a critical period, and the public of many valuable lives, by the cruelties which were inflicted upon them in their captive state. But this concern received additional poignancy from two considerations, which did not appear; one of which will never be known to the world, because I shall never palliate my own faults by exposing those of another; nor indeed could either of them come before the public, unless there had been such a charge as must have rendered an inquiry into the causes of this miscarriage necessary. The one was a non-compliance in General Greene with an order sent to him from White Plains, before I marched for the western side of Hudson's River, to withdraw the artillery and stores from the fort; allowing him, however, some latitude for the exercise of his own judgment, as he was upon the spot, and could decide better from appearances and circumstances than I, on the propriety of a total evacuation. The other was a resolve of Congress, in the strong and emphatic words following : —

" ' October 11, 1776. — Resolved, That General Washington be desired, if it be practicable, by every art and at whatever expense, to obstruct effectually the navigation of the North River, between Fort Washington and Mount Constitution, as well to prevent the regress of the enemy's frigates lately gone up, as to hinder them from receiving succor.'

" When I came to Fort Lee, and found no measures taken

towards an evacuation, in consequence of the order before mentioned ; when I found General Greene, of whose judgment and candor I entertained a good opinion, decidedly opposed to it ; when I found other opinions so coincident with his ; when the wishes of the Congress to obstruct the navigation of the North River, which were delivered in such forcible terms, recurred ; when I knew that the easy communication between the different parts of the army, then separated by the river, depended upon it ; and lastly, when I considered that our policy led us to waste the campaign without coming to a general action on the one hand, or suffering the enemy to overrun the country on the other, I conceived that every impediment that stood in their way was a means to answer these purposes ; — these, when thrown into the scale with those opinions which were opposed to an evacuation, caused that warfare in my mind, and hesitation, which ended in the loss of the garrison ; and, being repugnant to my own judgment of the advisableness of attempting to hold the post, filled me with the greater regret. The two great causes which led to this misfortune, and which I have before recited, as well perhaps as my reasoning upon it, which occasioned the•delay, were concealed from public view, and of course left the field of censure quite open for any and every laborer who inclined to work in it ; and afforded a fine theme for the pen of a malignant writer, who is less regardful of facts than of the point he wants to establish, where he has the field wholly to himself, where concealment of a few circumstances answers his purposes, or where a small transposition of them will give a very different complexion to the same thing."

WASHINGTON TO GORDON, 8 MARCH, 1785.

" But when, maugre of all the obstructions which had been thrown into the channel, all the labor and expense which had been bestowed on the works, and the risks we had before run as to the garrison, the British ships of war had passed and could pass those posts, it was clear to me from that moment that they were no longer eligible, and that the one on the east side of the river ought to be withdrawn whilst it was in our power. In consequence thereof, the letter of the 8th of November, 1776, was written to General Greene from White Plains ; that post and all the troops in the vicinity of it being under his orders. I give this information, and I furnish you with a copy of the

1 Sparks, *Writings of Washington*, vol. vi. pp. 328–330.

order for the evacuation of Fort Washington, because you desire it, not hat I want to exculpate myself from any censure which may have fallen upon me, by charging another." [1]

From these letters it appears that Greene, whose command included Fort Washington, persisted in the desire to defend it ; and by giving that advice relating to measures which he planned and was to execute, he made himself responsible for the result.

The "warfare in the mind" of Washington, however it may be judged, was due to two causes, — his desire to conform to the order of Congress until the condition on which discretion was allowed him by Congress should arise, and the persistently expressed opinion of Greene, that the condition had not yet arisen. If Washington had not cherished a tender regard for the orders of Congress, he would not have been the man to carry us through the Revolution ; but whatever may have been his merit or error on the occasion, it is undeniable that Greene as a counsellor gave the worst possible advice.

Such, as far as I know, was the unanimous contemporary opinion. Reed has written that the men and arms would have been saved; "but, unluckily, General Greene's judgment was contrary." [2] Graydon, not a mean authority, threw the severest blame on General Greene, and said : "Nor upon a cool consideration of all the circumstances, after a lapse of four-and thirty years, can I see full cause to renounce that opinion." [3] And, speaking of the opinion of the army, Wilkinson reports: "General Greene was chiefly blamed for attempting to hold the place." [4] The opinion of Jared Sparks in our day, I have already quoted.

I turn next to the charge numbered " XII. GREENE AT THE BRANDYWINE."

In the confusion of statements about battles, two trustworthy and independent eyewitnesses are to the historic inquirer as two separate blazed trees that mark the path through a forest. Knox, who was near Chad's Ford, is a good authority, that, on the news that Howe had turned the American right wing under Sullivan, Washington set off in a gallop toward the right. The question that is raised by General Greene's grandson is, whether Washington joined the right alone, or with troops. The grandson insists that Washington arrived in a gallop and

[1] Sparks, *Writings of Washington*, vol. ix. p. 101.
[2] J. Reed to C. Lee, November 21, 1776.
[3] Graydon's *Memoirs*, Littell's edition, pp. 179 and 211.
[4] Wilkinson's *Memoirs*, vol. i. p. 101.

alone, and quotes as his authority a letter written in 1845 by one Darlington, who says that he had heard his father say that he had heard one Joseph Brown say that he, Joseph Brown, though an elderly man at the time, and mounted on a strange horse, rode at full speed through woods and over fences before Washington as his guide, and that Washington was continually calling out to him, " Push along, old man ! Push along, old man ! " On the other hand, I follow the independent but coincident testimony of two men, Lafayette and Marshall, who on that day were both present serving on the right where Washington arrived. Lafayette says, in his autograph memoirs : " Le Général Washington arrivait de loin avec des troupes fraiches," — " Washington came up with fresh troops." The testimony of Marshall, afterwards Chief Justice, is to the same effect : " On the commencement of the action on the right, General Washington pressed forward with Greene to the support of that wing ; but before his arrival its rout was complete, and he could only check the pursuit." [1]

I was surprised that the " Review " should condemn me on what appears in the pamphlet as charge " XII. GERMANTOWN." The materials which set the attack on the British camp in that town in a clear light, are not readily found, and it is not strange that the critic had not seen them ; but why, then, is he ready with an adverse opinion ? After unwearied pains, continued through a succession of years, I succeeded in getting together trustworthy accounts of that battle, including three or four German accounts, and three English ones ; of American papers I have Washington's " Order of Battle " ; and of letters, one from MacDougal, two or three from Armstrong, one from Sullivan, one or two from Stephen, two from Wayne, one from Lacy, one from Heth, one from Walter Stuart, officers engaged in the fight, and writing their accounts of it immediately after the retreat.

That the right of the British position at Germantown was " accessible with ease," is the statement of Henry Lee, then present as an officer in the army, and greatly esteemed. That two thirds of the efficient force was assigned to Greene is established by the separate and concurrent testimony of Sullivan and Wayne. That the column under Greene was to endeavor to get within two miles of the enemy's pickets on their route by two o'clock in the morning, and that they were to begin the attack precisely at five o'clock, is proved by " the order of

[1] Marshall's *Washington*, vol. i. p. 157.

battle." The wing with Washington did arrive at two o'clock, took food and rest, and advanced to the attack at the hour appointed by "the order of battle," while the left column under Greene was not heard of till about three quarters of an hour after the attack from the right.[1] That the "windmill attack" upon Chew's house, which Washington had masked by a single regiment, was made by a part of the column under Greene, appears most distinctly and unequivocally from the testimony of Marshall, who, as he makes the assertion, takes care to add that he was an eye-witness; and of General Wayne, who, in a letter to General Gates of November 21, 1777, and to his wife of October 6, 1777, writes thus of the attack on Chew's house, and the loss of the battle. To Gates: "At Germantown fortune smiled on our arms for full three hours; the enemy were broke, dispersed, and flying on all quarters; we were in possession of their whole encampment, together with their artillery, park, etc., etc. A windmill attack was made on a house into which six light companies had thrown themselves to avoid our bayonets; this gave time to the enemy to rally; our troops were deceived by this attack, taking it for something formidable; they fell back to assist in what they deemed a serious matter; the enemy, finding themselves no further pursued, and believing it to be a retreat, followed; confusion ensued, and we ran away from the arms of victory ready open to receive us." To his wife: "After retreating for about two miles, we found it was our own people who were originally designed to attack the right wing of the enemy's army;" that is, a part of Greene's command. That Washington was dissatisfied and frowned, was long remembered by Greene, who, years afterwards, while he claimed merit for his exertions on that day, wrote, "At Germantown I was evidently disgraced."

The strangest accusation of all is " XV. WHY GREENE WAS MADE QUARTERMASTER-GENERAL." My simple account is as follows: " Driven by necessity, Congress won slowly a partial victory over their pride and their fears, and on the second of March they elected Greene Quartermaster-general, giving him two assistants that were acceptable to him, and the power of appointing all other officers in his department." The correctness of this

---

[1] The correct reading of a sentence in the letter from General Stephen published in Washington's *Writings*, vol. v. p. 467, is as follows : " The two divisions formed the line of battle at a great distance from the enemy, and marching far through marshes, woods, and strong fences, mixt before we came up with the enemy."

statement is undeniable and undenied; but it is insisted that his acceptance should have been described as "yielded only from a sense of duty to his country and personal devotion to the Commander-in-chief." I pray you keep in mind that I am blamed for nothing but silence about his motives.

When a man acts from a compound motive, it may be hard to analyze its elements; and we cannot know them, unless the actor himself gives us glimpses into the inner workings of his mind. In the present case these are not wholly wanting. Before Greene entered the army, he had been interested in profitable trade. Six weeks before the fall of Fort Washington, in 1776, he indulged in the dream of reaping "a golden harvest" on the sea, as the captain of a privateer, and devised a scheme for outwitting the enemy by "sufficient effrontery." In February, 1778, he wrote, not altogether in jest, "Money becomes more and more the American's object. You must get rich, or you will be of no consequence." In one of his letters "he freely confessed that the emoluments expected from the quartermaster's department were flattering to his fortune." From one of his own letters we also learn that "the committee of Congress promised him a fortune at the time he accepted the office." And in self-defense he called to mind the rule, "that the quartermaster-general in all armies is always liberally rewarded."

The system under which Greene retained his rank and pay as major-general in the line, and received other emoluments as Quartermaster-general, was not at all the device of Washington, but of Reed of Philadelphia, who was on the committee from Congress to the camp. Among those connected with Reed by marriage were John Cox and Charles Pettit. These two men he was able to persuade Congress to accept as assistants to the Quartermaster-general, with Greene as the head of the department. It was a cardinal principle with Congress to remunerate its Quartermaster-general by a fixed salary, which had been established at the pay of a major-general, and an extra allowance of one hundred and sixty-six dollars a month. To a continuance of that arrangement Greene would not listen; but, retaining his place and pay in the line, he insisted on an extra compensation by commission. Congress yielded. The commissions were to be shared equally between Greene and Cox and Pettit; that is, one third went to Greene, and two thirds to Cox and Pettit, and the three thus constituted a partnership. The rate of the commission Greene left to be named by his partners, and it was fixed at "five per cent. on all disbursements by the quartermaster-general and his agents." Such a system, though it might give the promise of efficiency, left little hope of economy. We know from the French Minister, whose business it was to be well informed, that the expenses were exorbitant, "that the service of the army of Washington for June, July, and August, 1778, cost seven millions of dollars, and that a European army of sixty thousand men would be well supported at the cost of fifteen thousand men of the United States."

Where so large a latitude was given to the disbursing officer, the public disliked to see him advance his relatives to lucrative agencies under him; but Greene did so, and his enthusiastic biographer "acknowledged that he was guilty of nepotism," setting an example followed by "dangerous consequences."

It is not conducive to administrative purity to regulate appointments to office by conditions of political partisanship; yet after Reed became President of Pennsylvania, Greene issued a circular, which, if I understand it, was intended, under a cloud of circumlocution, to confine the patronage of his office to the party which supported Reed.

As early as April, 1679, "growing clamors were heard in Congress. Thereupon, to cite Greene's own account of his representations: "I told the Congress, if they think my reward greater than my merit, I wish to quit the business." By midsummer of the same year, apprehensions of danger from popular resentment beset Cox and Pettit. Greene tried to cheer up his partners to the tone of defiance, and as to Congress, he wrote: " Governor Reed is much mistaken if he thinks that the voice of a member of that body is, as it once was, like the trumpet of an archangel sounding the alarm." [1]

Things went wrong, and complaints of a want of order and economy continued to increase. New rich men, who had gained wealth as officers of Greene's appointment, lived extravagantly, and the country resounded with murmurs. A Virginia poet wrote: —

> " Virtue and Washington in vain
> To glory call the prostrate train, ...
> Ruin with giant strides approaches,
> And quartermasters loll in coaches."

Of some of Greene's appointments in Pennsylvania, Joseph

[1] Greene to Pettit, July 24, 1779, in Sargent's *Loyal Poetry*, p. 187, note.

Reed, in April, 1780, wrote : " When such men make such a display of fortune, it is impossible to help looking back, and equally impossible for a people, soured by taxes and the continuance of the war, to help fretting." Nor were instances of dishonesty wanting. Greene having made it a condition of his accepting the department, that he should name all his own agents, Congress would have held him responsible for them. He resisted, and Congress replied mildly and firmly by a resolve, " That Major-general Greene, Quartermaster-general, be informed, in answer to his letter of the nineteenth of June last, that Congress, conceiving it to be essential to the public interest, as well as incident to the nature of all offices intrusted with the disbursements of public moneys, that those who exercise them should be responsible for such disbursements, whether it be made immediately by themselves or by agents appointed by and responsible to them, cannot consistently with their duty to their constituents, by any general resolution, hold up a contrary maxim ; but as they wish not to expose the faithful servants of the public to any unreasonable risks or losses, and are sensible that on the various branches of the Quartermaster's department abuses and frauds may possibly happen, notwithstanding all the customary precautions, that in all such cases they will determine on the circumstances as they arise, and make such favorable allowances as justice may require." [1]

Dissatisfaction increased to such an extent, that Greene thus describes his condition to General Schuyler : " Public distrust and popular abuse when joined together are intolerable." Greene was willing that the whole matter should be regarded as " a revival of the old scheme " of superseding Washington, as " a plan of Mifflin's to injure Washington's operations." He was mistaken ; even Pettit, one of his partners, doubted his opinions, and did not fully approve his measures. Congress was in earnest, and wisely, as I think, determined at all events to break up the system of partnership and compensation by commission, upon which Greene peremptorily resigned. The dilemma to which Congress was reduced, General Armstrong of Pennsylvania describes in a letter to General Irvine of August 8, 1780 : " General Greene's peremptory resignation in the business of Quartermaster-general, or refusal to act under the new regulation for that department, at this very critical moment, has at

---

[1] Journals of Congress, vol. iii. p. 499.

once disappointed and thrown Congress into a degree of vexatious distress greater than can be well expressed, or has yet happened in regard of any individual. Nine tenths of the difficulty arises from the importance of the present moment. The committee of Congress at camp appears to make General Greene's continuance of absolute necessity; so that if he is retained, the measures of Congress for reforming that department must be rescinded, and the censures of the public must remain against Congress, as deaf to their remonstrances for the reformation of abuses. . . . . Congress are as well disposed to do anything in their power that is in itself right, as men can be."

Nor was this all. Greene's letter of resignation was marked by what he called tartness, but what Congress looked upon as insolence. Of these expressions, Washington, who had read them, wrote to a member of Congress: "I do not mean to justify, to countenance, or excuse, in the most distant degree, any expressions of disrespect which the gentleman in question, if he has used any, may have offered to Congress, no more than I do any unreasonable matters he may have required respecting the Quartermaster-general's department." [1]

The words in Greene's letter of resignation which gave offense to Congress were: "Administration seem to think it far less important to the public interest to have this department well filled and promptly arranged than it really is, as they will find it by future experience." [2] Experience must prove that evil consequences followed the change, or this language was justly censurable. Timothy Pickering accepted the post of quartermaster-general on a moderate fixed salary, and he willingly undertook "to prevent the evils apprehended from a change, and to reform some of the abuses which had crept into the department."

The displeasure of Congress with Greene was very great. An upright patriot and warm friend of Washington wrote to him: "The manner of these demands, made in such peremptory terms at the moment of action, when the campaign was opened, the enemy in the field, and our ally waiting for coöperation, has lessened General Greene, not only in the opinion of Congress, but, I think, of the public; and I question whether it will terminate with the acceptance of his refusal only." [3] On this

1 *Washington's Writings*, vol. vii. p. 152.
2 *Ibid.* vol. vii. p. 514, Appendix.
3 *Ibid.* vol. vii. p. 150, *note.*

Washington interposed to retain him, not as Quartermaster-general, but in the line, saying of him : " As a military officer he stands very fair, and very deservedly so, in the opinion of all his acquaintance."[1]

I readily adopt the words of Washington. I doubt not that, with the fall of Continental money, the vision of wealth was not realized ; and I pray you not to interpret too unfavorably to Greene the notices which injustice has extorted. A strong sentiment of self is not absolutely inconsistent with great efficiency in war. I leave you to judge whether Greene's accession to the post of Quartermaster-general should have been heralded with a clatter about disinterested patriotism and self-denying devotedness to the Commander-in-chief.

I remember very well the remark of Lord Bacon, that " it is doubtless unpleasing to take out of men's minds vain opinions ; " and Sir Walter Raleigh warns of the danger to any one " who, in writing a modern history, shall follow truth too near." Yet I thought that in so honorable a purpose I might rely on the editors of the " Review " as a wall on the right hand and on the left. If you fail me, I must console myself with the teachings of the greatest of poets, where he says : —

" ' Di lume in lume
Ho io appreso quel che, s' io ridico,
A molti fia savor di forte agrume;

" ' E s' io al vero son timido amico,
Temo di perder vita tra coloro
Che questo tempo chiameranno antico.'

" La luce rispose: ' Coscienza fusca
O della propria o dell' altrui vergogna,
Pur sentirà la tua parola brusca.

" ' Ma nondimen, rimossa ogni menzogna,
Tutta tua vision fa manifesta,
E lascia pur grattar dov' è la rogna;

" ' Chè, se la voce tua sarà molesta
Nel primo gusto, vital nutrimento
Lascerà poi quando sarà digesta."

Or as it may be read in English : —

" ' From light to light
Have I learnt that, which, if I tell again,
It may with many wofully disrelish;
And, if I am a timid friend to truth,

[1] *Washington's Writings*, vol. vii. p. 152.

> I fear my life may perish among those
> To whom these days shall be of ancient date.'
> 'T was answered: ' Conscience, dimmed or by its own
> Or other's shame, will feel thy saying sharp.
> Thou, notwithstanding, all deceit removed,
> See the whole vision be made manifest;
> And let them wince who have their withers wrung.
> What though, when tasted first, thy voice shall prove
> Unwelcome: on digestion, it will turn
> To vital nourishment.' "

I remain very truly yours,

GEO. BANCROFT.

LETTER FROM PROFESSOR GEORGE WASHINGTON GREENE.

EAST GREENWICH, R. I., *May* 9, 1867.

To THE EDITORS OF THE NORTH AMERICAN REVIEW : —

GENTLEMEN, — Mr. Bancroft's letter in the last number of your " Review " may be divided into three parts — personalities, assertions, and the forms of discussion. With the personalities I have nothing to do. I proceed directly to an examination of the assertions and discussions.

First among the assertions is, that I " assume the appearance of fairness by a parade of documents and authorities, but that many of the documents are irrelevant, decisive ones are left out, and some of those which are confidently cited are unhistoric." It will, I presume, be allowed by every candid reader, that, in making assertions like these, the accuser is bound to prove them. I deny them all, and call upon Mr. Bancroft for his proofs.

Second. Mr. Bancroft claims to have used " in one sentence, fairly and without confusion, a letter of October 27th and another of October 29th." I believe that they were put together for the express purpose of conveying the idea that Greene was disposed to murmur at Washington's orders, and thus prepare the reader for the still graver charge of disobedience ; otherwise why conceal the fact that they were not only written on different days, but addressed to different persons — one to Washington, the other to Mifflin ? Where is the *murmur* of the following sentence, the only one in the letter to Washington which refers to the evacuation of Fort Independence ? " I think that Fort Independence might have kept the enemy at bay for several days, *but the troops here and on the other side are so much fatigued that it must have been a work of time."* So far from a *murmur,* is not this mention of the fatigue of the troops a proof that he too, thought that, after all, the evacuation was perhaps the wisest thing that could have been done ?

When he wrote to Mifflin two days before, he had not taken this fact so fully into consideration. The evacuation had come upon him by surprise, and he felt anxious about the effect of it upon Magaw's men, whom it exposed to a new danger. " I am anxious," he writes, " to know the state of the troops in the grand army ; whether they are high or low spirited ; whether well or ill posted ; whether a battle is expected or not. We must govern our operations by yours. The troops here and on the other side are in good spirits, but I fear quitting Fort Independence will oblige Magaw to draw in his forces into the garrison, *as the enemy will have a passage open upon his back. I fear it will damp the spirits of the troops. He did not expect it so soon."*

Neither of these passages will bear the construction that Mr. Bancroft has put upon them. He unites them to paint Greene complaining *" under the illusions of inexperience,"* and writing *" murmuringly to Washington."* Taken separately and in their chronological order, they show first, that the unexpected evacuation of Fort Independence excited very natural apprehensions in Greene's mind that Magaw's troops, finding themselves exposed where they had hitherto been protected, would lose heart. It did not require a very long military experience to show the probability of such an effect.

But — and here we come to the letter of two days later to Washington — subsequent observation led Greene to reflect that, although the fort might have been held a few days longer, yet the *troops were too fatigued* to hold it long, and therefore the evacuation was judicious. Such is the true interpretation of the *murmuring* letter to Washington. Can I doubt that this juxtaposition of the two letters was made with a purpose ? Not when I remember how closely on his 40th page he brings in the *despondent Greene* after Reed, " heartily sick of the contest," and wrote on the 187th, " no sooner did *Lee* find himself in a separate command than he resolved neither to join nor to reinforce his superior ; *and Greene* framed his measures on a system directly contrary to Washington's manifested intentions." Reed, Mr. Bancroft paints in very dark colors — and at what sacrifice of historic truth Mr. W. B. Reed has demonstrated. But why after painting him in such colors he passes so quickly to Greene, I cannot doubt. Lee was a traitor, as Mr. G. H. Moore has proved, and Mr. Bancroft has accepted the proof. Is there no purpose in connecting his name so closely with Greene's? Am I to suppose that Mr. Bancroft never read Hume's essay on the association of ideas, nor verified the effect of contiguity in time or space?

The next paragraph of Mr. Bancroft's letter being purely personal, I pass it by. In the third he summarily disposes of eleven sections of my pamphlet. He begins by saying: "Many of the charges are trivial and refute themselves, *making a muddle*," I use his own elegant expression, "only by their number. The first, which fills nearly a quarter of the whole pamphlet, is in part an argument to prove that *desperation* and not *hopelessness* is the *noun* corresponding to the *adjective* desperate; in part to make known that Greene was of a sanguine and hopeful temperament, which has been and is my own opinion." The first clause of the second sentence, however interesting as a reminiscence of the school-room, labors under the disadvantage of being wholly without foundation, a characteristic which it shares equally with the second clause. I shall do what Mr. Bancroft has neglected to do throughout the whole of this paragraph, prove my assertion.

In the first place, let me remind the reader that Mr. Bancroft's volume opens with a view of the effects of the Declaration of Independence, and the state of public opinion in July 1776. The following extract from his table of contents will show his point of view: "Independence the act of the people — Its aspect on the nations of Europe — Character of Lord Howe — His confidence of the restoration of peace — Lord Howe arrives at Staten Island — His declaration — His attempts at intercourse with Washington — He meets with a rebuff — His circular letters — His letters to individuals — Reed on the overture — Condition of America — Greene *despondent* — *Decision* of Samuel Adams — Of Robert Morris — Of Congress — Of Washington — "

It is evident from this summary that he intends to represent the people as united and decided on the great act of separation from England, — Samuel Adams, Robert Morris, Washington and Congress equally decided, and Greene despondent. The words of the text admit of no other construction. These eminent names, for they are all eminent, and some of them great, are brought forward as illustrations of the feeling which Greene ought to have had, but according to Mr. Bancroft did not have. Despondency, at a moment like this, was too nearly allied to treason to be permitted to take shelter under the veil of temperament. If Greene had desponded then, he would never have dared to look Washington in the face again. But he did not despond. This I have proved by his own letters, in which he shows himself perfectly aware of the danger, looks it calmly in the face, and points out the remedy with a wisdom which fully justifies Hamilton's estimate of his statesmanship. "There must be a good army established ; men engaged for the war ; a proper corps of officers ; and then after a proper time to discipline the men, everything is to be expected." "I am confident the force of America, if properly exerted, will prove superior to all her enemies, but I would risk nothing to chance ; it is easy to disband when it is impossible to raise troops." Why Mr. Bancroft, in the face of such evidence, brought such a charge against Greene, is made clear by the charges of *want of vigilance, disingenuousness, and disobedience,* which follow in the course of his narrative. Belief in the one was to prepare the way for the gradual acceptance of the others.

The course of my argument has led me into a minute examination of the general acceptation of the word *desperate.* To the word *desperation* I have made no allusion, and Mr. Bancroft's assertions that I have must be taken as assertions are taken which contradict facts.

Neither have I attempted " to make known that Greene was of a sanguine and hopeful temperament." Mr. Bancroft wrote : " Greene had once before warned John Adams of the hopelessness of the contest." [1] I have published Greene's letters to Adams to show that, while keenly alive to the danger of failure, he was convinced that if proper energy were displayed, and the proper measures adopted, the Americans would succeed. In each of those letters he urges the display of that energy, and the adoption of those measures. When a writer asserts that a certain thing has been said or done, and positive proof is given that the very reverse was said or done, can an attempt to cover up the original misstatement by another misstatement equally gross be accepted as a sufficient justification ? It is a matter of infinite unimportance whether Mr. Bancroft thinks General

[1] Page 40.

Greene sanguine or despondent, but it becomes a grave question when he selects him as an example of despondency at a decisive moment, and holds him up in that light in a work which claims to be the result of long and earnest investigation. Mr. Bancroft has misrepresented my position, and failed to meet my argument. As he makes no allusion to my documents, I presume that he regards them as belonging to that class which he has, greatly to his own convenience, discarded as " unhistorical or irrelevant."

" The second," (section) he continues, " is a gross and plain perversion of my words and meaning." The general law of interpretation requires that in endeavoring to ascertain the force of a particular statement you should compare it with the writer's other statements concerning the same or similar facts or persons. Throughout this volume Mr. Bancroft has manifested a fixed determination to degrade General Greene from the place which he has held in American history for well nigh a century. I have applied this fact to the passage in question, and drawn from it the conclusion that Mr. Bancroft's words were a covert insinuation intended to take its place in the reader's mind in connection with more positive statements, and aid in preparing it for the unfavorable impression which it was his intention to produce. Mr. Bancroft must venture beyond his entrenchment of mere assertions before he can reach my position.

" *The third is a silly charge of omission which could be scarcely urged against a biographer.*" Nor would it have been urged but for the reason just assigned. Mr. Bancroft's omissions, like Hamlet's madness, have method in them.

" *The fourth explains itself.*" It unquestionably does; but not in a manner favorable to Mr. Bancroft's reputation for accuracy of statement, as I have already demonstrated in the first part of this letter.

" *The sixth is a mere criticism on language.*" This also is true ; and as in the course of that criticism Mr. Bancroft is shown to have used an expression so strongly suggestive of *unscrupulousness* as *did not scruple*, in order to tell his readers that Greene did not hesitate to reinforce the garrison of Mount Washington ; nor to change Greene's words *any great danger* into *no great conceivable danger;* nor to assert that Greene "insisted that the evacuation (of Fort Washington) was not only uncalled for but would be *attended with disastrous conse-*

quences " when there is not a word in Greene's letter that is susceptible of such an interpretation ; when, I say, these things are taken into consideration, it will probably be admitted by every candid reader that my criticism on words becomes a criticism on acts. To what class those acts belong, it is not pleasant, though certainly not difficult to say.

" *The seventh complains that Greene is described as sanguine, which he certainly was.*" I need not tell the reader that the word I objected to in Mr. Bancroft's statement, was not *sanguine* but *easy.* Had he represented Greene as " indulging his sanguine disposition," I should have controverted the substance of the assertion, which is false, but should not have bestowed a thought upon the form which, as the mere expression of Mr. Bancroft's opinion, " does not merit my notice." But to my apprehension there is a material difference between an *easy, sanguine disposition,* and a disposition merely sanguine. A great man might have the one. None but a weak man can have the other. Such, too, appears to have been the opinion of Walter Scott, when in describing one of his favorite heroes, he couples *bold* with *sanguine,* as its natural attendant. As Mr. Bancroft can hardly be supposed to have been ignorant of so obvious a distinction, I am fully justified in interpreting this also as a link in the elaborate chain of defamation. Why did Mr. Bancroft omit in his letter the word *easy* which strongly inculpates, and take refuge in the word *sanguine* which merely defines ?

" *The eighth gains what plausibility it has by a confusion of orders, places, and dates.*" Here also, Mr. Bancroft meets argument and evidence by assertion. He says, and thereby shows us why he coupled *easy* with *sanguine* in his characterization of Greene's temperament, " Greene, indulging his easy, sanguine disposition, had neglected Washington's timely order to prepare for its (Fort Lee's) evacuation by the removal of *its stores.*" [1] Washington's words are, " You will, therefore, immediately have all the stores removed *which you do not deem necessary for your defense.*" This was written on the 8th of November. On the 10th Greene replies — " I have ordered the Quartermaster-general to send off all the *superfluous stores.*" Before Mr. Bancroft can claim absolution from the sentence, which this contradiction between his assertions and the indisputable evidence of the documents passes upon him, he must demonstrate the " *confusion of orders, places, and dates* " in which he takes refuge.

[1] Page 194.

In speaking of the 9th section, there is for the first time the shadow of an argument. But even this shadow melts away when we remember that the regular outguards were stationed, that the passage of the river was effected on a dark and stormy night, and that Washington, who had been on the ground, and consequently in actual command, six days, was as unconscious of the danger as Greene. If the success of the English was, as Mr. Bancroft insinuates, owing to an easy, sanguine temperament, whose was that temperament, Greene's who obeyed his orders, or Washington's whose duty it was to give them? Washington believed that Howe would cross over into the Jerseys. Had he, when on the spot, no responsibility in preparing to dispute his entrance? If Mr. Bancroft's censure were just, it is on Washington and not on Greene that it would fall. But neither Washington nor Greene can justly be blamed for a misfortune which the imperfect means at their command rendered inevitable.

" *The tenth is disposed of by the citation of my own language.*' Let us see. This language is : " The general officers, especially, Stirling, Mercer, Sullivan, and above all Greene, rendered the greatest aid in preparing the expedition." [1] Had Mr. Bancroft stopped here I should have had nothing to say. But on page 239, in his narrative of the second crossing of the Delaware and its consequences, he says, " Washington lost no time in renewing his scheme for driving the enemy to the extremity of New Jersey. . . . . While his companions in arms were *reposing he was indefatigable in his preparations.*' To this reckless assertion, for which there is not the shadow of authority, — if there is, let Mr. Bancroft produce it, — I opposed passages from " Hamilton's Eulogium on Greene,' in which he claims for him a share in the *conception* as well as the *execution* of the operations of this brilliant and decisive campaign. " Hamilton's Eulogium on Greene," says Mr. Bancroft, "is, like all other productions of that class, very far from being a safe historical authority." When the reader calls to mind that the writer of this eulogium was an officer in Washington's army, that he served throughout this campaign, that shortly after the close of it he entered Washington's military family and became his confidential aid, and that when he wrote these praises of Greene he knew that many of the members of the Cincinnati for whom they were written, had been actors in the scenes he was describing, and that Washington himself would probably

[1] B. p. 224.

be one of the audience — and in fact nothing but illness kept him away — when, I say. the reader remembers these circumstances, and gives them their due weight, he will probably conclude with me that they make this eulogium a historical document of the highest order.

" *The eleventh belongs at best to biography, and in my opinion not even there.*" What is the substance of the paragraph which Mr. Bancroft, with so absolute a tone, excludes even from biography ?

The English had landed at the head of Elk. The Americans were advancing to oppose them. Greene was sent forward to select a position for the army. He chose one which covered the country, and secured the lines of supply and retreat. Before his report was received, another position was fixed upon. When Greene saw it he objected to it as untenable. The British advanced, and the Americans were compelled to make a hasty retreat. Greene's prediction was fully verified. Mr. Bancroft describes the hurried change of position, and claims great merit for Washington's generalship. Greene's part, however, does not, he says, belong " even to biography, much less to history." A military historian would probably ask why a position was taken that made such a retreat necessary. Gordon, who had no rhetoric, but a sincere love of truth, told why. Most readers will, I am persuaded, thank him for it.

" *The fourteenth complains of my narrative where it is but the reproduction of the statement and almost the words of eye witnesses who were the most competent to give evidence.*" Mr. Bancroft can hardly be surprised if, remembering how he mutilates and suppresses in his quotation from Reed on his 40th page, and in those from Donop's Diary on his 229th, how on the same page he asserts that " Ewing did not even make an effort to cross at Trenton," when Washington in his report to the President of Congress says, " General Ewing was to have crossed before day at Trenton Ferry ; but the quantity of ice was so great that " *though he did everything in his power to effect it, he could not get over ;* how on all occasions he alters or omits essential words to suit his purpose, and everywhere uses documents, not as authorities by which he is to be guided, but as materials to be worked over and newly fashioned at will; Mr. Bancroft, I say, can hardly be surprised, if remembering these things, I decline to accept the testimony of his " eye witnesses " until he publishes their letters and narratives in full.

Third.   Having disposed in a manner so convenient for himself, though unsatisfactory to those difficult readers who require
arguments in answer to arguments, and regard documentary evidence as the only means whereby documentary evidence can be
rebutted, Mr. Bancroft selects four sections, the 5th, 13th, 12th,
and 15th, for "fuller discussion." I will follow him through this
discussion.   He begins with section 5th, the loss of Fort Washington.

I will not dwell upon the rhetoric of the first paragraph.   It
opens with Professor Agassiz, and " that cleft in the Jura," and
closes with Mr. George Bancroft on foot or on horseback, as the
reader may choose.   I prefer him in the saddle ; and, with its
hero in this position, the picture — for we have only t , add the
Hudson with its Palisades, and Spuyten Devil Creek with its
reminiscences of Antony van Corlear, the Dutch trumpeter, to
finish it in perfect keeping — is too charming to be rashly criti-
cised.   But I crave pardon of the genial and noble hearted
Agassiz, for introducing his honored name in such a connection.

The second paragraph contains a companion piece, superior
to the first in invention, but somewhat calmer in tone ; a quiet,
rural landscape, with Jared Sparks and George Bancroft drawing water "from the " same " well head." This is the second time
that Mr. Bancroft has attempted to force Mr. Sparks into an
impossible partnership with his calumnies.   Your own uncom-
mented addition of that part of Mr. Sparks' paragraph, which,
to borrow the suggestive words of Mr. G. L. Schuyler, concerning a similar omission, Mr. Bancroft's " clerk in transcribing
omitted," [1] is a sufficient rebuke for this unjustifiable attempt
to force a meaning upon the words of the honored dead, which
in life he would have indignantly disclaimed.

"Early in November," Mr. Bancroft says, " experience proved
clearly to the mind of Washington that Fort Washington ought
to be evacuated, and, knowing from the reports of Greene the
different opinion of that officer, he embodied in his order for
preparing for the evacuation the reasoning on which the order
was founded. . . . . When it is compared with Greene's con-

---

[1] " The letter you inclose from General Montgomery, is not the whole letter,
or a continuous extract from it.   Your
clerk, in transcribing it, has omitted the
closing words of the last sentence."
" Had you deemed it worth while to
have copied for my use the whole of this
letter as published in Irving's History
(vol. iii. p. 132), the bearing of your
extract, as in the case of General Montgomery's letter, would have been better
understood."— *Vide* pp. 20, 22, of Mr.
G. L. Schuyler's excellent pamphlet.

duct on receiving it, no room is left for doubt how that conduct is to be judged."

In the next paragraph we are told, "*First*, that it was not modest for the inferior officer, *who had already had occasion to explain his opinion*, to thwart the system of his superior." *Second*, that if every subordinate should insist upon his own plan, that harmony of action which it was the duty of the Commander-in-chief to secure would be destroyed. *Third*, that "the order to defend Fort Washington to the last was explicitly and unequivocally revoked;" yet Greene reinforced it. *Last*, that "a considerable discretion was left to Greene, and that he used that discretion in the most injurious manner." Two letters of Washington, one of the 22d of August, 1779, to Reed, and one of the 8th of March, 1785, to Gordon, follow. The discussion closes by evading the question of Washington's ultimate responsibility, throwing upon Greene the responsibility of "the warfare in Washington's mind," which was the immediate cause of the loss of the fort, and an assurance that, according to "the unanimous contemporary opinion, Greene as a counsellor gave the worst possible advice."

Such, I believe, is a correct analysis of Mr. Bancroft's argument. And now, in coming to an examination of it, please remember that in my pamphlet I waived in explicit terms the question of the correctness of Greene's opinion, and confined myself strictly to the inquiry, Who was responsible for the holding of Fort Washington after the 13th of November? Mr. Bancroft does not meet the question.

He says that "early in November experience proved clearly to the mind of Washington that Fort Washington ought to be evacuated." I, of course, have nothing to do with Washington's opinion except as it was known to Greene. There are, so far as I have been able to discover, but three letters of Washington to Greene in the first part of November. On the 6th he writes to the President of Congress: "I expect the enemy will bend their force against Fort Washington."[1] In this letter no doubt is expressed or even hinted of his power or intention to hold it.

On the next day, the 7th, he writes to Greene: "Conjecturing that too little is yet done by General Howe to go into winter quarters, we conceive that Fort Washington will be an object for part of his force, while New Jersey may claim the attention of the other part. To guard against the evils arising

---

1 Force, *American Archives*, 5th series, vol. iii. p. 543.

from the first, I must recommend to you to pay every attention in your power, and give every assistance you can, to the garrison opposite to you." [1]

Up to this date, therefore, there is no doubt expressed in Washington's letters to Greene about the propriety or possibility of holding Fort Washington. To the President of Congress, to whom any such doubt would necessarily have been communicated, he holds the same language that he holds to Greene. Mr. Bancroft's assertion, therefore, that Greene "had already had occasion to explain his opinion," has no foundation but in his own fertile invention. Thus far, then, Greene's intention to "thwart the system of his superior" could not have been formed, for no change in that system had been announced. Washington and Greene were still in perfect accord.

But after the letter of the 7th had been written, intelligence reached camp that "three vessels" had passed up the North River, and on the next day Washington wrote : —

"The late passage of three vessels up the North River, of which *we have just received* advice, is so plain a proof of the inefficacy of all the obstructions we have thrown into it, that I cannot but think it will fully justify a change in the disposition which has been made. If we cannot prevent vessels from passing up, and the enemy are possessed of the surrounding country, what valuable purpose can it answer to attempt to hold a post from which the expected benefit cannot be had? *I am, therefore, inclined to think* that it will not be prudent to hazard the men and stores at Mount Washington; *but as you are on the spot I leave it to you to give such orders as to evacuating Mount Washington as you may judge best, and so far revoking the order given to Colonel Magaw to defend it to the last.*"

If we apply to this letter the common rules of interpretation, we shall see, first, that it bases the idea of evacuation upon the impossibility of preventing the passage of the enemy's ships up the river, and speaks of the proofs of that impossibility as having been *just* acquired. Thus far, then, it confirms my position that, up to the 8th, Washington meant to hold the fort. The manner in which he speaks, in the letters of the 6th and 7th, of the enemy's designs against that post, inasmuch as they contain no hint of a doubt concerning his power to hold it, is also a confirmation of the correctness of my position.

Now what follows from this *just* discovered impossibility?

1 Force, *ut sup.* p. 557.

" *I am, therefore, inclined to think* that it will not be prudent to hazard the men and stores at Mount Washington." By what principle of interpretation was Greene required to accept this dubitative *I am inclined to think* as equivalent to a positive *I think?* Therefore, as the letter reads up to this sentence, there is nothing in it which could convey to Greene's mind the idea of a positive decision or a positive order.

But even if there had been, and the expression had been *I think*, what conclusion about Washington's decision would Greene have drawn from the next sentence? " *But as you are on the spot I leave it to you to give such orders as to evacuating Mount Washington as you may judge best.*" Is this an order, or is it a reference of decision on the ground of the Commander-in-chief's absence from the spot, and his consequent incapacity to decide correctly? Congress had instructed Washington to hold Fort Washington as long as possible. What if Greene had evacuated it? Would the language of this letter have justified him to a court-martial, or what to him was always of more importance than the opinions of man, to his own conscience, unless he could have affirmed that he believed it to be necessary? How the tidings of such an evacuation would have been received by the country may be conjectured from the general outburst of indignation with which those of St. Clair's evacuation of Ticonderoga were received.

The third count in Mr. Bancroft's indictment is, that " the order to defend Fort Washington to the last was explicitly and unequivocally revoked, yet Greene thought proper to reinforce it with some of the best troops and arms." How this revocation was expressed you have already seen. How it can be considered in any other light than as a logical sequence of the second clause of the sentence in which it occurs it is difficult to conceive. Magaw, who was in command at Fort Washington, — for technically Greene was never in command there, — had been ordered to defend his post to the last extremity. In authorizing Greene to use his own judgment about holding or evacuating it, a revocation of that order was a necessary part of the authorization. The last clause of the sentence is the necessary complement of the second clause. It conveys no opinion, contains no modification not already substantially contained in the second. Washington added it, as the qualifying *so far* proves, because he wished to express himself clearly and fully. He meant that Greene should feel himself justified in following his own judgment, and therefore told Magaw, through Greene, that he was no longer required to defend his post if Greene should order him to evacuate it. This is the only meaning that can be attributed to this clause, and the prominence which Mr. Bancroft gives it is utterly irreconcilable with every recognized law of interpretation.

I hold, therefore, that the so-called orders of the 8th were literally discretionary, or, in other words, that, throwing the responsibility upon Greene, they conferred upon him the power which was the necessary condition of that responsibility.[1] They contain, as I have fully shown, all that Washington is known to have said to him upon the subject.

From the 9th, therefore, the day on which Washington's letter reached him, Greene found himself in a new position. It became his duty to decide the question of evacuation according to his own judgment. It was a new question. Up to that moment, Washington's letters to him contain no allusion to it. So far from having, as Mr. Bancroft asserts, had occasion to explain his opinion on this question to the Commander-in-chief, the question had never arisen between them. The council of war of the 16th of October, which, with but one dissenting voice, decided that the river could not be effectually obstructed, decided also " that Fort Washington be held as long as possible." [2] Greene was not present at that council, but he believed that the free passage of the river might be obstructed, and the affair of the 27th October [3] shows that there was some foundation for his opinion. But this, as plainly appears from the minutes of the council, was treated as a separate question. Although the council decided that the river could not be secured, they also decided that the fort should be held as long as possible. Up to the 8th of November, Washington's words and conduct were in accordance with this decision.

What, then, was Greene's duty in this new emergency? Plainly, first of all to make sure that he had put the right construction upon Washington's letter; and next to tell him what that construction was. This he did, and in his letter of the 9th November, which, as I have given it in full in my pamphlet, I will not reprint here, he announces his difference of opinion and gives his reasons for it. It is evident, both from this letter and

---

[1] This view has been approved by two officers of high rank and extensive experience.

[2] Force, eighth series, vol. ii. p. 1116

[3] *Vide* my pamphlet, pp. 42–44.

from his conduct, that he interpreted Washington's " *I am inclined to think*," as the expression of indecision, and his " *I leave it to you to give such orders as you may judge best*," as a literal transfer of the power of decision to him.

Washington's letters of August 1779, and March 1785, upon which Mr. Bancroft lays so much stress, have nothing to do with Greene's knowledge of Washington's sentiments before the 13th of November 1776, and Greene's conduct as to obedience must be judged by his knowledge of Washington's decision. This is equally true of the letter of the 19th of November 1776, to Augustine Washington. Greene's only means of knowing what Washington thought was the letter of the 8th of November, and what construction a candid application of the simplest and most obvious laws of interpretation must put upon this letter I have already shown. To blame Greene for reading Washington's words as Washington wrote them, and interpreting them as he had always interpreted them, would be absurd, if the gravity of such a charge against such a man did not make it wicked.

On what day Washington received Greene's letter of the 9th I have no means of knowing; probably, however, on the 10th, certainly not later than the 11th. When he had read that letter, he knew what interpretation Greene had put upon his. It was the same construction which he had put upon Washington's answer to his letter of the 29th of October, about holding the lower lines. In that answer, Washington had referred the decision to Greene, because Greene was on the spot; and he had " not scrupled " to decide according to his own judgment. Eleven days had passed without a word of reproof from Washington, or even a suggestion that he had erred in his interpretation of Washington's words. Why should he hesitate to do now what he had done then ?

On the 10th he again wrote to Washington, unfolding his general plan of defense in Jersey. The letter of Harrison, Washington's secretary, to which this was an answer, has not been preserved, but it is fair to suppose that it was upon the same subject. On the 11th, Greene writes again. But from Washington, upon the holding or evacuating Fort Washington, there is no other letter.[1] His last word had been given in his

---

[1] But on the designs of the enemy and the general defense he writes on the 9th: —

WHITE PLAINS, *November 9, 1776.*

DEAR SIR, — Since my letters of yesterday two deserters have got in from

letter of the 8th. On the 13th, he arrived at Fort Lee. The reason for intrusting the decision to Greene ceased. The Commander-in-chief was now on the spot. If he disapproved Greene's conduct, why did he not countermand Greene's orders? Clearly, this was his duty as Commander-in-chief. Clearly, this was no time to balance considerations of delicacy. Clearly, if Washington hesitated, the fault did not lie with Greene, who had only an opinion to express, not an order to give. But Washington did hesitate, and during that hesitation the fort fell. It is not pleasant to accuse Washington of indecision, but it is not just to lay the consequences of that indecision at another man's door. Greene acted independently while it was his duty to act. He advised conscientiously when it became his duty to advise. Beyond this it was not in his " power to " go, and power is a condition of responsibility. If it was not modest in him to hold a different opinion from the Commander-in-chief, for such is the true import of Mr. Bancroft's words, it was neither considerate nor just in the Commander-in-chief to call upon him for an independent opinion. But no such thought ever entered the equitable mind of Washington. He saw that there was great weight in Greene's reasoning, and therefore took it into careful consideration. Unfortunately, before he had come to a decision, the opportunity of strengthening or withdrawing the garrison escaped him. Up to the night of the 15th, either of these might have been done ; and Washington was already on the spot on the 13th. This aspect of the question Mr. Bancroft evades. Let him prove that in the presence of the Commander-in-chief it was for the subordinate to decide, and I will accept the responsibility for my *grandfather*.

"*I turn next*," says Mr. Bancroft, "*to the charge numbered XII. Greene at the Brandywine. . . . . The question that is raised*

the enemy (at Dobb's Ferry), who relate many circumstances in proof of the enemy's intention of crossing into the Jerseys at or near Dobbs's Ferry, under cover of a cannonade from their shipping.

These deserters say that boats were to have been brought up (from New York they add, but possibly they may be brought from the Sound by the way of Harlem River) last night, and that their troops were ordered to have five days provisions ready dressed.

If there is a possibility of stopping these boats, it would be well to attempt it. A reinforcement is by this time, I expect, on the west side of the river, marching to your assistance. Other troops are passing upon this side, and will I hope be ready to cross to-morrow ; the force on your side under Generals Mercer and Stephens you will consider how best to employ. Keep an attentive watch upon the enemy. I shall soon be with you; in the interim, I am,

Dear sir,
Your most obed't and
Affect. serv't,
G. WASHINGTON.

by General Greene's grandson is whether Washington joined the right alone or with troops." Mr. Bancroft holds that he brought up Greene's division with him, and cites Knox, Lafayette, and Marshall; Knox, to prove that he "set out in a gallop" for the right; Lafayette, that he "came up with fresh troops"; Marshall, that he "pressed forward with Greene to the support of that wing."

I have relied upon Gordon, and upon Greene's letter to Marchant, to prove that Greene brought up one division of his troops himself, — Weedon's brigade; while the other, Mühlenberg's, took, by Washington's direction, another road. The statements of Greene and Gordon are positive, and admit of no modification. They must either be absolutely false or absolutely true. To these I have added the traditional testimony of Dr. Darlington of West Chester, Pennsylvania, as published by the Historical Society of that State. Mr. Bancroft's slur at this gentleman, whom he calls *one Darlington*, will hardly pass in Pennsylvania for an argument. According to Dr. Darlington, Washington, who was with Greene when the cannon announced the attack upon the right wing, took a cross-road, under the guidance of an old man named Brown, who had repeatedly told the story to Darlington's father. The point at issue, therefore, is, Whose testimony are we to receive?

Knox's declaration that Washington "set off in a gallop" shows that he must have "set off" alone, unless we are to believe that Greene's infantry "set off in a gallop" with him. Now as the troops of that day were not trained to the double-quick, they could hardly have kept up a gallop forty-five minutes, even if they had started in one. Knox, therefore, is, against, and not for, Mr. Bancroft.

But Colonel Pinckney, one of Washington's aids, in a paper dated thirteen days after the battle, positively asserts that he was with Washington, and Washington with Sullivan, when Weedon came up.[1] Therefore Washington must have been in advance of Greene, who was with Weedon; and to have been in advance — for they were together when the cannon was first heard — he must have come at least part of the way without him.

Thus Pinckney, with his fresh recollections of the battle, contradicts both Lafayette and Marshall, who wrote thirty years after the battle. But there is no need of taking either Lafay-

[1] *Proc. Penn. Hist. Soc.* vol. i. No. 8, p. 50.

ette's or Marshall's words literally. Neither of them enters into details. Both of them use expressions which are still correct as general narrative, if we suppose that Washington, after giving his orders, and seeing the march begun, "pressed forward" in advance, and was, as Pinckney tells us that he was, with Sullivan when Greene came up.

And, to come to the reason of the thing, why should Washington wait the tardy movements of infantry, when he knew, by the firing on the right, that he was needed there? Was it in keeping with his energetic character to walk his horse at so critical a moment, when a quarter of an hour's gallop would bring him where he could see and judge for himself?

But this is not the only issue between Mr. Bancroft and myself with regard to the Battle of the Brandywine. Permit me to call your attention for a moment to his narrative: —

" Howe seemed likely to get in the rear of the Continental army and complete its overthrow. But at the sound of the cannon on the right, taking with him Greene and the two brigades of Mühlenberg and Weedon, which lay nearest the scene of action, Washington marched swiftly to the support of the wing that had been confided to Sullivan, and in about forty minutes met them in full retreat. *His approach checked the pursuit.* Cautiously making a new disposition of his forces, Howe again pushed forward, *driving the party with Greene,* till they came upon a strong position, *chosen by Washington,* which completely commanded the road, and which a regiment of Virginians under Stevens, and another of Pennsylvanians under Stewart, were able to hold till nightfall."

And first let me remind you of Gordon's positive assertion that Mühlenberg, by Washington's orders, took a different road from Weedon, and that Greene, in a letter to Marchant, confirms Gordon's statement. I ask Mr. Bancroft for the authority by which he ventures to contradict authorities like these?

Next please to observe how Washington is made to stand alone at this stage of the narrative: " *His approach checked the pursuit.*" I would like to see this made plainer by authorities and detail. But — and do not overlook the sudden change — Howe pushes on, and, while Greene comes forward to be *driven,* Washington disappears from the field, suddenly reappearing, however, a *Deus ex machina,* the moment the driven Greene reaches tenable ground, and chooses it for him. I pass over minor points. I will not dwell upon the unhistoric absurdity of the picture; but I call upon Mr. Bancroft to give his authority for attributing to Washington the choice of the pass at which Greene made his great stand and saved the army.

For Greene always asserted that he had saved the army at the Brandywine. He claims it in a letter to Henry Marchant in 1778. He claims it in a letter to Henry Lee in 1782. Mr. Bancroft quotes this letter to prove, out of Greene's own mouth, that he fell under Washington's frown at Germantown, although the letter says no such thing. Why did he not quote the following passage? "I covered the retreat at Brandywine, and was upwards of an hour and a quarter in a hot action, and confessedly saved the park of artillery, and, indeed, the army, from the fatal effects of a disagreeable rout." Would Greene, in writing to Henry Lee, who was in the battle of the Brandywine, advance an unfounded claim to so conspicuous a service? Or is it "irrelevant and unhistoric" to name a Major-general in connection with the part performed by his division in an important battle?

Of Mr. Bancroft's paragraphs concerning Germantown I am at a loss how to speak, without using language which, however just in itself, and almost imperatively called for by the facts, would hardly become the pages of a literary journal. He has no condemnation for Washington's protracted discussion before Chew's house, the injudicious summons which cost the life of the gallant Smith, the time wasted in attempting to beat down its solid walls with light field-pieces, and the delay which all this occasioned in the advance of the right wing; but upon the attack upon it made by Woodford, under justifying circumstances, he dwells with minute complacency, as a blunder caused by a blunder of Greene; of the different circumstances under which the two halts were made, he is silent. He cites Marshall to prove that this "windmill attack" was made by a part of the left wing, and speaks of this part as having "*strayed to Chew's* house, ... halted there, ... and taken no part in the battle," except to "play upon its walls with light field-pieces." Marshall's words are: "*While rapidly pursuing the flying enemy,* Woodford's brigade, which was on the right of this wing, was arrested by a heavy fire from Chew's house directed against its right flank." Having thus boldly travestied Marshall's account of Woodford's movement, he with equal boldness ignores Marshall's statement that that part of the wing which was "led by *Greene in person,*" "pressing forward with eagerness, encountered and broke a part of the British right wing, entered the village, and made a considerable number of prisoners." [1] He carefully repeats that " the left column under Greene was not heard of till about three quarters of an hour after the attack from the right " ; but with equal care excludes from his text Sullivan's explanation of Greene's delay, and Pickering's assertion that Greene, having a large " circuit to make in order to reach his point of attack," the columns were " entirely separated, and at a distance from each other," so that " no calculations of their commanders could have insured their arriving at the same time at their respective points of attack." [2] It is also stated in a contemporary diary that " the guide of the left wing mistook the way." But this interesting and authentic document, although often within Mr. Bancroft's reach during " the succession of years " over which his researches extended, seems, like many other " trustworthy " documents, either to have escaped his " unwearied pains," or to have borne its truthful witness in vain. [3]

" *That Washington was dissatisfied and frowned,*" Mr. Bancroft continues, " *was* long remembered by Greene, who years afterwards, while he claimed merit for his exertions on that day, wrote, ' At Germantown I was evidently disgraced. ' " How far Washington shared this opinion may be gathered from the words — not cited by Mr. Bancroft — of the Henry Lee who,

---

[1] Marshall, vol. i. p. 169, ed. of 1848.

[2] Pickering's letter in *North American Review*, vol. xxiii. p. 429.

[3] Among the letters which Mr. Bancroft refers to, but does not publish, is a letter of General McDougall. Is it McDougall's letter of February 14, 1778, in which I read —

" Greene on the 5th of February, 1778, wrote to General McDougall : ' I wish you would publish the battle of Germantown. I think it would answer some valuable purposes.' On the 14th, McDougall wrote in reply . . . .

" ' I have endeavored to recollect your conduct in councils of war, but do not remember your dictating to the General, or using any other means to impress your sentiments on his mind than are common on such occasions ; and which were used by every member who spoke his sentiments. Nor do I remember your checking the spirit of enterprise by any part of your conduct which has fallen under my knowledge. And I have

reason to believe that the contrary insinuations are vile, groundless calumnies. Equally so are any charges to your disadvantage respecting your conduct in the Germantown battle. I did not see the least indication of your want of activity or spirit in carrying on the troops that day, but the contrary. Those of yours and General Stephens divisions marched so brisk, or ran to the charge, that they were some minutes out of sight of my brigade, although we formed and marched immediately behind your division, when its rear passed the corner of the fence where the new disposition was made. And as to the retreat, your endeavors were not wanting to bring off the troops in order, but could not effect it as the panic had seized them, and your conduct was far from showing any signs of fear. ' "

For this letter I am indebted to General McDougall's *grandson*, W. Wright Hawkes, Esq., who is preparing the life of that eminent man.

as Mr. Bancroft, trying, in another place, to use his testimony against Greene, tells us, " was then present as an officer, and greatly esteemed."

" The left column was under the order of Major-general Greene. Some attempts were made at that time to censure that officer; but they were *too feeble to attract notice* when levelled at a general whose *uniform conduct* had already placed him high in the *confidence of his chief* and of the army."[1]

And if this does not satisfy Mr. Bancroft, let him compare it with the following extracts from a letter of Greene's to Washington, October 24, 1777, and Washington's answer, October 26, 1777.

" I cannot help thinking, from the most dispassionate survey of the operations of the campaign, that you stand approved by reason and justified by every military principle. With respect to my own conduct, I have ever given my opinion with candor, and to my utmost executed with fidelity whatever was committed to my charge. In some instances we have been unfortunate. In one I thought I felt the lower of your Excellency's countenance when I am sure I had no reason to expect it. It is out of my power to command success, but I trust I have ever endeavored to deserve it. It is mortifying enough to be a common sharer in misfortunes; but to be punished as the author, without deserving it, is truly afflicting."

To which Washington immediately replies, after referring to " my letter of yesternight," —

" Our situation, as you justly observe, is distressing from a variety of irremediable causes, but more especially from the impracticability of answering the expectations of the world without running hazards which no military principles can justify, and which in case of failure might prove the ruin of our cause. Patience and a steady perseverance in such measures as appear warranted by sound reason and policy must support us under the censure of the one, and dictate a proper line of conduct for the attainment of the other. That is the great object in view; this, as it ever has, will, I think, ever remain the first wish of my heart, however I may mistake the means of accomplishment. That your views are the same, and that your endeavors have pointed to the same end, I am perfectly satisfied of, although you seem to have imbibed a suspicion *which I never entertained.*"

---

[1] " For the letter, *vide* Lee's *Campaign of* 1781 ; and for the extract, Lee's *Memoirs of the War in the Southern Department.*

It may not be without its significance to add, that Washington signs this letter, — written throughout by his own hand, — " with sincere regard and affection," — strong words for Washington to use to a man whom he had just before " frowned " upon for misconduct.

Mr. Bancroft professes a great veneration for Washington. Let him withdraw the charge to which Washington gives so distinct a denial ; or, if he still persists in asserting that Greene, on the 4th of October, " fell under the frown," so directly disclaimed in this letter of the 26th of October, let him bring his proof. Nor let him say in extenuation that he did not know of this letter. He knows that his applications to me for information have been courteously and promptly met, and that, if he had cared for the truth, he might have found it.

The last five pages of Mr. Bancroft's letter are chiefly devoted to my fifteenth section, ' Why Greene was made Quartermaster-general." His answer may be briefly summed up thus : Greene wanted to make a fortune, and gladly took an office which held out the prospect of one. To make sure of it, he insisted upon the appointment of Cox and Pettit as assistants, and by the aid of their relative, Reed, imposed onerous and unreasonable conditions upon Congress. The office thus gained he used for his own benefit and that of his relations. Failing, through the failure of the Continental currency, to realize his mercenary expectations, and alarmed at the public clamor which his mismanagement had occasioned, he threw up his commission in a pet at a critical period of the campaign. Washington, who thought well of him as a general, made no attempt to retain him as Quartermaster, thereby silently condemning his conduct in that office.

" When a man acts from a compound motive," is the grave opening of this grave charge, " it may be hard to analyze its elements ; and we cannot know them unless the actor himself gives us glimpses into the inner workings of his mind." The " inner workings of the mind," which explain Mr. Bancroft's difficulty in understanding Greene without the aid of metaphysics, are fully described by Sallust in a memorable paraphrase of Thucydides : " Ubi de magna virtute et gloria bonorum memores, quæ sibi quisque facilia factu putat æquo animo accipit ; supra ea veluti ficta, pro falsis ducit." [1] " When the glorious achievements of brave and worthy men are related,

<hr>

[1] Cat. iii. ; Thuc. ii. 35.

every reader will be easily inclined to believe what he thinks he could have performed himself, but will treat what exceeds that measure as false and fabulous." [1]

I do not purpose to enter here into the history of General Greene's Quartermaster-generalship. It belongs to another place, and, before that "half a lifetime" to which Mr. Bancroft alludes so impertinently is ended, may possibly be in print. My purpose here is merely to give the context and connections which Mr. Bancroft or Mr. Bancroft's "clerk" omitted in the extracts on which he founds the charge of selfish and mercenary.

"*Before Greene entered the army he had been interested in profitable trade.*" The expression in not strictly accurate; but strict accuracy, of course, I cannot expect. It may not, however, be unhistoric to add, by way of commentary, that this *trade* was one of the earliest attempts in that line of industry which has made Rhode Island one of the wealthiest States in the world in proportion to her population, — the transformation of raw material into articles of general consumption and use. General Greene was an anchor-smith. What the effect of this "trade" had been upon his habits of mind may be conjectured from the following passage in a letter of July 26th, to John Adams: —

" I will endeavor to supply the want of knowledge as much as possible, by watchfulness and industry. In these respects, I flatter myself, I have never been faulty. I have never been one moment out of the service since I engaged in it. My interest has and will suffer greatly by my absence: *but I shall think that a small sacrifice if I can save my country from slavery.*" " *Six weeks before the fall of Fort Washington in* 1776," Mr. Bancroft continues, " he indulged in the dream of reaping ' *a golden harvest on the sea,' as the captain of a privateer, and devised a scheme for outwitting the enemy by sufficient effrontery.*" I give the passage in full, that you may judge for yourselves how far it is to be regarded as a " dream " of personal gain, and how far as a suggestion made, in the intimacy of domestic correspondence, upon a subject of general interest; for, as you well know, the success of the Continental privateers was, at that time, a success of the Continental navy.

" This fall will be the last of the harvest. After this season all the navigation of Great Britain will go armed sufficiently to manage the small cruisers of America. If your privateers

[1] Rose.

should take any vessels bound to America or Great Britain, let the prize-master assume the character and personate the original captain ; if he should have the misfortune to fall in with an enemy's vessel, let him answer, bound to and came from the port mentioned in the ship's papers. If the captain or prize-master does this with sufficient effrontery, nothing but personal knowledge can detect him. It would be a good method to engage the crews of the prizes by giving them an opportunity to enter on board the privateer, and to share in all the prizes made after they entered on board. This may enable the captain of the privateer to continue his cruise and bring in a number of prizes, when he would otherwise be obliged to return home for want of men. And as to the fidelity and attachment of the sailors, you may depend upon it they will be as faithful, after becoming interested, as the generality of our own seamen.

"This fall is the golden harvest. I think the fishing ships at the eastward may be the objects of attention this fall. In the spring the East India ships may be intercepted on the coast of Africa. *Were I at liberty, I think I could make a fortune for my family. But it is necessary for some to be in the field to secure the property of others in their stores.*"

The only comment that I would make upon this letter, after asking you to compare it carefully with Mr. Bancroft's interpretation of it, is that it was written in the eighteenth, and not in the second half of the nineteenth century.

"*In February*, 1778, *he wrote, not* altogether in jest, 'Money becomes more and more the American's object. [1] You must get rich, or you will be of no consequence.'" Well may Mr. Bancroft say that these words were "not" written "altogether in jest." They are the outpourings of a saddened and anxious

---

[1] Greene, who was a daily reader of Horace, may, when he wrote these words, have had in mind : —

"O cives, cives, quærenda pecunia primum est :
    Virtus post nummos. Hæc Janus summus ab imo
    Prodocet ; hæc recinunt juvenes dictata senesque,
    Lævo suspensi loculos tabulamque lacerto.
    Est animus tibi, sunt mores, est lingua, fidesque ;

Sed quadringentis sex septem millia desint,
Plebs eris." — Ep. I. 1. 53.

"O citizens, citizens, the first thing to be sought after is money : virtue after money. Janus from top to bottom teaches these things ; young and old sing these maxims with their bags of counters and their tablets hanging on their left arms. You have spirit, you have morals, you have eloquence and fidelity ; but let six or seven thousand sesterces be wanting to four hundred thousand, and you will still be a plebeian."

spirit, asking itself, — for they occur immediately after the description of "a horrid faction which (had) been forming to ruin his Excellency and others," "Whither are our passions leading us? Where is this corruption to end?" "Ambition," he exclaims, "how boundless! Ingratitude, how prevalent!" Under no circumstances would a fair interpretation of Greene's words, even separated from their natural connection, as Mr. Bancroft has separated them, give them the meaning which he has attributed to them. But as the closing words of such a letter, how shall I characterize the attempt to convert them into an expression of the love of gain?

"*In one of his letters he freely confessed that the emoluments expected from the Quartermaster's department were flattering to his fortune.*" Here again I ask your attention to the context : —

"The emoluments expected from the Quartermaster's department, I freely confess, are flattering to my fortune, *but not less humiliating to my military pride.* I have as fair pretensions to an honorable command as those who hold them, and while I am drudging in an office from which I shall receive no honor and very few thanks, I am losing an opportunity to do justice to my military character. And what adds to my mortification is, that *my present humiliating employment* is improved to pave the way for others' glory. There is a great difference between being raised to an office, and descending to one. Had I been an inferior officer, I might have thought myself honored by the appointment. But as I was high in rank in the army, I have ever considered it as derogatory to serve in this office. It was with the greatest difficulty that I could prevail on myself to engage in this business. Nothing but the wretched state that the department was in, and the consequent ruin that must follow, added to the General's and the Committee of Congress's solicitations, could have procured my consent. *It was not with a view to profit, for the General and the Committee of Congress well remember that I offered to serve a year* (unconnected with the accounts of the department) *in the military line, without any additional pay to that I had as Major-general.*"

Such were Greene's motives as stated in a letter wherein Mr. Bancroft could find nothing but a confession that the prospect of emoluments "was flattering to his fortune." And this letter was addressed, not to a private individual or personal friend, but to Mr. Duane, member of Congress and head of the

Treasury Board, who could easily have verified its statements. The same motives are assigned in other letters. Mark what he writes to Washington in 1779 : —

"There is a great difference between being raised to an office and descending to one, — which is my case. There is also a great difference between serving where you have a fair prospect of honor and laurels, and where you have no prospect of either, let you discharge your duty ever so well. Nobody ever heard of a quartermaster in history, as such, or in relating any brilliant action. *I engaged in this business as well out of compassion to your Excellency as from a regard to the public. I thought your task too great to be Commander-in-chief and quartermaster at the same time. Money was not my motive.* For *you may remember* I offered to serve a year unconnected with the accounts, *without any additional pay* to that I had as Major-general. However, this proposition was rejected as inadmissible. Then I told the Committee that I would serve upon the same terms that Mr. Cox and Mr. Pettit could be engaged upon ; and I have nothing more now, although I have a double share of duty and am held responsible for all failures. . . . . Before I came into the department, your Excellency was obliged often to stand Quartermaster. However capable the principal was of doing his duty, he was hardly ever with you. The line and the staff were at war with each other. The country had been plundered in a way that would now breed a kind of civil war between the staff and the inhabitants. The manner of my engaging in this business, your Excellency's declaration to the Committee of Congress that you would stand Quartermaster no longer, are circumstances which I wish may not be forgotten; as I may have occasion, at some future day, to appeal to your Excellency for my own justification." [1]

You have seen how Greene wrote of his acceptance of the Quartermaster-generalship to Duane and Washington after he had been more than a year in office. See now how he wrote about it to Knox before he accepted it, February 26, 1778 : —

"The Committee of Congress have been urging me for several days to accept the Quartermaster-general's appointment. His Excellency, also, presses it upon me exceedingly. I hate the place, but hardly know what to do. The General is afraid that the department will be so ill managed unless some of his friends undertakes it, that the operations of the next campaign will in

---

[1] Sparks, *Correspondence of the Revolution*, vol. ii. p. 274.

a great measure be frustrated. The committee urge the same reasons, and add that ruin awaits us unless the Quartermaster's and Commissary-general's departments are more economically managed for the future than they have been for some time past. I wish for your advice in the affair, but am obliged to determine immediately."

Can Mr. Bancroft reconcile these statements — statements made to men who were familiar with the facts — with his representation of Greene's appointment as a device of Reed for the benefit of a partnership between Greene, Cox, and Pettit? Can he reconcile them with his assertion " that Greene would not listen " to the offer of a fixed salary ; " but, retaining his place and pay in the line, insisted on an extra compensation by commission " ? Can he explain how, upon this chief question of their mission, such men as Gouverneur Morris, Charles Carroll, Francis Dana, not to mention the less known Folsom and Harvey, were brought to lend themselves to Reed for the accomplishment of this scheme of private speculation upon public necessity ? Let him do this or blot out his narrative ; for on no other condition can it stand.

But I must hasten.

> " I' non posso ritrar di tutti appieno,
> Perocché si mi caccia 'l lungo tema,
> Che molte volte al fatto il dir vien meno."

> " I cannot all of (it) portray in full,
> Because so drives me onward the long theme,
> That many times the word comes short of fact."

Mr. Bancroft tells us, that " the public disliked to see him advance his relatives to lucrative agencies under him." Out of the hundreds of places in his gift, he gave only two to relatives. — the places of deputy commissary of purchases to his elder brother, Jacob, and to his cousin and intimate friend, Griffin Greene, men of unquestioned probity, and neither of whom grew rich in office.

I will not venture to ask you for room for all the documents relative to Greene's resignation of the Quartermaster-generalship. I will confine myself to a few of them.

Washington, having just learned that there was a movement afoot in Congress to dismiss Greene from his place in the line on account of the tone of his letter resigning his place on the staff, writes to Jones, saying, among other things : —

" In your letter without date, but which came to hand yester-day, an idea is held up as if the acceptance of General Greene's resignation of the Quartermaster's department was not all that Congress meant to do with him. If by this it is in contempla-tion to suspend him from his command in the line, of which he made an express reservation at the time of entering on the other duty, and it is not already enacted, let me beseech you to con-sider well what you are about before you resolve. I shall neither condemn nor acquit General Greene's conduct for the act of res-ignation, because all the antecedent correspondence is necessary to form a right judgment of the matter ; and *possibly, if the affair is ever brought before the public, you may find him tread-ing on better ground than you may seem to imagine ; but this by the by.* . . . . Suffer not, my friend, if it is within the compass of your abilities to prevent it, so disagreeable an event to take place. I do not mean to justify, to countenance, or to excuse, in the most distant degree, any expressions of disrespect which the gentleman in question, *if he has used any*, may have offered to Congress, no more than I do any unreasonable matters he may have required respecting the Quartermaster-general's de-partment ; but, as I have already observed, my letter is to pre-vent his suspension, because I fear, because I feel, that it must lead to very disagreeable and injurious consequences. General Greene has his numerous friends out of the army, as well as in it, and, from *his character and consideration in the world*, he might not when he felt himself wounded in so summary a way, withhold himself from a discussion that could not at best pro-mote the public cause. As a military character he stands very fair, and very deservedly so, in the opinion of all his acquaint-ance."

In this letter Mr. Bancroft finds only two passages worthy of quotation : 1st. " I do not mean to justify or to excuse, in the most distant degree, any expressions of disrespect which the gen-tleman in question, *if he has used any*, may have offered to Congress, no more than I do any unreasonable matters he may have required respecting the Quartermaster-general's depart-ment." 2d. " As a military officer he stands very fair, and very deservedly so, in the opinion of all his acquaintance." Having prefaced this last with, " On this," — that is, the receipt of Jones's letter, — " Washington interposed to retain him, not as Quartermaster-general, but in the line, saying of him, As a military officer," etc., etc., he supplements it by the following characteristic paragraph: [1] —

" I readily adopt the words of Washington. I doubt not that, with the fall of Continental money, the vision of wealth was not realized; *and I pray you not to interpret too unfavorably to Greene the notices which injustice has extorted.* A strong sentiment of self is not absolutely inconsistent with great efficiency in war. I leave you to judge whether Greene's accession to the post of Quartermaster-general should have been heralded with a clatter about disinterested patriotism and self-denying devotedness to the Commander-in-chief."

To facilitate your decision, I add a few passages from Washington and Greene which Mr. Bancroft's clerk forgot to copy.

On the 24th of April, 1779, Washington writes to Greene : —

" I am sorry for the difficulties you have to encounter in the department of Quartermaster, *especially as I was in some degree instrumental in bringing you into it.* Under these circumstances I cannot undertake to give advice, or even hazard an opinion on the measures best for you to adopt. Your own judgment must direct. If it points to a resignation of your present office, and your inclination leads to the southward, my wishes shall accompany it; and if the appointment of a successor to General Lincoln is left to me, I shall not hesitate in making choice of you for this command."

Mr. Bancroft asserts that " it was a cardinal principle with Congress to remunerate its Quartermaster-general by a fixed

---

[1] If Mr. Bancroft had wished to show his readers what Washington really thought of Greene, he would probably have quoted the following passage from a letter of March 18, 1777, — four months, that is, after the fall of Fort Washington, — to the President of Congress : —

" The difficulty, if not impossibility, of giving Congress a just idea of our situation (and of several other, important matters requiring their earnest attention), by letter, has induced me to prevail on Major-general Greene to wait upon them for that purpose. This gentleman is so much in my confidence, so intimately acquainted with my ideas, with our strength and our weakness, with everything respecting the army, that I have thought it unnecessary to particularize or prescribe any certain line of duty or inquiries for him. I shall only say,

from the rank he holds as an able and good officer in the estimation of all who know him, he deserves the greatest respect, and much regard is due to his opinions in the line of his profession. He has upon his mind such matters as appear to me most material to be immediately considered, and many more will probably arise during the intercourse you may think proper to honor him with ; on all which I wish to have the sense of Congress and the result of such deliberation as may be formed thereupon." — Sparks, *Writings of Washington*, vol. iv. p. 368.

This Greene of Washington's pencil is so irreconcilable with the Greene of Mr. Bancroft's painting, that he has found it convenient not to call the attention of his readers to the difference.

salary," and asserts, also, by implication, that the system of commissions was introduced by Greene. On the 15th of October, 1778, Greene wrote to H. Marchant, who was in Congress, and therefore familiar with the facts : —

"I readily agree with you that, so far as the commission allowed for doing the public business increases the expense, so far it is injurious to its interest; but I cannot suppose that I have given an appointment to one person who would wish to increase the public charge for the sake of enlarging his commission. However, I may be deceived. I wish it was possible for the public to get their business done without a commission ; but I am persuaded it is not. Be that as it may, the evil, if it be one, did not originate with me. The commission given to most of the deputies in the Western States under the former Quartermaster-general was much higher than is now given. The Board of War gave larger commissions for such persons as they employed in the department before I came in, than I would give to the same persons afterwards. I have got people upon the best terms I could."

The principle of compensation by commission, therefore, was not introduced into the department by Greene. I have already shown by his letters to Washington and Duane, that he offered to serve for a year without any addition to his pay as Major-general. Do not these facts form a part of the whole story ? Mr. Bancroft had seen Greene's letter. If he wished to tell Greene's story fairly, why did he suppress it?

As Mr. Bancroft refers more than once to Mr. Sparks, it may be interesting both to you and your readers to see how that accurate and truth-loving historian comments upon this passage : —

"General Greene had now served as Quartermaster-general for more than a year. *He had accepted* the *appointment reluctantly*, but had executed its duties with great zeal and ability, encountering obstacles of no ordinary kind, and rendering services of the utmost importance to the army. He was at this time in Philadelphia, endeavoring to effect some arrangements, with the concurrence of Congress, in relation to the business of his department. He found Congress so dilatory, and so little inclined to second his views and his efforts, that he became weary and disgusted." [1]

On the 3d of September of the same year Washington writes to Greene : —

[1] Sparks, *Writings of Washington*, vol. vi. pp. 229, 230.

" You ask several questions respecting your conduct in your present department, your manner of entering it, and the services you have rendered. I remember that the proposal for your appointment originated with the Committee of Arrangement, and was first suggested to me by them; that, in the conversations I had with you upon the subject, you appeared *reluctantly* to undertake the office, and *in one of them offered to discharge the military duties of it without compensation for the space of a year; and I verily believe that a regard to the service, not* pecuniary emolument, was the prevailing motive to your acceptance. In my opinion, you have executed the trust with ability and fidelity." [1]

" On the 21st of May of the following year, Greene writes to Washington : —

" *I would stop all commission business.* . . . . I shall be happy to render every service in my power to promote the proposed plan of operations, notwithstanding the injuries I feel, provided they are not accompanied with circumstances of personal indignity. *As to pay, I shall ask none, more* than my family expenses, and all the conditions I shall ask are, to have my command in the line of the army agreeable to my rank, and to be secured from any loss in the settlement of my public accounts. These conditions are so reasonable and just, and so flattering to the interest of the public, that I hope there will not be a moment's hesitation in acceding to them in the fullest latitude. No man has devoted himself more to the public service than I have; and I hope that I shall not be subject to the imputation of vanity, if I claim some consideration for past services. Your Excellency must know me too well to suppose my spirits flag at imaginary difficulties." [2]

On the 15th of August, 1780, two days after writing the letter to Joseph Jones, of which Mr. Bancroft has made such singular use, Washington writes to Greene as follows : —

" As you are retiring from the office of Quartermaster-general, and have requested my sense of your conduct and services while you acted in it, I shall give it to you with the greatest cheerfulness and pleasure. You have conducted the various duties of it with capacity and diligence, entirely to my satisfaction, and, as far as I have had an opportunity of knowing, with the strictest integrity. When *you were prevailed on* to undertake the office, in March, 1778, it was in great disorder

[1] Sparks, *Writings of Washington,* vol. vi. p. 339.   [2] Sparks, *Writings of Washington,* vol. vii. p. 54.

and confusion, and by *extraordinary exertions* you so arranged it as to enable the army to take the field the *moment it was necessary,* and to move with rapidity after the enemy when they left Philadelphia. *From that period to the present time your exertions have been equally great.* They have appeared to me to be the result of system, and to have been well calculated to promote the honor and interest of your country. In fine, I cannot but add, that the States have had in you, in my opinion, an able, upright, and diligent servant." [1]

Thus Washington wrote after Greene's resignation. It may interest you to see how he wrote before it. Mr. Bancroft will find this letter in Sparks's seventh volume, page 144, in most suggestive proximity to the letter to Joseph Jones. If he will give himself the trouble to examine the Washington papers he will find that, upon the Quartermaster's department, as upon almost all the great questions of the war, the opinions of Washington and Greene were in perfect harmony.

WASHINGTON TO GREENE.

"PEEKSKILL, *August* 6, 1780.

"SIR, — I have received your letter of yesterday. When you quit the department I shall be happy to give you my sense of your conduct, and *I am persuaded it will be such as will be entirely satisfactory."* (The Italics are of my adding. You will readily see why I add them.) "I cannot, however, forbear thinking that it will be unadvisable in you to leave the department before the success of the *letters written* from Paramus by the Committee and *myself to Congress* is known; and I *intreat* you to wait the issue of the application."

Greene waited. Congress rejected the recommendations of Washington and the Committee. It gives me a strange feeling to look upon Washington's letter as it came from his own hands (I write with the original before me, Harrison's text and Washington's signature,) and turn from it to the inexplicable pages of Mr. Bancroft. [2]

Such was the language of Washington to Greene, and of Greene to Washington. I could easily enlarge my extracts, but I have given enough to show that Mr. Bancroft has equally

[1] Sparks, *Writings of Washington,* vol. vii. p. 153.

[2] If Mr. Bancroft had not passed so decided a judgment upon Schuyler also, I would suggest to him, as a commentary upon the letter to Jones, a letter of Schuyler's to Washington, which Mr. Sparks has published, p. 427 of the second volume of his *Correspondence of the Revolution.*

misrepresented both of these great and good men. For the present I stay my hand; well knowing that it is not in his power to controvert one of my assertions, or impugn the authenticity of one of my documents. It is not merely as the grandson of General Greene that I protest against his perversion of the truth, but as a citizen of the United States I protest against his mutilation of one of the brightest pages of my country's history. Let no one attempt it who is not prepared to prove either that Washington's words are not the true expression of Washington's sentiments, or that he was weakly deceived in his estimate of a man who served for six years under his own eye in stations which required military and civil genius, a sound judgment, a resolute will, and the purest inspirations of sincere and earnest patriotism.

Mr. Bancroft closes his letter with a quotation from Dante. It would have been well for him if, before he ventured upon this bold misapplication of the words of the great Florentine, he had pondered the words of the great Roman: "Deforme est de se ipso prædicare, *falsa præsertim*, et cum irrisione audientium imitari militem gloriosum." "It is base to boast one's self, especially for what is false, and to the derision of your auditors imitate the vainglorious soldier (of the comedy)."

And as Mr. Bancroft, even in quoting Dante, has not forgotten to omit where the omission was convenient, permit me to remind you of the last lines of the same canto, which are well deserving the attention of every man who undertakes to write history: —

> "Ma nondimen rimossa ogni menzogna
> Tutta tua vision fa manifesta . . . .
> Che l' animo di quel ch' ode, non posa,
> Nè ferma fede per esempio ch' aia
> La sua *radice incognita e nascosa*,
> Nè per altro argomento che non paia."

Or as it reads in Longfellow's English: —

> "But ne'ertheless, all falsehood laid aside
> Make manifest thy vision utterly . . . .
> Because the spirit of the hearer rests not,
> Nor doth confirm its faith by an example
> Which has the root of it unknown and hidden,
> Or other argument that is not seen."

Very truly yours,

GEORGE WASHINGTON GREENE.

P. S. — I have hesitated about calling attention to Mr. Bancroft's statement of the commission paid to the Quartermaster-general, because there is the possibility of a clerical error. But upon a careful revision of the whole controversy, and a careful examination of the liberty which he takes with letters and other documents, I am led to quote the following passage from his letter, p. 478 : —

" The commission Greene left to be named by his partners, and it was fixed at '*five* per cent. on all disbursements by the Quartermaster-general and his agents.' "

Do me the favor to compare with this the following extract from the journals of Congress, Monday, March 2, 1778 : —

" That these three, *i. e.*, Greene, Cox, and Pettit, be allowed for their trouble and expense, *one* per cent. upon the moneys issued in the department, to be divided as they shall agree, and including an addition to the pay of the Wagonmaster-general and his deputy."

[*Foot-note to page* 417.]

" FROM you who knew and loved him, I fear not the imputation of flattery or enthusiasm when I indulge an expectation that the *name* of GREENE will at once awaken in your mind the images of whatever is noble and estimable in human nature. . . . . As a man, the virtues of Greene are admitted; as a patriot, he holds a place in the foremost rank; as a statesman, he is praised; as a soldier, he is admired. But in the two last characters, especially in the last but one, his reputation falls far below his desert. It required a longer life, and still greater opportunities, to have enabled him to exhibit, in full day, the vast, I had almost said the enormous, powers of his mind. . The sudden termination of his life cut him off from those scenes which the progress of a new, immense, and unsettled empire could not fail to open to the complete exertion of that universal and pervading genius which qualified him not less for the senate than for the field.

" In forming our estimate, nevertheless, of his character, we are not left to supposition and conjecture. . . . . We have a succession of deeds, as glorious as they are unequivocal, to attest his greatness and perpetuate the honors of his name. . . . . He was not long there [the camp at Cambridge] before the discerning eye of the American Fabius marked him out as the object of his confidence. . . . . His abilities entitled him to a preëminent share in the councils of his chief. He gained it, and he preserved it amidst all the *checkered varieties* of military vicissitude, and in defiance of all the intrigues of jealous and aspiring rivals." — ALEXANDER HAMILTON'S *Eulogium on Major-General Greene.* Delivered before the Society of the Cincinnati, July 4, 1789.

When we call to mind who the members of the Cincinnati were, and remember that, but for illness, Washington himself would have been present as their head, when this discourse was delivered, we shall see that it passes from the equivocal class of eulogies to the higher class of historical authorities.

CPSIA information can be obtained
at www.ICGtesting.com
Printed in the USA
LVHW100012181022
730905LV00003B/125